In all those years of travel he had never come across such a place as this . . .

He considered the possibility. Might it be pleasant to settle down after all this wandering? Might he make himself a home in such a town?

In which case, the inhabitants would have to get to know him. Understand what he was and bow down to him, yielding to his will. It was the natural order of things. They were merely mortal, after all. And he, despite his aged skin, was so much more than that.

He whistled a gentle, lilting tune, an old song of the Penobscot tribe. He'd learned it a full hundred years before the first ships from England had turned up.

In the old man's lap, the bulldog seemed to notice something. It sat up, changed shape for the briefest moment, growing larger. For an instant it was like a massive, green-eyed shadow.

Then it settled down, becoming merely a fat dog again. Made a snuffling noise, lowered its dense head, and began to lick at its front paws.

Which were both caked with drying, sticky redness.

Human blood.

By Tony Richards

DARK RAIN

DARK RAIN

TONY RICHARDS

An Imprint of HarperCollins*Publishers*

EOS
An Imprint of HarperCollins*Publishers*
10 East 53rd Street
New York, New York 10022-5299

ISBN-13: 978-7-60751-134-2

Printed in the U.S.A.

To Louise, with as much love as the first time.

ACKNOWLEDGMENTS

I would like to thank Alan Beatts and Jude Feldman for their invaluable help in the completion of this novel. Thanks as well to Diana Gill, Emily Krump, Leslie Gardner, Darryl Samaraweera and, of course, Louise Richards.

DARK RAIN

PROLOGUE

The ragged old man moved softly through the night. A storm was brewing, but he barely seemed to notice it. He just kept striding evenly, his footfalls barely making a sound. A rotund shape, a bulldog, trotted at his heels.

He was headed down a narrow country road in Massachusetts, and it felt slightly odd to him, since he hadn't been back here in a very long time. Trees crackled around him in the wind. There were no streetlights, and clouds covered up the sky. That didn't even slow him down, though. Darkness seemed to bother him no more than did the storm.

Every so often, he'd raise his head—the pupil of his left eye glinted when he did that. And sniff at the air, then murmur.

"Strange, Dralleg." He was talking to the dog. "There is something quite unusual round here."

He was in the middle of plain nowhere, not a hamlet or farmhouse in sight. Just low, rolling hills, heavily forested, the leaves still green as yet. It was late summer.

He could smell the woodland animals and hear a stream nearby. But it wasn't mundane things like those that had captured his attention. He was on the trail of something now. He had that kind of intent look.

When he lifted his head and sniffed again, his face

screwed up with puzzlement for a moment. Then, it became thoughtful.

"No, not just strange," he corrected himself. "Hidden."

And that last word? He swirled it around his mouth with relish. He was someone who loved digging objects up, revealing them. Learning things that he was not supposed to know.

He stopped at last on the bare crown of a hill, the only open place in all this verdure. Sat down on a boulder and let out a sigh. The bulldog settled in front of him, gazing up into his face. It had very pale green eyes that seemed to shine a little in the gloom.

The ragged man tickled the beast under its jowly chin with his long fingernails. "You can smell it too, can't you, boy?"

He gazed around.

"Now, what do we have here, exactly? What is someone trying to keep from us?"

His old eyes narrowed, and he stared into the distance, hard. But not even his gaze—flinty, hawklike though it was—picked anything out at first. Until . . .

From the thickest of black clouds above, a bolt of lightning suddenly shot down, thunder following hard on its heels, rolling like a wave.

Its glow brought the landscape into sharp relief.

And, deep within it, had he seen . . . ?

A second bolt confirmed it. The old man stood up, letting out a hiss and gazing to the west. *Now* he could see it. Streets and avenues and parks and squares and tall buildings, and many smaller houses. There was a whole town down there, cradled in a valley. Why had he not been aware of it before?

He gazed at the place for a good long while, trying to understand what he was looking at. And finally, comprehension dawned on him. A grin spread out across his withered face—a hungry one.

"Why, Dralleg." He was speaking into thin air by this time, the dog all but ignored. "This place shuns the outside world. Keeps itself to itself. And why? Because it has a secret."

His teeth parted and a laugh escaped through them. Then he glanced down at his four-legged companion.

"I love secrets. Don't you, boy? Let's go pay these folks a visit."

His smeared his hands down his coat, then continued on his way, heading downhill, the bulldog still trotting obediently behind him.

And went several more miles before he finally passed the signpost. It was wooden, and so old that it was practically falling to pieces. Parts of it were specked with mildew, other parts bleached by the sun. The words that had been carved on it could barely be made out.

But they read, "Welcome to Raine's Landing."

The ragged old man didn't even break his pace. He simply took note of it, then went striding on.

CHAPTER 1

"Evening, Ross."

"Evening." I nodded.

It was Jack Stroud, one of the neighbors on my street, out on his beautifully mown front lawn, doing unpleasant things to an emerging nest of ants. The light was failing swiftly, bleeding the color from everything around me. The white picket fences. The brown-roofed houses. The parked cars. The patterned drapes behind their panes of glass. The low rosebushes, and the ivy on the walls. Lights had begun to glow in a few windows, and the air smelled damp and mossy.

"Helluva storm we had last night."

"It was indeed."

"Feel the way the temperature dropped? Like an iceberg just blew into town."

"It got chilly," I conceded.

People in this neighborhood are always a little quiet and respectful around me, knowing as they do about my personal history. It's always made me uncomfortable, to tell the truth. But Jack peered at me curiously, wondering what I was up to.

"Just out for a stroll? Or is there something happening again?"

"The former," I told him mildly. "Stretching my legs and clearing out my head is all. There's no cause for alarm."

The man grinned ruefully and shrugged. "There's always cause for alarm in this town, and don't we all know it."

"Man, you've got that right."

I wished him a good evening, and continued on my way.

I like to walk long distances, and when I do that I get lost in thought. In memory especially. I never used to be so pensive, and it bothers me sometimes. But then, my life had become so different to the way it used to be.

Anyway, when my surroundings came back to me properly, night had fallen. All the ochre streetlamps had come on. It took me a few seconds to work out where I was. Not far from Union Square, near the corner of Meadows and O'Connell. One of the faintly seedier parts of downtown. The frontages were shabby, needed painting in some cases. There were balls of newspaper and candy wrappers in the gutter. The dimly flickering neon signs for bars and cheap eateries surrounded me. Across from me, its window darkened, was a scruffy little store full of rune stones and books on how to use them.

I thought I was alone at first, until I saw a shadow move out of a doorway. It was a woman, tall and slim. She propped herself against the wall, and watched as I approached.

Getting closer to her, I felt my jaw tense. She looked, otherwise, perfectly normal but had tiny pale-blue globes of light where her eyes ought to be. They were glowing, like they might be lit by electricity. But she didn't seem to be blind. Because her narrow, high-cheekboned face—reduced to a silhouette—followed me exactly.

She was dressed in a long leather coat and very high-heeled boots. And, when I got within a few yards of her, she let the coat drop open, revealing a black PVC miniskirt and a brassiere of the same material. And nothing more than that. She was very shapely and her skin looked pale as ice cream.

She crooked her right leg forward as if she was trying to

stop me with her knee. And met my eyes with those strangely glinting little spheres.

"Like some company for the evening, mister?"

Which was a good deal classier, I had to admit, than "wanna date." I paused and studied her.

If you discounted the eyes, she was actually quite attractive. Willowy and finely toned. Long golden hair dropped down across her shoulders in delicate curls. Her small chin had a dimple in it, and her lips looked faintly bee-stung.

But . . . her age? Twenty? Twenty-five? It was impossible to tell. Eyes give away volumes about a person. Not just their emotions but experience and character, and even time of life as well. Without normal ones, her face was just a pretty, passive outline sketched around an eerie glow.

The globes seemed to be studying me intensely.

"I can make it really good for you," she told me. "The best, guaranteed, you've ever had."

I wasn't interested in her services, but wondered what she was talking about. So, "How's that?" I asked her.

One slim hand came up, its fingers almost touching at the twin blue orbs. "With these? I can see what you really want. All your darkest desires and most secret dreams. The ones you'd never tell another soul about. I can see them in fine detail. I can act them out as well."

She paused, and brushed her lips with the tip of her tongue.

"We can negotiate the price."

I think I swallowed gently at that point. "And . . . is that what you wanted, when you used the magic on yourself?"

Her mouth pursed, the muscles at her jaw tightening. Creases formed in her pale brow. Those iridescent globes of hers still gave away nothing. But I guessed that—if she'd still had normal eyes—they would have taken on a distant, haunted look, dampening at the edges.

She glanced down at her boots. Then told me, "No. I wanted men to really love me, not just for my looks."

She gave a faint shudder.

"In a way, now, I suppose they do."

* * *

We've had magic in the town—real magic—for more than three hundred years. And, although it sometimes works the way it was intended to, it can just as easily go wrong. So encounters like that—and worse—are common enough. It depressed me all the same. Who said it? The suffering of a million people is a difficult thing to get your mind around. But the suffering of one can pierce you to the core.

Leaving her to ply her trade, I rounded the corner and went down O'Connell. Crossed Union Square, passing by the huge, bronze statue of Theodore Raine, our beloved founder. It was a pretty big square, as roomy as a couple of football fields. Symbolizing, perhaps, the importance of the Raine family here, and the hold that they'd always had over us. My footsteps clacked on the wide flagstones. I made my way to the nearby riverfront, the Iron Bridge, and stopped halfway across it.

There was, again, no moon tonight, no stars, The Adderneck splashed and gurgled below me as darkly as oil. I fished out a cigarette, noticing my hands were shaking slightly. Lit it and took a deep drag. Exhaled. Then started coughing. Damn it, why did I even bother with these things? I tossed it in the river, watched as it was spirited away.

Rubbed at my eyes, then looked around me. We New Englanders are pretty individualistic, don't you know. Rooftops of all shapes and sizes met my gaze. And below them, there were thousands of rectangular lights, the lit windows of houses.

For a town most people have never heard of, and few people visit, ours was a remarkably large one. But there's a good reason for that. I'll tell you about it in due course.

Don't get me wrong—the Landing's not a bad place on the surface. Everyone has work. There's a lumber mill and plenty of light industry, much of it high-tech these days. We have good schools, nice parks, public libraries. A transit system—of sorts. A theater, which doubles as a concert hall. All the courtrooms and the office buildings local governance requires, of course.

An average Massachusetts town, then, on the face of it. Except . . . the face is just a mask.

Why?

1692. You've heard of Salem, right? The witch trials. And you're correct if you think nineteen innocent people were taken to the gallows, hanged.

But the fact is, there were genuine witches in Salem. Clever and precognitive, they saw that there was trouble brewing, months before it came. Decamped from that town, and moved here instead. They married into the local population, picking husbands and wives from the wealthier families whenever that was possible. And Raine's Landing has never been the same since then. All kinds of weird things happen here.

By one means or another, these days, I usually find myself right at the center of it.

My cell phone began vibrating in my pocket. It was Cass.

"Trouble, Ross," was all she said, but that communicated volumes.

You see, in a place like this, there's minor trouble all the time. So common an occurrence that, after a while, you hardly even bother to comment on it any more. So when somebody—and *particularly* someone like Cassandra Elspeth Mallory—pronounces those two brief syllables, then what it means is "big trouble." Something pretty bad.

Her voice was breathless, like she had been running hard. And pretty shaken up as well. Which was unusual for Cassie, and just worried me all the more.

"Where are you?"

"Garnerstown."

Which was one of the older suburbs, to the south of here.

"And?"

"Something really horrible's just gone down. There's a lot of dead here."

A lot of what?

I stiffened and my head came up. This hadn't felt, originally, like an evening when death came visiting. But you can never be entirely certain.

"No telling exactly how many, yet," Cassie was continuing, "but it's got to be in good high figures. Something, possibly not human, went from house to house and took out an entire street."

Everything around me seemed to bleed into the distance for an extended few seconds. A jolt ran through me, and my mouth and throat went very dry.

"Ross?"

Cass sounded as shocked as I felt. That was hardly surprising. We've put in the hours, and seen a lot, most of it not good. But, if what she was telling me was accurate, this was the closest we had ever gotten to an absolute catastrophe.

There was a strong emotional quaver to her tone as well. So far as I knew, she had no friends down in Garnerstown. Which could only really mean one thing. Her one weak point, her Achilles' heel. An entire street had to include not a few children. And, given her own history, that had to hit her where it genuinely hurt.

Me too, come to think of it. My head had already started pounding, but I tried to keep calm and listen to what she was telling me.

"Mayhemberry P.D.'s here." Which was her name for the police department. "They stared. A few of them puked. And now? They're waiting for somebody to tell them what to do. You'd better get down here."

Not that I was a cop anymore. But the guys in the department listened to me readily enough. They knew that I'd a good track record, when it came to dangers of the supernatural kind.

"Okay?" she added, in a slightly desperate inquiring tone.

Then she rang off, unable to continue.

All my thoughts were spinning. I tried to steady them. My car was back at the house—it would take too long to get there, even if I ran. And there were no cabs in sight. So, my head and heart both working overtime, I retraced my steps to Union Square and waited by the bus stop. That might seem a curious thing to do, given the circumstances.

But not in a town like ours. I wanted to get down there as fast as I could, and this was the best way to do it.

I was alone. There was no reason for anyone to come here at this hour. The big public buildings had their doors all shut, and their shadows fell around me like great solid slabs of black. The glow from the streetlamps barely seemed to penetrate the gloom tonight. Or perhaps that was just the mood that I had fallen into. What was happening to us this time?

Within less than a minute, a vehicle turned up, as if somebody had read my mind. Perhaps somebody had. The bus was bright and clean inside, its windows shining with fluorescence. But there were no passengers. And no one at the steering wheel either. The thing was completely empty.

It chugged to a halt in front of me, its engine idling. The doors hissed open and I climbed aboard. It moved off again smoothly as I dropped into a seat. There'd been no destination indicated. There were no maps in view, no fixed route. But it would take me exactly where I wanted to go, in the promptest time that could be managed.

It's one of our newer services, provided by the good folks up on Sycamore Hill, the guys who really run this place. It was convenient, I supposed. One of the adepts' better notions. But normally, the things gave me the creeps.

Not this evening, however. There seemed to be much worse matters, and plenty of them, to worry about by this hour.

Cray's Lane was just an average little road—short, not even blacktop on it—out toward the bottom end of town. It was lined with wood-built, single-story houses, maybe thirty of them, none of them in mint condition. There was crabgrass on the front lawns, dandelions poking through the driveways. Rusty barbeques and swings out back. Most of the cars parked here were more than ten years old. Hardly a special street, in other words.

A stork had made its nest on a rooftop, I took note. Somebody, presumably a teenage boy, had a bumper sticker that read, "lurv instructor—first lesson free." Otherwise, all totally unremarkable.

Squad cars were blocking both ends of it, their lights casting red flashes across the entire scene. I couldn't see any patrolmen, though. They had to be indoors by this time. There was only Cass in view.

She was waiting for me on the first lawn to the right. She'd parked her Harley by the curb, and had a flashlight in her grasp.

Cass Mallory stands—in her thick-heeled, silver-buckled motorcycle boots—almost as tall as I do, and I'm six foot two. She was wearing her usual baggy, ripped jeans. A sleeveless white T-shirt. And a Kevlar jacket over that, she sometimes puts on and sometimes doesn't. It's not much use against magic, but defends against the claws and fangs that we occasionally find coming at us. She'd got the tattoos on her arms, a scorpion and a broken heart, back when she'd been a teenager. They were both faded now.

You had to wonder why she'd gotten those so early on, vulnerability and deadly violence juxtaposed like that. But then, I knew a few things about her troubled past.

Cass was fully kitted-out, as usual, Glock 9mms strapped to both her hips. Fastened to the Harley were a Heckler & Koch assault carbine on one side, and a pump-action shotgun—a brutal-looking Mossberg 590—on the other. She'd inherited her detailed knowledge of ordnance from her pa, who had taught her to shoot at a very early age, back when he'd still been alive. I also knew there were a variety of blades concealed about her person. Not someone who took chances, then, when it comes to dealing with the kind of trouble that we regularly address.

She nodded to me as I walked toward her. Back when I first met her, she used to wear her jet-black hair almost to her waist. But these days, it's cropped closely to her skull, emphasizing her cheeks and long, square jaw.

Cass believes in going into situations hard and fast, and keeping that momentum up until the thing's resolved. Tells herself she's doing it because . . . well, who else would? But the truth is, she's pretty much like me. She does it to stop thinking about past events. To try and make things right somehow.

Because she's lost people she deeply loved to magic, as have I.

Both of us shared the same dream as well. To bring the town's curse to an end. That was another of the things that genuinely kept us going.

Those eyes of hers—as black as her hair, and burning fiercely—were fixed on mine, and were the only part of her that was still moving. She could have been a statue, except statues never blink.

"You took the bus?" she asked me, once I was in earshot. "With this going on?"

She'd got over her initial shock, was trying to sound composed, and was making a half-assed job of it. There was too much stiff discomfort in her voice for her to sound in any way convincing.

Now that I was closer to her, I could see she looked exhausted. And it wasn't physical. Standing there in the dim light, she seemed mentally drained.

"I wasn't home." I pulled a tight face at her. "Sorry to have kept you waiting. What're we looking at here?"

"A bloody mess, literally." She had to pause before going on. "Almost all these houses had families in them. Moms, pops, even little kids."

She looked away from me a second, trying to hide the pain and anger in her gaze.

"All of them butchered with equal vigor," she continued, the words coming out twisted. "Not a shred of mercy shown."

My head reeled as I took that in. We'd had disasters in the town before, usually caused by magic. Fires. Explosions. Creatures being conjured up, or the conjurers themselves going berserk and lashing out around them. The dark arts can be an unpredictable and deadly thing. But there'd been nothing on a scale like this. I couldn't even start to imagine who might be responsible.

"Butchered how?" I asked, trying to keep my nerves intact.

It wasn't easy.

Cassie frowned as though her entire face were trying to draw toward the center. "Either knives or talons."

My God.

"Why would anyone do that?" I breathed.

Although, living where we did, it might just as easily be a *what* as a *who.*

"I've not the first idea. There's not a print that I can find, foot, claw, or paw. No signs of forced entry either."

"Someone got invited in?"

"I'd seriously doubt that."

One thing didn't figure, any way you tried to look at it. I stared around all over again.

"Bu . . . why here? What's special about this place?"

Nothing that either of us could see. Cassie let her shoulders jolt.

Then she drew herself up very straight and asked me if I wanted to take a look.

Not really. But what was the point of coming down here if I didn't?

The front door of the nearest house was open, blank darkness inside We headed for it. Had to skirt around a little pink tricycle on the driveway, ribbons tied to its handlebars. Cass didn't even glance down at it. She'd seen it before, and obviously wished she hadn't.

Her flashlight came back on, revealing faded, stripy wallpaper in the hallway, pink and white. A coat stand, with a baseball jacket hanging from it. A furled umbrella. A rubber plant in a big sepia pot. One of those embroidered *Bless This House* plaques hanging from a wall. Just an ordinary home of the low-income variety. A TV was still glowing from the living room, although its sound had been switched off.

Cass, I noticed, didn't follow me when I went in there. I just reached out, found the light switch, flipped it . . .

God. I wanted, straightaway, to turn it off again, for time eternal.

As I had been told, a family. There had been four of them. And, by the bloodstains on the couch and armchairs, they must have been settled around the box when who-or-what had paid them a visit. It seemed to have happened all at once. They'd had the time to jump to their feet—letting out a yell of terror, perhaps—before their new visitor had taken them to pieces.

The worst thing was, apart from the damage and the gore, they looked like they might at any moment get back to their feet and start moving around again. Only one thing separates the living from the dead, and that's intention. Corpses look like people who have plain forgotten what they want to do next.

My breath hissing in my lungs, I inspected the wounds more closely. Whatever had done this definitely wasn't human. It was far too strong for that. And the weapons it had used . . . there appeared to be several of them, tightly grouped, and each as sharp as scalpels.

The question rose again. If not human, then what? Someone must have created the thing. And I wondered who was crazy enough to work any witchcraft quite as dark as that.

And this had happened in all the houses on this street, according to Cass. In each of them, the same? How long must it have taken? Hadn't anyone heard screams, been warned?

The sickly charnel house odor was beginning to overpower me. I couldn't bear it anymore—my stomach started tightening. I backed out of the room, then squeezed my eyes tightly shut. Moisture was pressing up behind the lids, before much longer.

Although it wasn't wholly the sights, the smell. A realization had begun to settle over me. As I'd said, we have bad things happen in the Landing all the time. When so many of its inhabitants practice sorcery, it could hardly be otherwise. But something like this, the same awful scene replicated over and over again?

We were facing something different this time. Possibly a whole lot worse than we had ever encountered before.

The thought was like a heavy weight, pressing down on me. Was I strong enough to face this, whatever it was?

Cassie seemed to understand. One of her hands went gently to my neck.

"Take it easy, Ross."

"Right. How?" I muttered.

"Usual drill. Deep breaths."

I tried a couple, but they didn't even go down halfway.

"Why's it always us," I asked, "who have to deal with all the really lousy stuff?"

Her voice was still troubled, but was trying to sound practical.

"I could have just ridden away. You could have just hung up on me. It's gotta be someone, mister. What would you rather do, leave it all to the authorities?"

As if to prove her point, two of my old colleagues—Matt Chalker and Davy Quinn—had emerged onto the street when we came out again. They were slumped against a squad car. Had their caps tipped back, their faces white as flour. Their hands were on their hips. And they were staring about them with wide, glassy eyes, like they were trying to imagine they were dreaming all of this.

They're not bad guys, and not completely useless. It takes a lot of guts, let's face it, to try and serve as a peace officer when the normal rules are all blown to hell. But guys like Matt and Davy? They're not quick-witted or adaptable enough to deal with the way life here has become.

Because the truth is, there may have always been strange happenings in Raine's Landing. But they've gotten more frequent the last few years. No one was sure why, but it was undeniable.

It's a handful of private individuals who really make a difference, these days. Myself. Cass. DuMarr. Willets, when he can be bothered. And, of course, the Little Girl. If anyone can keep a lid on things, it's us. But the lid just kept on popping up, every time you turned your back.

Matt Chalker finally noticed me, and called out, "Christ, Devries? Would you *believe* any of this?"

Then he went back to his glassy staring, hands still on his hips.

"Is Saul here?" I asked Cass quietly.

And she nodded, her gaze steely by this time. As has already been noted, she doesn't have an awful lot of time for most cops. But she respects a few, and he was one of them.

"Fifth house on the left."

So I went across to consult with the Landing's one and only detective lieutenant.

CHAPTER 2

Think of Peter Boyle in *Young Frankenstein* and you've pretty much got the measure of Detective Lieutenant Saul Hobart, physically at least. Everything about him overly large and apparently ungainly. Big, thick fingers. Massive feet. Shoulders you could rest a dishwasher on each of, and an enormous, bald-domed head with stick-out ears and tightly packed, Chiclets-sized teeth. I am tall, but standing he tops me by several inches, except he's always slightly hunched.

He wasn't standing now, however.

He was sitting in the half-light of another living room, not dissimilar to the one I'd just left. Same ordinary furniture, same extraordinary carnage. *God Almighty, what on earth had hit this street?* He was gazing at something in his broad palm, and his head was bowed. He seemed entirely lost in thought, a saddened, brooding giant.

He was dressed as smartly as a man that size could manage. A charcoal pinstriped suit. A knitted woolen tie of the same color. A crisp white shirt, and a pair of gleaming black shoes the size of miniature kayaks.

The thing in his hand was a plastic doll with a sweetly smiling face, clad in a miniature pink frilly dress. Its owner . . . I looked quickly around me . . . wasn't here. So she had to be upstairs in her bedroom, in her nursery. I already knew that no one had been spared. And so the little girl who owned the dolly, whatever her age might be, wasn't going to get any older from this point on.

Saul had a wife and three daughters up in Vernon Valley, so this kind of thing had to get to him as badly as me and Cassie.

What do you say, around awfulness like this? My head was pretty blurred by this time, but that wasn't the reason that I couldn't come up with the right words. There were none. There never have been. No language had yet been created to express the feelings that a tragedy like this leaves you with. A rock hard lump formed in my throat.

. I felt for the man and his anguish, of course. But Saul had been my superior once. And so I stood there, waiting for him to make the first move.

·For a while, I didn't think that he was going to notice me at all. But then his head came up a little, and he greeted me in a voice far hoarser than was usual. There was a heaviness to it that spoke whole volumes about the crushed way that he felt.

"Hey, Ross. Noticed the dyke snooping round earlier. I thought you'd show up."

Which unstiffened me a little. Hell, he always calls Cass that, although there's never any pejorative in it. He jumped to that conclusion when he first met her, and has stuck to it ever since. So far as I know, he's wrong. I understand quite a lot of stuff about the ragged tatters of Cass's personal life, and it may have run in some unusual directions down the years. But toward her own gender isn't one of them.

Me, I was trying to breathe through my mouth and not my nose. Trying to keep my gaze away from the ruined bodies on the carpet. These ones hadn't been sitting down. They'd obviously heard yells from a neighboring house, and got up, moving for the window. But had not even reached that. Not even got halfway.

Hobart looked so far gone that he wasn't even taking in the view and odors anymore. And you could hardly blame him.

I stared across at the shabby mantelpiece. Family photos, china cats. A cheap vase with a plastic rose in it. Nothing of significance at all—give this stuff to a thrift shop and they'd throw half of it away. So what had brought the Reaper down on these folks in such a vile, tempestuous fashion?

It's no use holding in a question, unless you're around somebody like Willets or the Little Girl. So I asked it out loud.

Saul's head didn't lift any further, but he stared up at me through his beetling brows. His eyes looked wet and very distant.

"That's the thing, isn't it? Motive? These were all regular citizens, so far as we can tell. Heads-down, mind-your-own-business, get-on-with-your-life types. Hell, we've found a few crystals and rune stones, always do, in toolsheds or bed-rooms."

Most people in town used a little magic now and then, in other words. Most of them, except me. And why was I always the odd one out?

"But we're talking minor peccadillo stuff," Saul was continuing. "There are no adepts here. So what was this about?"

He looked down at the doll again, and stroked its nylon hair. Then tucked it, very gently, in his pocket.

"We've about seventy people dead, possibly more. And however rough things have gotten in the Landing, they've never been as ugly as this."

"Cass said no survivors?"

It was a question I asked with a very heavy heart indeed.

"Not that we can tell as yet."

"How about the neighboring streets?"

"No damage at all. Just this one."

"Didn't they realize what was happening? The people on the other streets?"

Hobart's eyebrows lifted and his expression became a little more numb.

"That's the other really weird thing. Nobody claims to have heard anything at all."

With all this mayhem going on? It seemed to confirm what I had already suspected. There was heavy magic, really powerful stuff, behind this.

"No witnesses, then?"

He shrugged. "None."

"So, what are you going to do?"

Hobart, at last, sat fully upright. It was an experience not dissimilar to watching an old sunken ship rising, prow first, from the depths. The gleam in his eyes had turned peculiar and doleful, slightly luminous. And the tautness of his features didn't slacken by an inch.

"I'm going to make sure everything gets bagged and tagged," he said. "I'm going to take a good number of trips down to the coroner's office, I'd suppose. I'm going to identify every victim, and inform nearest kin, when that is possible. I'm going to do my job in other words. That might take a while because, in case you haven't noticed, I'm pretty short-staffed."

And was that an accusation? Did he feel that I'd abandoned him, when I had quit the force? Nothing could be further from the truth.

I'd quit because I couldn't go on in the usual way, once my family had disappeared. I had to do something more than just follow procedure and routine. I needed to take a different course, one with fewer boundaries. But I was still, quite firmly, on his side.

I was waiting for more than the little speech he'd just delivered. He could see that, and his cheeks got flushed.

"Other than that? I'm mostly going to pray that this was just a one-off. Just the worst example yet of magic that went really badly screwy. Because my family? Live on a street pretty much like this one. And if anything like this happened again, anywhere *near* them . . . ?"

His frame gave a shudder, and that haunted look of his grew even worse. And then a hand went to his brow.

"I'm barely functioning, man. I know that. Perhaps it might be best if I just found a quiet corner, sat there for a while."

He took the doll out of his pocket again, and became oblivious to me.

Maybe he was finally losing it. And perhaps he had the right. Seventy people. Damn!

My own head had begun spinning gently again. I was just relieved to get back out into the open air.

A small crowd had gathered at the far end of the lane. People from the neighboring streets, a couple of them in their dressing gowns. They'd come wandering cautiously across to find out what was happening. Their faces were just indistinct, dim ovals in the flashing red light, their lips pursed and their gazes wide. Their heads kept on bobbing up and down. They were trying to spot something familiar, something they could make sense of. They'd probably had friends here. Their kids had, doubtless, played together. *What was going on?* was their collective thought. Matt and Davy were politely trying to make them keep their distance.

Cass was back in the position that she'd first been, standing by her Harley. In the time that I'd been gone, her features had become so hard they almost had a sheen, like metal. Her mouth was a rigid horizontal slash. Her own head kept moving around very slowly, side to side. But there was no suppressing the look in her eyes.

When she saw that I was coming back, she quickly wiped a wrist across her face. The fire in her gaze returned. She's like that, most of the time anyway. Faced with adversity, however bad, she usually drops into a no-nonsense, "can do" kind of mode. Solve the problem. Go back home. Save all the doubt and hurt for later.

"They've got nothing, huh?" she asked me.

I shook my head. And she grunted with annoyance.

"Freakin' Mayhemberry P.D."

"You're too hard on them," I said.

"I'm too hard on everybody. They deserve it."

She exhaled, and her lean, muscular body finally relaxed a little.

"So, where do we go from here?"

"There must be people living on this street who weren't at home this evening. Probably don't even know what's happened yet. It would help if we could find them."

"Oh, they're gonna love us, ain't they?"

And wasn't that the truth?

"They might have some insights. Otherwise? Hobart's claiming that there are no witnesses. That's never usually the case—there's always someone."

Cass's full lips puckered. I could see that she was coming around by this time. Letting all the trauma go, and getting back to her acerbic, hard-nosed usual self. It was a relief to see it, since I've relied on her for a good while now.

"Legwork? You know how much I hate that? Do you realize how long it's been since I've actually *shot* at anything?"

What was the point of having all that firepower, after all, if you never got to use it?

"Patience, Cass. Your time will come."

I'd been trying to put all the blood-drenched awfulness out of my mind, till this point. But my face had gone all sweaty again. I ducked it and rubbed at my lip.

When I looked back up at her, Cass was studying me closely, with a rather keener gaze than she'd seemed capable of before.

"There's something else bothering you, isn't there?" she asked.

She knew me all too well.

"We're standing in the middle of a massacre, for God's sake. Isn't that enough?"

Cass waited, folding her arms. There was something else, and she already knew it. The red lights flickered in her eyes.

I wasn't sure I wanted to voice my worst suspicions, just yet. But it seemed that I had little choice, unless I lied to her.

I struggled to gather my thoughts properly, difficult under the circumstances. Then . . .

"I keep on coming back to motive, Cassie. And I might be wrong, but I get this feeling . . ."

I knew the way that the really strong magicians in the Landing thought and acted, and it wasn't like this. A brand-new power had been at work tonight.

"First glance? Something just went on the rampage here. Magic gone wrong, like Saul is claiming. But what if it was deliberate? What would be the point of that?"

I gazed around another time.

"It can't be personal. Nobody can have a grudge against an entire street. Which leaves us what?" I asked her.

She had become very still again. And tipped her head, to indicate I should go on.

"Could it be whoever did this was seeing just how much damage he could inflict? And whether anything could stop him? Flexing his muscles for the very first time?"

"You're saying we've a new adept?"

"It could be that. I'm not quite sure."

She became deeply puzzled, so I summed the whole thing up.

"I hope I'm wrong. But *if* that's the case, this is maybe just some kind of trial run, someone testing us. And if it's that, then I'd imagine he's going to attack us again."

Which put a whole other complexion on the issue. Cassie took a little while absorbing what I'd said, her eyes becoming rather solemn.

And then she snapped back to full alertness, obviously deciding that I might be right.

"Okay, then," she said, with a little more enthusiasm. "Let's go do that legwork."

That was her to a tee. Face the problem. Do the job. Stop more innocents from suffering the way that she had done.

That's what we're really both about.

We'd divided out the streets between us, and were on the point of setting off, when another car appeared. It came entirely silently around the corner of Fairmont, and headed toward us. Its big round headlamps dazzled us at first. But soon we could make out its outline. Recognized the vehicle immediately. Anyone in town would.

It was a Rolls Royce, a classic 1968 Silver Shadow, its paintwork a bottomless midnight blue. Stenciled across it, though—all over the car, in fact—were magical symbols in a variety of colors. There were ankhs and pentagrams. Pyramids with staring eyes in them. Spirals of the type you find in ancient deserts, and more hierograms than you could throw a shoe at.

There were other symbols I could not identify at all, however. Some reminded me of snarling, fang-filled mouths. Of flying animals, and creatures that had never been. Who would do such a thing to a beautiful car like that? The world's ultimate spoiled rich kid, that was who. So insane, most of the time, so detached from reality, he treated most events, even ones as terrible as this, as if they were some kind of parlor game, like Clue.

I could already feel my heart sinking, and desperation setting in. Things were already quite bad enough, without an intervention from the Master of the Manor.

I waited till it had drawn up beyond a squad car. The back of the Rolls was empty, but the driver was there beyond the windshield, in plain view.

You would have needed a white stick and a guide dog if you couldn't see him. The chassis groaned when he got out. This was Hampton, Woodard Raine's trusted flunky, and the only person living at the Manor—still human at least—apart from Raine himself.

He took off his cap, and gazed at me in a refined, distanced manner that just oozed contempt.

Well?

"Master Raine would like to speak with you, Mr. Devries."

He had a high-pitched voice for such a large man. And in terms of girth was, literally, as broad as he was long. A hefty butterball of a fellow. Raine had got him all dressed up, though, in a tailored chauffeur's uniform of the same color as the car. There was a trace of perspiration at his collar, from his wattled neck. But otherwise, he looked the very picture of a stern and loyal manservant.

Two more things stood out about him. His face, as round

as a full moon's, was lightly tanned, a pale teak color. And the guy was walleyed, one iris bright green, the other a pale yellow.

I took a step forward, to make myself better heard. And asked him, "What if I don't want to?"

Hampton remained very still, those mismatched eyes gleaming in his flat pancake of an expression.

"He wishes to discuss with you this evening's . . ."

The man looked past me at the humble dwellings, obviously searching for the proper word.

"Unpleasantness."

Which wasn't it. That made me angry, and I wasn't in the mood to bottle any of it up.

"Man, he must be so upset," I snapped. "He cares so very much about the ordinary people in this town."

There's a big divide, you see, between the adepts, mostly born of Salem stock, and everybody else. And Woodard Raine epitomized it.

Hampton let his head drop, peering at his shoes. He hated to hear his master being criticized this way. It occurred to me, for a moment, that perhaps I was being unfair. Could even Raine be unmoved by a tragedy like this?

The chauffeur's eyes were burning as he looked back up at me. But he managed to keep his tone reasonable when he piped up again.

"Master Raine's only concern—which I'm quite certain you share—is to get to the bottom of all of this. He feels a sense of duty, sir. An admirable trait, surely?"

And then he waited for me to respond. I didn't see what option I was being given. Raine might be a deranged flake, but he had an awful lot of power. Saw things that most other people simply couldn't, except perhaps the Little Girl.

I sighed, and turned back to Cassie.

"Looks like you're getting *all* the legwork. You okay with that?"

She made another grunting noise. I already understood how much she disliked me having anything to do with our community's elite.

"I'll manage."

I hated leaving her alone out here. Knew how all of this had to be tearing her up inside. But choice can be a heavily rationed commodity sometimes, in this quaint town of ours.

The back door of the Rolls came open by itself, letting out a chilly gust into the mild night air. Me and Hampton both climbed in. There was no noise at all from the motor as it cruised back through the suburbs toward Sycamore Hill. Was that down to the fine engineering, or did this thing not even run on fuel anymore?

But there was one sound that was irritating me. Hampton can be as oblivious to reality as his master, sometimes. And now, hunched over in the driving seat, his stout hands on the wheel, he was humming to himself. Snatches of show tunes. On a night like this?

He kept on at it until I told him to shut the damned hell up.

CHAPTER 3

Me and Dralleg sitting in a tree, w-a-t-c-h-i-n-g.

Damn, it didn't scan at all. But the ragged old man smirked anyway.

He was high up, maybe forty feet up, in a massive, ancient oak that spread its branches out against the night sky a block down from Cray's Lane. Had a perfectly clear view of the whole scene from here. The black-and-white cars and the flashing lights. The goings, to and fro, of all these tiny-seeming mortals. He could see them. They could not see him, not even if one of them happened to look at him directly. He had made himself invisible. The furtive pleasure of the voyeur crept through every pore of his decrepit soul.

The tree creaked around him, and its leaves fluttered in the gentle breeze like swarms of tiny wings. He was perfectly comfortable up here. Had been born out of the deep primeval woodlands of New England, after all, long before the place had even had that name. He could stay up here all night, if need be, without the tiniest discomfort. The fact was, he had watched the very first humans arrive in the forest from a tall branch such as this. He'd gazed at them wonderingly, it slowly dawning on him what sport these curious, upright creatures could provide him with.

The bulldog was nestled in his lap. It had a squint-eyed, drowsy look, as though it had been busy. A terribly ugly example of its breed, the thing looked even older than its master. There was nowhere on its body where its skin was not in thick, uneven folds. Its basic colors were brown and white, in blotches. Except the brown looked more like a dark fungus, and there were rings of black around its eyes.

It was too fat even for a bulldog, its face, between the hanging jowls, all deep, distorted creases. Its protruding teeth were snaggled, razor sharp. Unlike most of its species, though, its tongue never came lolling out.

Something shifted, every few moments, underneath its skin. Ripples and bulges ran along its spine. As if a second creature was inside it, trying to get out.

Its master rubbed its bulbous head with fingers like dried twigs.

And continued to peer down, his eyes not even blinking. His left pupil—larger than the right—caught the flashing lights below and seemed to shimmer with a strange internal flame.

Cops and more cops. He sneered with contempt. He had known their type, whatever they might call themselves, since these forests had first been populated. People who tried to interfere. Human beings who tried to stop him. They thought their badges, warrants, and the weapons that they carried gave them power.

They were wrong. Had no idea what genuine power was. Hundreds of them, down the centuries, had learnt that to their cost.

They were temporary. He was ancient and, so far as he knew, forever. Could just swat them away like insects, any time he wanted.

There were two people down there, however—not in uniform—who interested him rather more.

First, the tall and slightly scruffy woman with her hair cropped like a man's. When she'd first arrived, he'd thought she was a gawker. A civilian who'd noticed there was something going on, and stopped around to watch. He'd quickly come to understand that she was more than that. She had purpose. Was dynamic, driven. Watching her as she scoured around the place was like staring at an acetylene flame, the heart of it penetrating, hot.

She had vulnerabilities as well. He could sense them, almost taste them. And would use them if he could. That was his special skill, one he'd honed down all the centuries. The thing he always did the best. But she was a strong one, and he had to admit that.

Then the tall, gaunt blond man had turned up. They obviously worked together. He was different to the woman. Just as driven, yes, but in his own far calmer and more solid way. There wasn't so much fire about him, really. More . . . a rock, standing firm against a swiftly moving current. He was powerful in his own way.

He would have to keep an eye on these two. Perhaps . . . test their limits? They seemed far smarter and more resourceful than the cops.

Would they even find, he wondered, the little calling card that he had left for them? Were they as clever as they looked, or just trying to be?

As for the rest of the town, the ragged old man was fascinated and amused. He'd wandered far afield since taking on a human body. It had been centuries since he'd been back to central Massachusetts. And, in all those years of travel, he had never once come across such an unusual place as this.

He'd really no idea such a community existed. They were in *his* business, yes indeed, of conjuration and the dark arts. Were stuck with it, it seemed. It was a path that they had no choice but to follow.

And he'd spent so much time out on the road. Never stopped for too long in one place. But perhaps . . . ? He considered the possibility. Might it be pleasant to settle down after all this wandering? Might he make himself a home in such a town as this?

In which case, the inhabitants would have to get to know him. Understand what he was and bow down to him, yielding to his will. It was the natural order of things. They were merely mortal, after all. And he, despite his aged skin, was so much more.

Below him, the large, dark, fancy car turned up. A man-servant of some kind got out and began to talk. And here was something else he'd already detected. Just how strong, exactly, was this Woodard Raine?

He continued staring, whistling a gentle, lilting tune under his breath. It was an old song of the Penobscot tribe. He'd learnt it a full hundred years before the first ships from England had turned up.

The blond fellow got into the Rolls Royce, and it moved away.

In the old man's lap, the bulldog seemed to notice that. It sat up, changed shape for the briefest moment, growing larger. For an instant, it was like a massive, green-eyed shadow.

Then it settled down, becoming merely a fat dog again. Made a snuffling noise, lowered its dense head, and began to lick at its front paws.

Which were both caked with drying, sticky redness.

Human blood.

CHAPTER 4

Sycamore Hill lies just to the west of the center of town, rising above the rows of lowlier rooftops like some vast carbuncle. Three of the streets radiating from the square, in fact, take you directly to the twisting, steeply rising gradient of Plymouth Drive.

The Rolls began to climb along it, after another while. I'd wound my window down a gap. The air became a little cooler, scented with the light odors of foliage. But it didn't do too much to ease the mood that I was in. I couldn't stop thinking about the scenes in those living rooms. All those severed bodies.

There were grander houses either side of us the first half mile of the slope, sporting high stone porches and wrought iron balconies, with expensive furniture glimpsed through the windowpanes. And then even those melted away, surrendering to open ground. Before much longer, it was high brick walls with spikes on top, and tall, neatly manicured privet rows. Concealed behind them were the dwellings of the Landing's elite. Judge Levin lived up here, as did Mayor Aldernay. There were various successful businessmen and -women, who managed to keep on getting rich despite the limitations on this town.

But it was old money that really set the agenda up on the

Hill. There were families going right back to the Mayflower, the Raines principal among them. It was they who'd benefited the most when the Salem witches first arrived here. A few of the adepts up here are self-made, the judge himself the most prominent of them. But most on the Hill were born to magic, had it in their blood, the descendants of those original refugees.

I'd become a little fidgety in my seat by this time. And it wasn't just what had already happened. There are more spells conjured up here than in the rest of the town combined. Powerful transformations are a regular occurrence. That's the thing about the rich, isn't it? They have so much already, and they always want some more.

And what if—for whatever reason—tonight's awfulness had its origins up here as well? It made my heart thump irregularly just to think about it. Could someone be quite *that* crazy? Woodard was a nut, I knew, but I didn't think him capable of savagery on this kind of scale. I tried to imagine who else it might be, but no one came to mind.

The plain fact is—peculiarly for somebody born in this town—I have always just plain hated magic. That was true even before what happened to my wife and kids. Maybe it was just my upbringing—my parents never used the stuff, understanding the harm it could do. Whatever, since an early age, I'd always shied away from using it. An instinct.

Because . . . the truth of the matter? However you might define it, whatever excuses you might make for trying to harness its powers, magic genuinely amounts to just one thing. Attempting to change reality, and bend it to your will. Trying to alter things you shouldn't, things that were designed to be immutable and fixed.

And that's just asking for trouble to my mind, any way you care to cut it.

My surroundings came back to me dimly.

Occasionally, we'd pass a massive gate and, catch a glimpse of the residence beyond. Most of them were large but fairly normal-looking. But one house that we went by looked remarkably like the Taj Mahal. And behind the barriers to the Vernon estate, a massive dog with three heads was on guard. Old Gaspar Vernon is, among other things, a classical scholar of note, and so I supposed that made sense.

Raine Manor, of course, was at the very top.

The original wood-built mansion burnt down at the turn of the last century. And was replaced by what must have been, even by the standards of its time, the Gothic monstrosity looming up ahead of me. Viewed sideways on, from the road, it was all dark shapes and shadows. But there were gargoyles at the guttering. Innumerable buttresses. There was a broad, low cupola—in the roof—that seemed to have no purpose whatsoever. And more wings than a swarm of dragonflies.

Woodard Raine's great-grandfather designed the place himself. So it's possible insanity always did run in the family.

The gates—both of them topped with a curlicued *R*—were wide open. In fact, they were rusted into that position. He doesn't exactly look after the place, our Woodard, and his sole employee was Hampton here. But the Rolls could only take me to the start of the broad driveway, and no further. Roots from the surrounding trees had pushed their way up through the gravel everywhere you looked. There were thick saplings climbing through it. The whole thing was impenetrably overgrown.

My door swung open, by itself again. Hampton just sat there, his strange eyes studying me in the mirror. He was waiting for me to make myself scarce. Lord, I hated coming up here, but I got out all the same.

The Rolls moved off a moment later. I looked back the way I'd come.

I could see fully half of the town from here. The center, with its statues and its spires and the wide, elegant bulk of the Town Hall. The northern and the eastern suburbs—I lived in the north—with their parallel rows of streetlamps and their postage-stamp-sized yards.

Churches and schools and movie houses. A hospital. A fire station. And the river running through it all, a darkly silvered snake, just like its name. A wholly ordinary provincial town, to the naked eye. Rather larger than it properly should be, but quite unremarkable apart from that.

If only that were true. I lit a cigarette. Took one drag from it, wheezed, and threw it down and stamped on it.

Then I turned around again, and started heading for the Manor.

Back when Woodard's father had been running things, this had been a beautiful garden, manicured to the last blade of grass. By way of a patrician thank-you, he'd invited us boys in the department up here once a year, for lemonade and crustless sandwiches on the lawn. There'd been a pagoda, a massive greenhouse, and even a bandstand. None of them remained in view, save for faint skeletons, dim, ivy-covered outlines these days. Almost like they had been slowly scoured away. They were completely overgrown.

Every single tree, and there were hundreds of them, used to have a small brass plaque screwed into its trunk, that told you what it was and which part of the world it had originated from. I supposed they were still there, but thick dark moss had covered them completely.

All the branches were deformed and spindly. There was not a single leaf. As though some poison had seeped up through the earth into them. Swarms of huge mosquitoes spun around beneath their barren branches, setting up a dismal whining.

It turned out bigger creatures were abroad as well. There was a sudden, heavy crackling from the dense undergrowth to my left. I caught a glimpse of something the size of a Labrador, and the shape of a potbellied pig. It was, doubtless, neither. All kinds of bizarre things here just come oozing out of Raine's imagination, taking root, of a sort, in reality.

And this was obviously one of them. But was it dangerous? I caught a glint of something off it that was probably a beady eye. But thankfully, no sign of claws or fangs. It moved parallel to me for a while, but got no closer, so I mostly just ignored it. I felt glad, however, of the Smith & Wesson snuggled underneath my coat.

The creature peeled away after a while, without revealing itself. I was still breathing slightly heavily, but for a different reason this time. The house itself was bobbing more clearly into view. And, as was usually the case, its owner had made a few more changes to it.

Not the west wing. That always remained the same. Half its windows were open to the night air, the glass in them shattered, heavy black soot-stains above them. That was where the blaze had started that had killed his parents six years back, a death as mysterious as any in this town. He'd not touched the place since then. Simply from respect for them, or out of guilt? I'd always wondered. Had he anything to do with it? There was no telling, either way.

Whatever, their passing had marked the start of Woodard's descent into total gibbering lunacy.

He had always been a wild kid, drugs and booze and sports cars, girls. A selection of dreadful friends. I'd even busted him myself a couple of times, although he never remained in the tank for very long. His family had too much influence for that to happen. But once his parents' wiser, calming influence was gone . . .

Well, you only had to look at the place to see what had happened to his mind.

Once, it had simply been a sprawling, ugly mansion house. But there was now, incongruously, a high spire on the building, just like on a church. Instead of a crucifix, the letter *W* stood at the very top. He hadn't built it in any conventional sense. He'd just made it appear one day, on a whim, which was the way he generally did things.

He'd hung wind chimes everywhere. But—there was still a soft breeze blowing—not one of them made a sound. A thin veil of mist clung about the place. None of the dozens of windows had an interior view beyond them, there was only darkness. And up at the guttering—I squinted—some of the gargoyles seemed to have changed position since the last time I'd been here.

As I watched, one of them abruptly straightened up a little. Then leaned forward and peered down at me, its stone face contorting.

Christ. That had never happened before. But a few more seemed to be trying to do the same. My heart slammed up against my ribs. I jogged the final few yards to the porch, went in through the open front door, and banged it shut behind me before the damned things got it into their heads to come on down from there.

Darkness folded its grasp around me, and I sucked in a breath.

Something scuttled across my foot. It seemed to make a faint chittering noise as it retreated. I didn't like to imagine what it was.

My eyes fought to adjust to the gloom. There was an extremely weak sheen of pale light coming down the stairway from the floor above. Heaven only knew what its source was. But it cast just about enough illumination to make out the dim outlines of antique furniture around me. Chairs that looked like Louis Quinze, a little table in the same style with a lamp on it, but not switched on. Were those crossed swords on the wall? Crossed muskets? Could that large bulk be a precious vase? I edged slightly away from it, worried that it might start moving too.

Woodard Raine's fruity tones came swirling to my ears, next moment. Not from any particular direction, you understand. From the thin air, so that they reverberated.

"In the ballroom, sport."

Another door came open at the far end of the hallway, a faint glow—yellow this time—emanating from it.

My footsteps echoed as I went on through. It wasn't just the floor that was wood, all the walls were paneled. It was a candle casting this more palatable light. A solitary black one on a plinth, not nearly bright enough to make clear the details of this massive, vaulting section of the house. The faint glitter above me, when I looked harder, turned out to be a crystal chandelier. And the silhouettes looming around me on the walls were portraits of Woodard's ancestors. But that was all I could make out.

Of the master of the house, there was no sign at all.

I felt more relaxed in here, though, than I had outside. Woodard Raine might be a nutbag with the power to squash me like an ant. But he had, curiously, picked up one concept from his father that he clung to almost religiously. That of "hospitality." Don't ask me why that one had stuck. Don't ask me why he arrived at any of the conclusions that he did. But if Raine invited you into his home, he would do you no harm while you were his guest there.

At least, that had been the case so far. Today? Tomorrow? Who knew?

But the truth is, if I don't use the arts myself, then I'm not much intimidated by their practitioners either. I could see no sense in being scared of something when I didn't even quite know what form it was going to take. My attitude to the whole business was, let the cards fall where they may, and play the game from there. Perhaps Raine, in his own peculiar way, respected that, and it was why he gave me so much leeway, letting me get away with things that others wouldn't dare.

I picked up the candle and approached the far wall. And there it was, carved into the dark mahogany, the Raine family tree.

Almost at the very top was Theodore Raine's only son, Jasper, who had married twice during his eighty years in Massachusetts. His first wife, Mary, had died mysteriously just short of her thirtieth birthday, and had borne him no children.

But his second wife, who'd more than helped him continue the bloodline . . . I stared at the lettering. Sephera McBryde, originally. And she had hailed from Salem.

This was not what I was here for, I reminded myself. I turned around, peering through the gloom.

"Where are you, Woody?"

He hated being called that. So I hoped it would provoke

him into finally showing himself. Other folks are deferential around him. Not me, not ever. I rarely felt anything but disdain for the man. Or maybe the correct word is repugnance. I never use magic, as I've said. He never uses anything else.

"What is this, Woods? Stop playing games!"

Just beyond the plinth that I had snatched the candle from, a pair of eyes suddenly blinked open. And I have to admit, it made me jump. Had he been standing there the entire time, and I'd passed close enough to touch him?

It was the type of game he liked to play. I think it just amused him. His eyes flashed, catching the flame that I was holding and then throwing it back sharply. They were massive eyes, far larger than a human's ought to be. And were bright gold in color, with the slit pupils of a cat. I could still remember the time Raine's eyes had been deep blue.

And when his lips parted, the teeth were slightly jagged, like a cat's as well. The rest of his face could not be seen at all. His gaze seemed to float freely in the dark. I wondered, for a brief moment, if he still had a body at all. But no, even he wouldn't go that far, would he?

As was usually the case, he looked a little bored and peevish.

"Do you *have* to call me that, old chum?"

"I'm not your 'old chum' and I'm not your 'sport,'" I told him. "And there are far worse things than 'Woody' I could call you."

The eyes blinked again, extremely slowly.

"You could simply call me 'Raine,'" he suggested. "It's such an interesting name. There are so many phrases one can conjure with it."

Conjure?

"'Hard Raine.' 'Raine of Terror.' ''Tis better to Raine in Hell than serve in Heaven.'"

He was always babbling these days. I was already sick of hearing it, and it hadn't even been a minute.

"Why have you brought me here, Woody?" I insisted.

He looked puzzled for a moment, as though he had plain forgotten.

But then, "I'm not really sure. I just thought that you could . . . help me figure a few things out."

I tried not to roll my eyes. "Such as?"

"What's been happening this evening. It's terrible. I'd really like to help, if I could."

Okay, then. Why not try that notion out?

"Did you see any of it?" I asked him.

He did not just see with his eyes, you have to understand. He had a power of second sight that extended well beyond these grounds.

"No. At least, not till after the event."

Which was odd. He hadn't left this house in years, I knew. Agoraphobia had become a part of his more general madness. But Woody usually kept a psychic eye on what was happening in town. He regarded it as his, after all.

"Why do you suppose that you saw nothing of the actual killings?"

He turned that over. "I think there was something blocking me."

But then his thoughts wandered off again. They were always taking new directions.

"All those poor dead people. Maybe I should try to bring them back?"

I felt myself go a little rigid at that, afraid he might try. That was definitely a bad idea. In the next moment, however, he seemed to remember something.

"Perhaps not." His bright gaze became a little sadder. "I tried it once with dear mama and pops. The result . . . wasn't very satisfying."

And then, he took a step toward me, his footfall clacking on the ballroom floor. The candlelight reached his face at last, revealing it to me dimly. It was gray and pale, with a high, stark structure and those leaf-shaped ears that were the mark of all his family. He'd grown a beard since I'd last seen him. Long dark hair now framed his features. Was he imagining himself, these days, as some form of Messiah? It wouldn't have surprised me in the least.

His head swung around slightly and he pursed his narrow lips.

"I would like to pay you for your services," he informed me, apropos of nothing.

What was he talking about now?

"I'm pretty sure, Devries, that something new has come into Raine's Landing. I can sense it."

What? That went completely contrary to Regan's Curse. Whatever had gone on tonight, it couldn't be blamed on any outsider. That just wasn't possible. No one ever came here. Or at least, no one ever stopped here long enough to make a difference.

But that wasn't completely accurate, now was it. Dr. Willets? Jason Goad? So I tried to accept what he was telling me might have some element of truth to it. It was hard to grasp, but not impossible.

"Don't you mean '*someone* new'?" I asked him.

"No." Raine was insistent. "Not a human being at all."

And he seemed so definite about it. For the time being, it was probably best to humor him.

"What kind of 'something,' then?"

He looked away from me a moment.

"I'm not sure, but I can feel it. I can tell it's here. It saw this place and it came in, and it doesn't want to go away again."

He was one of the most powerful adepts in this town, for all his lunacy. Could he tell me nothing more than that?

He seemed slightly affronted when I asked, like I was questioning his abilities. His yellow eyes narrowed. And for a moment, I was concerned that he might get agitated, even cross. I'd seen, several times before, unpleasant things come spilling out of his unconscious mind when that happened.

There was a sudden noise, a fluttering. Something with wings like a bat, moving through the air above us. Had it been there all along, or had he inadvertently created it?

But his face relaxed, he got himself under control. The noises went away, and I untensed.

"Whatever it is, it seems to be strong," he told me. "Strong enough that I can't look at it properly, or even tell exactly where it is."

He paused, thinking the matter through.

"Oh, and one other thing. I get this feeling—call it instinct—that whatever it's up to, it has only just begun. I suspect it has it in for all my little babies."

Which is what he sometimes calls the local populace. An irritating habit, but it gave me the opportunity to challenge him for once.

"You're the big cheese, Woody. You hold all the magic cards. So why don't *you* do something about it?"

He just stared at me as if he wasn't really sure what I was on about. His bright eyes seemed to lift a few inches higher. Had he levitated slightly? He sometimes did that as well, although I don't think he meant to. He simply forgot to stay rooted to the ground.

"How can I, when I'm not even certain what it is? You know how much I hate to go outside, old chum. And I've never been much of a one for the rough stuff. You, though, with your more prosaic talents? And your little band of chums?"

He looked like he was, any moment, going to move back from me and simply float away.

And that was typical of him. I felt my shoulders tighten. Partly, it was his aristocratic distaste for getting his hands dirty. In good part, though, it was also his dementia at work. He was reasonably lucid at the moment. But to him, most of the time, what happened in the world below had no more substance than a dream.

Today, he actually cared about what had just befallen us, enough to consult with me at least. But tomorrow? He might not at all. He might have completely forgotten.

Then he added quickly, "I will pay you handsomely of course."

There was a sudden rattle like coins clashing in the air, as if to emphasize that point. They were not there. He'd simply created the sound. I thought about all the people who had lost their lives this evening, and I gently swore. Which didn't seem to faze him even slightly.

"Tell you what. I'll put food on your table for an entire year. We'll call that a deal—let's not mention it again, eh, sport? A deal's a deal, you know."

For some reason, a row of blotches had appeared down one side of his face.

How far could I trust this thing that had once been a man? Everything that he had told me might be just a part of his more general lunacy. But it fitted in with what I had already seen. And he was the only person I'd met so far who had any insights whatsoever.

I shoved my hands into my pockets, then muttered, "Okay. I'll see what I can do."

"Don't toy with me, sport. You and that girly-whirl of yours? You're both already on it."

So I shrugged. "I'll keep you informed, then."

"Oh, no need," he told me airily. "I'll know."

The golden eyes slid shut as he said that. And I thought the interview was over. But they snapped open again.

"One more thing," he said. His voice had lost its distant quality, and taken on an urgent tone. "Whatever's come to visit us, it's all het up and hungry. It doesn't seem inclined to linger, loiter, ponder, take its time. I'd get a move on, sport, if I were you."

Okay. I took note of that.

On my way out through the ballroom door, I paused, turned. And asked him the same question that I always ask him when I come up here.

"Do you ever think about it? Trying to use your powers to lift it? Regan's Curse?"

I could only see his eyes again, by this time, staring at me from the dark. The candle had gone out.

"Why should I do that?" came his soft reply.

"Because then we could get out of here, and live more normal lives."

As usual, his gaze went rather puzzled. The typical re-action of an agoraphobic. It was cozy and familiar in the

Landing, so far as he was concerned. There was nothing wrong with the place at all. So why would anybody want to leave?

But finally, he saw my point.

"It's been tried so many times already. I just don't believe it can be done. Regan Farrow's magic was already very powerful. The pain of death just magnified it."

He let out a sigh.

"I think we're well and truly stuck here, chum. We can only pull our socks up, and get on with it."

And he actually sounded sane, for the first time in years. But it was not the answer that I'd wanted.

I made my way back quickly through the Manor's grounds toward the gate. Stopped there impatiently for several minutes. Neither Hampton nor the Silver Shadow came back into view. Goddamn.

So I started back on foot. It was a long walk home, but all of it downhill. And I had a lot of thinking to do.

CHAPTER 5

I never get to sleep quickly. The yawning chasm in my double bed is far too wide for that. There's still, even after two years, an indentation in the mattress where Alicia used to lay. But tonight, it was worse than ever. And it wasn't just the deaths in Garnerstown playing on my mind. What Raine had told me kept on ringing through it.

Did we have a visitor? I was lying in the darkness, but the moon had finally come out. A thin wash of silvery illumination made its way in past my drapes. The street outside was completely silent. But every so often a dog barked, several blocks away. And then I could hear a distant chiming as the Town Hall clock, down at Union Square, struck the hour.

When I was a kid, there was an owl in a tree near my home that used to keep me up for ages sometimes. Those unworldly sounds it made had me half convinced it was a ghost. I never told my folks, of course. My father wouldn't have understood. He'd been a cop too, just like my grandfather before him, both genuine tough guys in their own quiet way, capable, resourceful. I remembered the way that you felt safe around them all the time, and their casual, constant watchfulness. And all the time until I'd been in my teens—and begun the process of becoming independent—I had wanted to grow up just like them.

I hadn't grown *that* independent, I suppose, since I had wound up joining the force anyway.

But now? What was I listening for tonight? Something moving around out there. Something prowling—hungry—through the darkness.

Not knowing what it might be troubled me the most. And trying to guess exhausted me. By three o'clock, I had dropped into a restless doze.

That was when the dreams began, of course. I don't claim, the way some people do, to have the same one every night. But they all focus around the exact same subject. The same procession of circumstances and its terrible conclusion, just approached from different angles, separate starting points in time.

It was still there vividly in my mind's eye. A bright and sunny day, with just a faint hint of a breeze. People's front yards all in bloom, and a few traces of white blossom, a hint of pink contained in them, clinging to the apple trees. People were out walking, everywhere you looked. Despite what's happened to Raine's Landing down the centuries, it can be a pleasant, comfortable place. An environment you can enjoy, and even take satisfaction from. We'd all have gone crazy a long time back, if that wasn't the case.

I'd just got back from Calder Street, over in East Meadow, Cass's neighborhood. It had been an emergency call. Some would-be adept, nineteen years old, had gone berserk. And had—taking her cue from the Circe myth in Homer—attempted to turn her cheating boyfriend into an actual pig. That may sound amusing, except for two things. She hadn't succeeded the whole way—he was the right color, and made the right noises, but Old MacDonald wouldn't have him on his farm. And you only had to see the flaring terror in his eyes to recognize that this was not a joke.

In the end, Gaspar Vernon had agreed to come down from the Hill and sort the matter out. I left him to it. I suppose I might have been badly shaken up, if I had hailed from any other town. But a cop in the Landing deals with incidents like that the entire time.

My shift wasn't over for another couple of hours. But in those days, there was always a habit I had when anything unpleasant, caused by magic, happened. It put my mind at rest to drop by my own house, and make sure that my family was safe.

So there I was, cruising up through my own neighborhood of Northridge. There was nothing exceptional about the place, and that was how I liked it. Kids were playing on the sidewalk. They had balls and bikes and dogs. A postman was making his rounds. Old Ted Brampton already had the sprinklers on in his front yard, despite the fact that it was barely summer yet. Just row upon row of neat little houses, all of them well maintained. This was, and had always been, a respectable blue-collar neighborhood.

I turned the corner onto Kenveigh Street. Pulled up in front of my own garage, then walked across and rang the bell. And, when I got no answer, used my latchkey. There was no one home, but that was not surprising on a day like this. They'd obviously gone out.

I was writing them a note, to let them know I'd dropped by, when I heard a car backfire on the street. That drew me to the window. A fourteen-year-old rust-covered Toyota had just pulled up to the curb next to my squad car.

I squinted at it hard. And couldn't quite believe what I was seeing.

The thing had Nevada plates. Which couldn't possibly be right. My face went stiff and my pulse bumped over.

As I watched, a squat young man with shaggy hair got out. He went to the trunk, and hefted a massive, battered suitcase into view. I think my mouth must have dropped open at that point. This was obviously someone who was planning to stay awhile. Which was something that *never* happened here.

No one ever came here, unless they absolutely had to. And when that was the case, they got out again just as quickly as they could. Definitely, we had no long-term visitors. It was all part and parcel of the curse.

For the past three centuries, Raine's Landing hadn't been part of the regular world because of it. And it should have been working on this fellow now. I was absolutely certain of that. Every instinct in his body ought to have been screaming at him. *Turn around! Get out!*

Instead of which . . . was he smiling? He actually looked pleased that he'd arrived.

I finally unfroze, with difficulty. And went on outside, my original shock giving way to bemusement.

Oh, he was staying, all right. He was struggling with the big case, sweating. But there was this fixed, determined expression on his wide, lumpy face. His head swung around when I stepped down from my porch. And then his eyes narrowed when he saw my uniform.

That made me wonder straightaway, if he had been in any trouble. He just stood there, rather edgy-looking, as I walked across.

"Any problem, officer?" he asked.

His voice was flat and nasal.

I didn't like the look of him from the outset. He was pinkly chubby, like an overly large infant. Had to be in his late twenties. Stood about five six, and had let his dark hair grow out into unkempt cornrows. He had on a Hawaiian shirt, and denim shorts, brown sandals.

There was something about the look on his face, though. Something slightly twisted to it. And an unpleasant gleam in his tiny, deeply set brown eyes, like he had some kind of beef with the entire world.

"None at all. I live here, that's all—that's my house."

And, despite my misgivings, I extended a hand.

"Ross Devries. Most people just call me Ross."

He reached out warily and shook.

"Jason Goad."

There were large calluses on his palm.

"And what brings you here, Jason?"

I was still looking him up and down, and wondering how he'd even got here.

"That an official question?"

He didn't smile, asking me that. He was entirely serious.

"No. Free country. It's your business, I suppose."

But my throat was getting tight by this time. What the hell exactly was going on? I'd lived here my entire thirty-three years, and had never even *heard* of a visitor, save for Willets. And he was exceptional. Jason here didn't look as if he answered that description.

"Okay." He'd decided to lighten up a little. "I've rented a room, right here."

And he pointed out our neighbor's house.

I tried not to look dumbstruck as I squinted across at it. In all the time we'd been on Kenveigh Street, Mrs. McGaffrey, right next door, had inhabited the place alone. She'd had a husband once, but he had died in an accident at the lumberyard, a year before we'd turned up. And, since then, she'd had not so much as a relative drop around for coffee.

But we could barely communicate with the outside world at all, so how'd he managed to arrange that? Did he have some kind of special gift? If so, it struck me as bizarre.

I was still doing my level best to hide my astonishment. I wasn't sure how exactly. But somehow, this guy had managed to worm his way in here.

I was trying to think of what to say next. There had to be a way of finding out more without making it sound like an interrogation.

"All the way from Nevada, huh?" I tried.

"Right. Vegas. Ever been?"

When I shook my head, his pudgy features creased into a knowing smirk. So . . . how much did he know about *us*? What had he found out?

It suddenly occurred to me. Could this be somebody who practiced magic too?

"No, didn't think you had," he was continuing. His tone had become slightly superior. "I understand a few things about this place."

I stared at him again, less friendly this time.

"That a fact?"

"Sure. A few little rumors on the Internet, if you know

where to look. A bit of research, historical stuff. Late seventeen century stuff, if you really want to know."

Which was the period when Farrow had put all of us under her spell.

His gaze was studying my own, hunting for any kind of reaction. We're a closed community around here—to put it mildly—so I gave him none. Which didn't mean there weren't reactions galloping around inside my head.

"Population censuses," he told me. "Who lived where, and when. And where they came from. That and . . . how can I put this? I seem to have a special instinct."

I was waiting for him to go on. But, without any warning, his attention went elsewhere.

He looked past me, down the sidewalk. And I followed where his eyes had gone.

There was the faintest of mirages in the middle distance, caused by the day's growing heat. And from it were emerging Pete and Tammy and Alicia. They were coming back from the direction of the park. Pete was walking up ahead of them, growing confident at five years old. And Alicia had our daughter, two years younger, in her arms.

My boy spotted me and yelled out, "Daddy!" Tammy and my wife both waved. I should have returned the gesture. But a prickling of the hairs on the nape of my neck made me look back around.

Jason Goad was staring at the three of them like they were ice cream in the middle of a desert. Must have realized I'd noticed that. But he did not avert his gaze.

"That your family, Ross?" he asked.

I didn't like the tone of his voice. Not one little bit.

Particularly when he added, "Dude, is that chick yours?"

My alarm clock started ringing. My hand went across to slap it off. I awoke, but the dream hung with me for a little while. Maybe I was trying to rearrange the circumstances in my head, attempting to make them better.

I sat up suddenly, remembering what had happened yesterday evening. In fact, it all came flooding back.

My head seemed to ache with the pressure of it, and I rubbed my brow, blew breath out through my teeth.

It was seven in the morning. The house, as usual, seemed entirely cold and echoey without my family around. There was only one reason why I still lived here. I wasn't convinced they were completely gone. Was still hanging on to the faint possibility they might come back. Or was I just fooling myself? I often wondered.

Most things that I did, these days?—I did them just to fill the gap where my genuine existence used to be.

I took a long, hot shower. Didn't even bother to towel myself. Just pulled on a robe and then went through into the kitchen, where I got some coffee brewing.

Jack Stroud, I could see from my window, was back out on his front lawn, waging stage two of his war against the family Formicidae.

I popped a slice of bread into the toaster, then fried myself a couple of eggs.

It suddenly struck me that it was insane, the way I rattled around this place. Then I remembered the alternative. Rattling around alone elsewhere.

I closed my eyes a moment. Then I went into the living room, plate in one hand, mug in the other. It was the same way that it usually was. There were several tall shelves full of books. Alicia and I had always been big readers—she had been a teacher before Tammy came along. The half-dozen paintings on the wall were all by local artists. There was a large stack of assorted records by the stereo, although I'd not played any of them for a while. A checkerboard was open on a table in the corner, with the game half finished, gathering dust.

It was like the damned Marie Celeste *in here,* I thought.

Hung above the mantelpiece was a stuffed smallmouth bass. It was only seven inches long, but was the first fish Pete had ever caught—he pulled it out of the lake at Crealley Street Park, so we'd had it mounted anyway.

And arranged below it were a small cluster of baseball trophies, from my own days as a pitcher back in high school.

I'd had them tucked away in a box in the garage, but he'd found them, insisted we take them out, to Alicia's grins and my embarrassment. I could still hear his voice piping in my head. "It's an achievement, Dad! You've got to show them!"

At his age, Pete hadn't had anything like a proper arm yet. But I'd already started showing him how to hold the cheese for heaters, curves, and breaking fastballs, explaining to him what the different throws were for. I have to admit it, I'd had dreams for him in that direction.

And if this all sounds rather dull to you, then I'm not even going to apologize. I'd been just a regular guy—husband, father, cop—before all this had started. And I missed that more than words could say. If circumstances ever let me, it was a place I very badly wanted to get back to.

I found the remote under a paper on the couch, and switched the TV on.

It was tuned to RLKB. And the local news was being broadcast. The station's sole reporter, Marlon Fisk, was standing at the end of Cray's Lane, which looked rather less forbidding in the light. But a strip of yellow tape behind him bore the legend "Do Not Cross." A warning that had come rather too late.

". . . are calling this the worst single incident of magic gone wrong in the Landing's entire history," he was telling us. "Who caused it and why is still a mystery. But, for victims and survivors both, the consequences are all too real."

So that was how the powers-that-be were playing it. Had word come down from the mayor's office? I doubted Saul Hobart would announce that as a given quite so quickly. And there'd been my conversation at the Manor, late last night.

Fisk had mentioned survivors, though. People who lived there, obviously, who'd been lucky enough to be out that evening. That lightened my mood a little. Maybe they'd be useful.

My thoughts turned to Cassie. Hopefully, she'd turned up a new clue or a witness. I phoned her, but got no answer. Damn. Where to begin, when I wasn't even sure what I was looking for?

My appetite deserted me, the way it usually does when I'm under pressure. I put my plate aside, half eaten, then got dressed and headed for the office.

Banners were flapping around Union Square as I made my way across it. They had to have been put up at the crack of dawn this morning, since they hadn't been here yesterday. The wind was up from last night, and it yanked the fabric, making it crackle like sails. As though the looming gray buildings around me might be towed away at any moment.

The message on them read, 285th REUNION EVENING—THIS SATURDAY.

Three days away.

And I felt my heart sink even further. They were trying it yet again.

Face it, the whole ludicrous hoopla of Reunion Eve was no more than a dumb, pointless tradition these days. Something the town felt obliged to go through every year. There is no record of who first began it—maybe one of Raine's ancestors. But on the self-same date, for centuries, anyone who practiced even a little magic gathered here. And, under the direction of the mayor, took part in a mystic ceremony, trying to return the Landing to the normal world.

Regan's Curse again, in other words. Even when the most powerful adepts had joined in, they had not managed to lift it.

I could still remember my grandfather telling me the story when I'd been much younger.

"Most of the Salem witches fitted right in. Kept their heads down, at first. Kept their magic hidden. They behaved like regular citizens—which, of course, they weren't—at least until they'd borne children or sired them, and become established into the community."

The orange light from the log fire played across his features, which were solid even at that age. He rolled a cigarette and lit it.

"Regan Farrow, though? She was another kettle of fish. Proud of what she was, afraid of no one. She openly put spells on other women's husbands, took them to her bed."

"To sleep, Grandpa?"
I was wide-eyed.

"No," he chuckled, *"not to sleep. And anyone she didn't like, she'd turn the water in their well to bitter poison."*

"Did it kill anyone?"

"There's no record of that. Might have, though. However, in good time, the ordinary townsfolk just got sick of it. Got pretty scared, in fact, and mad. They came for her one night, like in that movie, Frankenstein.*"*

"Did they have pitchforks?"

"Yup, I guess they did. They knocked down her front door, and they came marching in. And Regan? She started to plead with them.

"'I'll go away,' she told them, 'and never come back. You'll never hear of me again.'

"They wouldn't listen, though. They grabbed her and they bore her up, and they carried her all the way to the village common, where Union Square is now. And all the while she's begging of them, 'Let me leave, there's no need to do this.'

"They," he sighed, *"bound her to a stake. Piled it all around with big bundles of hay and such. And then they set light to it."*

"They burned her?" I yelped, horrified.

My grandpa just frowned gently, and his gaze went sad. He had always been a decent and humane man, and he hated thinking about anyone in pain.

"That's what they did to witches in those days. They were meaner times. And so, the flames were getting higher. They were scorching at her petticoats. And Regan Farrow, knowing she was going to die, and already hurting, stared down defiantly at the town's inhabitants. Her eyes blazed and her face contorted. Just before the fire engulfed her, she yelled these words out.

"'If I cannot leave, then none of you ever shall. And you shall dwell alone here.'"

"That's her curse on this town, kiddo. That's how it's been ever since."

And how it was today. Nothing had changed, in all the passing decades.

Other folks, outsiders, could come here and go away again. But if you had the bad luck to be born inside Raine's Landing . . .

There can't be many of us who haven't tried to leave at least a dozen times. By car or on foot, the outcome is always the same. As soon as you cross the municipal limits, everything around you seems to slow down, then stops moving. The leaves don't shake in the trees anymore. There's no stirring in the grass around you, and no birds fly overhead. Not even an insect buzzes. The world becomes just deathly quiet, and bled a little of its color too, as though the sun has looked away.

You head down the road, but never reach an intersection. The horizon gets no closer. And no other buildings come in sight.

After a while, evening falls, and you're forced to head back.

It's a good part of the reason why our town is such a large one. No one ever leaves. And yes, these days we have to be careful about certain stuff. Who marries whom, for instance. There's an awful lot of cousins around these parts. But otherwise, we get on mostly fine. At least as well as a community like ours can manage. The rest of the world sends stuff in, we send it out. How could we survive otherwise? But that apart, we're cut adrift from it.

And—part of the curse too?—it gives us a wide berth, or else plain ignores us.

As Raine had said last night, we're stuck.

Reunion Evening hadn't shown a sign of working, on any occasion it had been attempted. I saw no reason to expect it would be any different this time.

But then, I can be too downbeat sometimes—I acknowledge that. And so . . .

Best of luck this year, folks.

*   *   *

Something else caught my attention, going past the big, dark statue of Theodore Raine. Standing by its bronze plinth, stock-still, was a raggedy old man I'd never seen before. He was stood straight as a ramrod, and was about as tall as I am, maybe slightly taller. Wore a shabby brown raincoat that reached right down past his knees, and had a shapeless, broad-brimmed hat planted firmly on his shaggy silver head. A beard of the same color hid most of his face. He didn't even seem to notice I was there.

There were a few derelicts in the Landing, and—to put it mildly—a few eccentrics too. He didn't fit onto the list of ones I knew about. But then, people's circumstances change all the time. He could have become newly homeless. Or he might just dress like that.

Beside him was a flabby, rather mangy-looking dog. A bulldog, pretty oversized for its breed, fast asleep. And the fellow had a placard draped across his chest.

"Repent," it read. "The End of the World Is Nigh."

The Landing's always throwing up some weird new character. He had probably just wandered in from one of the outer suburbs, drawn toward the center of town as if by a magnet. So I just gave him a sideways glance, satisfied myself he was not misbehaving, then continued on.

"The hour of doom is at hand!" he yelled suddenly, at my retreating back.

Oh yeah? What else was new?

CHAPTER 6

At twenty before eight, the big red truck pulled off the turnpike. It slowed down, wheezing as it reached the off-ramp—which was totally unmarked—then gathered impetus again. Before long, it was speeding down a narrow two-lane blacktop, the dense New England woodlands flashing by its cab.

Don Kozinsky, at the steering wheel, was sweating. God, he hated this part of his week. He'd been doing this run for two years, and he still hadn't gotten used to it.

The goods he was delivering slid around a little in the back. Big brown crates filled up with canned goods, any kind that you could think of. Beets, clams, tuna, creamed corn—name it, it was there. This was all he did, come rain or shine. Deliver the stuff to the grocery stores throughout the area. And he was usually happy with his lot. Not now, though. Not at all.

A bend forced him to slow down. But then he was gunning the big diesel motor once again. Quickly in, and quickly out. That was the way he preferred it.

You'd think there'd be at least one signpost for the place. A town that size? But he'd never seen one, except that ratty, ancient Welcome one on the town limits. You couldn't even find it on most maps. In fact, the only time he'd *ever* seen

it on a map was in the window of an antiques store in Fal-
mouth.

He'd lived in this region all his life—he was currently a
resident of Palmer. And most folks in these parts had never
even heard of Raine's Landing.

Not that he ever mentioned his trips here. Why was
that? He never talked about the place, once he was out of
it. He was pretty certain other truckers dropped freight
off here too. The place looked prosperous enough. And
he'd, on occasion, passed a rig speeding back the other
way. But at the stops he frequented, the talk was about
sport, and chicks, and other towns. But never once Raine's
Landing.

He considered going even faster—on a road like this? How
dangerous might that be? But it was hard to fight the temptation. Because by this stage of the trip, the heebie-geebies
were beginning to set in.

Again, he wasn't sure what caused them. But he'd felt
them his first visit here, and on every occasion since. He'd
been following the instructions that his boss had handed
him, scribbled on a sheet of paper. No maps available, remember?

He only had to get within a mile of the town's outskirts,
when the voices seemed to start up, deep inside his head.
*"Stay away." "You don't want to come here." "Turn
around—go back, go back."*

Oddly, they were not his own. They mostly sounded
female, a few deeper ones far in the background. And . . .
the first time it had happened, he'd been forced to pull the
rig over, almost putting its wheels in a ditch. He was that
badly shaken up.

They had to be just his imagination, he'd decided. But
they still had a strange, powerful effect on him.

Every fiber of his being seemed to pull at him, the opposite direction to the one that he was going. Every sinew,
every muscle, was attempting to rear back. His instincts
screamed at him to hit the brakes and get no closer. This
was not a place where he belonged.

But he'd been a trucker for twenty years. And always delivered his consignments. So Don gritted his teeth, peered fiercely through the windshield, and continued on.

The woods finally parted and the town came into view. It looked no different to a lot of places around here. A typical Massachusetts township, larger than a lot of them, but unremarkable in any other way. So why was his heart beating so? Why did he keep glancing down at his own dashboard, finding it hard to even *look* at the place for an extended period?

Concentrate on your job, man, he told himself. He had six stores to deliver to.

He took them, one after another, as though he were training for some newly created sporting event. Just dropped off the crates, and got the manager to sign for them. Jumped back in his cab, and headed for the next address. The streets passed by him in a blur.

The people that he had to deal with were all polite enough, even attempting to be friendly in some cases. But he simply mumbled at them, keeping his eyes lowered, his expression fixed like stone. He couldn't look at anything directly, not even a face, it seemed.

Within an hour, he was done. Thank the Lord—relief washed over him. He was heading back toward the turnpike like a man possessed.

Strangely, however, once he was passing through the trees again, the town lost from sight, his memory began to fail him. All of the anxiety that he'd felt earlier? What had it really been about?

He blinked . . . and found he couldn't recall precisely what Raine's Landing had looked like when he'd first approached it. Nor the layout of the streets he'd hurried down.

After a while, even the name of the place had begun dissolving from his thoughts.

He was back onto the turnpike before too much longer. And couldn't seem to quite remember why he'd ever left it.

Don's face creased with a gentle smile. He leaned across

and turned his radio on. It was promising to be a pleasant, sunny day, and all of his anxiety was behind him now, forgotten. He was already thinking about his next port of call. Frank's Roadside Tavern, and a big, cooked, greasy breakfast.

CHAPTER 7

I climbed the stairs, going up past the signs for accountants and dentists, till I reached my office door. The lettering on the frosted glass pane still looked reasonably fresh.

DEVRIES & MACDONALD—SECURITY CONSULTANTS

There's no MacDonald. I just thought that two guys sounded more secure than one. Cass only came in later, learning what I was all about and deciding to help. And "security consultant" in the Landing is rather more involved a business than a matter of fitting burglar alarms. But then, you've already figured that out.

Maybe it's the plain fact, once again, that I have never dabbled in magic. It gives me an outsider's perspective on the subject. I can see things clearly where a mind filled with arcana cannot. And what happened to my wife and children drives me too. It drives me constantly, in fact. I seem to be able to solve problems other people can't even get close to.

I could still recall—as I unlocked the door and then went in—those faintly colored flashes from the loft window next door. That was Goad, starting to practice genuine wizardry, then sharp-honing his skills. He'd bought all the books and implements he needed here, you see. They are freely available in town, and it's the way most people who don't have it in their heritage learn.

I'd done a little research on him by then. I had no computer, there were none at the department. We're, as you might imagine, a very inward-looking community around this neck of the woods. And few of our messages—part of the curse as well—ever seem to reach the outside world.

But the central public library had one. I found him on a cheaply put-together little website. He'd had a magician's act in Vegas. Apparently, not a successful one.

Here's the other thing you have to understand about Raine's Landing. It's not simply that people practice sorcery around here. It's more that, ever since the witches came, the whole place has become imbued with magic. It has dripped down through the soil, and soaked into the walls around us. The insects hum with it. The night winds breathe it. The whole place simply lends itself to woven spells and sudden transformations. And, in coming here, Goad had found what he had always really wanted. The ability to change things that he previously could not.

That creeping feeling on the back of my neck had become a regular sensation, a month after he first moved in. And it wasn't just the spells. There were even worse things than that.

I never actually caught him at it, but was sure that he was spying on my family, whenever they were out in the backyard. And on Alicia especially. I spotted his curtains twitch when she was sunbathing one time, and insisted that she come indoors.

"Ross, you're being paranoid!"

Except I wasn't. Not at all. Later events would bear that out.

My office was just one medium-sized room, not recently decorated that you'd notice. The white paint had gone rather dull, and specks of it had peeled away. Last year's calendar hung on the wall. The filing cabinets had come with the place—I barely ever used them. But there was an alcove to one side, with a washbasin and towel. I went to it, splashed some cold water on my face. Then, drying myself, gazed at my own reflection.

I'd always been on the narrow side, but these days I looked downright gaunt. My gray eyes didn't have the sparkle that they used to. And my wavy, pale hair—a couple of inches longer than I'd worn it as a cop—looked thinner at the front. I pinched it, with my finger and thumb, and a couple of strands came away. A curse escaped my lips.

The door banged open. It was Cass. Who else? She was still wearing the same jeans and boots as yesterday, but a cream-colored T-shirt instead. The Kevlar vest was gone. Her lucky charm bracelet was rattling at her wrist. She doesn't use magic any more than I do, but she can be super-stitious occasionally. It's just part of the way she is.

She looked rather squinty, as if she had had a restless night as well. And rather ticked off. I wondered who had just annoyed her.

"Who's that old guy by the statue?"

I shrugged. "Never seen him before. Why?"

"He told me that the world was going to end. And then he called me a harlot." She peered across inquiringly. "What'd I ever do to him?"

I just pulled another face at her. Cass, to put it gently, is quite capable of defending her honor if she needs to.

A residue of sadness still remained in her dark eyes. But, like me, she was trying to keep the lid on it by staying busy. She ran her fingers through her short-cropped hair, then sat down on the corner of my desk.

And announced, "Got something."

Nobody was ever going to hire her as a speechwriter, let's face it. I peered at her, interested.

"Why didn't you call me yesterday?"

"I tried—you weren't home. And your cell phone was dead. Still hobnobbing with the upper crust, I take it."

I had switched it off before I'd gone into the Manor. Woodard Raine, among other things, doesn't like new technology.

Cassie, for her part, doesn't like the people up on Sycamore Hill, and never has. She's pure Raine's Landing working-class—her father was a warehouseman and her mother a waitress. They both died in a road accident when she was seventeen—she'd had to make it on her own since then. I knew that she'd gone off the rails the first couple of years, although she'd never told me many details. But eventually, she'd sorted herself out. And there was nothing that she had in common with the self-styled aristocracy on Plymouth Drive. The wry twist to her mouth, the dryness of her gaze, reflected that.

Which slightly missed the point. I couldn't get things done at all if I didn't have dealings with the adepts. And besides, I was still waiting. What exactly had she turned up?

"Cassie?"

"Right. A few people came back to Cray's Lane, later in the evening. As you can imagine, they were in a pretty bad way when they found out what had happened."

I wondered what *that* had to be like. Going out for dinner or a movie. Ambling back after a pleasant evening, only to discover all your loved ones were gone. At least I'd been around when . . .

I moved away from that thought, trying to force it from my head.

"Most of them weren't in any state to talk." Her voice was tight, but she shook her head and got past it. "The few who were knew nothing. They were totally bewildered. But you were right about one thing. Someone *did* see what was going on."

"Terrific. Who's our witness?"

"A ten-year-old called Tommy Wilkes. He lives in the corner house on Amley Street, backing right onto Cray's Lane."

Better than nothing.

"Go on," I said.

"When all the yelling started, Tommy hunkered down and stayed put, just like he'd been taught. Except he was in his tree house, with a clear view of the street."

He'd been outdoors, then. Maybe that explained why he had noticed, unlike all the other people nearby. I was listening carefully. And . . . might we really find out what was happening through the eyes of a child?

"He was pretty scared," Cass went on, "but in a ten-year-old sort of way. Kept bobbing around and peeking. And, just as the screams began dying down, he caught sight of a figure moving away. A man, just in silhouette. But he was tall and pretty gangly."

She stopped at that point, blinking, something coming to her. And me too. I got up, started moving to the window.

When I looked down, though, the old vagrant with his placard was no longer in sight.

"Well?" Cass asked.

I shook my head.

"He's wandered off. Probably nothing."

If he'd been our guy, wouldn't he do something more than stand there shouting and then disappear? Both of us forgot about him.

"I've got something else," she said.

She was leaning back a little on my desk, with the beginning of a smug smile playing across her features.

"Am I going to have to wait all week to hear about it?"

"As this guy was leaving, well, he left behind a souvenir. Tommy saw an object fall from his hand to the verge. So—being ten years old—once he was certain that the coast was clear, he shimmied down and got it."

She reached into her pocket. Pulled out something the size of a matchbox, wrapped up in a handkerchief.

I went across, lifted it from her palm, unwrapped it. It seemed to glint very dully in the light above my desk.

My skin started prickling.

I emptied it into my palm. It felt very cool against my skin, far more than was natural. You generally only saw these in the museum over on Fairweather. It was a crude arrowhead, carved out of a lump of flint. The thing had to be hundreds of years old.

What was this about? I held it up between my thumb and forefinger. Its edges were still razor sharp, despite its age. And there were stains on it that looked like they might be blood, except that they were deep black, with the slightest hint of green to it.

I turned it over. Something on its surface winked. So I peered at it a little harder, adjusting its angle in the daylight from my window.

Lettering had been scratched into one of its flatter sides, so lightly I could barely read it. It looked like somebody had done it with a pin, or perhaps a fingernail. Block capital letters. I struggled to make them out.

SARUAK.

I had no idea what that was supposed to mean. A name? An invocation of some kind? But there was one thing I was pretty certain of, the more I stared. They were pretty recent, fresh.

"What is it?" Cassie asked me.

"What it looks like, I'd suppose."

"Why would he have left it behind?"

A new void had begun to open up inside me. A bewildered hollowness. Because this?—it answered none of our questions at all. Just posed new ones. If someone was playing a game with us, then I didn't understand the rules at all.

"Beats me," I said.

But that wasn't entirely the case. Maybe he'd dropped it there for us to find. Why, though? That was the real puzzle, wasn't it?

Extremely gently, I brushed the pad of my thumb against one of the sharpened edges.

And, to my astonishment, it cut me. A bead of blood sprang up.

A cold draft moved through my whole office, at the selfsame time.

The air in front of my desk began to waver gently. Only one thing could make that happen—some kind of sorcery. I held myself in readiness. Wrapped the arrowhead back up, though I held on to it.

Cass, alarmed, got up and went back several paces. Her right hand dropped to one of her Glocks. But the fact was, we could only stand there, waiting to see what was going to happen. And we'd both been in *that* impasse before.

The wavering grew heavier, like ripples on a pond. It didn't spread throughout the room, however. It was confined to a single area in front of me. A vaguely rectangular patch of air, its edges uneven but some five feet wide and rising eight feet off the floor. And that shape suggested . . .

Well, a doorway of some kind.

A drop of perspiration trickled down my brow. This *was* magic, I was certain. But a kind I'd never seen before.

A glance at Cassie told me she was equally dumbfounded. The bridge of her nose got all creased when she was like that, as if she was annoyed.

"Hey!" she blurted. "What *is* this?"

The rippling began to slow. As it diminished, something else began to take its place. Just a vague outline, at first. Then it quickly coalesced into a solid shape.

The air became completely flat and still again. But not empty.

Something was now standing in my office.

CHAPTER 8

It stood several inches taller than I did, and was considerably broader.

But, despite the fact that it had all the usual requirements—two arms, two legs, a head—it wasn't even remotely human. Was this the "something" Raine had warned me of?

Its shoulders were as wide as one side of my desk. It was superbly muscled, with a great barrel chest. At first, I thought it had fur. But then I saw that that was a mistake. It was smooth. An even, pale gray hue all over, a murky color that seemed just a little indistinct, like the creature was made partly out of dust. That was not the case, though. It was definitely solid. Its weight was making the worn parquet floor creak underneath it slightly. And I could smell its rank, meaty breath from here.

Its legs were bowed slightly, the feet massive. And its arms were unnaturally long. It had hands rather than paws—as large as catcher's mitts—but there were no nails on the ends of the fingers. There appeared to be something unusual about the tips of them, although I couldn't tell quite what.

It growled, a noise like rocks coming apart. My gaze went to its face. It was densely ridged and oval. There seemed to be something rather lupine about it. A suggestion of sharpness to the muzzle. A savagery to the heavy brow. Its ears were long, went to sharp tips, and were pressed back flat against its skull. Its eyes shone an iridescent green, and studied us both threateningly.

But it was its mouth that was the worst thing, for the moment anyway. Curving fangs protruded across the lips, distorting them. The beast was drooling gently, and it grunted as it breathed.

What *was* this? I took a step backward, becoming aware of something else. It had materialized between us and the only doorway out of here.

I tried to edge around it a little. Cassie, very gingerly, did the same. It responded by lifting those great hands of its a little higher. And, where I'd noticed something odd about the fingertips . . . ?

Retractable claws—about six inches long, and as sharp-looking as scalpels—all came snicking out.

It snarled again, hunched forward, and its mouth gaped open. There were several rows of fangs in there. I realized, in the dull shock of that moment, that at least we now knew what had been in Garnerstown last night.

I had a brief thought. *Who'd created this?*

And then, my hand was reaching for the Smith & Wesson in my coat.

Cass, as usual, beat me to it. Her gaze became cold, her features set like stone. And one of her Glocks came snaking up.

Her first round, fired almost at point-blank range, hit the creature, making it snarl again, but then bounced off it. It left a small, dull mark against the thing's gray hide, but that was all. I heard her curse.

But Ms. Mallory doesn't ever give up on the first attempt. She simply drew her other handgun, started emptying both magazines into the beast.

The creature stumbled back under the onslaught, but then started to fight against it, rapidly recovering.

I had my revolver out, was firing as well. But to an equal lack of real effect. The thing just took our heat, wincing with discomfort. And kept on pressing forward, trying to snatch the guns from both our hands. Its claws made a whistling noise, splitting the very air. *We* were the ones going backward by this time, and I didn't like that. You can't fight properly if you have to keep retreating.

It couldn't disarm both of us if we separated. So I stepped sideways, behind my desk. Gun smoke had already filled the room, my eyes were stinging gently. I was shaking slightly, wondering how to beat this thing.

The creature paused a moment, trying to decide which of us to follow. Its head went even lower, and its green eyes blinked. And then its shining gaze pinioned me. I'm not sure why. Cassie was the greater threat. But perhaps it had noticed that I still had the arrowhead in my left hand.

The beast suddenly lurched forward, ramming so hard into my desk it completely overturned it. My chair flipped over savagely, forcing me to jump back. I dodged across to one side, tried to fire again.

The hammer came down on an empty chamber. And the creature was stepping up onto my capsized desk by this time. I glanced desperately at Cass.

One of her slim eyebrows arched. She tossed me her second Glock. She uses the extended magazines, so she had plenty of shots to spare. The creature swiped at me with its long talons, missing me by barely an inch. I put three rounds straight into the center of its chest. It staggered back again, and let out something that I suppose might have been a moan. But then it just recovered, like the last time.

I could see there was no stopping it this way. We might as well be taking potshots at the side of a barn door. There was another handgun in the top drawer of my desk, a Magnum. Except my desk was lying on its side. And the creature had climbed on top of it once more.

I snatched up my fallen chair and hurled it, acting out of desperation. One of those huge arms simply batted it away.

Cass, though, had a clear run at the door by this time. I'd

at least succeeded in drawing it away from her. She took the chance that she'd been given, yelling back over her shoulder, "I'll be as quick as I can! Just hold it off!"

Thanks. I'd already figured that one out. I tried shooting at the creature's temples. That got me a slightly better result. It pawed at them and stopped for a few moments. But it wasn't backing off from me now. Not even a little bit.

I could hear Cass's boots hammering down the stairwell, and I knew where she was headed. I just wasn't sure what kind of condition I would be in by the time that she got back.

Perhaps it wanted the arrowhead? But that was the only solid lead we had. I wasn't about to give it up. I dropped it into one of my pockets, freeing up both of my hands.

I put another slug into the creature's face. Hit the corner of its mouth this time. It groaned again. Spat out a few flecks of darker gray liquid I supposed was blood. But I'd already noticed something else. Those faint marks we'd managed to graze its hide with were already fading. This beast was not only hard to damage. When you *did* hurt it, it healed up quickly.

I barely pulled my head away, as its claws went singing past my face.

I was backing off again, moving crabwise. Being forced into a corner. The chair I'd thrown was lying nearby, so I snatched that up as well.

By this stage, the creature wasn't even flinching when the 9mms struck it. It seemed to have grown used to them. Determination shone in those peculiar, glittering eyes.

A click.

The Glock was empty. I dropped it, then held the chair out at full stretch in front of me. Where the hell was Cass?

The talons came whizzing downward. The chair fell to pieces like balsawood. A second set of claws came swiping at me, but I ducked underneath the blow, dropping to the floor, rolling away. Then I lunged for my desk, and scrabbled around behind it.

Tried to yank it upright, which was not an easy job. It was

big, and built of stout New England oak. Difficult for just one man. But I kept on heaving, managing to get its top edge a few inches off the ground. The drawers slid partly open. I could hear the Magnum rattling around.

The creature—out of pique, perhaps—kicked the far end of it, sending it slamming into me. I found myself skidding across the floor, till I finally wound up against the far wall. I was bruised and dazed, but squinted back in the direction that I'd come.

The creature wasn't climbing *over* the desk, this time. It was wading right through it with those massive hind legs, trampling it to get to me. It made huffing noises as it progressed, spittle flying through the air, like it was filled with pressured steam and it was going to explode.

I thought of the arrowhead again. When I reached inside my pocket, though? It wasn't there. I tried the right one, with no better result. Maybe it had fallen out. I stared across the floor.

Too late. The beast was above me, like a storm cloud that had gathered. One of its hands was coming down again. I scrabbled to get out of its way.

Air rushed across my neck. I felt a tug, the back of my coat being torn. But otherwise, I got away unscathed. For how much longer?

In the ruin that had been my desk, I could see my other handgun, glinting dully in the wreckage. Still on my hands and knees, I went toward it breathlessly. And was just about to grab it, when a vicious pain ran through my leg.

The creature had just turned around, stepped forward. And—as casually as stepping on a bug—had planted a foot on my lower calf.

The muscles flared with pain. My leg was pinned in place like it had been nailed to the floor. Although the creature wasn't trying to crush it, merely stopping me from going anywhere. When I tried to wriggle loose, it increased the pressure slightly. When I reached out for the gun, it did the same.

I just took the discomfort, stretching my arm out until my

fingertips were shaking. They got almost to within an inch of the Magnum, but no closer than that.

I twisted around, to see what was happening.

Its right arm had come up once more. Its talons caught the light. This time, it wasn't going to miss.

The claws were sweeping down in the next instant. I was raising both my arms to shield my face, as though that would make the slightest difference.

When a loud explosion made the entire office rock.

The gray creature was almost lifted off its feet. It went back almost two yards, slamming against a cabinet and then nearly losing its balance completely. So it *could* be really injured. Its jaws split open as wide as they could, and it let out a shriek that nearly burst my eardrums.

Breathing hard, I hauled myself half-upright and then glanced toward the doorway. Cass was standing in it, triumph dancing in her gaze, the Mossberg smoking in her grasp. She didn't load the thing with ordinary cartridges, either. She used BRI "saboted" slugs, capable of blowing holes right through a concrete wall. And from the range that she had fired . . . ?

I looked back at the creature she had hit.

The round had penetrated slightly, leaving a dent in its stomach from which dark gray was leaking. A bruise the color of lead was becoming apparent around it. That looked more permanent than the other marks. I didn't think that it would heal real soon.

But it wasn't anywhere near dead. Obviously stunned, and in genuine pain. It remained to be proven if we could finish it for good.

Cass seemed eager to try. Her eyes narrowed and she bit her lower lip. She worked the pump, then stepped in closer, aiming for the head at nearly point-blank range.

The creature looked up, understood what she was doing. Its contorted features grew alarmed. I expected it to try and move away. Instead of which . . .

The air around it started rippling again, much faster than before.

And between one moment and the next, it had completely disappeared.

A long and breathless pause, as we stared at the empty space it had left, was finally broken by an aggravated "Damn!" from Cassie. She looked furious.

Not that I didn't sympathize. But—for my own part—I was just pleased that the thing was gone. It wasn't her leg that had gotten stamped on, after all.

I doubled over and massaged my calf. Cass, still holding the shotgun, came and stood by me, panting gently.

"You okay?" she asked.

"There's probably nothing broken. That's the upside. It still hurts."

"Sorry about leaving you like that."

She'd forgotten her annoyance. Her face was apologetic.

"No—you did the right thing. Thanks."

I stared rather numbly at the wreckage strewn around my office.

"Ever *see* anything like that before?" I asked.

"I'm sure I'd remember."

"Yuh."

But I started to wonder. I hadn't even told Cass about my conversation at the Manor yet, but . . . if this was the "visitor" Raine had talked about?

There was something missing. Whatever that creature had been, it seemed just an animal and nothing more, with no guiding intelligence. Why would it leave an arrowhead for us to find? It didn't even answer Tommy Wilkes's description.

And if it was just doing someone else's bidding, then what kind of lunatic would conjure up a monstrosity like that?

Cassie murmured "damn" again. Walked across to where the beast had last been, then stooped down and picked something up. Displayed it to me in her open palm. It was the saboted slug she'd fired, flattened to a pancake. It had caused some damage, certainly. But had not even penetrated fully. All the victory melted from her eyes by this time, and they glimmered with a quiet dismay.

This was definitely something quite out of the ordinary we were facing.

I edged across and finally picked up the Magnum. Then I stood up properly, carefully distributing my weight. My leg was aching badly. That would be the case for quite a while. But at least I was mobile.

I went to drop the gun in my pocket, but then patted at it in advance, and remembered it was empty. So, finally tucking the Magnum away, I began to turn in a wide circle, casting my gaze across the floor again.

"What are you looking for?" Cass asked me, a trace of suspicion in her voice.

"That arrowhead you found. I think I dropped it."

So she started hunting too.

She went off toward the window. Except, reaching it, she stopped.

"Er, Ross?"

Her tone was rather urgent, and my head came up. She was peering out numbly through the slightly smeary glass.

"You'd better take a look at this."

Cass's voice, uncommonly for her, had become reduced to a dull, low whisper.

CHAPTER 9

I'd come to know her well enough that, simply by the way that she was standing and the angle of her head, I realized that she could see more trouble brewing. A completely different kind of trouble, perhaps—she didn't raise her gun. It wasn't, then, the obvious kind.

She kept entirely still. So when I wandered up beside her, it was very cautiously.

I peered down onto Union Square. The shadow of the statue had expanded out across the wide flagstones. The doors of the municipal buildings were coming open, and a couple of cars were trundling by. There were a few pedestrians abroad by this hour of the morning, on their way to work. They were mostly on the far side of the square, and glancing nervously across and walking quickly. If the first shots hadn't quite been audible, then they'd certainly heard the final one.

Otherwise, it was entirely as it had been, with the banners flapping in the breeze. Except a pair of jet-black crows, big ones, were perching on the statue. They had not been there before.

And the ragged old man was back, and staring up at us. He might have been smiling—it was hard to tell with all that beard. His dog was at his heel, awake. And his placard was no longer there, as if he'd changed his mind about the world's demise.

He did have something to replace it, however. Something which, although much smaller, conveyed a whole new message.

He was twiddling it between the long, narrow fingers of his bare, outstretched right hand.

The arrowhead we'd been searching for just a second earlier.

He kept on fiddling with the piece of flint. I had no idea what it might signify. His gaze on us was steady and unflinching. There was something obtrusive about it too, which made my hackles rise immediately. I just have these instincts, sometimes. And I had them about him in spades now, so much that I wondered why he hadn't bothered me before. Perhaps he'd wanted it that way.

"Any idea at all who he might be?" I asked Cass.

"No." The bridge of her nose wrinkled up again. "But if he's the cause of all this, then he has to be a major adept. And a self-taught one at that."

I supposed so.

"And we know who all the adepts are," she pointed out.

"Or so we thought."

I told her, quickly—summing it all up—about my meeting on the Hill last night. Cass never usually gives the likes of Woodard Raine much credence. But on this occasion, even she looked shocked.

Below us, the arrowhead kept glinting dully in the morning's growing light. The old man hadn't budged an inch. He was waiting for us to come to him. And I wasn't sure if that was such a good idea.

Although, to tell the truth, I couldn't see too many other courses of action. So I quickly decided what we'd do.

"Stay here," I told Cass.

Her face swung toward me.

"Won't you need someone to watch your back?"

"You can watch it better from up here. You'll have a clearer shot."

I trusted her implicitly on that score. And she nodded. When it became obvious that I was coming down to talk, the old man nodded too. And, oh yes, he was definitely smiling now.

"Something," Woodard Raine had said. But this guy looked human. My stomach kept on flipping over as I went back down the stairs. There was nobody else in the stairwell or the lobby of the building. I was glad of that.

As I've said, the best way I'd ever found to confront powerful magicians was to not be overly impressed by them. Act normally. So I kept my tone light as I went out into the square through the front door.

"Hey, that was a neat trick. With the arrowhead, I mean," I called to him. "What exactly is that thing?"

The old geezer remained in place. The sharp flint kept on being twirled between his fingers.

"A Mohawk chieftain, a great warrior in his day, shot me through the heart with it once, just before I ripped his insides out."

Which sent another shock through me, although I tried not to show it.

His voice came as a dry, cool whisper from his wizened lips. There was something hoarse and very old about it. And an underlying gravelly quality as well.

I stopped dead, about three yards away from him. And felt my eyebrows raise.

"Excuse me?"

"After word of that had spread," he continued, barely noticing I'd spoken, "the Iroquois Nation never raised a weapon against me. Never once. Never again. A lesson that you newcomers, even after several centuries, have yet to learn."

His gaze shot upward momentarily. I didn't dare look back, but I knew that Cass was at the window with the shotgun at her shoulder. I could almost feel her watching us. This guy had noticed her as well. But his attention dropped back to me next instant. He was choosing to ignore her.

I stared at him more closely, taking in his height and bean-pole narrowness all over again. His shaggy hair and beard. His wide, floppy hat was a mud-brown color. And his tattered coat the same, buttoned the whole way up to his neck, tied around the middle with a length of rope. His pants, frayed at the cuffs, had once been charcoal gray, but were a variety of neutral shades by this time. He had on heavy black boots, densely scuffed, the laces broken and reknotted maybe half a dozen times.

His skin seemed faintly grimy. I had already taken note of how extremely straight his posture was. But he looked somewhere in his mid-seventies. Should a man so old stand quite like that?

His face looked hawkish and imperious under all that silver fuzz. There seemed nothing special about it. Except . . .

There appeared to be something odd about his mouth. About his teeth. I couldn't quite be certain. And his eyes, partway hidden in the shadow of his hat. They were very pale, and it was hard to tell which color. But one detail about them captured my attention. The left pupil seemed to be twice the size of the right. It winked at me, like a camera lens. Was there a faint, strange brilliance, a tiny fiery glow, within it? I just wasn't sure.

The crows behind him, cawing loudly, flapped up from the statue suddenly. They circled, and then vanished. When I looked back at the old man, though . . . ?

They seemed to have left some of their dark color behind, when they'd departed. He had borrowed it, perhaps. Shadow hung around him far more heavily by now. As though he'd stepped into this place out of the darkness of the previous evening, bringing some of it along with him.

He peered back at me, waiting for me to say something more. What *he'd* said made no sense at all. Mohawks? I kept on trying to hide how unnerved I was feeling.

An idea occurred to me. I glanced at the flint again.

"You didn't drop that accidentally last night, did you?" I asked.

There was a calculating look deep in his eyes, and I had noticed that as well. This was someone who did nothing just by accident.

He pressed his lips together.

"You were announcing yourself, like a calling card."

"Very good," he said.

And then he did something that genuinely startled me. He stopped twirling the arrowhead, held it up to his lips. Then put it in his mouth and swallowed it.

I could see the bulge as it slid down his throat. Remembered how sharp its edges had been. But he didn't seem in the tiniest bit discomforted. His eyes were laughing at me as the shape dropped lower, disappeared.

And when his mouth had opened . . . had his teeth been filed down to sharp points? Or were they naturally like that?

I could hear Cass push the window open wider, obviously alarmed as well. But I raised a hand quickly, before she could do anything else about it.

My breath was hissing in my lungs. What exactly was I standing in front of? The few pedestrians around us, I could see, were giving us a wide berth, glancing at us oddly. Even they had noticed there was something wrong.

"Why did you do that?" I asked.

"Just putting it back where it belongs, Ross."

And how did he know my name?

"Have we met?"

"Not exactly, Mr. Devries. But you know what I am called."

My head reeled slightly. What was he talking about, if this was the first time we'd come face-to-face?

"You've seen it," he added.

"Where?"

His brow creased a touch.

"Oh, Mr. Devries! I'd assumed you were the observant type, more than capable of putting two and two together."

But I was already observing more than he had recognized. My own gaze had, a few times, flickered down to his old dog. It was pale, with diseased-looking brown patches on its hide. Its eyes were a gently glinting green. And its big belly was hanging on the flagstones . . . but was that a large, deep bruise I could make out? A deep gray color, just like . . . ?

It looked back at me balefully, its snaggled jaws mashing together, and let out a snarling noise that sounded a touch familiar. A chill ran through me, and my pulse worked a little faster. What *was* all this? But, not sure what was going on as yet, I simply stood my ground.

The only thing I really knew about this guy was that he owned that arrowhead. And scratched on it there'd been some lettering. So . . .

"Saruak?" I tried.

"Bingo!" It came almost as an abrupt laugh. "I knew you could do it!"

Then he peered at me expectantly, like I ought to welcome him to town.

My feet were trying to move away all by themselves, but I wouldn't let them. It felt like a caterpillar was crawling up my spine. I hated even standing near to this guy, he let off such a hateful aura. It was a struggle just to keep on sounding calm.

"And where are you from?" I asked.

"Around these parts, originally. After that? Nowhere in particular. I travel a lot, you see."

"What do you do, exactly? And what brings you here?"

"As to the first, the Iroquois tribes used to call me 'Matchi Manitou.'"

I knew what that meant. "Evil spirit." *That's crazy,* was my first thought. Such a thing could just not be. But when you considered where we lived . . . ?

His features stiffened, as though he'd heard that.

"The Penobscots, who knew me first, had another name for me. Quite hard to translate. But roughly, 'The Dancer in Dreams.' As for your second question . . . well, it seems a pleasant place, this town. I thought I'd hang around awhile."

Which was not how people usually reacted to Raine's Landing, and I told him that.

Laughter flickered in his eyes. "I understand that. Yes, I know."

I studied him all over again. He remained passively still under my gaze, his face blank, like he had absolutely nothing that he wished to hide. How much *did* he know about this place?

"Did you kill all those people last night?" I asked him outright.

His expression didn't even twitch.

"Is this how you treat newcomers? You're being very rude."

"You're saying you didn't?"

Saruak shrugged. "It hardly matters, either way."

I thought of all those butchered people, their dead faces staring. And it was of no consequence to him? When I tried to speak again, it felt like a fishhook was embedded in my throat.

"Because?"

"I've seen so much death, down the centuries. A human life, passing?—is like a drop of rain hitting the soil. A perfectly common occurrence. One that happens several hundred times a minute."

Which didn't sound like any philosophy I wanted to subscribe to. But how old, precisely, was this Saruak claiming to be?

My gaze dropped back to his ugly dog.

"My guess? It wasn't you personally doing the killing last night, was it?"

Once more, his face split with delight.

"Spot on again, Mr. Devries! I *knew* that you were one of the sharper tools in this particular box! Meet Dralleg."

And he reached down, patted the beast's head. It blinked at me, its eyes seeming to glow a little brighter.

"Strange name for a dog," I commented.

"Strange dog," he grinned. "But I'm wasting my breath. You've already guessed that."

It couldn't do what it had done in that form. But another native concept came to mind—shape-shifter. I wondered how safe I was, standing here. Any moment, it might change back into that creature in my office.

But it just sat there like a miniature blimp with half the air let out. My lip curled.

"Where did you find something like that?"

"I didn't. I thought him up. Dralleg is a product of *my* mind."

"That's some imagination you have."

"I'll take that as a compliment."

I was getting angry with his flippant manner. "Why did you kill all those people?"

"You've already asked."

Which was no answer. I just gazed at him.

"To prove a point," he told me.

"Being?"

"I am the new boss round here, or soon will be. Forget your Sycamore Hill, your adepts and your mayor. And Woodard Raine."

I'd heard that kind of speech before. It got me wondering not only how much he knew, but how on earth he had discovered it.

There was a deeply mocking gleam back in his eyes. When his voice came oozing out once more, it sounded exactly like Woody's.

"'Whatever's come to visit us, it's all het up and hungry . . . I'd get a move on, sport, if I were you.'"

I jolted.

"Ross?" Cass yelled, behind me.

I sucked in a breath, then quickly looked around. She was leaning right out of the window, with her shotgun trained on the old man. I shook my head, indicating that I was all right. Then peered back at Saruak, dumbfounded.

He had somehow been listening the entire time last night. And Woodard Raine, for all his powers, hadn't even known. That spoke volumes by itself. What was this guy capable of? And we had always thought, here in the Landing, that there was no magic greater than our own.

My hand went to the Magnum in my pocket, out of reflex. But the man didn't seem in the tiniest bit bothered.

"Look, there's nothing for you here," I told him.

But he shook his head. "I disagree."

"What, then?"

"A place to rest. Do you know how long I've been on the road? Practically four hundred years."

Longer than we'd been under Regan's Curse, in other words. But, again, what did he mean exactly? On the road where? And for what purpose?

His gaze and expression, they had both become impenetrable.

"Why stop, after all that time?" I asked.

"This problem that you have. This isolation from the world. It seems to bother most of you. But me . . . ?"

The dog made a faint noise and looked up at him.

"It gives me a captive audience. And I've always wanted that. Most humans run away from me eventually. But the plain fact is, you people cannot. You are rooted to the spot. And we can . . ."

His eyes took on a sickly sheen as he hunted for the right way to put it.

"Get to know each other properly. We can commune, in depth."

He could do anything he wanted with us all, in other words. And take his own sweet time about it. It didn't sound like any kind of idle threat. I kept wondering how he was going to act on it.

"What are you, really?" I inquired.

Saruak's arms became slack at his sides.

"Are you sure you want to know? It might prove more than you can handle."

I stared at him wordlessly.

"Very well, then," he responded. "See you again soon, I'm sure."

The air around him began to waver, just as it had done inside my office. Just before the old man disappeared . . .

I caught a glimpse of him in his true form.

Blood was pounding in my temples, and I couldn't breathe. I couldn't seem to move at all.

My insides became frozen. The world tilted or . . . no, my knees were buckling. I went down on them hard. And then curled forward, till my head was pressed against the paving stones. And I stayed there with my eyes squeezed shut, just trying to get some air into my lungs.

CHAPTER 10

I could hear Cass pounding up behind me before too much longer. Then her hand was on my shoulder, gently squeezing it. I *still* couldn't get my forehead off the ground, and sweat had drenched my face.

"Ross?"

Waves of nausea were rushing through me. I grit my teeth, trying to fight against it.

"Ross—what did he do to you?"

"He . . . he's not a man, Cass. Isn't even remotely human."

"What are you talking about?"

"Did—?" I tried again. "Didn't you see it?"

She explained to me that she'd seen Saruak flicker very slightly, just before he'd disappeared. But that was all. The revelation of his true form had been purely for my benefit.

Cassie crouched down and started to massage my neck.

"You're fine, bud. No real damage done."

I took a deep breath through my nose that made me dizzy.

"I'll take your word on that."

"I'll bet you've seen worse."

"Don't be so sure."

One of her arms was going around me next. And then she

was helping me back to my feet. Something seemed to be wrong with the way my legs were working. So Cass propped me firmly up, then guided me inside. It's a tribute to her strength and determination that we made it the whole way to my office without even pausing.

I was starting to calm down by the time we got there. All the same, she put me in the only unbroken chair, and then brought me a glass of water. She was gazing at me closely, real worry apparent in every pore.

I described to her, once my breathing had steadied, my entire encounter with Saruak.

"And you think he's for real?" she asked.

"From what I saw, yes."

And Woodard Raine already believed he was a genuine threat.

She examined the notion carefully. "If he was capable of taking this town over, surely he'd have already done it?"

Which was a good point. What was stopping him?

"I said it last night, Cassie. He seems to be testing us."

She stuck out her lower lip. "Which means he doesn't fully know . . . ?"

"What the people here are capable of. The adepts in particular."

"He'll keep on coming at us, then."

I nodded. "Till he knows our limits. And is confident that he can win."

There was an unfazed glint in Cassie's eyes. Faced with anything that posed a threat, she tried to find the positive side.

"If we have weaknesses, he's got to have some too."

I'd already figured that one out.

"Any clue what they might be?"

"I don't have the first idea," I told her. "But I know someone who might."

Which only made her look unhappy again. Worse than she had when I'd consulted with Woody.

It was time for me to go and see the Little Girl.

* * *

I drove off from the square and headed west, passing along streets that were only moderately busy. And then, when I left the center, not busy at all. More reminders of the impending ceremony were visible around me, as I cruised along the empty avenues. Posters were displayed in storefronts, had been stuck to trees along the roadside. When I passed a schoolyard, there too, another large banner had been draped.

Between Garnerstown and Sycamore Hill—not physically, you understand, but in terms of status—lies a district known simply by the name of its main street, Marshall Drive. Not as low-rent as Cray's Lane, nor as high-toned as the mansions, it's a part of town that can be summed up with the one word: "comfortable." It had no pretensions of being anything else. A classier version of my own area, in other words. The cars sitting on the driveways were all new and brightly polished. The flowers in the front yards were expensive, cultivated ones. I even caught a glimpse of an occasional pool out back. A contented neighborhood, then, maybe even a little smug around the edges. But the last place in the world you would expect to come across a strange phenomenon like the one I was about to visit.

My gut was still flipping gently. And the backs of my eyeballs felt raw, like what I'd seen had actually seared them. Every time I blinked, I got another flash of that last image. Saruak in his true form, all fumes and fangs and heavily scaled tentacles. So I tried to stop blinking as much as I could.

This was a low-lying part of town. Beyond its furthest rooftops, the beginnings of the forest could be seen. That was where the Landing ended. A couple of hawks were circling out there, reminding me uncomfortably there was another world beyond our own.

I went by a young mother pushing a stroller. She had auburn hair but was slim, and reminded me a little of Alicia. Most attractive women did. I drove quietly down Bethany Street until I finally came to a halt outside the house that I was looking for: Number 51.

Just stared at it silently, at first. I always do. There was a Chrysler parked in front of the garage. Neat drapes at the windows, and the lawn was trimmed—by whom? There were strands of ivy on the walls, but not too much of it. Nothing in the tiniest, in fact, to differentiate this place from all the others on the street. What it contained *within* its walls, though?—there was nothing normal there.

The front door was hanging slightly ajar, with no lights on beyond it. Was it always this way, I wondered, or did it just come open for my benefit? I pushed it gently back, then paused a moment on the threshold.

I could see the hallway and part of the living room from here. Nothing remarkable about them in the slightest. Maplewood furniture, framed prints of classic paintings, and a vase of artificial flowers on a cabinet. Exactly what you'd reckon on seeing in a home like this.

But whose had it been? Who'd originally lived here? I'd searched the whole place several times, and turned up nothing. Not a checkbook or a document, a credit card, a bill. Nothing with a name on it. But surely someone had to own this place?

Right now, there wasn't time for any idle speculation. I just went quickly up the stairs, then headed for the nursery.

It was at the rear of the house, overlooking the large, neatly tended backyard. I found myself looking at another door set slightly at a gap. An electric blue glow was spilling out across one wall. It was a steady one. Light cast by the most powerful magic almost never flickers.

Oh yes, the Little Girl was home.

She never seemed to leave.

She'd known that I was on my way, of course. How could she not? She sees more than the rest of the Landing's inhabitants combined, including Woodard Raine. And as I stepped into her room—becoming suddenly immersed in that blue glow—I felt the skin across my entire body tingle. Felt the hair lift on my scalp a touch. My clothing clung to my body more tightly than before. There was a strange energy in here, all deriving from one source.

Oddly, it was a pretty normal nursery apart from that. Pretty much what you'd expect for a child of her age. There were dolls scattered everywhere, houses to put them in. There were fluffy toy ducks and rabbits, and a rather battered teddy. A My Little Pony duvet lay across the bed. A mobile dangled from the ceiling, silver moons and leaping moo-cows.

The wallpaper was fancy, a cartoonish depiction of the sky, with billowing white clouds, songbirds, and a rainbow.

But the curtains—in the same design—were firmly closed. And had been ever since I'd started coming here.

The room's occupant, you see, did not need anything so mundane as a window.

At the direct center of the nursery, floating some four feet off the thick pile carpet, was the Little Girl herself.

As usual, she was rotating placidly, with her eyes firmly closed. You wanted to ask her, "Hey, what are you doing up there?"

Apart from the two noticeable facts that she was airborne and emitting colored light, she was just a child of first grade age, fair-skinned and with pale blond hair that hung down past her shoulders. She was clad in a blue gingham dress, white socks, and buckled-up white shoes. That made it all the weirder.

Her arms hung limply by her sides. Her expression was smooth and calm, as if she might be sleeping, although I knew that she was not. Her long, fine lashes quivered almost constantly. And beneath her lids, her eyeballs were moving the entire time.

Her lips twitched. Her expression tautened slightly. Maybe she'd been thinking about something else, and had only just remembered I was there.

"Hello, Mr. Ross." It was her usual greeting.

Her voice always startled me slightly. It had an echoing quality to it, as though the words were being spoken sev-

eral times, and layered across each other. And it sounded
far more distant than it really was. A sound like someone
calling to you from the far depths of a cave.

She kept on turning, turning. Her small face disappeared
from view a moment, and then swiveled back again.

"There's no need for the 'Mr.'"

I had told her that before.

But her brow only furrowed. "No. That wouldn't be polite."

Okay then, I thought, have it your way. I already knew that
she could hear that, just as clearly as if I had said the words.
It's not the most pleasant of sensations, realizing there's
someone rooting around in your mind the whole time you
are in their presence. But I'd gotten used to it.

I could only stare up at her, wondering exactly who she
was. When we had first come across her, Cass and I had
canvassed every house in this whole neighborhood. And nobody—just no one—had the slightest memory of any family
at this address. We had gone to the Town Hall as well, and
scoured the records. There were none for this place. Not so
much as a passing reference to 51 Bethany Street.

It seemed she had just popped out of thin air one day.
Where were her parents, if she even had any? And how had
she become this way? I was still no closer to uncovering an
answer. But there was one thing I knew for sure.

The Little Girl could help me in ways few other people
could.

"You've come about the bad things?" she asked me suddenly.

And I nodded. "Yes."

"What happened last night?" Her face puckered up a
moment. "It . . . it made me very sad."

"You saw it?"

"I saw the start of it. Then I got upset and looked away.
But I could still feel it happening."

That was the weirdest thing about her. She seemed to possess enormous power, but she just stayed in her room and
watched. She never went outside, or intervened. I had often
wondered, was she trapped here?

"Do you know *why* it happened?"

"I suspect you're right. Our vulnerabilities are being probed."

"He wants to see if anyone here can fight back?"

"Yes." Her lips twisted into a brief, rather bitter smile. "He was surprised when Miss Cassie managed to hurt his Dralleg."

"Not too badly, though."

The Girl considered that and nodded. Her expression became blank again.

"Is he capable of worse?" I asked her.

"Certainly, he comes from a race of massive power."

"From the spirit world."

"Yes. He is a tree spirit, and an extremely ancient one, born out of a poison oak and the start of the first forests. The Iroquois knew all about him and were very cautious of him. Rightly so."

"And?"

"He respected them, as much as he was able. But us?" And she frowned. Did she regard herself as part of humankind? "He regards us as interlopers, and despises us. Loves to trample us like ants. He's spent the last few centuries traveling across the nation, visiting communities and bringing death down on them. He does it for sport."

Which all sounded bad enough. But he wasn't just visiting, in this case. He had told me he was planning to stay. Which brought us to the million-dollar question.

"And can he be stopped?"

She turned that over carefully, her brow becoming tense. The creases made her look far older than she seemed to be. Shadows overtook her face. Her body seemed to blur for a moment, its outlines going indistinct.

Then she became simply a little child again.

"His power must be fed, if he is going to perform great feats of magic," she told me.

What exactly did that mean?

"He draws it from us, in large part."

I was still waiting for a proper explanation. The Girl

seemed to understand that. Her hands suddenly twitched and lifted a few inches, and her head tipped slightly back. And I could almost sense her peering outward, despite the fact her eyelids were still shut.

"It is . . . a matter of belief."

Uh-huh?

"A matter of perception. The more that we allow Saruak to dominate our actions and our thoughts, the stronger he'll become. Bending us all to his will, even though we do not know it—that's what truly nourishes him. The larger he swells in our consciousness, the more powerful he'll grow."

I swallowed. "Could you be a little more specific?"

"Have you ever had a mildly bad dream?"

I remembered what the Penobscot had called him. That was where he liked to dance.

"Yes, plenty."

Since none of my dreams were mild these days, that was not quite the truth. I should have had more sense. The Girl looked agitated for a few long seconds, like she might be on the verge of reprimanding me. But then, she calmed down and continued.

"They barely bother you. A seriously bad dream, however? It makes you sweat and thrash about, and then wake up and even scream. It affects you, you see. Has power over your whole body. Saruak is the same way—an expanding and engulfing nightmare."

I still wasn't sure that I entirely understood her. But there was no mistaking just how definite she looked.

"Why bring that nightmare here? Why us?"

"It's our own magic, Mr. Ross. That's what drew him to Raine's Landing in the first place."

She stopped rotating for a while, and simply hung there, facing me.

"This place, unlike the normal world, is far more like the dimension he came from in the first place. Magic fuels more magic, see? Spells lead on to stronger ones. The Landing is like rich dark soil in which he's planted his first roots. And when we use our magic, Saruak drinks deeper."

But *I* never used it at all. Maybe that was what had drawn him to me. Was there something about me . . . that was puzzling him?

Another thought occurred.

"Then why send his creature after me, if he's so all-fired powerful? Why didn't he just snuff me out himself?"

"I said that he came from a *race* of great power. But he has been on the road a long time since his last stop, and has barely fed at all."

At last, I—and the whole town—were being given a lifeline. *Now* I could see what she was driving at.

"So it's all potential?"

The Girl nodded, then began slowly rotating on the air once more.

"He needs time for his strength to gather?"

Her smile was gentler, this time. "Yes."

I should have let Cassie shoot him from the window, I could see. Taking that on board, I almost kicked myself. But maybe it wasn't too late. If I could get to him again, before he fed . . .

"Where is he?" I asked urgently.

My chest was thumping with the prospect of it. Might we have another chance?

But one glance up put paid to all of that. It's hard to look unhappy with your eyelids closed, but the Little Girl still managed it.

"He is an expert at concealment, I'm afraid," she told me apologetically.

I felt stunned and abandoned. Even her?

"He's had centuries to practice it. I'm sorry, Mr. Ross."

I could see it on her features. She was conscious that she'd let me down. And was taking it badly, exactly the way a girl of her age might.

There she hung, revolving on the blue-tinged air. Apparently just a child. And . . . what was she even called? Where had she come from? How'd she get like this?

We'd simply found her one evening, drawn to her by the strange blue glow behind her drapes.

There didn't seem to be anything more that she could tell me. So, trying to make her feel better, I thanked her for the help that she had given.

"You're welcome," she murmured back, all softly and politely.

She'd given us some degree of hope, at least. Given us some kind of fighting chance. And that was worth more than all the riches on the Hill, wasn't it?

I shot one last glance back at her, as I went out through the door. She was still rotating at the same languorous speed, and seemed to have forgotten I was even there. Her expression was blank again. And her eyes remained tightly shut.

You want to know what I think?

Well, despite the fact that she has simply watched events unfold so far, I'd guess that she has other gifts. Enormous power of her own, maybe. I think that one day—who knows when?—her eyes will finally open, something new will be unleashed here in the Landing. Although whether for good or bad is anybody's guess.

There are times I even play with the idea that she's not genuinely a Little Girl at all.

In which case . . . what is she?

CHAPTER 11

I found myself going past a public library on my way back. So I parked by the curb just beyond it, headed back on foot into its mildew-scented dimness. The amber light was low in here, and there were green-shaded lamps switched on. There were a load of little grade-school kids, reading up on some class project about the town's history, and so the noise level was slightly buzzier than it should have been. I went past them to the section on mythology, prized out a tome on Iroquois folklore, and learnt what more I could about Matchi Manitou.

They were as old as the continent itself, born out of its lakes and rivers and its woodlands. Were secretive, mysterious beings, masters of concealment. They ranged, in nature, from the mischievous to the downright malevolent. And the worst of them were pretty damned powerful things.

They could not only do tricks like changing their appearance. They could call up lightning and storms. Get into people's minds and play with them in bizarre ways. And possess a human body, controlling it as if it was some living marionette.

They could even shift the very borders of reality, and re-create the rules.

One odd thing began to strike at me, after a while. In every reference that I came across, the same thing was repeated.

They had just one serious limitation. Because they had been born from natural elements, they were tied to the area where they had first come into being. That was a pretty big one, when it came to the New England woods. And Saruak hailed from these parts, for sure.

But the Little Girl had told me—and he had implied—that he'd been wandering the entire nation, these past centuries. And it made me wonder. How'd he managed that?

Nothing that I read lifted my mood even slightly. Nothing gave me any better cause for optimism. We were up against a Big Bad Something, without any doubt.

Study, so I've always heard, is good for the mind. But mine didn't feel any better by the time that I went out of there.

Which begs the question, Who thought that old proverb up?

There were more people about, in cars and on the sidewalk, as I headed back toward the office. And I studied them when I slowed down at an intersection or a set of lights.

A few of them were going about their business just as usual. Hardy souls, battle-seasoned, who were used to taking what the Landing threw at them and just getting on with their lives. Living proof that human beings can adapt to almost any circumstance.

Most of them, however, the majority . . . ?

It wasn't the case that they were doing anything out of the ordinary. It was far more that they seemed to be doing it at a slightly warier, slower pace than they had yesterday. Eyes were a touch wider, faces stiffer. And the near distance was being studied constantly, to see if there was anything wrong. Brief glances were being thrown at corners, over shoulders, or at rooftops, at the sky.

A whole town on edge, in other words. Worried and—with no small justification—paranoid. Everyone had to have heard what had transpired down in Garnerstown last night. And they were starting to form small huddles now, on street corners and storefronts, and at bus stops and park benches. And the question being asked—I didn't need to be able to hear it, to know what it was.

What had happened last night? Might it happen once again?

I kept on thinking about what the Little Girl had told me, regarding Saruak making his presence known and gaining power that way. And, although these people didn't even know that he was here, I felt sure that I was watching the start of the whole strange process she'd described. People were afraid of something, even if they couldn't put a name to it as yet.

And once they could? How strong, then, would our visitor grow?

I went right on the lights at Fairmont, past a shoe store with a half-price sale on, heading down to Union Square. Everywhere I looked, it was the same. It occurred to me. Was consciousness of Saruak's evil seeping through the town the same way Salem's magic had once done? Would insects soon hum with the knowledge of him, and the night winds moan his name?

It ground at me, the whole thing, almost to the point of sheer infuriation. Because there was nothing I could think to do about it. Not yet anyway.

There'd be parking restrictions on Union Square by this hour of the morning. So I stopped the car in a little alley just behind my office, and then went in the back way.

Cass had been trying to tidy up—fairly unsuccessfully, she's not much good at stuff like that. In fact, she'd already given up. And was crouched over the pile of matchwood that had been my desk, with her cell phone to her ear. Apparently, she was on the line to her half sister, Pam. Her tone was light and comfortable—she obviously didn't want to freak the woman out. But she made her excuses quickly and hung up when I walked in.

Her expression was an apprehensive one. But not for the same reason as the people on the street. She always hates me going to 51 Bethany. Has only ever met the Little Girl one time. And got so upset by the experience, she's never ventured back.

"Jesus Christ! You trust *that aberration?"* she was fond of asking me.

The real reason for her abhorrence, it had to be said, was probably a good deal closer to home. Cass had once had a family of her own, just like me. Three little kids, to be precise. And she'd lost them to magic too. One—I'd seen the photos, many times—had been a girl of exactly the same appearance and age, except her hair had been a few shades darker. And so going into that blue-lit nursery had to be—to her—like seeing the ghost of her own baby, still in the world, just floating there. It had startled her far worse than all the monsters we had fought put together.

"So?" she asked me, her features rearranging themselves gently. She was trying to look unconcerned. "The weird kid have anything to tell you?"

I arranged my thoughts as best I could, then started in. And Cassie became more and more subdued as I conveyed it all. Until, by the time that I was finished, she was not even looking at me anymore. Still squatting on the floor, she'd put her elbows on her knees, and was staring at the bare boards with a tired exasperation.

"He's really that much of a threat?"

I was forced to clear my throat before I answered.

"If everything that I've found out is true, then he's the worst kind by a long chalk."

"The way that he gains his power? If we just ignored him . . . ?"

"My guess is, he's going to make that pretty difficult."

Cassie finally looked up, her eyes filled with a quiet dread. "There's going to be more like last night?"

"I'd reckon. Or perhaps worse still."

She peered at me questioningly.

"You weren't there, Cass, talking with him face-to-face. Didn't see the way he really looked at me, the way he gloated. He's malevolent to the core, and very cruel. I think that it's just in his nature."

She absorbed that, her lips parting just a crack. But all she did was gnaw her lower lip. The muscles in her shoulders had bunched tight. She was preparing herself, mentally, for whatever was coming our way.

"What now, then?" she asked in a hollow whisper.

"First? We pass this information on."

There were plenty of figures of authority in our town. Hierarchies, powers-that-be. And if they didn't know the full story already, then they at least needed to be warned.

It wasn't exactly the longest walk to the Town Hall. We took it slowly all the same, wondering how the information that we'd gathered up was going to be received. Edgar Aldernay—our esteemed mayor—was a good administrator, but not exactly famous for his bedside manner. He was as likely, we both knew, to blow up in our faces as to listen to us sensibly. The only consolation was that he was just a mouthpiece, any way you looked at it. A figurehead or, if you wanted to be cynical, a puppet. There were other forces, far more savvy and intelligent, lurking in the shadows just behind his throne.

Union Square was busier than it had been before. At the northern end, two huge flatbed trucks had pulled up. One was loaded with dismantled scaffolding, the other with big stacks of wooden boards. Burly guys in hard hats were carefully bolting it all together. The stage for this season's Reunion Evening was already taking shape.

Down at the opposite end, two pale blue vans were parked, their rear doors open. Guys from these were paying out long reels of cable, and attaching loudspeakers to the lampposts around the square.

It might work. Probably wouldn't. But the authorities were making sure this year's Reunion Eve was going to be an impressive show.

We went up the steps, under the huge clock and past the big stone lions. There was nobody to stop us when we went inside. It's pretty much a come-and-go-as-you-like kind of place, with no real need for security. People were standing around talking in the lobby, some of them with files under their arms. But all they did was glance at us, then go back to their conversations.

We knew the way and headed up toward the second

floor, the ornate ironwork of the stairwell taking us in broad ascending circles. A mail-room boy was going along the main corridor, when we reached it. From the office doorways that we started passing, electric typewriters chattered, photocopying machines let out a busy hum. As I've already said, computers have never really caught on here. The whole building smelled of ink and aged oak and history.

The mayor's personal assistant for these past twenty-five years—Mrs. Dower—wasn't at her desk when we went in. But beyond it was a double doorway, open just a fraction. We could hear the great man himself, shouting on the phone.

"No, goddamn it, I do *not* accept that this could happen again! It was a one-off and that's *all* it was! A freak accident—*that's* the official line! Everybody's panicked quite enough, thank you! If the slightest word to the contrary slips out from anyone in your department, I will have your goddamn *badge!*"

So I supposed that he was yelling at Saul Hobart.

We went in as he slammed down the receiver. When he saw that we were there and looked up, he was florid-faced. Which is not an unusual complexion for Mayor Aldernay. There are days when he seems barely capable of staying calm at all.

He was a man of mediums, both in terms of height and stoutness. But impeccably dressed as ever, in a sharp Brooks Brothers suit. His slightly greasy brown hair reached down almost to his collar. And he sported what I've always thought of as an overly thin moustache. His eyes were rather dull and far away. His nose had a few pink blemishes that might be down to alcohol. I'd never seen him drink too much in public, but who knew?

The man eyed us fiercely. He was either wondering what we wanted, or just wishing we would go away. He didn't look in the mood to be bothered.

"Don't people even knock these days?" he asked. "I'm still the goddamn mayor, you know."

I murmured, "No offence intended."

Cass just looked away. She has as much time for official-dom as for the adepts—namely, none.

To give the man credit, he seemed to figure out pretty quickly why we were here. The fire in his gaze eased off a little. Aldernay tented his knuckles underneath his chin. Glanced down for a second, then puffed out his cheeks.

"Let me guess? You have your own two cents to put in about what went on last night."

"Might do."

"Well?" he said. "I'm listening."

"That 'happen again' part you mentioned on the phone? That's what we need to talk to you about."

"A *what?*" he exploded, several minutes later.

Well, so much for him being reasonable. His fingers pressed down on the desk. I thought that he was going to stand up, but he didn't. Just sat there, his knuckles going white.

"Have you gone *insane*, Devries? An ancient spirit? That is simply *horse manure!*"

I stood my ground, unimpressed by his show of anger. It was pretty much what I had been expecting, after all. There's a theory as to why our mayor descends, so often, into such atrocious moods. Just gossip really, but . . .

Edgar Aldernay hailed from one of the most distinguished families in the Landing, when it came to the practice of magic. His late father was the renowned Rufus Aldernay, so skillful at his craft he earned the title of Grand Adept. His grandmother was Beatrice Bratt, who had ended the drought of 1931, when the Adderneck ran almost dry. And the Salem witch who started his line was Constance McBryde, cousin and close friend to Sephera herself.

And rumor had it that—in spite of all that—Edgar here was no good in the slightest at the hocus-pocus stuff. He tried and tried during his early years, but couldn't find it in himself. He couldn't get so much as a puff of smoke out of a cheap cigar, much less fill a river up.

Maybe that is why he's clung on to his job so fiercely all

these years, when others would get tired of it. It makes him believe he's in control, and good at something. And it would certainly explain the way he acts—like the whole world knows his guilty secret.

You had to sympathize with him, on one level. But his manner was exasperating, all the same.

"I think you've got the wrong idea," I tried to explain to him.

But he was having none of it.

"Oh really? And what are you going to tell me next? Ghosts are going to come along and rob our banks?"

If he could get annoyed and shout, then I could do the same.

"You'll have to come to terms with this sooner or later, Edgar! Saruak *was* responsible for what happened yesterday evening!"

And that slowed him down a little, although the red glow in his cheeks remained.

"He *could* be some new adept that we didn't know about," he finally conceded.

"That's what we first thought. Just one problem. He came from outside town. Surely that has to tell you something?"

He had been immune to Regan's Curse, in other words. He had not shied back, or turned away. Which made him rather special, rather different to normal humans.

Aldernay's gaze met mine sharply. "Even that's not totally unprecedented. Look at your friend Willets."

Now, I wouldn't call Willets a friend exactly. I don't think he has any of those. But the mayor did have a point. Could Saruak just be someone who'd gained power, and then adopted this whole "spirit" persona? Not the first time something of that kind had happened. We'd had a self-taught adept, once, who'd thought that he was actually Merlin.

Things around here were often not quite what they seemed to be at first. Were all of us, even the Little Girl, being suckered by some lunatic or fraudster?

I couldn't get that moment out of my mind when he had revealed himself to me. My head might try to deny what I had seen, but my instincts couldn't. I was certain it was real.

So I went on to explain to the mayor what the Little Girl had said, about the way that Saruak drew his power. Aldernay looked more and more confused, his gaze becoming darker.

"First he's a spirit. Now he's a nightmare. Lord, can't you make your mind up?"

"We need to find some way to stop it happening," I persisted. "Maybe your friends on the Hill . . . ?"

"Goddamn it, Devries, you still haven't convinced me. And I'm quite busy enough as it is."

"With?"

The man went noticeably sweaty at that point. He picked up a pen, for want of anything better to do.

"Reunion Eve, of course!"

Was he kidding? I asked my next question as politely as I could, which wasn't very.

"You seriously think that's more important?"

"I'd thank you to keep that tone out of your voice."

"This guy is planning to take over the whole Landing. He's doubtless going to harm more people, plenty more. You *seriously* think your magic show is a priority, compared with that?"

The mayor stared at me, frozen with embarrassment.

"Well," he grumbled finally. "If what you say is true, it might be our best bet. Since—if it works—then we can all get out of here."

Cassie's eyes rolled, at that point. I took a slow step forward. Aldernay was almost in denial by this stage, trying to pretend that there was really nothing to get too concerned about. So I explained the facts to him as firmly as I could.

"Reunion Evening hasn't achieved anything—the last time I counted—on two hundred and eighty-four separate occasions. And you're putting all your faith in that? What in God's name are you thinking of?"

The mayor, though, had another odd trait, apart from his volatility. When shouting at people didn't do the trick, he just ignored them and switched off.

He stared down at his desk again. Scribbled something on a pad. And refused to even look at me.

"Well, it might work this time," he murmured, talking to thin air.

We were obviously dismissed. Frustration boiled through me. But we'd had this kind of attitude from Aldernay before, and had got along perfectly well without his help.

We were about to turn away when the phone on the man's desk rang. He glanced at it surprisedly, then snatched it up.

All the color on his face drained away within the next half minute. He was silent, merely nodding, listening carefully to whatever he was being told. Cassie and I exchanged glances. You didn't need to be a psychic to figure who was on the other end.

As I've already mentioned, there were shadows massed behind that chair of his. Bright eyes back there, which watched intently. I could spell out some of the names, but you will hear them later anyway. Not Woodard Raine, in case you're wondering. Woody—it's been pointed out before—is too far gone, aloof.

But there were others, peers of his, who took a far more active interest in the business of the Landing.

By the time he set the handset down a second time—far more gently this time—Aldernay's face looked like a balloon with a puncture in it. All I did was stare at him. He cleared his windpipe, then leaned forward in his chair.

"I've been asked to tell you—"

His voice was hushed, almost croaky. He swilled the next words around in his mouth before finally spitting them out.

"—that your observations have been duly noted, and are receiving proper and intent deliberation."

Which was all I'd really come here for. The powers-that-be knew everything that I'd discovered now.

I thanked him. He just nodded briefly, his dull eyes going rather glazed.

And then, without another word, Cassie and I were out of there.

CHAPTER 12

The bearded missionary stepped up . . .

It was all there in his mind's eye, as clearly as if it had only happened yesterday. Nearly four hundred years, in fact, had passed since the event. But it had altered Saruak's existence so completely he could still smell every odor and hear every tiny sound. Some finches chirped in the trees. A gentle wind blew through the branches.

He, as usual, had been perched up on a high one, gazing down.

The bearded missionary stepped up through the tree line, entering the vast New England forest with a taut expression on his face. You would have thought that he was stepping off the very edge of the world. He had on a black hat, a coat of the same color, britches. A large wooden crucifix was clutched between his fingers. The dense carpet of leaves beneath him crunched with every step he took. In comparison with the local tribesmen, this was an extremely clumsy individual. And he was mumbling to himself as he progressed. Saruak listened closer. He was mumbling a prayer.

This man's name was an extremely plain one—John Jones. John, son of John, in other words. And was that all? When you compared it with the poetry of some Iroquois names . . . how odd!

He was unmarried and twenty-six. Had come here from a place named Cardiff, in a far-off country simply known as Wales. The religion that he practiced was a version of this one-god nonsense that the newcomers had brought with them. But a newly founded version, known as "Baptist." They believed—the more Saruak read this human's mind, the harder he found it not to laugh—in throwing people in a river, cleansing them of sin that way. Was John Son of John really planning to do that to any of the Iroquois? They'd take his ears to remember him by, then feed him to the dogs.

He was brave, admittedly. He carried no weapon, and did not believe in them. All he had were the clothes on his back, a small bundle of supplies, his Bible tucked in among them. And his crucifix, his prayers, his faith. However frightened he might be, he just pressed on in a determined fashion. He was going to find some "savages"—that was the word he used—and convert them, to save their souls.

He began to sing, as Saruak listened. It was all in rhyme, all "see" and "be" and "thee" and "me." What simpletons these newcomers were. They knew practically nothing about the way the cosmos really worked.

He didn't even know where he was going. There was an encampment twenty minutes north of here. From the tree-tops, you could even see the smoke. But the missionary was heading due west. Why hadn't he even hired a guide?

But then Saruak read his mind again, and caught hold of another thought. "The Good Lord shall steer me true."

It was all too much. And this time, he did laugh.

The noise rang out among the tree trunks. The Welshman stopped dead in his tracks. Saruak already knew that his laugh did not sound like a normal one, to human ears. It sounded far more like the noise an animal might make, in pain. It chilled them. As he watched, the missionary's fingers stiffened on the cross. His gaze went darting around. Saruak supposed, at first, the man might change his mind about this whole excursion, turn around, head back the way he'd come.

But, despite the fact that he was shaking, John Son of John merely stopped a short while, then pressed on.

His song got louder—"be," "he," "we," "sea."

He was moving further away now. Saruak followed him quietly through the higher branches.

It wasn't just an idle fascination guiding him by this time. An idea had begun occurring to him.

Ever since humans had first started living in these forests, he'd considered them fair game. The finest sport he'd ever had, in fact. They were intelligent enough that he could twist it around and fool them. Stubborn enough that they'd not run away. Courageous enough that they would try to fight him even when their cause was lost. And stupid enough that they could never grasp the truth . . . he'd always win.

But after several hundred years of this, the Iroquois had become used to his trickery. They had no defense against him, of course. There was none. But when he greeted them with an illusion these days, they saw through it more often than not. When he planted crazy ideas in their minds, they tried to force them out again, ignore them. "Dancer in Dreams," they would mutter. "Take no notice of the evil one."

They'd grown wise to him, in other words.

These interlopers? They had no such wisdom. In truth, with their one-god and their church, they were considerably dumber than the tribesfolk. With them around, he could start to play his deadly games all over again. But a far grander plan was taking shape in Saruak's ancient mind.

Stupid though these pale folks might be, there were more of them arriving all the time. They were driven, industrious, and had one quality the Iroquois did not, ambition. He could almost see the way the future, from this point, was going to unfold.

They would not stop here. They would not be happy with a mere few coastal settlements. They'd press inland and spread out, like termites. Go to places on this continent he'd never seen.

And that was his only limitation. The one thing Saruak had ever been bound by. He resented it. Matchi Manitou he

*was, born out of these woodlands when they had been sap-
lings. And he could not leave them, ever. He was physically
tied to this place.*

*To see deserts just for once, or mountains. He could smell
them sometimes, very far away. To watch the sun set on a
different lake, or walk the banks of those enormous rivers
that he knew were out there. These newcomers, down the
next few hundred years, would do all that. But he?*

*They had an advantage, then. It struck him as unfair. It
angered him. Unless . . .*

He toyed gently with the notion.

Unless he went with them.

Stop singing a moment, John Son of John.

The lyrics froze in the Welshman's throat.

*I've become a missionary too, you see. I want to convert
you to my own religion. Like yours, there is just one god.
That deity is me.*

*By this time, he had gotten ahead of the human's line of
progress and was shimmying down a tall pine trunk to in-
tercept him. He had made himself invisible, so far. But not
for very much longer.*

*John Son of John had stopped moving again, and was
clutching the crucifix to his chest, gazing slightly up. Maybe
he had heard something, a rustling from the pine needles?
Or perhaps he simply sensed that there was trouble on the
way? Whatever, his face had gone extremely pale, the lips
pressed together and the pallid eyes wide.*

*Saruak reached the ground some thirty yards ahead of
him, and then began moving toward him swiftly.*

"Who's there?" the man suddenly called out.

*He seemed to believe he'd found some natives. Because
the next moment, he reached into his bundle, pulled out the
Bible from there. Lofted it above his head, then started to
cry out.*

*"I bring thee salvation! Yea, I bring thee the good
word!"*

*"And which good word is that?" Saruak shouted. "Be?
Thee? We?"*

He was just ten yards away by now. The man could still not see him. But the sound of the voice brought his head swinging around. He went entirely rigid, almost lifting himself out of his hard shoes. His features were completely white. His eyes gleamed like a madman's.

Saruak's pace did not slow, not a little bit.

"I'll give you a good word!" he hollered at his victim. "Me!"

And, in that moment, he revealed himself.

This was not like the other times when he'd possessed a human. Those had been temporary events. Whereas, this was going to be permanent, a taking over rather than a borrowing.

The man's screams echoed through the forest for a good while after that.

When it finally quietened down again, he was still standing there. Not the real John Jones any longer. His eyes were far more colorless than they'd originally been, and one pupil was larger. His teeth had changed as well, becoming far more like a predator's. But all his consciousness was gone. There was only his body left, a shell for Saruak to occupy. They were fused, the man's flesh and his own dark spirit.

He tried turning back to his original shape, and managed it easily. All he had to do was rearrange the substance of the body that he was in and the clothing around it. But a human appearance suited his needs far better from this point on. And so, he stuck to that.

He was still holding the Bible. Saruak turned it over, gazed at it, then tossed it into the undergrowth. The crucifix went the same way, as did the bundle. Such supplies were no longer required. The suffering of all those he tormented would sustain him well enough.

West, he had been going. Yes, that seemed a good direction to head. Laughing quietly to himself, Saruak continued on his way.

The scene hung in his head a moment longer. Then his left eye gave a flicker, and his surroundings returned.

Poor John. He had perished with the knowledge that his one-god could not save him. His soul had blinked out of existence like a tiny flame. Only his frame was left, only his bones and skin. They had aged very slowly down the centuries, but were still good enough. Occupying this body had set him free, taking him out of the forests at last, moving toward limitless horizons.

He had traveled with wagon trains, then ridden on steam ones. Sailed on rafts, and then on riverboats. Gone from coast to coast of this vast continent, and brought down suffering on humans, everywhere he visited. Fires and floods. Murders and mass suicides. He had been in San Francisco in 1906. He hadn't caused the largest quake, but he had been there for the aftershocks. In New Orleans a few years back—the same. And in southern California, several recent summers.

He had been precisely there, in fact, when a vagrant breeze with the scent of woodlands on it, blowing in from the northeast, had begun drawing him back, finally, to New England.

And now, he was sitting on the high roof of a church on Greenwood Terrace, with his back against the steeple. Dralleg nestled in his lap. There were no tall buildings to overlook him, and the humans passing by below couldn't see him all the way up here. This was the way he preferred to be—very much present, but completely unobserved.

His inner vision scoured the whole town. Ross Devries was making himself busy. He'd expected that. The boys in the police department were trying to stretch their limited intellects, and failing dismally.

As for the rest, the only being that he couldn't really fathom was this creature with no name, just called the Little Girl. Every time he looked in her direction, all that he could make out was a brilliant pale blue sphere of light. What genuinely lay within it? There seemed to be no way of telling.

She'd been passive up until this point, but he would have to keep an eye on her.

Otherwise, there were powerful magicians here, oh surely. Sorcerers nearly as strong, in their own way, as the shamans of the olden days. But they'd never met his kind before. Had no clue how to deal with him.

And his strength was already growing. Being fed by all the panicked speculation he'd set flowing through these people's minds. He couldn't take these "adepts"—as they called themselves—head-on as yet.

But soon he would be able to. He smiled. Very soon. Come evening, he would make his next move, strengthening his grip.

He reached into his ragged coat, pulled out a silver pocket watch. He'd got it off a merchant he had waylaid by the roadside in the eighteen hundreds. It was such a pretty thing. And he watched the secondhand revolve, his smile widening into a massive grin.

For all this curious township, time was running out.

CHAPTER 13

There are times when the work that I do these days mirrors, far too closely, what I used to. And the worst thing, always, about working as a cop . . . ?

The waiting.

We didn't go back to the office. No, we headed over to my house instead. I got coffee brewing. Cassie made some sandwiches from the odd items I had lying around my fridge. Then we just sat out on the front porch, waiting for whatever came down on us next.

I'd gotten used to it down the years, learning to be patient when I needed to. But Cass had never got the hang of that particular trick. She was an incorrigible pacer, twitcher, fiddler. She kept getting up for no particular reason, looking around, then sitting down again. Sometimes, she would walk the whole way over to the sidewalk and peer down the street, like she was expecting to see something headed in our direction. It was as if she'd rather something bad happen than nothing at all.

It was fairly exhausting watching her. In spite of which, I sympathized again. I understood her tension, and the slow burn in her eyes. We'd both much rather have been direct and aggressive, gone straight after this intruder. But how could we, when we didn't even know where he was hiding?

All that we could do was wait for him to move again. And hopefully, he'd do it before he had got much stronger.

I'd brought a scanner out, and turned the dial until I found the police channel. Nothing much at all seemed to be going on. A placid murmuring, edged with a soft fuzz of static, drifted out across the still afternoon air. Any hint of wind was gone. Birds made short hops from the nearby branches to my roof. You could hear a few kids yelling happily, somewhere in the distance.

"You're certain," asked Cassie, "he'll attack again?"

My face tensed up a little. "I'm not sure of anything."

"Then . . . ?"

I thought of that first encounter. The dry confidence in Saruak's tone. The way those eyes of his had studied and then challenged me.

"He didn't strike me as the type to bide his time, that's all. If he comes at us again, he'll do it pretty quickly."

Then I swung my gaze away from her, across the rooftops of the town. It pained me to see how normal-looking it all was. On the surface, another extremely pleasant day. Sunlight dappled the houses and the sidewalk, fading a little every so often. I looked further up. The sky was littered with small, fluffy clouds. But they were barely moving either, drifting only very slowly, like abandoned little boats in some calm harbor.

A bee went humming past. So placid, the entire place. Just like any other quiet New England town. I'd never been to any others, so I had to take a guess at that. But everything seemed so serene.

A few hours later on? I shook my head, scarcely able to believe that anything as bad as last evening might bear down on us once again.

Obviously bored out of her skull, Cass had got back on her cell phone, and was talking to Pam again. Who, of course, wanted to know what was going on. And, to give Cassie her due, she was noncommittal about that. The same happened when she phoned up Bella, another of her close-knit little coterie of girlfriends.

What, you thought she only had me? She'd probably have gone crazy a long time ago, without her small clan of bosom buddies.

You could hear the faintest hum of traffic from downtown. Very tiny in the sky, a jet plane was going overhead. They pass by every so often, always quite high up. I could hear its engines, like a soft murmur of thunder from a continent away.

Could they see us, when they looked down? Watching those occasional planes, knowing that I'd probably never ride on one, always made me feel slightly lonely, lost and cut adrift.

There were more pressing things to worry about now, however.

Saruak had to be looking down at us, as well. Of that there was no doubt. And with precisely what intention?

The sun dropped lower. All the shadows around us stretched, and the gentlest of breezes finally began to blow. The scanner kept murmuring in the background, but it had nothing significant to say. There was no trouble.

The calm before the storm. It put me in mind of another afternoon, not unlike this one. I'd been driving watchfully down Crowland Street, still a cop back then.

I dropped back a little in my chair, letting my head settle. Then my eyes drifted shut.

And it was all there, flooding through my memory again.

It was four months after Goad had arrived. And it seemed as though his presence here had triggered something. We in the P.D. had never been so busy for the past few weeks. People, casting spells, had simply vanished, or turned into things that they'd not wanted to. One middle-aged couple had set half their street alight, and we still weren't sure if it was just an accident. The Circe girl, who had been locked up months ago, had managed to conjure herself out, and it had taken us nearly a week to find her. And a certain Mrs. Carey, up on Johnson Avenue, had decided that a basilisk would be the ideal pet for her backyard.

"It's just a small one," she kept telling us.

The Landing had become a pretty frantic place for those in law enforcement. And nobody had ridden two cops to a car for days. There were too few officers for that, and too much going on.

Except the hubbub had all died away, this particular afternoon. Things had, without warning, settled down. It was as if all the previous mayhem had never taken place. I was just cruising around, taking a grateful breather.

I was about to turn right onto Vine, when my radio crackled.

"Ross?"

The dispatcher was Elvie, who I liked to kid around with. I picked up my handset.

"Talk to me."

"We've got reports of a possible disturbance."

Possible?

"Can you try to be more specific? What's that mean?"

"Nothing seems to have happened yet. But some sort of weirdness might be going down."

I said, "Surprise me." And was smiling gently, till she gave me the address.

I hit my brakes, dead in the middle of the pavement, and a pickup truck behind me hooted and went past.

"That's your street, isn't it?" Elvie was asking me nervously across the ether, her voice blurry-sounding and unreal.

My head was spinning by this time. Because it wasn't just my street. It was the house next door to mine.

And my very next thought was, *Goad!*

I didn't even put my siren on, but was screeching up in front of my house several minutes later. Slamming my wheels across the curb, then stumbling out. My hand was on my holster, but I didn't draw my weapon straightaway. I had two small kids to think of, didn't I?

"Alicia?"

No answer came. I stared around. The entire block was silent, with no signs of anything amiss. But then I peered a little closer at the front door of my house. It was slightly ajar, and my wife never left it open.

"Tammy? Pete?"

Someone came out clumsily onto his own porch, at that point. Joe Norton, two houses down.

"What's happening?" I yelled at him.

His face was like a porcelain mask, and it occurred to me that maybe *I* was frightening him.

"It might be nothing, Ross, but we thought you ought to know. Some half an hour back, Alicia and the kids went into Mrs. McGaffrey's place. There was something weird about them. And they haven't come out yet."

I could only stare at him frustratedly, wondering what was going through his head.

"Why take so long reporting it?"

"It didn't seem . . . to be actual *trouble* as such. Just peculiar, that's all."

When I looked over at my neighbor's front door, it was open too. So I forgot all about Joe and his lack of action, at that point.

Hurried toward it at a crouch, drawing my firearm carefully. I kept half my attention on the windows. Was I being watched? But there was no sign of any movement beyond them. Jason Goad's room, I reminded myself, was out back in the loft.

I jabbed at the door with my free hand. And it swung wide open soundlessly. Shadows and the scattered shapes of furniture were all that I could see inside. I went through into the living room, my heart pounding with every step. My surroundings were clean and tidy but threadbare, the hallmark of genteel poverty.

Of my family? Of Goad, though? Not a sign.

"Mrs. McGaffrey?"

I noticed her suddenly, in the corner. She had been just like another shadow, until then. Was sitting in a rocking chair, but didn't move or look at me, even when I spoke.

Her eyes were open, but they seemed to be unfocused. And I thought at first she might be dead. But when I ventured over, put two fingers to her throat, I could feel an even, steady pulse.

She didn't respond in the slightest to my touch. Had she been put into some kind of a trance?

A low creaking took my attention to the ceiling. Leaving the old woman there, I started heading up.

The only light on in the entire place was up there at the very top. I took the next couple of flights three risers at a time, my chest pounding like an engine, my lungs tight against my ribs.

Something was completely out of whack. All the years that we'd been neighbors, Mrs. McGaffrey had used energy-saving bulbs. She scarcely had the money to pay her regular bills. And so, the windows of her house had always had this chilly, warmthless, glow.

Except . . . this new light that I could see was pale, but intensely bright.

I reached the top, a far more narrow landing. Looked at the scene beyond Goad's open doorway.

And my entire body froze . . .

"Ross!" Cassie was yelling at me.

My eyes snapped back open. Jesus, for how long had I been dozing? How much time had passed?

I took in my surroundings rather numbly. The sun had dropped the whole way to the rooftops, scattering them with its reddish glow. A few people were returning from work, and there were more cars on the drives than there'd been earlier.

Cass was on her feet again, and stooping over my scanner. "Ross, there's something going down!"

Dream and reality merged for just an instant. Then I pulled myself together, and sat stiffly up.

We listened to the babbling coming from the set.

"Pulling onto Greenwood Terrace."

It was Davy Quinn's voice I was hearing. Greenwood Terrace was a mere half-dozen blocks from Cray's Lane, at the northern edge of Garnerstown. Not *there* again?

"There's people running everywhere!" Davy was shouting. "Some of them are injured. They seem to be coming from the church. Get backup here, for chrissake!"

We could hear hurried, crunching footsteps next. St. Nevitt's was on Greenwood Terrace, I knew. And it had a gravel drive. But . . . a church? This was a Wednesday.

"There's dead on the steps here!" Davy yelled. "A lot of blood. Some people really badly injured! I . . . there's something moving! Oh my God, what *is* that?"

There was a clatter and a hiss, then the transmission went completely dead.

We both started running, me for my car and Cass for her Harley.

CHAPTER 14

The light was starting to fail properly, the sky phasing
through increasingly deeper shades of vermilion and the
shadows growing dense. A few streetlights were coming
on, but not casting a proper glow as yet. Everything
looked indistinct, half formed. I squinted through my
windshield.

Cassie had already gone a good long way ahead. Me? My
knuckles seemed to almost crack as I worked the steering
wheel. I could still get plenty of speed out of my old Cadillac, but I had to jam the pedal down the whole way to the
floor to do it.

All the streets were quiet until I reached the area I was
heading for.

Greenwood Terrace was the precise opposite. There was
howling pandemonium every place you looked. Frightened,
damaged people milling everywhere. Some were clutching
handkerchiefs or even hanks of clothing to their wounds.
There were screams and siren wails and urgent shouts.
Every emergency vehicle in town seemed to be descending
on this spot. Squad cars, ambulances, and even fire trucks
were pulling up the whole time. Householders along the way
were coming out and trying to help.

There was plenty of strobing red light, just like yesterday

evening. It broke the scene around me into jerking, ragged fragments.

I could see, just beyond the church, Hobart's dark blue Pontiac approaching. Cassie had her shotgun out, and was advancing steadily toward the building's gaping doors.

I clambered out. It looked like a bomb had gone off here. All the windows in the building had been shattered. Except there was very little glass on the surrounding verges. Had the windows shattered inward? What could have caused that?

Faces stared up desperately at me. A lot of the injured were just sitting on the ground by this time, some of them waiting for help, others unable to stand. A few had passed out, or maybe worse. But the paramedics and cops were moving quickly. The worst cases were already being attended to.

I leaned in a couple of times to see what damage had been done. And was, once again, surprised. From my fight with the Dralleg, I'd been expecting clean straight cuts in almost every case. Parallel rows of them. But that was not what I was looking at. These people had jagged wounds, uneven lacerations. One poor guy had had a lump of flesh the size of an apple torn out of his scalp, and was clutching it, still conscious, groaning.

"What happened?" was the question being asked by the authorities.

But they didn't seem to be getting any coherent answers. These folks were either babbling or numb, trapped at opposite ends of shock's narrow spectrum.

Whatever had come down on them, I felt pretty certain it was not the Dralleg this time.

A middle-aged woman was having a large shard of glass pulled out of her wrist. A friend of hers was trying to soothe her. Which provided me, at least, with a partial answer. Were those smashed windows the only wreckage here?

I checked my gun, thumbing off the safety before returning it to my pocket. Then I headed for the porch myself.

I didn't quite make it. Saul Hobart came flashing across my field of vision, moving very fast for such an obviously ungainly man. There were corpses up ahead of us, as Davy's last report had said. Except that, by this stage, there was one in uniform as well.

Something heavy formed in my gut. Davy Quinn had joined the victims he was trying to help. We'd gone out for beers together, maybe twenty, thirty times.

His radio was lying beside one open hand, the fingers curled. And there was his gun, still in his grasp. He'd gone sprawling backward on the steps. His face was tipped to one side, and his eyes were wide, reflective. His expression was frozen.

There was something of a pale brass color sticking out through the middle of his chest. And I thought at first it was a knife, until I realized it had no proper handle.

It was a narrow crucifix. My eyes stung, looking down.

Saul knelt over the man, feeling for a pulse. And then his mouth came open. I suppose he groaned. There was too much noise around us to be sure.

A pair of paramedics were approaching, but he waved them back. His head stayed down. Perhaps he just didn't want anyone to see his face.

I tried to think of something to say, but it wasn't only my throat that had gone rigid. It was everything, even my mind.

In the end, I just reached down, and touched the man on the elbow.

He didn't respond, at first. But then he suddenly stood up, easing back his shoulders and then straightening his tie. His eyes were damp around the edges, but he didn't even try to wipe them.

"Okay," he muttered quietly. "Let's find out what did all this."

Cass was at the doorway but, unusually for her, had not gone in. She was standing stock-still on the very threshold, peering inside. What had stopped her?

We went up to join her, picking our way through the bodies and the debris. There was plenty of the latter, a great deal of scattered glass. One of the cadavers nearest the entrance looked like a porcupine, there were so many shards protruding from it.

This was not the time to focus on details like that. I tried to keep my feelers out, and take in my surroundings. One thing, I was sure of right away. This was dissimilar to last night in several aspects. In the first place, there were plenty more survivors. There had been no walking wounded in Cray's Lane. And, second, all these victims seemed to have been felled by objects, rather than a living thing.

There was a big pewter goblet lying by a woman's head. Her skull was partly crushed. Had Saruak simply hurled it at her?

Another victim had a narrow metal curtain rod jammed in between his ribs. It looked to me like every inanimate object in St. Nevitt's had, somehow, come alive.

Behind us, an RLKB television crew was rolling up. But . . . were we still in any danger? I took my gun out again, Saul following my cue.

When I stepped forward, something crunched under my heel. Staring down, I saw a crystal on a narrow length of cord. It had been dropped in all the panic.

They were scattered all over the place, when I looked closer, as were all the stones and amulets that people employ when using magic. The good folks of Raine's Landing might still worship at the altar of a single God. But they bring along these trinkets too, since God is not the only power they believe in.

We joined Cass, either side of her. All three of us stared in.

With no moon up yet, the interior was pitch-dark. All the lights had obviously been switched off, or else been smashed. But there was just enough illumination, filtering in through the high, shattered windows, that you could make out shapes after a while.

There were plenty more corpses in here. I thought one of them might be wearing the robes of a pastor. And not one of them so much as twitched—there was not the tiniest moan. They were covered with an even frosting of glass, for all the world like sugar sprinkled on them. And the *smell* in this place. Once again, I found myself trying to avoid breathing through my nose.

But there was more than that, and even worse. The entire pulpit had been ripped away from the far wall. A figure was lying underneath it, obviously crushed. And the body next to that one had apparently been brained with a statue of the Virgin Mary.

My mouth got very dry, but I felt so numb that I didn't even try to wet my lips.

"See anything?" I asked Cassie.

"Plenty," she replied.

"Anything moving?"

"Uh-uh. There's no Dralleg here."

"What?" Saul blurted. But we just ignored him.

I was still trying, furiously, to figure all this out. Why on earth attack a church? And why, come to that, had there been so many people in it early evening of midweek?

My gaze drifted to a poster nailed to one side of the door.

"THIS EVENING, 6 P.M.," it read. "PRAYERS FOR OUR GOOD NEIGHBORS IN CRAY'S LANE, WHO THE LORD TOOK TO HIS BOSOM LAST NIGHT."

It hadn't been the Lord at all, responsible for that. But I stared around urgently at Hobart.

"Jesus Christ Almighty, Saul! Is this the only place?"

"Speak English. What only place?"

"Where they're holding a memorial service this evening?"

He gawked at me like he was wondering where I had been all day.

"Hell, no. They're happening all over town."

And this was just perfect for our new visitor. We'd gone and played straight into his hands. I thought about it. Hundreds of ordinary citizens, all clustered together in a single place. Thoughts elsewhere but on the present, heads bowed blindly as the axe began to fall. How could a creature like Saruak resist the temptation?

If this wasn't stopped immediately, Cray's Lane would look like a mere overture in his grand opus, his symphony of destruction.

"You've got to break them up!" I yelled.

Saul took a step backward, squinting.

"Are you serious? Why?"

Cass was staring at me too, but in a more receptive way. And maybe it was just a hunch, but my spine was prickling by now, and my thoughts racing.

"This?" I told them, gesturing at the carnage. "It's going to happen again, *that's* why."

CHAPTER 15

The amulet was a small, round iron one, with a creature called a griffon engraved on its face. His father had given it to him on his fifteenth birthday.

Ike Mackenzie grasped it between his forefinger and thumb, savoring its coolness, as the memorial ceremony went on around him. An organ was playing, its doleful chords echoing through the confines of the church. And Ike hated sad occasions. Which was why, perhaps, his thoughts had retreated, back into the past. He was remembering when he'd been a teenager—the day that his father had given him the gleaming piece of metal he was holding.

At first, he'd squinted at it dubiously.

"Is it for good luck, Pop?"

And his father had smiled.

"Oh, partly. But it can do much more than that."

"Like what? Make magic? Conjure me up stuff?"

Which got a sharp cluck from Pop's tongue.

"Objects like the one you're holding have to be used wisely, son."

"And how do I know what 'wise' is?"

"Well, that amulet? It has a voice." His father's smile became a little tighter. "You don't believe me? Listen to it very carefully—you'll learn how in good time."

"And what . . . what'll it tell me?"

"How to use it well. And that's what wisdom is."

Pop had been right. Down the twenty-one years that had followed, he had learned how to detect that voice. And the amulet had benefited and enriched him.

It had helped him find his wife, Ethel, now standing by his side with their three children. It had transformed their home into a dream one, without the expense and inconvenience of workmen. And it had brought good fortune into every aspect of his life.

Neither the other Father, Son, nor Holy Ghost had managed anything like that, which was why he barely ever came to church. But this was a different matter. He had *known* some of the people who had perished on Cray's Lane, last night. Two of them, in fact, had been employees of the landscaping company he owned. Mark Breville and Sarah Whiteman. Jesus Christ almighty!

"Hymn thirty-seven, from your books," Reverend Swain was announcing, from in front of the altar. "'Nearer my Lord to Thee.'"

Ethel had a pleasant and harmonious voice, when it came to this kind of singing. Surprisingly, so did all his children. None of them seemed to have inherited the dying-bullfrog gene he carried around inside him. Ike had actually known people to frown and try to edge away from him when he was in full voice. So he flipped to the correct page, but only mouthed the words. It was a better deal for all concerned.

His amulet slipped tightly into the palm of his left hand.

Looking around him, he could see that plenty other of the congregants had brought gewgaws of their own. Medallions winked and crystals glittered. Ike smiled briefly, and then had a thought.

He read extensively these days, nonfiction mostly. And especially about the world beyond this town, the one he'd never known. And yes, there was a parallel between the way the people of Raine's Landing went to church and other strange religions. The slave ones in particular, voodoo and Santeria.

It looked quite like Christianity on the outside. But there were other beliefs—older, darker—hidden deeply in it.

The hymn trailed to an end. Then the reverend began reading out the names of last night's victims. And Ike stiffened, recognizing some.

"Clarice Kilpatrick. Martin Howell."

"Ike Mackenzie," came a completely different voice.

What?

That wasn't the reverend. No, someone else had cut across him, his tone dry and crackly, and cold, and faintly mocking. The voice was emerging from nowhere in particular. But it reverberated just as loudly around the church as the organ music had been doing, a few seconds back.

"Ethel Mackenzie," it continued.

His wife.

"Irving Trevellian."

Who was sitting just two rows away. Ike watched the man get to his feet with a gasp.

What on earth was this? People's heads, the whole way along the rows of pews, were jerking around alarmedly.

"Margaret Krause. Samuel Hamner. Peter Fynch."

They were *all* the names of people in this church, for heaven's sake! And this might have been a joke, a very bad one, if it hadn't been for what had happened on Cray's Lane last night.

The reverend was flapping his hands, trying to keep everybody calm, but not succeeding very much. A ripple of horror went through the whole congregation.

There was a sudden, whooshing noise in midair, like a vacuum sucking inward.

And that was when every lightbulb in the place exploded.

Somebody wailed, obviously cut by flying glass. There was such utter, pitch-darkness that it seemed to drain the breath out of Ike's lungs. Then, something even more startling began to happen.

Up until now, there had only been the electric lighting on. There were plenty of candles scattered around the church. Till this point, they'd not been lit.

But then a tiny point of yellow brightness, dazzling to look at, appeared near the front doors of the building. Every last head swiveled around to gawp at it. Before the congregation's gaze, it rapidly danced from wick to wick like some demented firefly.

Little flames started to grow and waver all around them. Shadows overlapped each other, trembling like phantoms. A few people started shouting worriedly. A little boy let out a squeal.

"This part of the service, Reverend?" someone up at the front called out, although that seemed to be a case of wishful thinking on his part.

Reverend Swain didn't even answer. He could only watch like everybody else, his face so frozen and his eyes so glassy he looked almost hypnotized.

The whole interior was lit up gently, before too much longer. And the yellow brightness that had ignited the candles winked, then disappeared. Ike tried to keep his wits about him, peering warily around.

The faces of the saints up on the stained glass windows all looked very lofty, distant. Even Jesus on his cross, behind the altar, seemed to have a vacant gaze. Most of the congregants that he could see had been reduced partway to silhouettes. The entire church looked like a mausoleum. The faces nearest him seemed colorless, and horribly drawn. Cavernous shadows yawned.

This wasn't right. This looked like a building full of half-dead people. And they had come here this evening to *honor* the dead, not *join* them.

Ike reached out carefully for his youngest daughter's hand. This wasn't going *at all* to plan. So they were getting out of here.

Which was precisely when the glass above them started to bulge inward. The narrow bands of lead between the panes let out a creaking noise. It was like some force, outside the church, was pressing in at them.

And that couldn't last for very long before they broke,

he knew. His wife was staring at him with her features distended and her blue eyes bright with fear.

He wanted to shout out something. What though? He decided. *Run!*

His mouth came open. But he heard another sucking noise. And the windows all imploded before he could get the word out.

The broken glass didn't behave in any way that you'd call normal. It came flashing inward, breaking up the candlelight into a million dazzling fragments. But then it seemed to all get caught up in some current on the air, some silent whirlwind. And, with barely a scrap of it reaching the floor, began to spin around.

It kept on going like that until it had formed a floating cylinder of shards. And then it plowed into the pews up at the front. The people caught within it . . . they were torn to pieces within seconds, the way a tree branch might be when you fed it in a shredder. Thank God that they'd been slightly late, were sitting further back.

Piercing screams rang everywhere. Reverend Swain had staggered back against the altar and was clutching at his throat. And other people . . . ?

My God, he could hardly bare to look. Nausea and shock rushed through him, rendering him motionless. All the people around him were trying to scramble to the door.

But that was when practically every object in the church took to the air as well. The crosses and the statuettes. Light fittings were ripping from the walls. Ike came to his senses again. Just turned around and concentrated on bundling his wife and children out of there.

It occurred to him, in the next instant—might his amulet protect them?

But there was simply no time to find out. A low humming noise, pushing insistently through all the chaos, made him look back the way he'd come.

The big silver collection plate had risen into the air. It

caught what light remained, and flashed. The thing was revolving like a circular saw, as fiercely, as insistently.

It came hurtling toward him. And Ike, simultaneously, understood three things.

It was heading for his neck.

It was going to take his head clean off his shoulders.

And he didn't have time to get out of the way.

CHAPTER 16

Saul Hobart was still eyeing me as though I'd slightly lost it.

"Do you know how many churches there are in this town?"

I understood precisely what he meant. My patrols had taken me the entire length and breadth of the place, when I had been a cop. And there were dozens.

"And how am I supposed to get word to them, Ross? All my men are here. And people switch their phones off when they go into a church, you know."

I just looked at him. "Well, you'd better start somehow."

The pandemonium around us was dying down a little, although the red lights still made everything look fractured, disconnected. Some of the ambulances were moving off, taking away the worst of the injured. There were more shocked sobs, by this stage, ringing out than screams.

"Exactly what are you basing your assumptions on?"

There was plenty that I hadn't told him yet. Plenty that I knew, he didn't. He had sensed that and, being a detective, didn't like it very much. His mouth was set firm. There was a stony glitter to his gaze.

"The creature who caused all this—" I started telling him.

"This 'Dralleg'?"

"No. He's called Saruak."

Saul just blinked slowly, and then stuck out his lower lip.

"Last night was only the beginning. He as much as told me so."

"You've *talked* with him?"

"Which is not something I'm pleased about, believe me. He wants to hurt us all until we can't stop screaming, Saul. He wants dominion over us—that's his ultimate goal."

"What *is* he?"

I was just about to explain it to him, when the radio in his car began squawking urgently. He made his way across to it, picked the handset up.

And, when he turned back to face me, it was stiffly. He looked pretty shocked.

"God, you were right," he mumbled hoarsely. "It's happening at St. Agnes's this time."

Which was six blocks due northwest of here.

St. Agnes's was on Devon Street, a placid avenue normally, lined with leafy, spreading maple trees. But we arrived to find the same kind of confusion that we'd seen on Greenwood Terrace. Except that even fewer people seemed to have got away from the destruction, this time. Those who had were mostly in a noticeably bad way.

Cassie was already off her Harley, carrying both heavy weapons, one across each shoulder. I went across to Hobart as he got out of his Pontiac. He'd drawn his service-issue pistol, but I quickly shook my head.

"We'd be better off with shotguns."

He peered at me, obviously wondering how I knew all this. Then murmured, "In the trunk."

He tossed a riot gun, a Winchester, to me, then pulled out a second for himself.

"It would help if I knew what we were up against."

His tone was reproachful. I could understand that too. But there just wasn't the time.

People were spilling out across the curb, many of them hobbling or clutching at their stomachs. We made our way through the retreating throng, trying to keep up with Ms. Mallory.

"Cass, slow down!" I yelled at her. But that got no result.

She had already vaulted up the front steps and was almost in the church. She'd readily go in alone, but I wasn't sure that was a good idea. I already knew this Saruak was tricky. If he managed to split us up, what games might he play with us?

Once again, though—and thank God for that—she stopped at the doorway. You couldn't help but wonder what exactly she was looking at.

I reached her side and peered in. Holy hell, there were *dozens* of corpses inside, layered across each other in the copper-scented dimness. Some of them looked like they had practically been torn to pieces. There was one cadaver near the entrance that was minus its whole head. This was even worse than Greenwood Terrace. Was Saruak honing his skills?

Total silence reigned, in there. But behind us, the sounds of the injured just kept swirling around like some dismal, haunted wind. A girl was crying, and wouldn't stop. My gut felt leaden. Bile rose to my throat.

It suddenly occurred to me. All of the emergency teams were still back at the first church. There was no one to even *help* these people. Only three of us were here, and there were scores of wounded, everywhere you looked.

A young woman nearby held her arm out toward me. From the way that it was bleeding, an artery had been cut. So I went over to her, and made a tourniquet out of my belt.

Once I was certain that she'd be okay, I walked off from her and threw my head back.

Yelled out, *"Saruak!"* into the dim night air.

As you might suppose, I don't lose my temper an awful lot. But when I do . . .

My fists were bunched. There was a flaring pain inside my chest.

"Saruak, you son of a bitch! Stop hiding! Just *show* yourself!"

A hoarse, echoing laugh brought my attention back to the church door. I hurried up the steps again.

Sprawled across the altar was the body of a clergyman. And the air beside it rippled suddenly. Not slowly, like when the Dralleg had appeared. Between one heartbeat and the next, the ragged man was standing there.

His monster was with him, lurking just behind his shoulder. I could hear Saul Hobart gasp. Its green eyes glowed balefully. It hunched forward again and held its claws out, but did not advance.

Cassie aimed her shotgun at it. She had hurt it once already, and that seemed to give her confidence. She just wanted the chance—I knew—to finish off the job she'd started.

Saul Hobart was a different kettle of fish. He'd seen creatures conjured up plenty of times before. But now, his features were like putty. This wasn't like the ones that he'd seen in the past.

I ignored them both and gazed at the altar.

Saruak's left pupil was glittering again, despite the fact there was no light to make that happen. And he looked entirely satisfied. The faintest, dreamiest of smiles was playing on his features, as if all this death were nectar to him, he was savoring its taste.

I think I only took on board, at that point, just how vicious and dangerous he really was.

His voice came toward me like the creaking of branches in an ancient wood.

"Why, hello again, Mr. Devries. Nice to have the pleasure of your company once more."

Then he did something that genuinely appalled me. He raised his right hand, and set his palm down in the middle of the dead clergyman's chest. And leant against it, for all the world like some huntsman with a trophy. I remembered what the Little Girl had said. He killed for sport.

The bile got so thick in my craw it almost choked me. But the sight dampened my anger down at the same time. It made me cooler, more determined. All the heat in my thoughts bled away.

I could feel all my energy becoming steady. And my voice was calm when I replied.

"Are you having fun, Matchi Manitou?"

I could feel, rather than see, Hobart gawk at me again. But I paid that no attention.

"Yes, a little. But the problem with human beings is, their bodies are almost as soft as their minds. So, of course, they die far too easy."

Out of the corner of my eye, I saw the muscles tense in Cassie's arms. She was apparently thinking of trying to prove him wrong, but I put out a hand to still her.

Saruak seemed amused by that.

"It would seem your girlfriend disagrees. I'd be happy to demonstrate, if she likes?"

I ignored that as well. "Are you done for tonight?" I asked.

I was already deeply sickened by the way he kept on crowing. This was not a game. These people were not pawns.

But we differed on that too, it seemed.

"Not completely. Not yet. No."

I edged a little forward. "Why can't you just leave us be?"

"Far too much temptation, I'm afraid. I simply can't resist it."

Then his strange gaze swung in the lieutenant's direction.

"'Do you know,'" he mimicked, "'how many churches there are in this town?'"

When he chuckled this time, it was a profound, rumbling noise, as though from a deep cavern. The church seemed to fill up with it. And once again, the shadows around him thickened.

The Dralleg stirred behind his shoulder, like some dog responding to its master's tone of voice.

I wasn't fazed at all. I was remembering what the Little Girl had told me about him.

"He's not at full strength yet," I whispered to Cassie, being careful not to turn my head.

And she got the general idea, and murmured, "Yeah?"

"We might be able to take him."

I was keeping my voice as low as I was able. But . . .

"*Might* you?" Saruak yelled back.

He had heard us clearly, all the same. Took a few steps toward us, his arms swinging loosely at his sides. His whole face was lit up with an ugly, twisted mirth. The Dralleg trailed along behind him, letting out a hissing sound.

There was no point being patient by this stage. And so I shouted *"Now!"* with my next breath.

Saul Hobart had caught on too. All three of our shotgun barrels swung toward the ragged figure, opening fire simultaneously.

The salvo caught him squarely in the gut. He stumbled back a couple of paces, and I thought we'd got him. His knees bowed slightly and he wobbled. I just stood there, watching, patient and grim, hoping that he'd fall.

Both his palms went to his stomach. But when he pulled them back, and when he held them up for us to see . . .

They were clean. Not a trace of blood. He straightened up. And his delight was obvious and massive. He'd been toying with us all along. I'd read, hadn't I, that mischief was a characteristic of his kind?

Growling issued from the Dralleg's throat. It had no sense of humor, and was annoyed at what we'd done.

But its master just stepped forward, almost laughing.

"Nice try, Ross. And this morning, it might have worked. But I've already gained so much strength, just from what I've done so far."

Cass was taking aim again. He simply thrust his lean face at her.

"You can't shoot me!" he crowed. "Because . . . I'm not really here at all!"

I was wondering what he meant by that, when both he and the Dralleg crumbled to fine dust. Two piles of it were settling where they'd been. The rank odor of leaf mold reached my nostrils. It smelled like a compost heap in there.

An illusion, that was what we had been looking at and

talking to. His sort could play with minds, and with the borders of reality. So, if he wasn't here, then where exactly *was* he?

I'd thought we'd actually had a chance at him. My teeth grated. An infuriated Cassie kicked the doorpost, for want of anything better to kick. Hobart let out a slow breath and leaned against the jamb.

"Who the hell was that?" he asked.

I didn't even bother to answer. Saruak was going to attack again—he had already told me that, I didn't doubt it. So I just turned, and headed for Saul's Pontiac. Snatched a map out of the glove compartment, and then spread it on the roof.

"What are you doing?" Saul yelled at me. "He could turn up anywhere!"

But I was remembering that business with his name, making me try to guess it when we had first met.

"This guy likes to play games," I said, scanning the outlines in the pale glow of a streetlamp. "He hints at what he's up to, and then waits to see how long it takes you to catch on."

How do you know all this? was the question in his eyes. But he could see how urgent matters were, and held his tongue.

"If there is a next attack, then it will not be random. There has to be a pattern. And the only one that I can see?" I jammed my finger down. "Maybe he's moving in a straight line, due northwest. And the next church in that direction is . . ."

I peered a little harder, feeling a sharp pang of dismay. There were two. The House of the Good Word on Savory Street. And St. Cleary's on Van Ness Crescent. Both within a block of each other, and both in the area known as Marshall Drive.

Hobart got on his radio again and shouted at the dispatcher.

"They must have phones in their office? Raise somebody now!"

He waited practically a minute and then shook his head. "No dice."

I imagined the massed congregations in their pews. Prayers being read out. Music playing. And two phones in separate back rooms, ringing hopelessly, ignored.

There was nothing else for it, so I glanced at Cass. I didn't like the thought of any of us having to face Saruak alone. But I couldn't see any other way we could cover both places.

She nodded, her gaze darkening a little more.

"Fine. I'll take St. Cleary's."

None of us knew how long we had. So, speed was of the essence.

By the time I'd got back to my car, Cassie and her bike had melted to a single faint shape in the distance.

Which, howling furiously, dwindled. And then vanished as I watched.

CHAPTER 17

We headed back into the tidy, well-heeled area I'd visited earlier, and quickly found Savory Street. The House of the Good Word was visible from a good way off. As you would expect, it was a fairly modern building, red brick and a lot of broad plate glass. Brilliant lights were on inside, so that the structure shone like a massive jewel. Fairly pricey, mint-condition cars were parked outside. And as we marched in through the front door, an electric organ was playing. And the congregation was in voice, singing "Abide with Me."

A few heads swung around. There were smart suits and fancy hats everywhere that my eyes took me. And just like the other churches, this place was completely packed.

We made our way quickly down the red carpet of the central aisle, drawing a few murmurs from the worshippers. I expected Saul to pull his badge out, but he didn't seem to need to.

"I know the minister," he whispered to me.

The man up front, leading the service, stopped and peered at us. He was short, rotund, with striking silver hair, and wore a plain gray business suit. His eyes kept growing larger behind their gold-framed spectacles, the closer we approached him.

"Saul? What are you doing with those guns in here?" His mouth pursed with reproach. "Land's sake, this is a house of God!"

"I'm afraid God needs a bodyguard this evening, Dr. Purlock," Saul replied.

He hurried up ahead of me and began talking in the reverend's ear.

My nerves were singing like taut wire, as I looked around. Because there was *so much* glass in here. And if it came to pieces, the way it had done at St. Agnes's . . . ?

Other faces were studying mine. This congregation didn't seem to like my appearance. Perhaps I seemed a little rough-looking, to their eyes. I'd had a long, hard day, not over yet, and couldn't fully blame them.

Saul had finished all his explanations. Dr. Purlock seemed to take them quickly in.

"People?" he yelled, raising both his arms above his head. Their attention swung away from me. I could see the man was well respected.

"People, I'm afraid we have a situation! If you'd care to, very calmly, make your way to the exit? No need at all for panic—we can do this all in an orderly fashion, can't we?"

His congregants just stood there and blinked at him. It wasn't that they were refusing to move. It was that no one seemed to understand what he was asking of them. What was this about?

At which, the reverend simply reached across. Took the riot gun from Saul's grasp, and pumped a slug into its chamber with a loud, decisive clack.

"Folks?" he asked them mildly. "Would you like me to repeat myself?"

I immediately saw why he and Saul were on good terms. Boy, this was no ordinary minister.

In less than a minute, we were all outside. People were milling around numbly on the sidewalk, wondering what was going on. But at least they were not missing body parts, or bleeding. It was rather different to the scenes we'd left behind.

The murmur of voices around me sounded like the clatter of soft wings, a gentle sound. A few small children in the crowd seemed to think this was some game, and they were beaming. Let them believe that, if it made them happy. I just felt relieved.

Then I took in the fact that Saul was still consulting with the reverend. And the little man was nodding swiftly.

Purlock's arms went up again.

"My brethren? I need a few seconds more of your attention!"

He looked around at them anxiously.

"Some of you have medical experience, don't you? Even first-aid training, anything of that sort?"

At least a dozen people nodded and spoke up.

"Okay, then. You need to come with me to St. Agnes's on Devon, right away. There are brothers and sisters there who are badly in need of our assistance."

He began organizing them.

Hobart came across to me, looking bluntly satisfied. We both gazed at the building, which had all its lights still on.

"So we beat him to it," Saul growled.

But surely he could move a good deal faster than us? In which case?

I took my cell phone out, and speed-dialed Cassie's number. There was no reply.

CHAPTER 18

A similar-looking crowd was swarming around outside St. Cleary's, when we arrived. They were not *exactly* the same. These people seemed just as well off, but even more buttoned-down and formal. A lot of black in evidence, and even veils on some of the women's pillbox hats. There were long dark gloves in evidence, black ties, and black fur stoles. These folks looked shadowy, exactly like a witches' coven. And everywhere that my gaze went, crystals flashed and talismans glittered.

And this bunch seemed less happy than the crowd outside the Good Word. They were talking rapidly among themselves, obviously agitated about something. Cassie can have that effect. Puzzled gazes battened on us as we climbed out. And this time, Saul did show his badge.

I stared past them, at the church itself. It looked eighteenth century and was built of roughly hewn gray stone, as solid as a fortress. All the windows were intact, but the lights were off inside. Cassie's Harley was beside the porch. Of its owner, there was not a sign.

"Anybody seen a woman, about so tall?" I held out a palm. "Cropped hair, tattoos, probably heavily armed?"

About a dozen voices all chimed up at once, most of them affronted.

"Is she your friend?"

"She tossed us out of our own church!"

"She shot a hole in the ceiling."

"She was *very* rude!"

None of which I doubted. But where was she?

"She's still inside," somebody else explained.

And . . . what was she doing in there? I was still wondering why, when a triple burst of shots rang out from the interior of the building. The stained glass windows were illuminated briefly by the flash of Cassie's Heckler & Koch.

Hobart and I were at the entrance, shoulder to shoulder, a bare couple of seconds after that. I don't know about him, but my heart was trying to beat the minute mile. The darkness was broken by another triple flash, and a burst of fire that made our eardrums ring.

Silhouettes leapt into being. Narrow, fluted pillars. A crisscross of rafters over us. A huge crucifix at the rear. An ornate stone pulpit, with a huge angel, its wings outspread, engraved across the front of it. Then, they were lost into the blackness once again.

Saul had had the presence of mind to bring a flashlight with him this time, and he flicked it on. Its wide beam swept along a rear wall lined with plaques and wreaths, until it started picking movement out.

Cass was standing just down from the altar. And standing squarely, her boots planted shoulder-width apart. She couldn't use both of her guns at the same time. So the Mossberg was lying at her feet, where she could snatch it up. And she was shooting with her carbine, firing from the hip.

Why was she still here at all? If the same happened as at the other churches, she was risking being torn to shreds.

But it appeared that Saruak had grown tired of that game. And gone back to one that we were already familiar with.

As I watched, she swung around to the left and pumped another burst at just a shadow, something I could barely see.

The flashlight dipped in its direction, just in time to catch the Dralleg stumbling back, then sinking away completely into the dimness.

But I thought I could make out another large shape in the gloom. And this time, it was moving up behind her.

Hobart swung the light again. And yes, it was the same damned creature, coming straight toward her back, its arms already raised, and its claws gleaming. How had it gotten around there so fast?

I didn't have time to figure it out. Just leveled my own gun at it, firing a charge of pellets.

They didn't have the same effect as Cass's heavy slugs. The Dralleg simply shuddered, coming briefly to a halt. But it was enough to warn her. She pivoted on the spot, then handed out the same treatment she'd given it the last time.

It wailed and abruptly vanished. With no wavering on the air on this occasion. God, with no delay at all! That startled me as much as anything I'd seen so far. Had Saruak's power risen even further?

Cassie glanced across at us. And my chest went very tight at that point. She looked as startled as I'd ever seen her, genuinely afraid. Her face was pasty, sweaty in the flashlight beam. I could see it in her eyes—she had miscalculated badly.

"Get *out* of there!" I yelled.

She'd got everyone else out, after all. Why'd she not taken her own advice?

I got my answer a few seconds later. Two things happened practically at once. The beam picked up yet another glimpse of the hulking Dralleg, closer to us this time, trying to circle around her through the gleaming wooden pews.

And then the circle of light . . . flashed across a second one. And then a third. *That* was why she wasn't moving. *That* was why she hadn't left. There wasn't just the one of them. There were several. And they had her surrounded. My pulse skipped its next few beats.

Each creature was identical, so far as I could see. But what was going on?

A familiar dry, mocking voice came skirling down from the high rafters.

"Ever play Find the Lady, Ross?" it asked me. "Well, you'd better, before Death finds yours."

We both looked up, and Hobart shone the light there. But the ragged old man was not in view.

Cassie's carbine thumped again.

I tried to figure out what Saruak was implying. He had used illusion at the last church, hadn't he? Made us believe that he was actually there? And could this duplication of his monster be the same?

Which meant that only one of these hunched, drooling creatures was the genuine Dralleg. I saw the game that he was playing with us. We had to decide which.

Almost as soon as I'd figured that out, though, things started to become more complicated.

Because more of the beasts began appearing, all throughout the church.

Hobart glanced across at me. He squinted.

"They're not real either?"

He could be smarter than he looked sometimes.

"One of them is," I told him.

"Damn."

Cassie, however, still hadn't got it. Or maybe it was simply that she didn't have the luxury of waiting to find out. She was firing at anything that got close enough to harm her. Three, four, then five of the beasts came lunging at her, and she gunned them down in quick succession.

They weren't even pretending to be injured anymore. They simply crumbled to fine dust when the bullets hit them, the same way the one at St. Agnes's had done. That rotting stink filled the interior once more.

It felt like spiders were unfolding in my gut. New beasts were appearing all the time, replacing the ones who'd vanished. And in the darkness, among all this mayhem, the genuine Dralleg was lurking somewhere.

I could still remember, from my first encounter, its ferocity and massive strength. There were two sets of real claws out there, then, both as sharp as scalpels. Two enormous arms to swing them. Shimmering green eyes to guide the blow. Caliban, with murder on its mind. And if it managed to sneak up on her, while she was distracted . . . ?

Hobart and I exchanged looks. We couldn't just stand by the doorway any longer.

"Cass!" I called to her. "Stay where you are!"

"That's what I'm *doing!*" she howled back furiously.

"We're coming to get you!"

"Any time this week?"

Dozens of pairs of shining eyes all swung toward us momentarily. But we weren't the one who they were after. Their focus went back to Cass.

The next time she tried to fire, her carbine gave a hollow click. She dropped it and snatched the Mossberg up in the same fluid motion. Put a saboted slug into the beast that had got nearest to her. It, like the others, came apart into a sprinkling of fragments.

"Why the hell are they doing that?"

"They're just illusions!" I yelled. "But the real one's here as well!"

"Where?"

"I don't know!"

And *now* she'd got it. She had crouched down slightly, gnawing at her lip. Her gaze was hunting through the dimness for any slight sign of the genuine monster.

Hobart swept the flashlight around, and we began to edge inside. At least six of the creatures looked at us again, when we did that. Their eyes burned with warmthless light. A rumble sounded from their throats. Then, several of them were swiveling around, and loping rapidly toward us.

Which one was the real Dralleg? There was simply no way to tell. We opened fire on them, cutting them all down. Each of them dissolved to powder. A fine patina of the stuff was settling everywhere.

More materialized into being. This was like fighting with a Hydra. Chop down one—two more appeared. I was getting more concerned with every second. How strong had our visitor become?

Time was going at a crawl now. And with every single slow moment that passed, the pattern was the same. Crouched gray shapes, one after another, would come surging through the dark at us. We'd hit each of them with a barrage of pellets. Only to find out it was a wasted effort.

Several of them got so close that I tensed up. It was pointless—the pain never came. But there were scores of them. Which one was the creature we were looking for?

Cassie's gun kept roaring too, the spent cartridges ringing as they struck the flagstones. And how many rounds did the Mossberg hold? Nine, I remembered. All of us were getting low on ammunition. Maybe that was part of the plan too.

Sweat was dripping down my face, and my breath was coming in ever shorter gasps. This wasn't working. We weren't getting any nearer to Cass, with these things coming at us all the time. Was there any way that we could sort out the reality from the deception?

And then something popped into my head. Something quite remarkable, in fact. Because the only things there, usually, were my own thoughts. And this definitely wasn't one of those.

There was—suddenly, behind my eyeballs—a pale flash. Electric blue. There was only one place that I could think of where I saw that color.

The Little Girl's home was not far from here. And . . . had she just communicated with me, in some way?

She had opened a small doorway in my mind, it seemed. Caused me to go back. A recent memory.

That first tussle with the Dralleg. One of its hind paws pinning me down. The monster rearing up, ready to finish me. And then Cassie's shotgun announcing its presence, and the thing stumbling back.

And when I had looked over at its injured gut . . . ?

I reached across, without a word. And snatched the flashlight from Saul's grasp.

"What?"

He'd been playing it at head- and shoulder-height, until this point. But I shone it lower, seeking out the pale gray bellies all around us. Another of the things came leaping at me with a high-pitched growl. Its skin, though, was completely unmarked.

Saul fired, and it turned into a billow of fine particles. Then he noticed that I hadn't even tried to shoot the thing.

"What are you *doing?*" he yelled again.

I just kept sweeping the beam around. And, an instinct taking hold of me, aimed it close to Cassie. There were four more of the creatures around her. Three to the front—her attention was fixed on them. But another one, slower and more stealthy, was creeping up on her, directly to the rear.

The stomachs of the first three were as flawless as the rest had been.

But on the one behind, there was a massive, ugly bruise, a souvenir of its last encounter with the Mossberg.

I looked frantically at Saul.

"That one!"

Its claws had already lifted. Two more steps, and it would be all over her, taking her apart like kindling. Saul finally got what I was driving at, and we both charged in its direction.

Several of the creatures that we went past swiped at us. I felt their claws pass through me like a blast of ice-cold air. But they were insubstantial, and did no harm. There was no injury.

"Cass!"

The riot gun exploded in my grasp, and Hobart's did the same. And from this close a range, there was much more impact. The real Dralleg went lurching back a step.

Its jaws parted, fangs glinting. It howled massively. Cass spun around, her face almost childish with fright for the briefest moment. She could see how close the thing had got.

And then she scowled, her eyebrows knitting. She went forward and fired at the beast herself.

It threw its ugly head back, let out a reverberating shriek, clutching at its torso once again. Hobart and I responded to that by emptying our last rounds into it.

It glowered at us, letting out a strangled noise. Then vanished.

When I looked around, the rest were gone as well.

My lungs just wouldn't slow down. I felt like I'd keep breathing this hard for the entire remainder of eternity. My hands were quivering. I could feel dampness running down my spine.

Cass and Hobart looked pretty much in the same condition. Perhaps we should have simply pulled ourselves together and got out of there, before Saruak tried out any more such stunts on us. But we didn't have the strength to move, not right away.

My thoughts went, rather muddledly, to that flash of light inside my head. It was hard to figure. For the first time since we had discovered her, the Little Girl had done something to genuinely help. She'd personally intervened. But why exactly? Was the danger we were facing so serious it had finally awoken her, stirring her into action?

A new sound made me forget all of that, and straighten up again. It was a slow, dry hand-clap, echoing and loud. And, again, it was coming from above us. There was no way to be sure of which direction.

A couple of sirens were pulling up outside. Hobart must have called for backup on the way here. But details of that kind were lost on me by this time. My eyes peered up and hunted through the gloom.

Saruak's voice, all venomous, came spilling down toward me.

"Bravo, Mr. Devries!"

"Show yourself!" I bellowed back.

But he obviously had no intention. He preferred to remain hidden when he could. I had read that too about his breed.

"You've acquitted yourself better than I thought. You catch on quickly, sir."

He paused a moment.

"But I'm only warming up, you see? The big event is still to come."

And what might that be? I spat out an oath, still trying to catch a glimpse of him. He just wasn't there, I understood before much longer. The only part of him here was his voice.

"What are you talking about?" I called out.

He didn't reply at first. And I was starting to think that he'd gone away, when he spoke up again. But he ignored my question.

"By the way, Ross."

I just stood there.

"One more thing about me that you have to understand. I am *not* magnanimous. *Not* the type to shrug and say, 'You've won this round.' Don't make that mistake about me."

With so many people dead, I was hardly about to.

"I have to admit," he went on, rather mildly, "that I can be spiteful when I'm bested. And—just to prove my point—look. There appears to be something wrong with that curious female companion of yours."

I peered around startledly at Cassie. She was still on her feet, and seemed perfectly okay. There was not a scratch on her that I could make out. So what was he talking about?

There was a crackling sound above us. It was coming from one of the stained glass windows. Was it going to implode, and cut us all to shreds? I tried to move away from it.

But it wasn't the whole thing that came apart. Just one section broke free. It was about six inches long, a triangle, glinting at its narrow tip.

It hung in midair for a second, flipping over, catching the flashlight's beam.

And then it suddenly shot forward, hissing through the dark. And embedded itself deep in Cassie's stomach.

CHAPTER 19

As I watched that happen, my heart seemed to stop beating and then rush right up to block my throat.

Cassie could only stare back at me, her mouth dropping open. But no sound at all came out.

Her shotgun fell away, crashing to the flagstones from her nerveless grasp. Both her hands went to the wound. And then her legs started giving way, her whole face crumpling up.

By the time she'd fallen to her knees, she was tipping over to the side as well. She went down. The pain hit her badly. On the cold stone floor, she curled into a fetal ball, an anguished grunt finally escaping her. Tears were pushing through her eyelids. She was hissing quickly, trying to stay conscious and alert.

I was at her side immediately. Put one hand across her arm. Was the violent shaking hers, or mine? My thoughts weren't even coherent anymore.

In all the time we'd worked together, I had never seen her hurt as bad as this.

"Cassie?"

Her teeth grated—I could see them clench and shift. Her palms were clasped across her stomach. Not enough, however, to stop the blood from spilling out.

A pool of it grew as I watched, jet black in the flashlight's beam.

"Cassie? I want to see how bad the damage is!"

She tried to ease her hands away, but didn't get them very far. Because, as soon as the pressure eased, something began to bulge under the skin there.

Something had been torn or severed. So I made her hold on tight again. *Oh good God, was I watching her die?*

Several cops had entered, moving warily through the dense shadows. Hobart spoke to one of them, then shook his head. He came across and bent over us, his face apologetic.

"There are no ambulances left," he murmured.

Which made sense, after the other attacks. But it didn't exactly help.

"One of our cars can take her to the hospital, Ross. That's her safest bet."

But my mind was unclouding by this stage. Raine General was at least ten minutes from here, even with a V8 engine and a siren. And the ER ward would probably resemble a field hospital after the battle of the Somme. I recalled how many injured there had been. They'd be running short of blood reserves as well. And Cassie needed plenty.

I put my mouth to her ear and said, "I'm going to get you to my car. It's going to hurt. You ready?"

Her eyelids fluttered, and she managed to give me a tiny nod.

As carefully as possible, I rolled her into my arms, then stood up. It obviously pained her like crazy, but she kept her jaw tight and didn't make a sound. I admired her for that. Except, for somebody so wiry, she wasn't exactly light.

Hobart stepped out of my way, wondering what I was up to. I just headed for the open street.

She was practically unconscious when I eased her into the passenger seat. I ran around to the driver's side, then gunned the engine.

* * *

"Lawrence L. DuMarr," read the lettering on the glass door. "Apothecary. Acupuncture. Spiritual Matters Addressed."

It was on a short brownstone block, called Exeter Close, at the furthest edge of Marshall Drive. The only storefront with any lights still on. All the rest were dark. But when you looked at them, you could see that they were all of a kind.

If you practiced magic, you could do all of your shopping on this single street. It was straight, with broad, neat sidewalks. There were no trees or shrubbery whatsoever. And the stores were all packed side by side.

Some specialized in pendants, fetishes, and amulets of every description you could think of. Others carried the ingredients for potions. One establishment stocked only crystals, in every shape, size, and color imaginable. And there were several bookshops, naturally. The subject? You can guess.

But none of those instruments, that knowledge, could help Cassie, and I knew it.

I'm the first to admit that magic, wielded properly, can cure a sickness, a disease. Actual wounds, though, are another matter. Most powerful adepts think twice, then three times, before trying that.

It's a matter of understanding, you see. Proper magic begins in the head, by visualizing something. And in this case, visualizing the body itself, the damage to it. How to fix it. How to make it right.

Cells mending, and closing around each other. Severed vessels joining up. Muscles readjusting. Blood starting to flow along the correct routes again. There's far too much to take account of. Far too much that could go wrong. And, whatever condition Cassie might be in, I couldn't take that chance. I wouldn't risk it.

Lawrence L. DuMarr was something rather different.

There was a Closed sign turned around in the door. Beyond it, I could see hundreds of neatly arranged glass jars with fat cork-stoppers, on a row of shelves. They were filled up with dried fungi, dried dead beetles, God alone knew what else.

But another door, at the rear of the shop, was slightly ajar, a chink of ochre light apparent from behind it.

The air was faintly misty as I lifted Cassie out and carried her along. It formed soft, yellow nimbuses around the streetlamps, like the breath of some strange phantom, and made my surroundings seem a touch unnatural. Rather like a dream, in fact. If only it were that.

Cassie was unconscious. Her head lolled slackly on my forearm. All the blood had gone from her face. She was still breathing gently, and no longer in pain, at least. But my heart was beating like a hammer. How much longer did she have?

I couldn't push the doorbell without letting go of her. So I simply kicked the frame till Lawrence noticed that. His face came poking out of the back office, looking annoyed at first. But then he saw what was going on. His expression changed to one of alarm, and he hurried across to let us in.

"Cassandra! What's happened?"

"Picked the wrong fight," I told him, as I hefted her inside.

DuMarr ushered us through, sweeping all the papers off his desk. I set her down. She made an unpleasant bumping noise, like a dead weight of potatoes. Blood began spreading almost immediately on the wood.

The man peered at her anguishedly. He was on the scrawny side. In his middle forties, but with prematurely white hair that swept down across his shoulders. And, despite the fact that he'd been born here, looked more like he came from Oxford, England, in the pre-War days. A friend of Tolkien, perhaps. He had a goatee beard, the same white as his hair. Wore a maroon velvet smoking jacket with cigar burns on the sleeves, a silk shirt of the same color, and loose bell-bottomed pants. There was an embroidered skullcap on his head, a tassel swinging from it. And a gold pince-nez was balanced on the sharp bridge of his nose.

His eyes were watering. He was genuinely mortified. For some reason—despite the fact that they're as different as chalk and cheese—DuMarr had always utterly adored Cass, ever since he'd met her. Not in an amorous way, you understand. It was more to do with admiration. He liked her straightforwardness, her vitality, I think. Whenever she was around, he'd fuss over her until it drove her to distraction. And when not in her presence, he would talk about her like some kind of heroic princess.

"I feel *so* much safer, knowing she's around," he'd tell me.

He inspected her wound, as carefully and gently as if he were handling gossamer.

DuMarr, you have to understand, doesn't practice magic any more than I do. Has the same suspicion and disdain for it, in fact. But years ago, hunting through our libraries, he came across another art, and one that fascinated him.

It's a Chinese practice. The guidance and manipulation of the power inside ourselves, the life-force called the *chi*. He'd taught himself the skill, and has demonstrated it to me numerous times. This was its most important and skillful application. He wasn't going to heal Cass. He was going to try and help her body heal itself.

Once he had surveyed the damage, he put his middle finger to the spot between her eyebrows. It's a vital area, known as the third eye. I imagined he was trying to tell just how much life-force she had left. His own myopic gaze slipped shut. You could almost believe he'd gone into a coma, he became so still.

My eyes darted briefly around his office. The ochre glow in here was coming from a big old oil lamp, with a hint of jasmine to its fumes. It cast strange shadows around us that seemed to sway, as if we were at sea. There were dark wooden shelves and cabinets, with books and boxes of instruments on each. Thumbtacked to the walls above them was a dozen massive charts. Each a different aspect of the human body, with dotted lines drawn all over the skin. These were the meridians through which the energy flowed, he'd told me. And the round dots spaced along them were the pressure points.

His eyelids drifted open again, the lamp reflected in his glasses. His face was grave when he looked at me.

"You barely got her to me in time," he muttered. "Maybe I can help her. But there's no guarantee."

He had to be hurting terribly inside. I certainly knew I was. But the man was a picture of composure by this time, his every gesture measured. Her survival depended on him alone. On no one else in the whole world. He'd not give in to panic, and he would not let her down.

The palms of his hands started to move very gently up and down her body, tracing its smooth contours without touching them. Both palms came together just above her navel, at the area called the *dan tien*. I thought I saw the bloody shard of glass move slightly.

"Come, Cassandra, breathe. As deeply as you can," he murmured. "Breath and *chi* are one. Draw in good, new life-force. Push out bad."

Even unconscious, Cass seemed to respond. Her nostrils flared slightly, and her ribs began to lift and fall.

Her jaw dropped open, and she let out an incoherent moan. DuMarr stooped lower, coaxing her quietly.

"Yes, I know it hurts. But you have to try. Where's all your courage when you need it, huh?"

But he was smiling at her.

Not much later, I could feel a gentle prickle on the hairs around my wrists, like a mild electric current was now flowing through the room. I understood what this was too. He'd explained the whole process. He was not merely using the force in her own body. He was drawing it from outside, what is known as universal energy. The life-force of the world itself, and even the stars beyond.

It may seem strange that a man like myself, a practical man, accepts this kind of stuff. But the fact was, I'd seen it work. And right now, that was more than good enough.

I could only stand and watch, though. And I felt utterly helpless. The racing and the pounding in me had faded away, replaced by an awful leaden feeling. My thoughts just kept on getting darker. Cass had already bled out so much. Could even Lawrence save her?

His empty palms continued to move in fixed patterns across her. The glass actually did lift an inch from her stomach, the third time he completed that. He reached down smoothly and pulled it out, flinging it aside. Then his hands were circling the wound, making the bleeding stop.

And I understand what you are thinking. I have done a little reading on the subject for myself. And know that, in the outside world, the skills DuMarr was demonstrating do not work as powerfully as this.

Maybe it's simply the case that, steeped in the arcane the way Raine's Landing is, anything that's in the realm of metaphysics just works so much better here.

Cass was breathing far more evenly, I could make out. Her face was still like ivory, but it looked a little more serene. The tension in my body eased for the first time in quite a while. Were we going to be lucky after all?

I don't think DuMarr believed in luck. He just kept on at it. His gaze never left her once.

I swear there was the faintest lambent glow under his palms by this stage.

Oh yes, and one other thing. The wound was starting to close up.

CHAPTER 20

"Make her a tea of this when she wakes up," he told me, handing me a small glass vial with some nondescript brown shapes in it.

I didn't even like to guess what they were.

"Full of iron," DuMarr assured me, "far more than in a tablet. Otherwise, make sure she rests. Which will be hard work—yes, I get that."

He looked utterly exhausted, but delighted with himself. Cass was in an armchair, heavily wrapped in blankets. Still completely out of it, but a glow was finally returning to her cheeks.

I started to express my thanks.

"No need, no need," the man said, brushing me off quickly. "I did what I could. It's up to you now. Take her home."

We turned, at long last, onto Rowan Street, a wide, non-descript avenue in East Meadow, one of the rather shabbier parts of town. Not as dingy as Cray's Lane—at least the road was paved. But a lot of the old wooden houses had been partitioned off into—in some cases—curiously shaped apartments. And the whole place had an air of neglect about it

I'd been here a good deal, back when I'd been on the force. Nothing very major ever drew me here, you understand. Mostly domestic disturbances and the handling of pilfered goods. It's the sort of community, in other words, that stretches concepts like relationship and economy past their normal limits. The sidewalks were empty. A fox appeared in my headlamps for a moment, and then vanished like a ghost.

The neon sign outside her place was turned off, but I could still read it. "Cassie's Diner." That was what she used to do, before her whole world got turned head over heels. It had a low flat roof, big plate-glass windows, and you could make out the shapes of the tables and chairs inside. A deep fryer. A coffee machine. A sign on the door read "Ask About Our Specials." It was peeling away at one corner.

She owned the place free and clear, and had done okay with it. I'd dropped in many times, when I'd still been a cop.

I drove around the back, stopping just outside her apartment door. The screen was torn. There was a bug lamp to one side, but it hadn't been switched on in months.

The sky above us was a hazy, starless charcoal murk. Something flittered across it that I thought might be a bat.

I looked Cass over carefully. She was sleeping soundly, her breathing mildly sonorous, and I felt grateful just for that. I fumbled with my key chain till I found the one for her place. We keep each other's, for situations just like this. And then hefted her again—she didn't make a sound.

The instant that the door came open, there was a mewl from near my feet. Her big old tabby cat, Cleveland, was staring up at us with those dusky amber eyes of his. When he saw that there was something wrong, though, he beat a retreat, disappearing off into the back. The goddamn coward.

Once inside, I bumped the light switch with my elbow.

And there they were, even in the hallway. The children she'd once had. Staring at me, tiny, from the walls, in dozens of framed photographs.

Kevin, six years old. Angel, five. And Little Cassie, only three.

Trapped at those ages forever, motionless and two-dimensional.

I knew her story. Not all of it, but enough.

Cass had never married, but there'd been plenty of men. The problem was that—strong and hardy and dependable herself—she'd always had a penchant for, been drawn to, total losers. Flotsam on the sea of life. Guys who wasted their existences, and used up other folks' along the way. Drinkers. Gamblers. Semi-criminals. She liked them the same way other people took a shine to stray dogs. She would move them in and feed them like you would a scruffy, homeless mutt.

It never lasted long. After a few months she'd get bored, and then show Mr. Wrong the door. Cass had never been the sort of person to get all tied down. So I guess that, on one level, she preferred her life that way.

Her kids, as a consequence, each had a different father. But she loved them deeply, fiercely, all the same. I'd seen her with them, in the old days. She was like a tender lioness, with them around. When she needed to be firm with them, she always did it kindly. They were her whole life. So imagine how she must have felt, to turn around one day and find . . .

She still felt pretty weighty, but I didn't mind a bit. Not when you considered option number two. I shifted her in my arms, and headed slowly toward the next door down the corridor.

She had never told me the full details. Couldn't bring herself to do it. Every time she tried, the words just piled up like a car wreck in her throat. I'd got the gist of it, however, down the last couple of years.

She'd been out front, flipping burgers. Her kids and her new paramour were here in the apartment. He'd gone out that day, despite the fact that it was freezing cold, and brought back something with him. Some kind of ornate talisman, a black stone at its center. Where'd he even get it? Stolen it, more than likely.

"You be careful with that thing," she'd told him.

She was busy at the time, with a new raft of customers out front.

"Don't let the little ones touch it."

A normal day, then. Flipping burgers. Snow on the pavement outside, and the windows of the diner misting up continuously. The griddle sizzling. The smell of coffee on the air.

She had somehow sensed that something was wrong. Just a mother's instinct. And come running back inside, to find an utter, yawning vacuum where her family had been.

Cassie had searched for hours after that, first in every corner of her silent and deserted home. Then through the white-clad streets outside. One of her regulars had called the police. It was no use at all, none of it. That man of hers, and all three of her kids, had simply . . .

"Vanished, right?" she managed to ask me just one time, the tears pouring freely down her cheeks. "Not forever, though? Not dead? Just like your family . . . right, Ross?"

Right, I'd told her. But the plain fact was, I didn't know for sure, in either case. There was simply no way of telling.

Not then, and not even now. It drives me practically crazy sometimes.

I bumped my elbow on another switch, at the entrance to her living room, revealing flimsy nylon drapes, cheap-looking ornaments, a threadbare rug. The kind of furniture you had to screw together, which looked secondhand from new. A TV set that belonged in some kind of museum. There was clothing of hers scattered everywhere—I've already told you she's not tidy.

The walls had been painted light pink a considerable while back. There were biker magazines in a heap on the coffee table—she'd owned a chopper since she'd been eighteen and run with a bad crowd. Propped against the couch was the Gibson acoustic guitar she liked to strum sometimes.

And there were hundreds, literally hundreds more of the same kind of photograph. Kevin, Angel, and Little Cassie, happy, innocent, and beaming.

I'd seen them many times before, but never quite got used to them. How could she come home every night to this? And I was better placed than most to understand how it tormented her.

Just like me in my own house, all the children's toys were packed away. "For safekeeping," I suppose she tells herself, the same way that I do. There were hardly any books. She had a stereo cabinet, the equipment pretty old.

And over in the corner, about three feet tall, was a shiny, gleaming tinsel tree. There were colored lights strung all around it, but they'd been unplugged a good time back. The silver star at the top was hanging partway off.

And that was the worst of it, the grimmest aspect. Her children had disappeared just two weeks before Christmas.

Something hard and dry moved in my gullet.

Forget it now, I told myself. Then looked away. I always hate the sight of that damned tree.

I carried her through into the bedroom. Set her down and covered her up, making sure that she was comfortable. I hovered there for a while, with the lights turned off, just watching her. Then, leaving the door open a small gap, I went into the kitchen.

It was all perfectly clean, don't get me wrong. But she'd just set things down wherever it was most convenient, not even bothering to stow them away in cupboards, so the work surfaces were a big jumble of pans, skillets, crockery, and cups.

She'd never really cared about stuff like that, not even when the kids had been around. Neatness and respectability? They were just diversions, to her way of thinking. The only thing that really mattered was the degree of happiness with which you lived. And that had been intense until . . .

Until happiness had been torn from her grasp, leaving her with nothing to hold on to except what we did.

I went across and got a beer from the fridge. My hands smarted gently as I yanked the cap off. I felt like I'd run a marathon. My muscles were aching, and my body was filled with a tiredness so profound it seeped right through into my bones.

What an evening this had been. I'd never known one similar. I gazed around again, taking a slow pull from the bottle.

My mind couldn't find release, however exhausted I might be. It kept banging away at the same questions. What might Saruak be planning for us next? What else did he have in store for this peculiar town of ours?

The answer came a good deal sooner than I had expected. In the very next second, in fact.

A sudden vivid brightness flared outside the kitchen window. And then it began to spread, and grow.

CHAPTER 21

S

The single letter hung, in blazing fire, high up against the night sky. Too far away to tell how large it really was. But smoke was trailing from its edges. It was massive, and illuminated this entire district. I supposed it was lighting up almost all the town.

I'd gone outside, around to the front of Cassie's diner. And was not the only person out here. Everywhere I looked, folks were spilling onto the sidewalk, drawn there by the vivid glow. And this had to be happening everywhere. Heads were angled back. Eyes mirrored the churning flames. Their faces were lit up, flickering yellow. I was reminded of those neighbors back on Cray's Lane the other night.

They looked uncertain and afraid. Precisely what was happening now?

Another letter began to appear, like it was being traced there by some invisible pen.

A

There'd been a television crew back at St. Nevitt's. It had, almost certainly, gone on to St. Agnes's as well. Most people had to know what had been going down this evening. I remembered what the Little Girl had said. Awareness of the evil spirit. That was how he would tighten his grip on us, until it squeezed us half to death.

R the moving finger wrote. And, having written, moved on to a *U*. It was our friend again. There was no doubt on that score.

He was impinging on the consciousness of this whole town. Growing larger in its people's thoughts, until he obsessed them. They already knew that horror, in its purest form, had descended on the Landing. It had been a shapeless and an unknown form up until this point. But now it had a name. They knew exactly what to call the thing they'd grown to fear.

I gazed up defeatedly as the second *A* and final *K* sprang into being, knowing there was nothing I could do about it anymore. *Saruak.* It would be in people's dreams tonight. More likely in their nightmares. It would trip from the mouths of infants, and be the first word people thought of when they woke. It would hang there in their minds, the way the flames were hanging. And then, as the Little Girl had told me, it would take root, grow.

I could almost feel the heat of the huge letters from down here. Even the adepts up on Sycamore Hill would be watching, I knew. And how long before they became involved?

Was there nothing we could do to stop him?

After a while, it all began to fade away, crackling into nothingness like marsh gas. But its impression remained. I could still see that word every time I blinked. I couldn't be the only one.

The heat must have been so intense that it had actually seared the night-borne haze away. The stars were winking down at me again, very cold and distant. I turned my head from side to side. A few people were still looking upward. Most of the rest were gazing at each other with their mouths hanging open.

"What did that mean?" I heard several times.

Something in me wanted to tell them. But I got the feeling that they'd all find out quite soon enough.

I went back in to check on Cass. She was fine, still sleeping. Lucky to be out of it. This room was as big a mess as the rest of the house. But there were clumps of lucky heather on her dresser, and a four-leafed clover set in a cube of acrylic on her nightstand. I'm not superstitious personally, but I brushed my fingertips against it all the same.

Cleveland had returned, and was now dozing on the quilt down by her feet. She called him that because she'd always wanted to see other places, and that one sounded—to her ears—like it had a cool, exotic ring to it. I had read enough about the outside world to understand she'd got that wrong, but I'd never had the heart to tell her.

They both looked pretty cozy, just like everything was all right with the world. And that eased my dark mood a little, making me feel slightly better.

So, leaving them to it, I went to get another beer, then slumped down on the living room couch, making the guitar hum slightly. I didn't think I'd actually sleep.

But tiredness can descend upon you like the most silent of traps. *I'll just settle back a moment. I'll just close my eyes.*

And then, I was pounding up the stairs at Mrs. McGaffrey's all over again. Coming to a stiff halt at the top, in front of Goad's room.

What I was looking at? I could scarcely believe it.

Pale white light was flowing from the room. A solid stream of it. It didn't flicker, which meant this was magic at its most extreme. And it was so intense I found it hard to look into. I shielded my eyes with my free hand, and squinted. It was still so bright that I could only make a few vague shapes out.

But they were human, four of them, dim smudges in the brilliance. Two were taller than the other pair. And one of them was broad as well. I already understood who *that* had to be.

Goad stepped toward me, spreading out his arms. I could see, as he got closer, he was wearing some kind of cloak. His sandals were gone too, and his feet were bare. I couldn't tell what his expression was, but just knew from his tone of voice that he had to be smirking.

"Hey there, neighbor! Keeping well?" He said it cheerfully, like we had just bumped into each other in the park.

Was he kidding me? I moved forward carefully, with my gun held out. But it got knocked from my grasp, clattering to the floor, the instant that my hand drew level with the opening. My knuckles stung like they'd been hit with an iron bar. I'd run into some kind of barrier, invisible to the naked eye.

"Oops, sorry about that," he chortled. "Man, I should have warned you."

I recovered quickly, slamming at the thing with my forearm. It just made a dull thudding sound, and did not yield a millimeter.

Goad let out a snort. He was right up close to me by this time. And I could make out his features, although they were indistinct. A sloppy grin was spreading over his face. Dressed the way he was, he looked like Nero after an extended nap.

I tried to stare him down, but he looked unimpressed.

"Mr. Authority personified!" he crowed. "But you've got none around here, dude!"

I pressed myself against the barrier.

"Let me in, right now!"

His head shook delightedly. "No can do."

And so I looked over at the vague shapes behind him, mostly made of heads and shoulders, just a vague blur underneath. None of them were moving. And they didn't seem to be conscious that I was even there. It ripped at my insides to see them that way. He wouldn't deliberately hurt them, would he?

"If you've touched one hair on them—"

I thumped at the barrier again, with the heels of my hands this time. Goad just peered across his shoulder, then returned his nasty gaze to me.

"If I've touched your *wife*, you mean? Not to worry, Rossie. All I've done so far is bring them up here for the ceremony."

Which was the first time that word had come up. What in God's name was he planning to do?

He turned around and walked toward them. It was only when he stopped that he gave me his full attention again. He put an index finger to his chin.

"Know what your problem is, huh, Ross?"

Humor him, I thought. So I asked, "What?"

"You just think so very small. Here you are, surrounded by actual living magic, and you don't even grasp the opportunity. You roll around in your patrol car and let all these boundless possibilities drift by. That's okay by you? Each to their own, I say. But your family . . . ?"

He pointed to them.

"Your family deserves a whole lot better. Alicia in particular."

I couldn't stand to hear him speak her name, but there was nothing I could do about it. He was really scaring me, since his tone was getting louder, wilder.

"She's a goddess, don't you understand? I knew that from the start. And now? I'm going to be Zeus to her Hera."

The power had gone completely to his head, the way it often did to people with weak natures. I began pounding at the invisible shield. All I wanted was to get my family out of there. But the barrier wouldn't give. It seemed impenetrable.

"Forget Sycamore Hill!" he was yelling. "Forget the dumb-ass adepts! I'm going to be the most powerful sorcerer the Landing's ever seen. A great man, yes, superb. And great men need families, Rossie. How else can they build dynasties? I don't have one, so I'm taking yours. I'm doing them a favor!"

He was going to try and conjure something huge, in other words. My sense of panic escalated massively. He'd only been learning for a bare few months. He might have managed, somehow, to create all of this energy. But did he have the knowledge, the experience, to control it? Things could go in all kinds of directions from here, I could tell. Including very badly wrong.

"Don't do it!" I shouted. "It's not worth the risk!"

All Goad did was sneer and take another step back, gazing at me like I was some kind of vermin.

"Oh sure, 'be cautious.' Typical of you. But look what I've already done? There *are* no limits! I can make happen whatever I *want!*"

Then I noticed that something was glimmering around his neck. I couldn't see it clearly, but it seemed to be some kind of pendant, a jewel on a silver chain. Although the brightness wasn't coming from it, it just seemed to hang there passively. I wasn't sure what part it played.

Goad raised his arms, the sleeves of his cloak falling back.

"By the power that is in me!" he shrieked, throwing back his head. "By the magic that is mine alone, I seek to transform us!"

Transform?

"Please, stop!"

But he just ignored me.

I started yelling out Alicia's name, and then my children's. There was not even a flicker of response from them. Could they even hear me?

"I shall make us all immortal!" Goad was howling.

His short legs were dancing underneath the folds of his cloak.

"I shall make us gods on earth, and the wind shall sing our names!"

Alicia remained motionless. But, to my relief, Pete and Tammy started coming around. Then it struck me forcibly. Was that a good thing, or an indication that he didn't have as much control as he thought he did? They peered around rather sleepily, then saw that I was there and both came hurrying toward me.

"Daddy! Daddy!"

There wasn't even time to warn them. Their outstretched arms hit the barrier, and they both fell back. I collapsed to my knees in front of them, desperation setting in. They were mere inches away from me, but were completely out of reach.

And then the quality of light in the room suddenly transformed.

It got fiercer until, in a bare few seconds, my eyes hurt just trying to cope with it. The kids were reduced to wildly moving silhouettes, still trying to reach me. I was bellowing at the top of my voice, but had no idea what sounds were coming out. My entire face was wet.

As I watched, the searing brightness started pouring into all four of them, through their mouths and eyes.

"You see?" Goad was hollering. "You see what I can do?"

The glow was filling up their bodies. They no longer resembled people. They looked more like angels. Maybe this would work, I tried to tell myself, though I was shaking furiously. They'd be changed, but still okay.

The light . . . abruptly went a much deeper hue, almost a bronze color. The kids became just vague shadows inside it. My heart froze in my chest. I tried to think of something I could do. Or was it already too late?

Tammy screamed.

That went through me like a knife, jarring me back into action. I was scrabbling around, next instant, retrieving my gun. If I couldn't break through this damned barrier, then perhaps a bullet could.

I swung back around, yelling a warning to my kids to get out of the way and thumbing back the hammer.

And the light inside the room . . . ?

Transformed to pure black, in the exact same moment. I never even got that second chance to try and save them.

The darkness faded gradually. Until at last, it revealed the loft room the way it had originally been. An unmade single bed. A bare dresser. And a very smeary window looking out on the backyard, a palm print distinctly visible on it.

There was no one left in there at all.

Jason Goad, and my whole family, were gone. . . .

I woke with a yell, sitting violently upright. Children's faces were staring at me when I looked around, and for a moment I thought they were my kids. I had completely forgotten where I was. Then the truth sank in. These were Cassie's photographs, nothing more.

I peered more slowly around the living room, then rubbed at my hot cheeks. The dampness on them wasn't merely sweat, just like in the dream I'd had.

I missed my wife and kids so much. All I had left to cling on to, these days? The same belief that Cassie carried around with her. I hadn't seen them actually perish. They might still be alive, someplace else. Perhaps on some different plane of existence—I'd heard adepts talking about stuff like that. And I told myself that same thing, every single day.

After a while, I went through into the bathroom. Wiped my face down with a dampened towel. Stared at myself in the mirror. My face was distorted by the glass, which was streaky.

It was still dark outside. As quietly as I could, I went down the hall and pushed open the bedroom door again.

Cass was still fast asleep, her lean face in repose. Yellow light from a streetlamp was filtering through her drapes. With her cropped hair and her gaunt appearance, she looked entirely different to Alicia. They'd been cast from very different molds. Not that she was unattractive, far from it. And how did I really feel, deep down, about her? It had been so long since anyone . . .

But no, I couldn't think about her in those terms. If I ever went that route, I'd be practically admitting that my wife was gone for good.

Finally, I just scribbled her a note and left it on her nightstand, with the vial DuMarr had given me.

She'd turned over on the mattress by that time. Perhaps an indication that she wasn't hurting anymore. And a corner of her pillowcase was sticking in her eye. So I leant over, gently rearranged it.

Her warm breath touched against my hand when I did that. Cleveland woke up, peering at me suspiciously.

Back in my car, I went to light a cigarette, then changed my mind. Cass's dried blood was all over the seat beside me, reminding me that, damn, this had been the closest of calls.

I didn't feel right, just leaving her alone like this. So I called her friend Bella's cell phone number, left a message on her voice mail. Could she drop around later, make sure everything was still all right? I wasn't too specific about how she had been injured. But then, her pals are used to Cassie getting into scrapes.

Then I turned the engine over, and headed for my office. Wound my window down on the way there. The air rushed around me coolly, bringing me properly awake.

At least I'd be able to watch the sun rise. But how many dawns did any of us have left?

Something else was nagging at me, gnawing like a rodent at the edges of my consciousness. I couldn't get a handle on it, though.

A faint, silvery gray line had appeared on the horizon when I parked in Union Square. The darkness had not faded yet, but it was going to, and soon. A soft breeze was still blowing, and the banners that had been strung up all flapped around like living things. Their lettering wavered as I stared at it.

And that was when it finally hit me, so obvious it almost struck me dumb. Saruak drew his strength from us, from our perception of him. And if that turned into a massed, collective one?

This was something people *really* needed to be warned about.

I climbed the stairs, wondering if any of the powers-that-be were up and around at this time of the morning.

The answer came before I'd even opened up my door. The phone was ringing on the desk, inside.

I hurried in and grabbed at the receiver, to be greeted by a familiar voice.

"You wish to meet with us, Devries?" Judge Levin asked me.

He felt no need to announce himself. How long had they been watching me? Did they already know?

"Yes, I do," I told him, although I made sure not to sound too deferential about it.

It's never wise to throw your lot in wholly with the Sycamore Hill crowd. They have their own agendas, mostly to do with status and position. And us humbler folks, the way they see it?—our job is to serve those ends.

But sometimes, they're the only game in town, when it

comes to the kind of threat that I was dealing with. And out of them, the judge was one of the most reliable. He had some kind of a moral code, at least.

"It's agreed, then," he told me quietly. "A few of us will be gathering at Gaspar's place within the next half hour. We'll look forward to seeing you there."

CHAPTER 22

The huge wrought-iron gates to Gaspar Vernon's mansion were open when I finally arrived. Its grounds stretched out beyond them, as motionless in the dimness as some vast oil painting. The three-headed dog that usually guarded the place was nowhere to be seen, thank God. I wondered what size kennel they put *that* thing in.

I followed a driveway of fine reddish gravel toward the portico. My gaze kept flickering around the entire time. I barely ever came up here.

This was nothing like the seething mess Raine Manor's gardens had become. Perfectly trimmed lawns, as neat as golfing greens, stretched out around me in the predawn light. There were even, when I looked a little closer, croquet hoops out there. Every verge was filled with flowering shrubs, or elegant topiary cut into the shapes of mythic beasts. I went by a phoenix, and a Minotaur. They looked so real that I half expected them to wake up, like Raine's gargoyles had done. Man, that would have really made my day.

The house itself was low and broad, and built along classical lines. The portico had Grecian pillars. Several cars were parked out front. Judge Levin's pale cream Bentley was there. And I thought I recognized the classic Porsche right next to it.

The front door opened as I walked toward it, although not by any magic this time. Vernon's butler was standing there, a rigid little silver-haired man in a funereal black suit and a shirt with a winged collar. I never had found out his name. His head was tipped back very slightly, so that he could stare at me more easily along the bridge of his hooked nose. His lips bunched up as I approached, becoming even more bloodless.

"Glad you could make it in such good time, Mr. Devries," he announced, unconvincingly. He didn't sound particularly glad about anything. "If you would kindly follow me?"

He led me off into the mansion's depths.

I was soon surrounded by an aged elegance. The tiles under my feet were white marble. The urns along the walls were all Minoan. A statue of Hermes would have been raising its arms to the heavens, if it'd still had any left. Some of the lyres and flutes in their display cases long predated Christ. He hadn't purchased any of this stuff, since there was nowhere in town you could get hold of it. He had simply conjured it up, using photographs in books and magazines for reference.

Gaspar Vernon—as I have already mentioned—was a classical scholar among other things. A patron of the arts. A connoisseur of fine wines, and a superb cook. All of which made you wonder why he presented himself to the outside world the way he did.

We reached a door, at last, no different to the dozens of others we'd been walking past. But the butler raised one slender hand, and rapped it with his knuckles. Then, without waiting for an answer, he pushed the handle down and ushered me inside.

There was a study in there, quite small for a place like this. Just one weak lamp was switched on, over in the corner. Don't ask me why, but major adepts always seem to prefer clinging to the shadows. Sinking back into them, getting partly lost, however powerful they have become. It's not simply a conceit on their part. More as though, the deeper into witchcraft that they get, the more darkness becomes a part of them.

There were four of them seated behind the broad desk in here. They were reduced to partial silhouettes. I recognized them, all the same.

At the center of the group, standing out the way a buffalo might do in a cabbage patch, was the owner of all that I'd surveyed, Gaspar Vernon himself. He was as tall as me, but a good deal burlier. His flat-topped head was largely bald, and he wore a drooping, off-white mustache. He had on what he always did, a checkered shirt, the sleeves rolled up as though for business. Doubtless a pair of blue jeans as well. The desk was hiding them. A corncob pipe hung, unlit, from his mouth. It was unfilled, in fact. Frankly, he looked like some kind of hick.

Who did he think he was fooling? I already knew he was a cultured, educated man. But Gaspar Vernon hailed from woodsman stock. The lumber mill out on the edge of town was the business that had built up the start of his family's fortune. By his manner and the way he dressed, he never seemed to let himself forget that. Nor anybody else, for that matter.

Sitting to his right was his close friend and peer, Judge Samuel Levin. I knew his history as well. His people had been Dutch-German tinkers, living on the edge of town, back in the Salem days. They'd come a good long way since then.

The man was only five feet four, and was as narrow as a snowflake's chance in summer. But as usual, he was immaculately turned out, right down to the manicured gleam of his fingernails. His thumbs were tented underneath his chin. Cufflinks glinted at his wrists. His hair was thick and black, with only the lightest dusting of silver in it. His eyes were slightly narrowed, and they studied me intently from behind the rimless spectacles he wore.

Off to his side was Kurt van Friesling, number one son of the town's most aristocratic family after the Raines. He was in his late thirties, blond and handsome in a rather flat-faced way, with eyes so very pale a blue they looked like spots of water. He had thick lips that carried an ironic twist around with them. Back in his own wild youth, he'd been a leading member of Woodard Raine's rat pack. But these days, he'd transformed himself into a responsible citizen, and took the town's well-being very much to heart.

At the far end—even deeper in the shadows—was a woman in her forties with her hair piled up. This was either Cynthia McGinley or her sister, Dido. They were not twins, but looked so similar they might as well have been. Spinsters both, they presented themselves to the outside world like they were the last word in gentility.

I had watched them turn a man who'd welched on a gambling debt into a pool of molten slurry, once. He had been still alive, and had screamed nonstop. Gaspar here had made them change him back, but they had only done it grudgingly.

Whichever this one was, she had intense green eyes that followed me like a cougar's. The rest of her face could barely be made out at all.

I felt my windpipe tighten a little. All four of them were gazing at me closely, not a smile anywhere to be seen. There was a chair already set out for me, but I stopped just short of it.

"Well, don't just stand there!" Vernon rumbled around the stem of his pipe.

He never just said anything. He roared it or he growled it. Or, if agitated, spat it out.

"Sit down, man! Sit down!"

So I did that.

I was still wondering what they were all doing up at this time of the day. A closer look provided me with the most likely answer. Their eyes were red-rimmed, and they all looked drawn. I guessed they hadn't been to bed at all last night. They must have been at the hospital. Not that they'd have been treating any wounds. I've already explained how magic generally cannot do that. But they'd have been helping any way they could, I had no doubt.

They had the slightly pummeled expressions of people who had tried their best, and been found lacking. Just how many casualties, I wondered, hadn't been as lucky as Cass?

There were rows of massive books, on artwork mostly, on the shelves behind them. I studied them a moment, then my gaze went back to the four faces in front of me, and held there, waiting.

"No one ever tell you that it's rude to stare?" Vernon inquired.

For some reason, he had never particularly liked me. I just made a small motion with my shoulders, keeping my expression blank.

"Land's sake, Devries! Every time I meet with you, it's like an object lesson in disrespect. Why don't you just tell us what you think is going on?"

"In your own time," Judge Levin put in, his tone more generous than his companion's.

So I did precisely that, recounting everything I had found out. For once, they all listened intently and they didn't interrupt.

"Let me get this straight," Vernon grunted, once I'd finished up. "You're telling us this Saruak is deriving power from the people in this town?"

"That's the Little Girl's opinion."

"That brat?" he snorted.

They had always been suspicious of her, and perhaps rather afraid, since she was such an unknown quantity.

"Tell us what *you* think," Judge Levin asked.

I leant back. "He's struck where he wants, whenever he wants. I know that. He's done enormous harm. And now? The people have a name to put to all the shapeless fear that's gathered. It doesn't look random in any way. I'd say it's all part of his plan."

"To what end?"

"The Reunion Evening."

"What?" van Friesling blurted.

So I explained it to them calmly.

"Believe it or not, the mayor got it right. He told me what everybody will be thinking. 'If it works this time, then we can get away from Saruak.'"

I glanced around at them.

"Everyone'll have that foremost in their minds, when they turn up for the ceremony."

"And . . . ?"

"The larger he is in our thoughts, the stronger he becomes. Everyone who uses magic, gathered in one place? It's the perfect opportunity for him."

They took that in slowly and uncertainly.

"And what do you suppose that we should do about it?" Vernon asked.

"Call it off."

"And if people still show up, and try to hold it on their own?"

Which they might do, I conceded.

"Stop them. Use force if necessary."

It was Levin's turn to get annoyed. His spectacles flashed in the dim lighting.

"Outlaw free association? Whatever else the Landing might be, this is still America. Besides, if most of the town shows up, we won't have the manpower."

The woman beside them abruptly leant forward, till the details of her face became apparent. Oh yes, this was Cynthia. Dido had suffered a mild stroke last year, which made her left eyelid droop.

Her mouth was crumpled up, and her brow furrowed. She looked like she wanted to sneer in my face, and only her upbringing was preventing her.

"Why should we take your word, sir, or that of some maladjusted child? Reunion Evening has become our town's oldest tradition."

And its most useless, I pointed out.

"All right, let's look at what we genuinely know," Judge Levin intervened. "We already have proof of what this Saruak is capable of. And I suppose we're pretty certain what he is. He has this *thing* with him as well, this . . . Dalek?"

"Dralleg."

"Quite. We're in no doubt of the havoc that this pair can wreak. But to take over the entire town?"

"Is that really likely?" Vernon asked. "We're talking about thousands of people, after all."

At which point, I felt myself groan inwardly. I'd been here plenty of times before.

The constant use of magic, as I've noted, leaves you detached from the real world. And these guys, for all their wealth and power, sometimes weren't much of a step up from Woodard Raine. They approached reality cautiously, as if it might turn around and bite them any moment. If me and Cassie moved or thought as slowly as them, we'd have both been dead a long time back.

They seemed to sense my irritation—they were that aware, at least.

"Is there any possibility of *talking* with this Saruak?" Levin asked. "Persuading him to back off? It's an option."

I reminded him about the Manitou's penchant for trickery. And added, "Best of luck with that."

His face went hard as granite.

"There is another way," put in Kurt van Friesling, before an argument broke out.

I looked across at him. And he was smiling at me very gently.

"The real problem, as I understand, is in finding him. He's not strong enough, yet, that he's invulnerable—correct?"

"Perhaps."

"Which is a matter I've been working on."

That certainly captured my attention. Everybody else's too.

Kurt produced a bag from underneath the desk and pulled out something that looked, at first, like a large compass. It seemed to be a jet black disk of stone, with golden symbols engraved around its edge. I looked at them closer, and concluded they were letters in some cabalistic script.

At the center, for a needle, was a spike-thin dragon, also made of gleaming gold and with bright, tiny crystals for its eyes, its forked tongue poking out.

It swiveled around till it was pointing due east of here.

I stiffened in my chair, my nerves singing a little. He had

obviously been doing some research. And had he discovered a way to find our newcomer?

"I say to hell with negotiation," Kurt went on, a little more vehemently. "Too much blood has already been spilled for that. I say, hunt him down and finish him. Who's with me?"

Levin's features became very thoughtful. Vernon's eyes went dull a moment, then began to smolder. He bit down on his pipe stem.

They were all—I could see—starting to come alive to the idea, their earlier reserve forgotten.

Cynthia McGinley cleared her throat, and then said, "Count me in."

She stared in my direction, her predatory green gaze seeming to devour me.

"You?"

I felt as surprised as anyone by this new development, but I nodded.

What else was I going to do? Ever since I'd first met Saruak, I had been waiting for a chance like this.

CHAPTER 23

Only Kurt came back outside with me. I wondered what the rest were going to do. He tossed me a set of keys and nodded to the black Porsche 911, which was sitting on the gravel with its roof down, looking like a cross between a bullfrog and a fighter plane.

"You drive," he told me. Then, by way of explanation, "I'll need both my hands."

For what? But he seemed eager to get on with it, whatever it might be.

Above us, the sky had grown slightly lighter than it had been when I'd gone inside. The sun had not come up as yet, but it was due. The whole eastern horizon was tinged with paler shades of dimness and then, along the world's edge, a soft band of platinum, which was growing as I watched.

Another crow, or perhaps a magpie, just a tiny cutout shape, flapped out of a little copse of trees and wheeled toward the growing light. The town lay below us, motion-less, its roads empty and its windows black. The streetlamps crisscrossing it shone like distant candles, the whole place slumbering and unaware.

What kind of dreams were the people down there having? Ugly ones, I would imagine, centered around the same events.

The wind up here was stronger, cooler than below. I shivered slightly as I approached the car. Or maybe that was the adrenaline. This might be the morning that we finally gave Saruak the unpleasant reception he'd been asking for since he'd arrived.

I climbed into the driver's seat. Turned the key and put my foot lightly on the gas. Felt my pulse race a little, as the engine's vibrations ran through me. I never got *that* sensation from my Caddy.

Thankfully, there was a manual shift—I've never much liked automatics. I went up swiftly through the gears as we headed back out past the gate.

Van Friesling set the black stone disk down carefully on the dashboard. Its needle was still pointing where it first had done, toward the east.

"I just follow it?" I asked.

"What else? It's exactly like a compass, but is drawn to supernatural forces, rather than magnetic north."

My excitement didn't seem to be affecting him a great deal. Kurt had always been the languid kind, that translating to an air of coolness when he'd been a teenager. He just settled back into his leather seat, his expression calm, relaxed.

We were just starting down the hill when a low thudding noise behind us made me glance up at the rearview mirror. And I'm pretty sure my jaw dropped open at that point.

I could see the Vernon mansion back there, of course. It was just as dim and still as every other building in my field of view. Except that three of the windows in the topmost story had, all at once, come blasting open. And the objects that came surging out . . . ?

I craned around to get a better look at them.

They seemed to be three rolling, churning clouds. Or three dark palls of smoke, perhaps. But smoke had never moved like this. It didn't come apart.

They all came hurtling across the mansion's grounds, in the same direction we were heading. Then began to climb as they reached Plymouth Drive, getting harder to see the further they rose, until the murk above had almost swallowed them.

All that you could make out, before too much longer, was a faint motion against the dormant sky. A bolt of lightning flashed across it briefly, but no thunder came.

"Were those . . . ?" I asked, my head still back.

"Yes. Just watch the road," van Friesling told me.

We were coming up on the first of the bends.

By the time I had a chance to look up again, a fourth cloud had come soaring along to join the others. Judging from its direction, I supposed that Cynthia McGinley's sister, Dido, was counting herself in as well, minor stroke or not.

Another chill ran through me. And it definitely wasn't from the cold this time. In all the years I'd lived here, I had never seen the adepts change themselves in quite this way.

Saruak and his Dralleg had better watch their step, from this point. Salem's most gifted descendants were now on the move.

Coming down a steep part of the hill, we went around another hairpin bend. The golden needle swung with the motion, still pointing directly at the center of town. Union Square itself. Did Saruak have the gall to still be loitering around down there? It was where we'd first met, after all.

But then we passed a line of trees, and the square came properly into view. We were close enough to make out detail. And a quick glance through the windshield confirmed that, not only did he have the nerve, but he had it in spades.

The broad, rectangular buildings of Union Square still looked pretty small, from this distance. But I could make out a paler dot, directly on the Town Hall roof. As I watched, it detached itself from the chimney it was standing by, and began to pace across the broad expanse of grayish green tiles.

I glanced over at van Friesling, who had lost a little of his detachment, and seemed rather stunned as well. *Son of a bitch, how long had Saruak been up there?*

The road straightened for the last time. We'd reached the lower stretches, where the normal houses stood. There was no need to watch our speed, no traffic in the way. And so I powered down the last half mile as quickly as I was able.

Kurt van Friesling sat up in his bucket seat, when we skidded off the Drive. And then, as I raced through the narrower streets, he reached into his pocket. His casual air had slipped away. He produced a jangling metal object, which he fastened around his neck. It was an intricately wrought, large pendant, made of strands of black-enameled metal. The shapes were slim sinuous dragons, like the golden one on top of the disk. But writhing ones, all wrapped around each other. Their talons were extended and their jaws gaped. There were red stones for the eyes.

And it must have been the car creating the effect. But for an instant, I thought I saw one of them shift position very slightly. I tried to pay that no attention.

"It's called Black Morgan's Talisman," Kurt told me, with a tight, wry smile. "Not all my family is Dutch. My many-times great-grandmother brought it to Salem with her, all the way from Swansea."

"And what does it do?" I asked.

We were having to shout above the wind and the roar of the engine.

"Wrong question. It's what it helps *me* do. It magnifies the power that an adept has. In this case, a Spell of Binding."

And he settled back again and closed his eyes, preparing his mind for the task in hand.

When I got another look at the Town Hall roof, the dot on it had resolved into a vaguely human shape. And had stopped between the two flagpoles directly at the center, Old Glory and the crest of Massachusetts fluttering above it. We were still too far away to tell, but I felt sure that Saruak was watching us.

He could disappear at will, I knew. So the fact that he was waiting for us didn't seem to bode too well. I tried to tell myself he was just being overconfident, or didn't understand what he was really up against this time.

Van Friesling opened his eyes again, spread his hands apart, the palms facing each other. And an electric bolt danced between them, so bright that it dazzled me. What the hell was that?

The streets had grown even narrower, too many flat roof-tops obscuring our view. Which made me uneasy. What might Saruak be doing while we couldn't see what he was up to?

Van Friesling had begun muttering under his breath, although not in any language that I recognized. Starting up his spell, I didn't doubt.

We finally burst into the square. I braked, and we swerved to a halt.

It was dead to the world, its windows vacant. Shadows were layered heavily across it, just the same as they'd been the last time I was here at night. The wind, trapped by the buildings, made a heavy moaning sound.

And there he still was, in between the banners. I could see his outline clearly. He was just waiting for us, his left eye glinting faintly. A bulge against his shoulder and a twin green glow told me that he was cradling his dog.

The sky had turned a little brighter. Saruak was black against it, and I could not see his face. Had no idea what his expression was.

He was staring at us, though. He didn't seem to move a muscle.

Van Friesling held out both his palms. A huge web, like flaringly bright electricity, came shooting from them, reaching up across the square.

At the exact same moment, there was another flash of lightning from above. Those four dense, boiling clouds had gathered high above us, I could see. And they were circling. One of them detached itself, came hurtling down toward the roof.

It made a thrumming noise, parting the air as it approached. The flags crackled more fiercely. Saruak looked up.

Gaspar Vernon's face appeared at the center of it, strangely disembodied, as if somebody had lopped his head off. Enormous, though, as big as a house, and rather two-dimensional.

His eyes blazed and his mouth was gaping. I had never seen the man look so angry and determined. The humming noise turned to a shriek.

The web that van Friesling had cast tried to wrap itself

around Saruak. But he just flailed with his free arm and brushed it off. The strands came apart, then vanished. And, before Vernon could get to him, he disappeared, along with his dog.

The other three clouds wheeled around a little faster. Shining bolts flashed in between them, once again. Gaspar Vernon just hovered above the rooftop, staring down at us frustratedly.

"Kurt?" his voice boomed out, so loud it made my head ring.

Van Friesling could only look apologetic.

"I'm sorry. It's been a long time since I did anything like this."

But had that been our only chance? I glanced down at the black stone disc. The needle had swung around again, and was pointing southward.

"He's still here," I said.

But how far away exactly?

I backed up the Porsche a little, swung it around, bumping the front tire on the curb. Then put my foot down hard. The howling motor started eating up the distance. And it wasn't very long before the taller buildings started giving way to a low, suburban sprawl.

The needle flickered slightly to the right, halfway down May Avenue. I swerved at the next intersection, went across a block. There was a cold, hard feeling growing in my chest. Could we be heading . . . ?

Greenwood Terrace lay ahead of us. The scene of one of his crimes last night. He seemed to be fond of revisiting places. And had he gone back there?

Van Friesling had leaned back again, his blond hair fluttering in the draft. His lips weren't moving anymore. But the look on his face was so intense, I felt sure that he was concentrating hard. Focusing on, and trying to strengthen, the next spell that he was going to cast.

His palms lifted, the same way they had done the last time. Dozens of electric sparks danced in between them, like a tiny firework display.

I spotted a narrow silhouette ahead of us, at the next intersection. And tensed for a moment, thinking that it might be Saruak again. But it wasn't. It was just an ordinary man, the first that I had seen so far on this particular morning. The dimness robbed him of all his normal hue. And his back was bent, as though to take the weight of the approaching day. He was climbing onto a push-bike, heading into work presumably. His head came up, at the sound of our approach. And he gawped at us astonishedly as we went hurtling by.

He was lost into the background a few seconds later. Just a regular Joe with a regular life, completely unaware of what was going on around him.

I'd been like that, once upon a time.

When I got the chance, I glanced up again. There was still movement in the sky above us. The adepts' first attempt might have failed, but they were not anywhere near to giving up.

We crossed another junction, and a spire became apparent up ahead of us. The needle shifted again, pointing directly at it.

My teeth clenched, and I almost spat enamel. My God, he'd gone back to St. Nevitt's!

We swung around the corner. Saruak came clearly into view a second time.

As did other things, high up in the air, to either side of him.

Vernon was hanging back, this time. It seemed to be the turn of the others. Two of them swung around to the left of the church, and one more to the right. And then they started to descend.

There was no humming noise accompanying them this time. And no faces I could see. As they grew closer, they changed shape, lengthening and spreading out.

A sound did reach my ears, at last. But it was a steady, heavy flapping. As the shapes resolved, it finally became clear what they were. The adepts had transformed themselves into massive birds.

To Saruak's left were a pair of buzzards, but far larger than normal ones. Their wingspans had to be at least eight feet. And what was the betting, if you got up closer to them, they had nasty emerald eyes? It was impossible to tell from this far away.

To his right there was a truly gigantic eagle. A bald eagle, I guessed, since Levin had always been a patriot. I couldn't tell for sure, because there was no visible detail or color. All the birds looked the same shades as the original clouds had been.

Saruak peered around at them slowly. And if he was taken off guard, then he didn't show it. Because his next act was to stoop down, drop the bulldog from his grasp. It ran around in small circles on the church's rooftop, growling furiously at the approaching shapes.

Then the ragged figure straightened. And spread both his arms out to the sides, for all the world like some enormous scarecrow. These weren't crows, though, and did not slow down. He was in silhouette again, and I still couldn't see his face.

But he yelled out something, a single guttural word. In some Iroquois tongue? There was no way of telling. But the beginning of a spell of his own, I was pretty certain.

I began to slow the Porsche down, about fifty yards away. And, without any warning, Kurt van Friesling stood up in his seat.

His hands shot toward the roof. A massive net of sparks, far larger than before, leapt out at it. They moved faster than they had done last time, wrapping themselves around the man up there.

He didn't have the chance to lash at them this time. Saruak began struggling in their grasp.

There was a solid beating noise. A shadow slid across the roof. The great eagle reared its body back and struck at him with its massive talons.

One of them took purchase. And the Judge began to lift the figure up into the air. Saruak writhed abruptly and broke free, dropping to the roof again. But the bright web still surrounded him; he could not get away.

The eagle was turning for its next attack.

Saruak was on his hands and knees, still trying to get up, when both buzzards hit him at the exact same time.

For the first time since I'd met him, he let out a yell of pain. These two weren't trying to grab hold of him. They were mauling him like enraged Harpies, their wings churning the air with a furious clattering sound.

My gaze went tight. Had they finally got him? When I looked around at van Friesling, his face was all lit up.

The buzzards were screeching, their bills agape. And the eagle had rejoined the attack, adding its great curving talons to the onslaught. Saruak couldn't even get back to his feet. He'd managed to work one of his arms loose, and had a hand clasped to his head, trying to protect it. But the howls that he was letting out were wild, agonized ones.

I think I smiled when I heard that.

But I'd forgotten about the Dralleg. One moment, it was barking at them helplessly. The next, it swelled to its full size, a pale gray mound of flesh and muscle, something of the wolf about it, rearing up and then stooping forward against the backdrop of the brightening sky. Its green eyes flared. It roared.

"Good God!" van Friesling whispered.

I thought I saw its claws come out. And then the monster lurched into the fray, swinging at the birds around it. The eagle flapped up out of reach. But one of the buzzards wasn't so lucky. The Dralleg managed to catch hold of its right wing, and there was a big explosion of shattered plumes before the huge scavenger got free again.

It soared away, but flying oddly, listing to one side. Lord, I hoped that wasn't Dido.

The second of the pair kept coming at the creature, trying to attack its glowing eyeballs. The Dralleg just hissed back and swiped at it defiantly. The buzzard continued circling, but could not get close enough.

The creature's master was still down on all fours, still in the grip of the shimmering net. But the Dralleg stooped toward him, next, and swiped at the strands. They parted, blinking out of existence. Beside me, van Friesling cursed.

If he'd been hurt, there was not any lasting damage. Or

even, apparently, lasting pain. Saruak stood up and laughed.

How could that be? I felt staggered. Maybe agony was just a fleeting thing for him, a sensation felt like a gust of air against the skin, and then forgotten. He was nothing like a human, I reminded myself.

Both the figures vanished as I watched.

I wiped a hand across my face, and peered down at the black stone disk.

The needle, again, was pointing due east. And I squinted in that direction, puzzled. It was the district of Greenwood that was being indicated. There were just poorer suburbs that way, single-level houses for as far as your eye took you. Not a single taller building. Why the hell would he go there?

A shaft of pale yellow light sprang up at the far horizon. The sun was finally rising. And, as a few birds started singing in the trees nearby, my stomach tightened. A terrible suspicion had started to grow in me.

I pulled back onto Greenwood Terrace all the same, and got us on the move once more.

It was a long road, dead straight, traversing the town west to east. The needle kept pointing relentlessly ahead of us as we went down along it. Not a flicker. Not a waver. He was right in front of us.

But how far? We went past sleeping houses and the shadowy windows of stores. A couple of lights had come on by this hour. But there was still nobody around. A scruffy dog yapped at us from behind a chain link fence. It was the only living thing in sight.

The last few intersections went by. And the last few rows of homes. Then there was just an untidy stretch of waste ground and some bushes, a low heap of rusty, scattered motor parts.

And beyond that . . . ?

I stopped the car.

We were on the very edge of town. Its furthest limit.

Regan's Curse took over, if you went any further than this.

And the needle was still pointing directly ahead.

CHAPTER 24

The Porsche's engine made a clicking sound as it began to cool. It was the only noise I was aware of, for a while. I just gazed out toward the edge of the horizon. Kurt van Friesling, beside me, was silent and stunned too. This was something he'd not been expecting.

More yellow rays were lancing up ahead of us, brighter than the first. And finally, the top edge of the sun came boiling up. Its edges seemed to ripple. Everything looked pitch-black against it. I shielded my eyes with one hand, still peering out ahead.

As night fell away, the view out there got clearer. Most of our town is surrounded by forest, coming right up to the borders like an army of stern, wordless giants. But in this particular spot, there were rolling green fields stretching for several miles before the tree line swallowed them again. The woods were an aquamarine blur in the distance. A few wild poppies dotted the landscape in between, but little else.

Except that, a fair way ahead, perhaps the best part of a mile off, the grasses rose and formed a hillock. At the top of it stood the remains of a lightning-blasted elm. It looked fossilized, against the morning sky. You could paste its photograph against the word "unmoving" in your dictionary.

But I could just make out a tiny shape sitting in one of its branches. Guess who? I was surprised I could see him at all, from that far off. Perhaps he wanted it that way.

His voice came rolling across the green sward toward us, much louder than it should have been, considering the gap between us.

"Me and Dralleg sitting in a tree, savoring our victory!"

The kind of thing a child might say. That was the first thought that came to me. This guy was capable of being so violent. Where he'd cast his shadow, there'd been death not far behind. But now, he was chortling about the whole affair, the way a schoolboy might.

There were different sides to his nature, apparently. And none of them very good.

We got out of the car. I did it slightly warily. But Kurt van Friesling looked, in equal measures, infuriated and amazed. He couldn't quite seem to understand how easily he had been bested. His pale eyes glittered, his wan complexion deepening a notch. And he had taken several steps forward before he remembered himself.

None of us, not even the most powerful, were immune to Regan's Curse.

Large shadows were passing over us. There were sounds like the air being funneled inward. And the four who'd taken to the skies came back to earth, around us.

Levin had his judge's robes on. He always wore them when he practiced magic. Dido McGinley was clutching at her right arm, which was bleeding, and her sister went across to help her. They all looked frustrated, and I couldn't blame them. Some of the most skillful sorcerers in town and—even when they'd worked as a team—this new enemy of ours had slipped through their fingers like water.

Another hoarse laugh came from Saruak's direction.

"Are we finished, ladies, gentlemen? Oh, but we were having so much *fun*! What seems to be the problem?"

All their faces swung toward him, and their gazes burned.

And I could see what was happening to them by this stage. We had well and truly fallen into his trap. Because *they* were becoming obsessed with him as well. He was filling up their every thought. A matter of perception, as the Little Girl had said. He had only worked his spell on ordinary folks till now. But, once that he had captured the attention of the adepts . . .

How much stronger would that make him? How much vaster would his power grow?

The sun was more than halfway up. It looked like the open doorway to a furnace. Saruak was a tight black figure at the center of the growing disk. I couldn't look in that direction very long. But I could see that, from his high perch, he was swinging his legs idly. Again, just like a little boy. And all of this? Some kind of idle entertainment, to his mind.

My eyeballs were smarting, and I turned my head away.

"Can't bear to look me in the face, Mr. Devries?"

I swore under my breath, but didn't move a muscle.

"Do I remind you of your numerous failures, perhaps?"

My pulse started thudding in my temples. He had almost made a new profession out of taunting me.

"You couldn't even save your family. How do you expect to save this whole town?"

He thought that he could do just anything he wanted. Thought that he could toy with us and play his spiteful tricks, and we'd just sit there helplessly, allowing him to do it. But the same few words were pounding in my head. *The hell with that.*

"And what about that *friend* of yours?" he was crowing.

He was really laying it on thickly. Showed no inclination to give me a break. Perhaps he was trying to affect my mind, like all the others. His voice seemed to echo in my skull.

"Oh, she looked so *sexy* when she needed your help!"

That finally made me snap. That was *it*!

My fists clenched and I marched toward him with my head tucked slightly down.

"Devries?" I could hear Gaspar Vernon yelling after me. "What do you think you're doing, man?"

The truth was, I was barely thinking at all, anymore. I just wanted to wrap my fingers around Saruak's throat. Squeeze and watch his eyes bug out. Keep on squeezing till his lips turned blue. But, the moment I crossed the town limits, the inevitable happened.

The grasses up ahead of me had been stirring very gently in the morning breeze. But now, they slowed and stilled.

There'd been a few bees and other insects ambling around. I could not see or hear them any longer.

No birds flew overhead. All their song had disappeared. And the color had started bleeding from my surroundings, becoming fainter with every step I took. The field around me was no longer such a vivid green. It was more the kind of shade that you'd see underwater. And the bright red poppies went a far duller hue. The sky absorbed some gray into its blueness until it looked dull and overcast, despite the fact that there were hardly any clouds.

Even the sun no longer blinded me, when I glanced at it. It was reduced to a pale primrose circle. I could stare right into it. Saruak was still in front of it, his outline as dark as ever.

I left the paved road, the grasses crackling underneath my tread. It was the only noise that came to me at all, apart from my own breathing. As if the rest of the world had just faded away.

I must have kept on at it for a good five minutes, trying to reach the figure in the tree. I even tried running at one point. It was useless effort. Got me no closer to Saruak at all. My legs were aching slightly, by the end of it, my lungs heaving up against my ribs.

His silhouette remained at the exact same distance. His dangling legs kicked the air with glee, and I could see the bulldog shift position in his lap, as though to get a better look at me.

"Catch me if you can, Mr. Devries!" he bellowed. "But it seems a rather hard task for you. Why *is* that?"

The simple truth of it bore down on me. He'd had the upper hand on us all along, and had doubtless known it.

None of us could leave the Landing, ever. But *he* could, any time he liked.

In the end, reason gave way completely and I pulled my handgun out. Fired at him, once, then twice.

The shots rang out across the grass. They echoed, and then quickly faded.

And the only sound, once they were gone?

Saruak's mocking laughter, beating at my ears.

CHAPTER 25

I should have gone and checked on Cassie, once that I had
headed back to the Vernon residence and got my car. But I'd
got barely any sleep last night. And hadn't eaten a bite since
yesterday afternoon.

I stopped for a waffle on the way home, at the diner that
I've regularly used since hers closed down. The staff all
knew me, and were friendly enough. They noticed how
drawn I looked and inquired after my health. I just said
something vague in reply. And the food they served was
usually good. But my breakfast, this morning, tasted like a
wad of cardboard, and went down about as well. My senses
were pretty numb, I had to admit. Enjoying anything was
difficult.

A couple of regulars went by the table, and I nodded "hi"
to them.

A TV was murmuring over in the corner, and the patrons
and the waitresses all started watching it. RLKB's Marlon
Fisk was, once again, facing the camera.

"And the question on everybody's lips this morning? Who,
or what, is 'Saruak'?"

Good question, Marlon, I thought. *Except you don't really
want to know the answer—and I wish I didn't either.*

Exhaustion was washing over me in dull, cool waves when

I got back home. I went around shutting all the drapes, which made the place seem even more bereft of life than ever.

It hasn't changed an awful lot since my family vanished. I'd tidied all the kids' stuff away, storing it carefully in boxes. But I hadn't moved a thing of Alicia's—there's still a bottle of nail varnish sitting on the corner of the washbasin, still waiting to be used.

The living room was in its usual state. Several copies of the local newspaper—the *Landing Ledger*—were piled up at one end of the couch. There was a mug of coffee that I should have rinsed out days ago. Not a pigsty, in other words. Just normal, casual messiness, the entropy that gradually surrounds us when we're more concerned with other things.

All I wanted to do was rest. But something kept on tugging at my thoughts, the way it often does.

I went across slowly to a cabinet by the far wall. Hunkered down and opened it.

That awful moment when my family disappeared came back to me. Jason Goad's loft room darkening, then returning to its normal state, completely empty.

Except for one thing.

That little pendant that he'd worn around his neck. It had been lying there, gleaming in the soft light from the windowpane. And when I'd picked it up, it had felt a little warmer to my grasp than it ought to be. There seemed to be a tiny black flaw inside, when you tipped it at certain angles.

What was it? What part had it played in everything that had happened? There were no immediate answers. But I'd kept hold of it, all the same. I gazed at it and, not for the first time, wondered where he'd got the thing.

I'd never touched it since the first day that I'd brought it here. The idea scared me a little, since I wasn't sure what it was capable of. But perhaps it would be the key, one day, to getting my loved ones back. Or was that just wishful thinking, clutching at the narrowest of straws?

It glinted, despite the fact that there was no illumination touching it. It seemed to be made up of three separate parts.

The chain was just an ordinary silver one, like a couple of dozen that Alicia had owned. The gemstone at the bottom was a tiny one, no larger than a pea. It was mostly clear—the flaw apart—but had a bluish tinge to it, the faintest sheen, like the surface of a pond. And it was round, a faceted globe.

Which made its setting even odder, since it was four times the size of the jewel. It was made of silver too, but looked much older than the chain. It was in the shape of a claw, with five digits, bright talons, clutched firmly around the gemstone, as if they were trying to squeeze it till it broke. Etched into the top were little symbols. They were simple, crude ones, but not childish. No, they looked extremely precise. I'd never seen their like before, and had no idea what they signified.

I eased my fingertips toward it, but not the entire way. What was I playing at? I needed rest. I forced myself to close the cabinet again.

Then I went across and threw myself out full-length on the couch. The springs creaked heavily. My eyes slid shut without any further prompting. Darkness filled my head for an unmeasurable while.

Someone . . . called my name.

I recognized the voice immediately. It had been a long time since I'd heard it, except in my dreams.

My eyelids snapped back open. They seemed to be the only part of my whole body that was capable of movement right then.

Pale and almost spectral in the dim, filtered light, Alicia—my wife—was standing there.

Shock rose through me. I untensed a little and managed to sit up. And gawked at her. All she did was smile back gently. The living room hadn't changed a bit, except that she was standing in it, calmly, one hand on her hip.

She looked real. I could even smell her perfume. It was the one she always wore.

Of course, my first thought was, this just has to be a

dream. But there's a trick for that. I knew it. A doctor that I had helped out explained it to me once.

I reached across quickly, switched the lamp by the couch on. The bulb immediately brightened. And that doesn't happen, when you're dreaming. Cause and effect don't work in the same way, and you can't turn on any lights.

My hand dropped numbly from the switch. I could barely take in what had just happened. If I wasn't dreaming . . . was this *real*?

Alicia didn't move at all. She just gazed at me from the edge of the yellow pool of illumination, waiting to see what I'd do next.

She was wearing what she'd had on that last day, before I'd gone to work. Faded blue jeans and a white blouse tied above the midriff. Bare feet. And her blond curls were tied back, except for one lock that had escaped and flopped across her brow. Her blue eyes sparkled at me, and her smile was very wide and white. She had never had to use cosmetics much— her high cheekbones had a natural flush to them, her lips were pink as rose petals.

"Aren't you pleased to see me, Ross?" she asked, after another while.

Her voice was *exactly* as I remembered it. And hearing it made me ache. I wanted to get up and hold her in my arms.

I remained where I was, though. Because I was certain there was something wrong. How could she have simply popped back into existence?

The muscles in my jaw ached as I tried to form the words.

"Who are you?"

Alicia looked disappointed, and then raised a narrow eyebrow.

"That's a stupid question, darling. How could you ask that?"

But her voice was far too calm, I realized. Wouldn't she be getting all emotional as well?

"How did you get here?" I asked her.

"I've been around the entire time. I didn't die, if that's

what you think. That goes for the children too. We were simply trapped in some weird limbo."

I was trying to stay rational, but that was pretty hard. The children? Where were they, if she was here? And part of me was fiercely drawn to her. I just couldn't help it. I missed her company so very badly, her beauty and gentleness, the touch of her skin.

But I still held myself back. *Where are the children? Focus, focus!* It was hard to even talk. The words were sticking in my throat.

"How come you're here now, after all this time?"

"I've come to warn you."

If I wasn't dreaming, then I had to have gone insane, I decided. I answered her anyway.

"Warn me of what?"

Her gaze was sparkling, but a little coldly, and her mouth went firm for a brief second.

"Don't try to fight Saruak anymore, Ross. You can't win. Keep on at it, and you'll simply die."

I stared at her incredulously. How did she know anything about it? Had she come back just to tell me this?

But she looked utterly convinced. She seemed quite determined to get her message across.

"If you give in, persuade the others, he'll go easy on you."

And I wasn't buying that at all. Not from what I knew of him.

"He'll let you live. And let me stay. And bring the kids back too."

My confusion was sliding away the more of this nonsense she spoke. I'd started to work out what was going on by this time. And could see that I was being had.

I kept a poker face, studying her closely all over again.

"And how do you know this?"

"He told me."

"You're on speaking terms?"

She smiled again. "He's not so awful, when you really get to know him. He's just . . . misunderstood."

And she *had* to be joking. But the truth was unfolding in my head. Whoever was telling me all this, it just wasn't Alicia.

The cruelty of it. To use *her* against me. I peered a little closer at her heart-shaped face.

I stood up carefully. She made no move to back away. Her expression grew happier.

"Yes, that's it, Ross. Hold me, like you used to."

I took a slow step. She looked even more genuine, right close up.

"Touch me." Her voice had become so soft that it was practically hypnotic. "I've been waiting for that, such an awfully long time."

When I swallowed, it hurt. Everything did, talking, moving, breathing. God, just looking at her hurt. Part of me still wanted this to be real, not a trick.

I lifted my right hand toward her face. She grinned.

"Go on, darling."

I had noticed something while I'd still been on the couch. The lock of blond hair that had flopped across her brow? It was hiding most of her left eye. Taking great care not to touch her skin, I shifted it to one side with my fingertips.

Her left pupil was far larger than the right.

Her smile became a twisted one. And when she opened her mouth again, Saruak's voice came out from between sharply pointed teeth.

"My, you are perceptive! Well spotted, Mr. Devries."

I stepped back, out of reach of him.

"What the hell do you want now?" I blurted.

The shadows were thickening around him again. And I could feel the malevolence of his presence, the massive force and energy of it. I reminded myself, uncomfortably, that we were alone here. Fear was working its way through my pores, but I managed to hold my ground.

"Just trying a little . . . how to put it? . . . gentle persuasion. I thought that I might even get you on my side."

Which astonished me. Did he imagine he could ever do that?

"Why don't you just finish me off, if you're so damned powerful?"

There was the thrill of the victor in his gaze. I could smell his breath. It was like the dust in the churches, leafy, moldy.

"And what fun would that be?" he asked.

Then he pulled a casual face.

"Well, see you later!"

And he was gone, in the blinking of an eye.

It had all happened so fast, it struck me. Thinking she was back, then being confronted with the harsh reality. My emotions had been yanked back and forth like a child's swing in a playground. And now, they were backing up on me.

My head began spinning. I couldn't think straight any longer.

So I did what seemed to be the next best thing. I went into the kitchen, and threw up.

Washing my face and drying it with a cloth, I came fully back to wakefulness. I still felt tired. I wasn't even sure how much sleep I'd managed to get.

My hands were shaking gently, and my skin felt tight, vibrating too. Even though it had been an illusion, what I'd seen still pained me very badly.

I couldn't get it out of my mind. That first moment when my eyes had opened. I had imagined that and ached for it for two whole years. The savagery behind the deception . . . it simply took my breath away.

But what else did I expect from a creature like him? Anger began setting in again.

I didn't let it take me over. Something else had just occurred to me. Why did Saruak keep on coming at me in particular? Time after time, he had singled me out. It wasn't like I was an important figure in the town. Hobart or Mayor Aldernay would have been far better choices. But he seemed to be obsessed with me. He'd been around at every turn.

My thoughts swam some more, and then returned to the present. How was Cassie doing?

I could hear some chickens clucking as I parked outside her place. One of her neighbors had a coop out back. A kid was yelling, in one of the nearby houses. And a radio could be heard, from an open bedroom window.

A small mongrel ran up and started barking at me, but when I just ignored it, it got bored and sat down in the dirt, watching me rather mournfully.

A light was on in her kitchen, so obviously she was up. And hopefully, much better after a night's rest. God, would she be pissed when she found out what had been happening while she had been asleep. Even though we'd not succeeded, she'd have wanted to get involved.

I let myself in with my key, went down the hall. Stopped dead in the doorway of her living room.

Cassie was up, and fully dressed. A black top and gray jeans this time. She had her gun belt on. And was standing in the middle of the room stock-still, with her head bowed. She was clutching another of her shotguns in both hands, a Winchester. What was she doing, cleaning it?

That was when I noticed a shock of curly red hair, on the floor beyond the couch. What on earth was Bella doing down there?

I got my answer when Cass's face lifted—totally deadpan, no expression at all in her dark, wide eyes.

And then she raised the gun at me, and squeezed the trigger.

CHAPTER 26

I didn't even think about it. There are times when conscious thought just isn't fast enough.

I threw myself off to the side and backward. The charge of heavy shot—she wasn't using the saboted slugs this time—passed so close to my face that I could feel the rush of heat off it. But none of it, so far as I could tell, even managed to graze me.

I hit the carpet of the hallway so hard that it knocked all of the breath out of me. Then another shot came slamming out, blasting the photographs on the wall above me, sending glass and chunks of wood frame spilling down. These were photos of her own children she was hitting. And the Cass I knew would turn her weapon on herself before she did anything like that.

I took a quick glance at her, as I rolled out of her line of fire. Her face looked odd and strained, as if caught between two separate emotions, fury and bewilderment. It was like she didn't want to do this, but she couldn't help herself. What sense did that make?

She was out of sight again, as soon as I pushed myself away. But her shadow began moving in my direction. She began to speak, her tone far colder and more gravelly than it usually was.

"I've been thinking about what you said, Mr. Devries. And you're right. Why *not* just finish you? You're not the only game in this town—not by a long chalk."

But it wasn't Saruak's voice this time. Hardened it might be, but it was definitely Cassie's. This wasn't the Manitou taking on her shape. I remembered what else I'd read about them.

An entity like Saruak could adopt any form he wanted. I'd already seen that demonstrated, in the worst imaginable of ways. But he also had enormous power over people's minds.

There'd been nothing different, that I had seen, about her eyes. It really had been her that I'd been looking at when I'd walked in. And so . . . had he taken control of her? Had she been possessed by him?

And the conflicted expression that I'd caught a glimpse of. Did it mean that Cassie was still in there, trying to fight back?

She was getting—very quickly—closer. I was on my hands and knees. And trying to scrabble for the front door didn't seem to be a clever move. It was too far away. Where else?

I pushed myself up to my feet, and ran.

To my left, coming up fast, was another door. And I believed it opened onto one of her kids' bedrooms. I'd never been in there before. I heard the clatter of the shotgun pump behind me. Kicked it open and lurched through it, just as another shot went past my neck.

She might be trying to fight against this, but was apparently not succeeding. She'd nearly taken my head off that time. *Damn.*

I slammed the door and bolted it, for all the good that that would do. I backed away swiftly, my breath fouling up in my throat. One hand had gone to the gun in my pocket. But could I even contemplate that? This wasn't an illusion. This was actually Cass.

I stared around quickly. This had to be the eldest boy's room. Kevin, six years old. It looked to me like he had wanted to be a pilot. There were plastic model airplanes and posters of jet fighters everywhere you looked. One for the movie *Top Gun* too. Perhaps he had dreamed of joining the Marine Air Corps. At that age, you're far too young to understand how straightforward realities limit you.

Just past his narrow bed was a small window. It looked out onto the back alleyway. I went across and tried to open it, but it wouldn't budge. The wood had swollen in the frame.

To my left, there was just another wall. I thought quickly, and remembered that, beyond it, was the rear end of the diner. If I could only get through there.

I heard her stop outside the door. She tried the knob briefly, then grunted.

"That won't stop me, Ross. Good Lord, you're being such an infant."

The voice might be hers. But the derisive tone was entirely his. I didn't even want to kill him anymore. Just jamming a cork in his mouth would be sufficient.

The air filled with splinters as the lock blew out.

I'd been in this house often enough to know the walls weren't exactly industrial strength. You could hear a bluebottle in the next room, if it flapped its wings hard enough. So I took a step back, covering my face with my arms. Then flung myself at it.

It turned out to be just a single sheet of board with a thin veneer of plaster on it, and I went straight through. I'm not going to say it didn't hurt. But, compared with remaining where I was . . . ?

I slammed into the back end of the diner's counter. The rest of the air was knocked out of my lungs, and my ribs felt like they would be aching till Thanksgiving. But I'd made it. For the moment, at least.

Chairs and tables lay around me in half-shadow. They were all covered with dust. Fluorescent strips were suspended above me, lightless, speckled with dead flies. Unlike out back, all the crockery was stacked in piles, although not neat ones. The faint smell of rancid grease was coming from the fryer to my right.

This had once been a friendly, welcoming place. I could

still remember Cassie with her hair down almost to her waist, gossiping with her female customers and joking with the male ones. I'd spent some happy times in here, back when happiness had not come at a premium.

The shotgun pumped again. I vaulted across the counter, barely making it in time. The next shot came right on my heels. Most of the laminated wood behind me flew into small pieces. And I was running out of places to go. I slid under one of the tables.

For God's *sake*! My hand went to my gun again. I didn't want to hurt her—this was not her fault. But what else could I do?

"Cassie, *fight* him!" I yelled out.

The tabletop above me broke apart with a resounding blast. I scrambled for the next one, getting closer to the front. But the door was padlocked, I already knew. So where exactly was I going?

I caught a glimpse of her, as she came striding along the aisle. And by now, there was no conflict left in her expression. It was blank and stiff. I got the weirdest feeling that this wasn't even Cassie I was looking at, merely an empty shell. Was there any part of her that I could even reach?

I didn't get the chance to find out. She spotted me, and aimed. I was forced to flatten out again. The next shot did hit something, though. There was a brittle crash behind me, telling me the charge had hit the window. A whole section of plate glass came thundering down.

I was back on my feet the instant that happened, hurrying across the broken shards, then jumping out onto the street beyond them. A couple of locals had stopped on the far sidewalk, wondering what the commotion was about. They made themselves scarce quickly enough. Because Cass was stepping out across the glass as well.

And where was there left to retreat to? There was no cover here except for a few lampposts. Cassie kept advancing, and I slowly backed away from her, stepping off the curb, my arms held out in front of me, till I finally came to a halt on the broken white line down the middle of the pavement.

"Cass!" I bellowed. "You don't have to *do* this!"

Her only response was an ugly grin that contorted her deadpan features.

"I can only imagine how it must feel," she remarked in that tight-sounding voice. "Dying at the hands of somebody you're close to and you care about."

She was just being used as a mouthpiece, I knew. Was Saruak even here at all? Or controlling her from a distance? He could still be in that tree branch, out beyond the edge of town, I understood.

Cassie's hands pulled at the Winchester again. Except that this time . . .

No slug pumped into the chamber. It was empty.

When her face contorted this time, it was with astonishment. What had Saruak imagined?

He'd got lost in the moment, I could see. Become so intent on finishing me off that he'd forgotten the mechanics of it. He hadn't remembered to reload.

If Cassie had been herself, she wouldn't even have paused. She'd have let go of the Winchester, and gone immediately for the side arms on her belt. But with the spirit in control, she seemed to be trying to figure out what she ought to do next.

It was the only chance I'd had so far. I took it, and began running toward her.

When she saw what I was doing, her whole frame jerked with alarm. And then, finally, her right hand started dropping. This was going to be a very close contest. It was still her body, her reflexes, and I *knew* how fast a draw she was.

Her hand closed around the butt of the Glock. She tugged the pistol into view, her arm straightening as it lifted.

It was almost in my face, only a foot away. I shoved my left palm into her wrist, deflecting the shot.

And then I slammed her on the jaw with my right, felling her like a log.

By the time she came around, I had divested her of all the weapons that I knew of. Not just the shotgun and the pistols.

There was the stiletto taped between her shoulder blades, the straight razor in her back pocket, and the short serrated knife in her right boot.

They were all in a neat pile behind me, where she couldn't get to them.

Oh, and I had made a pillow for her with my coat, and was crouching over her attentively. This was the second time that she'd been hurt in twenty-four hours, and it filled me with unease, not to mention guilt. A few of her neighbors had come over rather nervously, offering to help, but I'd politely sent them all away.

None of this had really been her doing. She'd probably feel terrible about it when she came around. Relief washed through me when her eyelids fluttered, and her gaze came slowly open. She squinted, trying to figure out where she was.

All the same, I took my gun out, for precaution's sake. Her eyes focused on that. She leant up on one elbow, blinking fiercely.

"What . . . ?" Her voice was back to normal, although groggy-sounding and extremely surprised. "What am I doing here?"

"You okay?" I asked her.

"I think so."

She rubbed at her chin and winced, then peered at my weapon for a second time.

"You're going to shoot me, just for lying in the street?"

So she was definitely back in control, Saruak long gone. I put the gun away, then carefully explained to her everything that she had done. She listened closely, trying not to look as troubled as she had to feel.

"It was weird," she told me, sitting the rest of the way up. "At first, I could see what was happening. But like, from a tremendous distance. There was nothing I could do about it."

Her jaw quivered.

"Then it all went black. Completely. Like I wasn't there at all anymore."

There was something else worrying me, and she could see it on my face. Cass sucked in a tense breath.

"If he can do that to me? He can probably do it to anyone, in the whole town."

And what a problem that might be, if it proved to be true.

She touched her chin again. There was a bruise appearing there by this time.

"I don't believe it. Ow! You actually *hit* me?"

"I'm afraid so. Sorry about that."

She thought about it, and then favored me with a tight smirk.

"I'm sorry about trying to shoot you too, seeing as we're handing out apologies."

Then she twisted around, and gazed at the damage that had been done to her place.

"Hey, who did that?"

"You," I told her, glad I didn't have to make any more confessions.

She took in the wrecked tabletops and the mounds of shattered glass. Then stared beyond them

"And I made that hole in my wall?"

"Er, no. That was me."

Cass let out a long, slow breath. "Great. Just what I've always needed. Extra ventilation."

And that was when Bella stumbled out through it, clutching at the back of her head.

"Holy Christ!"

CHAPTER 27

We got her sat down, got an ice pack for her, tried to help her understand what had been happening. Then we finally took her home. She only lived a block away.

"Just what friends are for," she kept on mumbling.

Cassie's eyes were still bright with dampness as we walked back to her place.

Her arsenal was still there, in a small pile in the middle of the street. No one had dared touch it. She stooped down and picked it up, replacing it in the appropriate pockets, holsters, hidden nooks. Then we headed back in.

"I could ask Frank Benson to fix this up?" I suggested, glancing around at the wreckage.

But she only shrugged again, and thrust her lip out. "Nah. I'll do it myself."

She was so capable at everything she turned her hand to that I didn't doubt she would.

As usual, she was trying to take adversity in her stride, smiling wryly and making little jokes while she inspected the damage. But her expression dropped—I'd thought it would—when she saw the hole in Kevin's bedroom door. And when she stepped into the hallway, and the shattered photos came in sight . . . ?

I'd been trying to prepare myself for this. But all I could do, in the end, was stand there.

All of her composure dissolved in an instant. She was lunging forward, going down on her hands and knees, and trying to scoop up the fragments, careless of the broken glass. And she was murmuring under her breath.

"My *babies*! Oh *no*!"

My gut filled up with emptiness. It felt like she had gone a hundred miles away. Her face suddenly looked a decade older than it had before. Her eyes were glossy, covering the windows to her soul. She was rocking slightly back and forth.

I finally crouched next to her, and put an arm around her. I could feel her trembling.

"It's not your fault," I kept on whispering. "You weren't in control."

She found something and picked it up, holding it in her open palm. A torn fragment of Little Cassie's face. She stroked it gently with her index finger, like she was trying to make it better.

Whispered, "I'm sorry, sweetheart."

Then she put it in her pocket, wiped away a tear.

"I'm being stupid, right? They're only pictures."

Which was to avoid the point. Her children hadn't just been the focus of her life. They'd been, for parts of it, her only genuine happiness. And without that, what was she? I felt sure that there were times she didn't even know.

It took her a while to pull herself together, but she finally managed it. Then she started to clean up, refusing to let me help. She gathered all the bits of photo up into a dustpan. Separated them as best she could from the pieces of frame and glass. Then emptied out a drawer in her bedroom cabinet and tipped them—very reverently—into it. Murmured to them for a couple of minutes, recounting things—I supposed—she needed to say. And at last, she slid the drawer shut.

A small, quiet funeral ceremony then, for all those images of what her life had been. I just watched her from the doorway.

She had calmed down completely, by the time that she was done. However hard she gets hit, Cassie always seems to bounce right back.

She got some sodas from her fridge. And we were now sitting out back of her place, the town coming alive around us. A garbage truck was making its way down the far end of her street, we could hear the trash cans clattering. Cleveland had shown up again and was huddled near her feet.

"If he wanted to kill you, why not simply take *your* mind over?" she asked me. "Make you stick your gun into your own mouth, and just blow yourself away? Why this fandango?"

Which wasn't the most delicate way of putting it, but I ignored that. It was a good question. Either Saruak was simply messing with us for his own amusement, reveling in the spectacle of us at each other's throats. Or there was something else, something deeper, going on here.

The same thing had been bothering me for quite a while.

"More to the point, why does he keep coming at me specifically?"

Cassie peered at me, her dark eyes barely blinking.

"There's something special about you, when it comes to all this hocus-pocus. Surely you must realize that?"

I wasn't quite sure what she meant. She had never told me anything like this before.

I frowned. "And what might that be?"

Her mouth twisted awkwardly. As though she felt embarrassed, saying it out loud.

"A . . . purity," she told me. "That's the best word I can think of. You've never used magic yourself, or even tried, not once. Do you know how unusual, how rare, that is for anyone over fifteen, here in the Landing? Even I . . ."

She trailed off, her eyes going slightly distant. She'd never mentioned that before. This was turning out to be a morning of big revelations.

"Really?" I inquired.

"Of course. In my teens, I mean. All that power at your hands? All those boys, and fun to be had? What's a girl to do?"

Her nose screwed up. She looked away a moment.

"But you," she went on, "you're like a lifelong teetotaler in a room full of alcoholics. And that gives you a special . . . what? A power of your own."

She leaned a little closer to me.

"Do you understand how much you've changed since— you know—Jason Goad?"

My shoulders tensed at the mention of that name. I wondered what she was getting at.

"That thing with the cigarettes, for instance. You keep lighting them and then putting them out. Back in the days when the diner was open, you were a regular smoker. Never did it at home—I recall you telling me that. Not in front of the kids. But here?"

That couldn't be right, could it? My mind seemed to have gone rather blank.

An awful chill had started creeping over me. If what Cass was telling me was true . . .

Why should there be holes in my memory? There seemed to be no reason for it. Had something happened to *me*, the day that Goad had made my family vanish? I stared at the ground between my shoes, trying to understand it.

"Don't you remember?" Cass was asking me.

I just . . . wasn't sure.

The blood seemed to have drained from my whole frame. I told myself that couldn't be the case, and finally looked up at her.

"Is there anything else?" I asked her.

Her expression became unreadable.

"You always were a good cop. But these days? There's this tight focus, this clarity, to everything you do. You notice things that other people don't. You're attuned to everything that's going on around you. It's almost like . . . you're on a mission. Almost like you have a purpose."

I tried to take that in. It was no easier than it had been the first time.

Then, for want of anything better to say, I grumbled, "Yeah, I'm Sir Galahad, looking for the Holy Grail."

Which came out rather more tersely than I'd intended. The whole thing simply stumped me, the more I turned it over. None of it made any sense. I was just an ordinary man.

What on earth had made her come out with all that guff, when she's normally so sensible?

Cass could see I wasn't buying it. She squinted peevishly, and then said, "Okay, forget it."

Which I was glad to.

I took her to retrieve her Harley. There was even less traffic than usual. Maybe some folks had decided to stay home today, in view of what had been going on. And those who had ventured out onto the street? It made my heart sink, seeing just how nervous and jumpy they were.

There was yellow tape fluttering at the doorway of St. Cleary's. When we peered inside, Cass's guns were no longer there. So I got on the phone to Saul Hobart.

"How is she?" he asked.

"Back to normal."

"Well, I'm not sure that's a blessing." But I was pretty sure I heard him grin. "You're calling about those cannons of hers, I take it. They're here in my office. She can come and sign for them any time she likes."

I relayed the news to her. Then, as she was climbing on her bike, I went back to my Cadillac.

"Where are you going now?" she asked me.

I tipped my face toward her briefly. "What you don't know won't harm you, right?"

"Willets?"

"I'd suppose."

"Watch your step, then. Promise me?"

There was no need, so far as I was aware. But most of the town was frightened of the man. And she was no exception.

"Promise!" she yelled as I climbed into the driver's seat.

I nodded, then drove off.

But the way that she had shouted at me seemed to follow me most of the way to the commercial district.

CHAPTER 28

It covers the northeast edge of town, and is hidden just
beyond a narrow stretch of parkland with a double row of fir
trees, a couple of broad avenues leading in and out. A lot of
the townspeople have jobs up there. But nobody lives there,
with one exception.

Big warehouses and four-story office blocks were going
past me before too much longer. Looming behind them was
a huge Victorian smokestack that's not seen use in years.
The grid of streets was quiet, almost no one out of doors. It's
always struck me as an unwelcoming place, with little in the
way of human touches.

There were signs for all the companies, pretty much what
you would expect for an area like this. Printers, office suppliers,
packagers, business goods. We make a lot of furniture in this
town—trucks show up from the outside world and haul most
of it away.

At one intersection, I looked right and caught a quick
glimpse of the green walls of the lumber mill. It has been
there since the early thirties, and is still a working concern.
Just because folks can't leave this town, it doesn't stop them
walking off into the forest with a chainsaw, dragging back
a log. A flatbed truck piled high with them was reversing
toward it at this very moment, a man with a hardhat and
thick leather gloves signaling to the driver.

There were higher-tech ventures here as well, mostly in the smaller and more modern buildings. Ironically, one of them produced a top-selling video game, called *Witch's Curse*. You were trapped at the center of a medium-sized town, and had to find your way out past the warlocks and hobgoblins.

Artifice imitating life, in fact. Except that nobody outside this place had any way of knowing that.

I reached the final street, out on the edge. It was just trees, beyond that. The shadows in the forest seemed to peer at me, as I got out.

The pavement was all broken up, and full of weeds. And there was just one building here. Its dark red brick had become faded down the decades, and was crumbling at the corners. Where the sun could not reach, there was moss. No lights were on. Its windows were smeared and murky, those that were not broken. Apparently abandoned. But everybody knew the place still had one lone inhabitant.

Dr. Lehman Willets, quite uniquely for this town of ours, was not born here. He came from Charleston, South Carolina, originally. Had taught comparative religion at Boston U. But his main interest was in a field far more peculiar than that. He wrote books about, and investigated, paranormal phenomena.

What had brought him here? The same research as Goad had undertaken. That and a keen sixth sense when it came to the supernatural.

"I could hear the voices, telling me to turn back, yes," he'd told me once. "I could feel this freezing chill inside my bones. But I'd encountered that before, in haunted houses and the like. And it wasn't easy, but I kept on going."

When he'd arrived, people had kept gawking at him. And his first thought had been, *What, you've never seen a black man?*

It had gradually dawned on him what was going on, just the same way it dawned on the townsfolk. Some were suspicious, some relieved. An elderly couple from Vernon Valley had eventually taken him into their home.

And Lehman Willets, using all the town's resources, had started to learn about real magic.

I walked quickly to a door in the side of the building. It was metal, and looked more like it belonged on a ship. A lizard scuttled away from my advancing feet and disappeared through a gap in the brickwork. There was a wasps' nest in an air vent near the top—I could see the humming specks going back and forth.

"Sanderson's Supplies," read a huge sign painted overhead. Supplies of what? No one even remembered what this building had been used for.

I tugged down on the handle of the door and pulled it open. It let out a rusted creak.

And then, the music came skirling up toward me. A distant-sounding, rather frantic saxophone. Willets was playing his jazz again. But I'd already been expecting that.

Back when he'd begun his study of the Salem arts, he'd been puzzled at first, but then learned quickly. Had turned out, after about a month, to be better at it than he ever could have dreamed. Perhaps he was just a natural adept. Whatever, his power grew exponentially after that. He became capable of massive feats of witchcraft in mere weeks, and sometimes even days.

He could fly before long, without becoming a cloud or a bird the way the Sycamore Hill set had to. He could transmogrify objects, or summon them up. Change the weather. Make himself invisible. He didn't even *need* a crystal or a talisman.

Then he started healing people, pulling tumors out of them, and getting them up out of their wheelchairs. It was the highest art of all.

But that was where it all went wrong.

This doorway didn't lead into the main part of the building. There was just a flight of dingy metal stairs below me, leading to the basement. It was where the man had lived for years now. Ever since . . .

"Come to me, people! Let me share this glory with you!"

The magic had affected him, driving him completely over the brink. You're still wondering why I don't like the stuff? It was normally the feeble-spirited who went this route. But his power had become so vast that it had overwhelmed him. He'd harbored messianic aspirations long before Woodard Raine.

My tread reverberated on the first step. The frame seemed loose and trembled a little, so I grabbed onto a rail. There were cobwebs all around me, and some dark mold on the walls. Only the dimmest light was visible, below.

"We can all be holy! We can all shine with a bright, pure glow! Gather, brothers, sisters! Let me show you how!"

He'd been floating just above the struts of the Iron Bridge, the river gurgling beneath him. The air around him practically danced with the power surging from his body. And most people gave him a wide berth. They'd learnt, a long time back, to be wary of a force as strong as this.

But twelve, mostly young folks, credulous, approached.

He smiled at them as though they had become his children.

"You are my special ones, beloved," he'd told them. *"The mysteries of the Universe will be revealed to you."*

He had spread his arms, and then his fingers. Bolts of light had shone out from them, far more dazzling even than the webs I'd seen van Friesling throw. They had leapt from individual to individual.

Some of the charred corpses, in the end, were so heavily fused to the sidewalk, they'd had to pull up entire paving stones and bury those.

The madness had died from his eyes, to be replaced by an unbearable remorse. And he'd fled society, become a hermit. And had lived here ever since.

So far as I knew, I was the only person who ever visited him. Not that I felt easy about that. My heartbeat quickened slightly as I made my way down. There was no blue glow, no electricity, like stepping in to see the Little Girl. But I could feel his power all around me, moving the air and making it stir in unnatural ways. The shadows were far blacker than they should have been. The dimness almost seemed to inhale and exhale.

He could hear me coming, obviously. But he'd have known that I was on my way if I had trod as quietly as a mouse, although he didn't respond in the slightest to my presence.

He was sitting on his folding camp bed, over by the far wall. And his head was down. His hair was gray and curly. He was wiry, medium height. Was wearing his usual tweed jacket and a pair of blue serge pants.

The place couldn't have been more sparsely furnished. A single naked bulb hung from the ceiling, about forty watts. A small, neat fire of twigs was burning over in the corner, with a black iron kettle suspended above it—where did the smoke go? He only had the clothes he wore, although those remained impeccably clean, just the same way that he never sported stubble and his hair was always the same length.

Here was a man frozen in time and recollection.

Hundreds of books kept him company. He just conjured them up whenever he needed one. Huge leather-bound tomes, for the most part. Since he had no shelves to put them on, they lay in neat piles all over the floor. Some of the lettering on the spines was gold leaf. And some of it was in an alphabet I didn't even recognize as human.

At the center of the room, there was a matt black plinth with a turntable on it. His pride and joy. No amplifier. No speakers. But, all the same, the saxophone chords kept churning out.

If he had one passion left in his whole wounded, dried-out heart, it was his music.

"Morning, Devries," he mumbled, still not looking up.

"Quite a morning," I replied.

He must have understood what I was talking about, but he ignored me.

"You know who this is?" he asked me, nodding at the turntable.

I glanced at the spinning vinyl disc, but couldn't read the label. Alicia had been fond of jazz, however, so I knew a bit about it.

"John Coltrane?" I ventured.

And he nodded again, slowly.

"Know the tune?"

There were other things, far more important, that I needed to talk to him about. But with Willets, you took it slowly. Let him set the tone, the pace.

"It's from *The Sound of Music*, isn't it?"

"'My Favorite Things.' 'Whiskers on kittens' and lah-dee-da. As white-bread as they come. I think that 'Trane chose it deliberately, because of that."

He hunched down a moment, listening to the track intently.

"Hear what he's doing? Plays it normally at first, and then starts taking it apart. Like an expert mechanic with an engine block, until it's all lying across the floor in little pieces, nuts and cogs and bolts. And then what does he do? He puts it all back together again. Deconstruction. Reconstruction. The perfect demonstration of bebop. *That's* magic."

From another person's mouth, it might have all sounded enthusiastic. But Willets's tone remained a somber one. Deeply brooding. Deeply pensive. As though he felt sure that he was missing something here. Was he wishing he could reconstruct those dozen souls?

I looked around, then up. We might be the only humans here, but we were not alone.

The ceiling was so dense with cobwebs, it was like a great translucent canopy that shimmered in the bulb's weak glow. Its inhabitants were moving around, and they were large ones.

Something else came writhing from a low vent in the wall. It was the largest millipede I'd ever seen, rustling along the floor, its black carapace gleaming. There were other good-sized bugs down there as well, massive beetles. And from the darkest corner gleamed two shining sets of eyes, a pair of rats. Motionless. Just watching him.

Not that the place was dirty. But it had been this way for a good while. It was the energy that I had felt, coming down the stairs. It simply drew most living creatures to him. They never came close. They just stared at him from a safe distance. But they barely ever turned their gazes away. Maybe they were wondering what he was going to do.

Nothing at all, I knew, if he could help it. Ever since that day on the bridge, he'd kept his use of magic to the barest minimum.

His head came up at last. His narrow face had deep lines on it. Not wrinkles—he was only in his forties. More like a perpetual frown. His eyebrows were salt-and-pepper, and his lips looked like he chewed at them a lot. His gaze was a medium chestnut brown.

Except for his pupils, which were definitely not commonplace. The size of pinheads, they glowed a searingly bright red, as if coals had been lit inside that pointy skull of his. They always made me stiffen up a little. It was something you could not get used to.

"But you haven't come here to discuss bebop, have you?" he whispered through the dimness at me.

Which was stating the obvious. I understood how bad, how guilty the man felt. But nothing could be done about it. Perhaps he ought to try starting to let it go a little, a process that began with forgiving yourself.

I wasn't even sure, though, he was capable of that.

He twitched the fingers of his right hand. The plinth and the turntable blinked out of existence, the last chords dancing around the cellar and then fading off. A straight-backed chair appeared on the same spot. For my benefit, you see. I nodded my thanks to him, and then settled onto it.

"You're aware of what's been happening?"

"Of *course* I am!" he snapped impatiently. "What do you suppose I am? Blind? Stupid?"

Just sitting here, I knew, he'd sensed it all.

He was never in the best of moods. Today was no exception. And he doesn't get much chance to hone his social skills, you understand.

"Then you have to know that I'm here for your help."

His gaze grew slightly hotter, and he scowled at me. "Can't give it."

I hadn't been expecting *that* fast a refusal. He peered at me from his folding bed like I was wasting his valuable time.

"You must know what's at stake here?" I came back at him.

"You don't *understand*." His voice was practically a hiss. "I'm not indifferent, or chickening out. If there were any slightest way that I could help this town—"

It might ease him toward redemption, after all. And that's what I'd been banking on.

"We're really up against the ropes," I told him.

"Yes, I get that! Do you honestly believe anything else? Look at me, Devries, what I've become!"

A tight ball of self-loathing, if the truth be told.

"But you cannot see what's really going down," he went on. "You don't get the whole picture."

Okay. I eased a little further back into my chair. "Enlighten me."

His hands wrapped themselves around each other. And his eyes, thankfully, closed. His brow creased deeper as he tried to sort his thoughts into some kind of manageable order.

"Down here all these years, I've had the chance to think about most things involving magic. Really study them, and examine them hard. Peel away the layers, to reveal an inner truth."

He made an odd rumbling noise.

"You see all this in terms of a shootout—who has the better aim, the faster draw? And there's some validity to that. But the deeper reality is, there's a hierarchy to it all."

Which was something I had never heard before. I waited for him to go on.

"It's like a pyramid. At the bottom, there're the dabblers, folks who use a little magic to improve their lives. Next? The adepts. Vernon, Levin, Raine. Myself. I *am* merely an adept, Devries, whatever people might think. And we occupy, I'd say, some kind of middle level."

I already didn't like where this was going, but I held myself in check.

"And Saruak?" I asked him.

"Saruak, at full-strength—and he's close to that by now—comes somewhere near the apex. His race is phenomenally ancient. They've visited plagues on entire populations, crushed whole dynasties beneath their heel. We'll never know how things might have been different, if it wasn't for the Manitou."

He'd tensed himself, as though the ground beneath him had become unsteady.

"The most powerful of us are only human, at core. But *they* occupy a level no adept can reach. A good way to describe them? You could call his kind . . . Destroyers."

I could almost hear the capital, when he said that. And some of his dark mood was affecting me by this time, settling down around me like a shroud.

"But you said near the top," I pointed out. "What trumps a Destroyer?"

"Only one thing." And his eyelids finally came back open. "A Changer of Worlds."

Then he sat there like a bright-eyed shadow, taking in the sight of my blank face.

"A Changer doesn't need to use magic as such, Devries. The Buddha was one. Jesus was. Christopher Columbus. Edward Jenner. Einstein. But in this case, I'd imagine, we require one with special powers, rather more than changing water into wine. Can you think of anyone who answers that description?"

He waited for my answer, knowing there was none, then let out an exasperated sigh.

"Anyone, in this whole town?"

"Maybe if you really tried . . . ?"

But his features screwed up, almost with contempt.

"I've already *told* you! I'm only middle management in the pecking order of the dark arcane. I just drive a fancier car than most."

"You're seriously telling me there's no one who can face him down?"

"At the beginning, maybe. But it's far too late, by this stage. He has pushed his way into our every conscious thought. And he'll keep on using that, until he makes his final move."

I wasn't giving up, however.

"How about the Little Girl?"

Willets pulled a strange expression, mildly amused by my persistence.

"Her? I'm not quite sure what she is. I'm not even certain that she's sure."

And what did that mean?

"But I don't think that she's our savior, no. In fact, I'd lay good money on it."

"There's no hope for us at all, then? I can't bring myself to believe that."

"Which is your strength, and I envy you for it. But it won't help you this time. I'd love to give you a happier answer, one that you'd prefer to hear, but —"

He spread his slim hands, showing me how empty they were.

"— honesty forbids me. I am genuinely sorry about that."

Then he just hunkered down a little in the shadows, peering at me from his bed. His back was bent. His frame and his whole manner reeked of sheer exhaustion. Just how long had he been sitting there exactly, before I'd arrived?

What *was* it about the stronger forms of magic? Raine. The Girl. And now my somber companion here. This town was staring into the abyss, and they were being no real use at all.

I think I saw the truth of it, right then. Because magic does away with all the normal laws, it cuts you loose, leaving you marooned beyond reality. Although that wasn't only true of him, the more I thought about it. It described us all.

"You're right about one thing, the ceremony," he told me gently, trying to make up for his lack of helpfulness so far. "It's going to be Saturday he makes his final move."

I thanked him for that and started getting up.

"You want to know what I believe?" he breathed, stopping me. "When people get into the habit of overturning the natural order of things, they're tempting Fate in the most perilous fashion. We've all been ducking and weaving for a good long while now, surviving somehow. But it's finally caught up with us. And—you know what?—we've no one but ourselves to blame."

Which was a judgment that I simply wasn't willing to accept.

My greatest strength, he'd said? Perhaps my greatest weakness too. But it was better than his attitude. I wished him a good day, then headed back toward the street.

As I pushed the metal door back shut, that saxophone came floating, once more, from the subterranean dimness.

I could still hear it as I walked away. Except that, now, it was inside my skull.

CHAPTER 29

In the electric blueness of her room, the Little Girl revolved. Her eyes were moving swiftly again, under their closed lids. And her smooth brow was furrowed up with intense concentration.

She'd felt so terribly unhappy, during the course of the last couple of days. All those people she'd seen dying, all that pain and loss and injury. And some of it had been inflicted upon little children like herself. She would have cried for them, if she'd known how. Something in her desperately wanted to reach out and touch them, heal them. Maybe even bring them back to life.

But perhaps that was not such a good idea, the more she turned it over. She'd seen very bad things happen, when magicians had tried that.

Although, like most other things that happened in the town, she'd only ever watched it from a distance. Mr. Ross was right about that. No, she never left this room. And never got particularly involved in anything that was going on beyond it.

She'd been listening to his thoughts, the whole time he'd been talking to Dr. Willets. And . . . was he cross with her?

He didn't understand, though. She was bound to this

place, could not leave. She wasn't exactly sure why. It was just a fact that she had always been aware of.

She kept on listening, as Mr. Ross discussed things with the red-eyed adept. And one thought of his, in particular, stood out.

Staring into the abyss. They're being no real use at all.

She felt her limbs stiffen.

Oh, I'm sorry, Mr. Ross. I want to help. I really do!

"I'm not quite sure what she is," Lehman Willets said. "I'm not even certain that she's sure."

She considered that. And he was right as well. Sometimes, there was only hollowness inside her head. A yawning vacuum, desperate to be filled up. Others, there was such a babble of conflicting voices that she couldn't separate them out, or even tell which was hers.

If she was going to achieve self-knowledge at some point, then which point? What was keeping it?

But that wasn't the most important issue. There were other matters, far more pressing, which required her attention. And she needed to be helpful now. She needed to take part. If she didn't, if she just did nothing, then Mr. Ross might become a good deal more displeased with her. Might not visit her any more.

Mr. Ross, in fact, might . . .

No, she couldn't bear to think about that. There'd already been more death than she could stand.

She turned over everything that the adept had been saying. And yes, when she looked at it more clearly, she could see that he was quite correct. She'd never thought of magic in that way before. A hierarchy, yes. A pyramid. *Clever Willets!*

And Saruak near the top of it? She cast her gaze toward him. He was no longer even trying to hide himself, and she could see him clearly, still perched in that tree beyond the boundaries of the town, kicking his scuffed boots and chortling to himself.

Her temples creased up even further. Oh, that bad, bad man. She had watched him hurt so many people. And a flare of hatred ran through her. She wished that she could hurt him back.

But then, her mind grew calmer, and she started dwelling on the other things that Willets had explained.

The only thing that could beat him was this Changer of Worlds. She had never heard of that before. But the doctor was a very wise man. If he said so, she would take his word for it.

And if she wanted to be helpful, she would have to find this Changer.

So she began to cast her gaze out, like a lighthouse beam, across the entire town.

Look, Mr. Ross, look! I'm trying!

Are you happy with me now?

CHAPTER 30

Halfway back into town, my cell phone went off. I was still floundering in a pool of dark emotion from my meeting with our learned friend, and didn't feel much in the mood to talk. But I answered it. Cass was on the other end.

"You okay?" she blurted.

"Fine."

I heard her let out a breath.

"Get anything out of him?"

"A seminar about pecking orders."

"Huh?"

"Exactly. Oh, and a brief lecture on the subject of deconstructionism."

She sounded slightly boggled as she took that in. I wasn't sure she'd even heard of the word before.

"Er, what's being deconstructed?"

I sighed. "Us, apparently."

Then I noticed her voice sounded echoey, like she was out of doors. And there was some kind of hubbub going on around her. Dozens of raised voices were competing with her own. It was hard to tell from this far away, but they sounded tense and angry.

"Where *are* you?" I asked her puzzledly.

The background din rose a notch, so she was almost having to shout to make herself heard above it.

"Union Square! Out in front of the Town Hall!"

"What's happening? Who're all those people I can hear?"

"Maybe you should get down here and ask them?" she came back at me. "Because, personally, I just can't *believe* what's going on!"

The sun was high and very bright as I headed back into the center of town. The sky was a clear eggshell blue. I could see the river glimmering. The perfect day to be out of doors, tossing a ball around or just shooting the breeze with your friends. Except that the majority of us knew better.

The top end of the square, when I arrived, was half filled up with people. They were all ages, all sizes. And more of them seemed to be showing up the entire time.

There were no adepts here. None of these folks seemed to be anything special. Just the ordinary citizens of Raine's Landing, coming here to make their point. By this hour of the day, most of them should have been at work, or school. But they seemed exercised, and had a slightly frenzied air about them. Normal life had been forgotten, or at least set aside for the time being.

"We want answers!" someone yelled.

When I looked across, I could see it was a shopkeeper I knew, Hoyt Dinsmore. I had never even heard him raise his voice before.

The stage for the ceremony was practically complete. Gaily colored bunting had been strung around it, fluttering the way the banners did. There were microphones in place, and chairs, but they'd been covered up. The gathering crowd completely ignored all that. They had flooded around its girders to the steps of the Town Hall, the big stone lions gazing down at them impassively.

Mayor Aldernay was at the top, directly beneath the clock. He had his suit all neatly buttoned up, and there was a sup-posedly placating smile on his broad, tired-looking face.

"People, people!" he was begging them.

Just like Cassie, he was having to shout just to make him-self heard. But his tone, even at this higher volume, was noticeably more mellifluous in public than it ever was in private.

"Surely you can understand what happened yesterday? It happened to people who were gathered in large groups, like this one! Go home, please! It's far safer than being here!"

"That's *why* we're here!" a woman in an apron bellowed back at him.

"We'd be safer if we could get *out* of this place!" her friend, standing next to her, added.

The rest of the crowd murmured their agreement. And I wondered, was this turning into a mob?

Halfway down the west side, just a few yards from my office door, were Saul Hobart and several of his men. The guys in uniform had their expressions blank, their hands set on their hips. They were trying to look stolid and implacable. But their eyes gave them away, becoming more anxious the larger the crowd grew.

This was a town where people knew each other. Nodded, smiled, and exchanged pleasantries when passing on the street. If things turned ugly, what exactly were they going to do about it? I understood their dilemma. I'd have been in the same position once.

Saul was leaning up against a mailbox, taking in the scene with an unhappy air and shaking his big head.

Cassie had her Harley parked at the south corner and was standing beside it, with her Mossberg at the ready, her head going constantly around. It wasn't the humans she was worried about. She was scanning the whole area for any sign of trouble. Dralleg trouble in particular, I guessed. When I walked across to her, she didn't even notice I was there at first.

"Hey!" I said.

Her face jerked around. It was set like concrete.

"When did all this start?"

"I'd reckon, half an hour ago."

"Completely out of the blue?"

She seemed almost as puzzled as I was.

"Looks like."

But it hadn't been spontaneously. I had figured that out by now. The Landing might have its shortcomings, but angry mob scenes generally weren't one of them. And so . . .

I wondered what kind of bearing Saruak had on all this.

"What is it these people want?" I asked Cassie.

But the answer didn't come back to me from her lips.

"Hold the ceremony right away!" an elderly guy shouted from the center of the crowd.

I turned around and stared at them. What in heaven's name were they talking about?

"What are you waiting for, Aldernay?" another voice put in. "More innocent people to be slaughtered?"

"There's no point hanging round till Saturday! We could all be *dead* by Saturday!"

Aldernay's cheeks, true to form, turned a noticeable shade of puce. The shadows underneath his eyes grew darker. He was trying to remain calm, but he failed quite badly, going stiff, flapping his hands in what he obviously presumed was a placating manner. I could see some people looking even more annoyed, when he did that.

"All the plans for the ceremony are in place, folks! If you'll just be patient—"

The rest of what he was trying to explain was lost under a fusillade of catcalls.

"Get one of the adepts here!" someone demanded. "Let's hear what they have to say!"

And I'd never heard an ordinary Joe demand to see an adept before. Why on earth would anyone do that?

I could sense the crowd's whole mood becoming nastier and more intense. And this might be partly the Manitou's doing, I could tell. But not entirely.

There'd been three massacres in just two days. Parents and loved ones lost, whole families wiped out. Everyone was panicked, very badly. There was no way you could blame them.

But this insistence on the ceremony? The idea that it could save them? It had been tried—and they all knew it—countless times, and achieved nothing. From where had the notion come that two eight five would be the charm?

That *had* to be our visitor. It was what he wanted from them,
after all. Willets had already confirmed it. Reunion Evening
would bring Saruak to the high zenith of his power.

He was handing them the pen with which to sign their
own death warrants. And I couldn't see any way to snatch it
from their grasp.

"The adepts are getting ready!" Aldernay was insisting
above the growing hubbub. "If we're going to do this thing,
we need to do it right!"

There were a few derisive whistles.

"That's bull-flop!" Hoyt Dinsmore yelled, his glasses
looking all steamed up. "They can conjure anything they
like, so long as it's for their benefit! Why can't they do something to help us?"

"It's not *them* getting butchered!" someone else joined in.

But the fact was—I could see it clearly—nobody was suggesting anything new. There was nothing startling about the
concept. Several adepts had attended most Reunion ceremo-
nies, down the years. And it hadn't made the slightest difference. Regan's Curse had remained intact, and everybody
knew that.

Except . . . they seemed to have forgotten it. I could only
think of one person who'd want to make that happen.

I was starting to get really worried. It had been bad enough
when Saruak was influencing one human being at a time. If
he could cast his spell on this many, then why not the entire
population?

It gave me a queasy feeling, imagining what that might
entail.

The mayor threw a hopeful glance at Saul. Who, to his
credit, just stood there like a spectator. Aldernay's focus returned to the crowd.

"I *will* consult with them, I promise you!"

"That's not enough! We want their answer, and we want
it right away!"

If there was such a thing as "pucer," Edgar's face became it.

"Things aren't done that way! You know that! We can't go
demanding—"

Fierce yells cut him off again.

Saul was on his cell phone, calling for more help. His men were standing at the ready, and had put their hands across their nightsticks, although they hadn't drawn them. This showed every sign of turning bad.

I noticed, out of the corner of my eye, a shadow moving through the sky toward the square, from the direction of Sycamore Hill. It passed over the crowd, making them all glance up. There was a dull rushing noise, and Judge Levin appeared beside the mayor.

He was wearing the same suit as when I'd met him earlier, but had discarded his robes. His hair looked mildly rumpled, and his face was gray and drawn. But his presence, mild and solemn, seemed to have a dampening effect on everybody else.

I heard someone mutter, "At last."

And then the people started quieting down.

Asking to see an adept was one thing. Having one stand right in front of you? Another. The families up on the Hill had exercised such power, for so very long, that people grew up naturally respectful of them. As I watched, a few averted their gazes.

Levin peered around at them slowly, taking in every last face. And then he stepped forward, making sure he could be properly heard.

"Ladies and gentlemen, be assured," his voice rang out imposingly. "We genuinely understand your concerns. The events of the past couple of days have been appalling, truly so. They have been foremost in our every thought and deed."

He glanced briefly in my direction, looking for confirmation. I'd not had the time to tell anyone about the way we had gone after Saruak this morning, and could only shrug back. But there was an urgent question in his gaze as well. He was wondering, as I had been, what had gotten into everyone. They'd never behaved like this before.

The man had the sense to cover up his true feelings about the matter. He was managing to look as if nothing out of the ordinary was going on.

"And something will be done about it," he continued. "That much is for certain. As for the Reunion ceremony? It's an option, I'll concede that. But we've recently been approached with the opinion that it might somehow be used against us, rather than for our benefit."

I started to exhale with relief, but could see that I was being premature. Because that didn't last for long.

"Who's idea was *that*?" the woman in the apron asked.

Levin was careful not to look at me again, and I felt grateful for that, at least. If these folks found out it was me who'd tried to get the evening canceled . . .

"That doesn't matter. The one thing we're sure of is we're dealing with a very tricky adversary. Merely the suggestion, from a reliable source, means that we have to consider it."

So it seemed I'd gotten to the adepts, after all. They had been so stubborn, back up on the Hill, so heavy with objections. But, for all their shortcomings, all of them were smart. And they'd had examples, at firsthand, of what our visitor could do, so maybe they were beginning to see my point.

The ordinary people didn't, and were starting to become restless again.

"*What* source?"

"Where's the *evidence* of that?"

Then a young girl yelled out desperately, "We just want to leave!"

Levin retained his composure. I had never seen him lose that, come to think of it. He was standing like a rock, his hands folded in front of him. An understanding smile was playing on his face. He waited for the noise to die down, then opened his mouth to answer them.

He never got that far. Next moment, a completely different sound rang out across the square. Then another. Then a whole load of them.

Over to our left, the air was being torn apart by anguished, high-pitched screams.

CHAPTER 31

Gazes started jerking around. Mine, the crowd's. Even the guys up on the Town Hall steps. Hobart and his men all stiffened. And Cassie took a couple of smart paces forward, hoping to bring her shotgun to bear. But on what?

Nothing had happened to the crowd that any of us could see. There was nothing attacking them. The screaming wasn't coming from this area at all.

Every eye swung toward O'Connell, to the west of here. The street where I had wound up just a couple of nights back. The neon lights were off by this hour, and most of the bars were closed. But there were cheaper stores dotted along its dingy length, and it was always fairly busy.

There was pandemonium down there. Some people were running, I could make out. Others were just standing, howling, frozen in the grip of terror.

The traffic in that direction had stalled, and a few folks were abandoning their vehicles. For some reason that I couldn't really see from here, a town bus had stopped dead, slewed off to an angle, in the middle of the blacktop.

I threw a glance at Cass, and then at Hobart and his men. We all had the same idea. We started going forward, at a jog at first, then running.

Yesterday hadn't been quite enough. Not for Saruak,

apparently. His taste for mayhem seemed insatiable. My own gun was in my hand. The cops all had their sidearms drawn.

And all of it too late, by the time we got there. We were too late to do anything but call for more assistance, which Hobart promptly did.

The bus was one of those driverless kinds. It was full of passengers, and its doors were wide open. But nobody was getting out. Even before I got the whole way there, my heart began to sink.

A middle-aged man's head was leaning against the inside of one window. He was wearing a smart business suit, a stripy tie. And he might have been fast asleep. Except his eyes were open.

And his mouth . . . his throat . . .

There were straight, clean wounds across his windpipe, parallel ones. The Dralleg again. I forced myself to pull my gaze away. Everywhere I looked, along the glass panes, there was blood. Most of it had been spattered there, for sure. But some of it was smeared.

Fingertips and palms had done that. I imagined all these injured people, scrabbling to escape. Trying to push themselves away from danger. Precious few had managed it. There were a couple of wounded lying on the asphalt, and Hobart's people were tending to them. A young man came running out of a store with a blanket and some bandages. Some motorists were going to their trunks for their first aid kits.

But all of it was after the event. There was no way of stopping this from happening time and time again, or even of predicting it. I felt completely numb once more. But Cassie didn't pause.

She went up immediately through the doors, her gun at her shoulder. Swung it around carefully, saw that the culprit had already left.

Then she stooped down and called out, "We've got someone alive in here!"

And disappeared from view.

When I looked inside, she was kneeling over a thin guy in his thirties, pressing down with both palms on a severed artery. She didn't look like she needed any help, and the ambulance crews would be here soon. They were getting plenty of practice, let's face it.

As for the rest of the passengers? My God, it was remarkable anyone was still alive at all. The Dralleg had gone through here like a lawnmower through grass.

Sirens were approaching. I was getting rather too accustomed with that sound.

I tried to think. Saruak . . . why would he do this, other than from sheer malice? He was capable of that, but he'd already made his point, hadn't he? Captured our complete attention?

Then I took in the gawping faces all around me on the street—more people were approaching all the time. And looking at their expressions, I believed I understood what this was all about.

In broad daylight, this time.

I could see it in their eyes. I could almost hear it in the way that they were breathing. The first attack had been at night. The later ones had come in the evening. And they'd all happened in enclosed places, churches and in private homes.

Whereas, this attack was in broad daylight, and plain public view. I began to see where this was heading.

There was a growing horror in their gazes. They all looked the same way, and were coming to the same conclusion. Nowhere in the Landing was safe, at any time. The nightmare that the Little Girl had talked about was taking shape, becoming wholly tangible and real.

A few more people were unfreezing, moving in to help. But then, one teenaged girl started wailing.

"Did you *see* that thing?"

Her fingernails went to her cheeks. She was on the verge of complete hysteria, shaking furiously and almost dancing on the spot.

"Did you see it? It . . . it just appeared, out of nowhere! Is *that* what's been killing people? Oh my God, is it coming for *us*?"

Someone tried to calm her down, but she jerked out of his grip and began crying.

You had to hand it to Saruak, he'd timed this just perfectly.

As if to prove the point, the rest of the crowd from Union Square started showing up and mingling with the people here. Judge Levin pushed his way to my side. He climbed up on the step and took a good hard look inside. I could hear him suck in a breath and curse. And when he got back down, his face was even more ashen than it had been.

There was a glint, the bead of a tear, in the corner of his eye. But his mouth was rigid. And he held his shoulders squarely. He was fighting to stay calm. After all, he had an example to set.

Everyone behind him started pushing in, then groaning when they saw what had transpired. He turned to face them, his spectacles glittering.

"You're going to just 'consider the matter'?" someone demanded, when he tried to open his mouth again.

He shut it.

"How many more times does this have to happen before something gets done?"

"What else are you offering us? What else *is* there but the ceremony?"

Other voices lifted in agreement. Even people who had not been part of the original mob were joining in. All Saruak had had to do was unleash his creature once again, and this was the result.

Levin might have had dignity and weight, but he was losing his authority with all this going on. There was no way that he could just ignore these people. I watched as he took in that fact, and it was not something he was used to.

He looked slightly flustered, running a hand through his hair. His lips formed a tight circle, then unpuckered. If the townsfolk were demanding action, he could no longer deny it.

He cast a helpless glance at me, as if to say, "What can I do?"

Then he cleared his throat, puffing out his chest inside his sharply tailored suit.

"Very well, we'll bring it forward. But we can't hold it immediately."

"Why not?"

"If we're going to make it work this time, the adepts must *all* gather in the square and bring their full powers to bear, at once. And that will take some organizing."

Except that Saruak thrived on magic too. I thought about so much arcana concentrated in one place. Oh, this just kept on getting worse.

When someone else tried to argue with that, the judge stared him down angrily.

"Would *you* like to carry the responsibility for this, sir? No? Then kindly take my word for it."

And was he telling them the truth, or giving me some kind of temporary reprieve?

"It will take us at least a day to get everything ready. We shall bring Reunion Evening forward to tomorrow. Friday evening, eight o'clock. That's my final word on the subject. I'll see you all there."

They still weren't exactly happy about it, but there was nothing else that they could do. Even the dumbest person here had to realize the ceremony didn't have a chance of being successful without the adepts showing up.

Squad cars and ambulances started rolling up around us, uniformed men pushing their way through. A paramedic went up to take over from Cassie, and some of the civilians began moving out of the way.

They started wandering off, dispersing, murmuring un-happily among themselves. All the stores and cafes around us were now empty, except for a few remaining staff. The cops had begun moving the abandoned cars out of the way. O'Connell, never the most cheerful street, seemed sunk in gloom, despite the brightness of the day.

I felt the deepest pity for these people, watching them all

go. They were so determined, sure that they were doing the right thing. And had no way of knowing they were running headlong into a deadly trap.

If I could only get Willets down here to explain it to them. But they'd probably run away from him. I wondered why I couldn't choose more personable allies.

Cassie came back down. She'd got hold of an old cloth from somewhere, and was wiping the blood from her hands, grumbling under her breath and looking pretty sickened. It became perfectly clear to me the way she lived two separate existences, her life at home and the one out here. Whereas, I only ever seemed to have the one.

"He okay?"

"He'll live," she told me.

So my gaze went back to Levin. He was staring at me grimly, his eyes bright behind their thin glass disks.

"I think I've taken the right action," he said.

"Really?"

"Maybe *you* are wrong, have you considered that, and this really is the town's best hope. If you can prove otherwise, Devries, then you've a day left to convince me. Otherwise, Reunion Evening goes ahead."

He became a depthless shadow, which just disappeared in the next moment. Leaving me to wonder how in God's name I was going to manage that.

CHAPTER 32

There's a saying that goes, "If you've dug yourself into a hole, stop digging." And what exactly had I been achieving up till this point? For the most part—between bursts of violent activity—just doing the rounds, making inquiries. Pretty much like the workaday cop that I had, for a long while, been.

Considering the danger that was crashing through the walls of our world, all I'd managed, really, was to plug up a few cracks.

Which wasn't nearly good enough, and I could see that. It had got me nowhere. And I'd just been told the truth of the matter, by one of the highest authorities possible. I was running out of time, and very badly.

Cass and Hobart were looking at me. They could both see what the problem was. Only the most persistent voyeurs from the crowd were still hanging around. The final rescue teams had shown up, body bags were being shipped down from the stricken bus. Not a job that anybody ought to have to deal with. But we were all doing what we could.

I turned to my old boss.

"Can you make sure," I asked him, "that, at least until tomorrow, there are no more gatherings like this?"

A gleam of annoyance came sparking up in his usually mild eyes.

"Since when did I start taking instructions from you?"

We'd all been left, let's face it, pretty jumpy by what had just taken place. And I'm sure he didn't mean to sound so hostile, but the strain was showing in his whole demeanor.

"No such thing," I told him calmly. "Only a polite request."

"Well, I'm not sure I have the power to do that. People gather, Ross. That's what they do."

I could see the sense in what he was telling me, but it wasn't good enough. There had to be some way . . . ?

I couldn't think of one immediately. And Hobart just stared back at me and worked his jaw around.

Thank God we had Cassie with us. She might not have too much in the way of education, but when it comes to getting her own way, she can be pretty shrewd.

"Hey?" she suggested lightly.

She turned to Union Square, and took a few steps back there, her boots clacking.

"What's that I can smell?" she asked us. "Maybe . . . gas?"

There was no such odor. But she raised her head and flared her nostrils all the same, like she was perfectly convinced that she had noticed it. Saul and I glanced at each other.

"Um . . . yeah," the Lieutenant offered. "I think you might be right about that."

"Do you suppose it's coming from in front of the Town Hall? A cracked main, maybe?"

And she had a point.

"I could call the gas company in, when I've time to get around to it," Hobart began suggesting. "And in the meantime, I suppose, put up some barriers, for safety's sake. Sure, I could do that."

Which would do the trick for the time being. Things were bad enough already, without any private citizens getting it into their heads to try and start the ceremony early. They'd have to evict the Town Hall too. I could just imagine Mayor Aldernay's face.

"And how about me?" Cass asked. "I can't go round telling people what to do."

Armed the way she was, that was a statement I took issue with. But there was nothing I could think of at the moment. I was going to be headed, before too much longer, in directions that she very definitely wouldn't want to go.

"Best thing you can do," I said, "is to patrol the town, the next few hours. You've always had a pretty good nose for trouble. Why not use it now?"

But she looked unconvinced.

"You want me to just ride around in circles?" she asked, a knowing gleam appearing in her eyes. "Why do I get the feeling that you're trying to get me out of the way?"

I gazed back at her squarely.

"Let's just say you're not going to like what happens next, Cass. This far in? I think we have to use the biggest guns we've got."

The wasps were still humming back and forth when I pulled up outside Sanderson's Supplies again and killed the engine. They had a casual, almost lazy air, like they didn't even understand that these might be their last few hours before darkness fell for good.

The sun had tilted over to the west. Shadows were leaning all around me, a reproach, reminding me how rapidly the hours passed. A jackdaw landed on a branch out in the forest. There was a rustling that might have been a deer. I had my window wound down again, and could hear it clearly.

Christ, I should have done all this the first time that I'd been here. I rummaged in my glove compartment for the two items I needed. Stuffed them in my pockets. Then got out, headed across.

The music of another saxophone came floating up to me, when I pulled open the metal door a second time. It was deeper, more melodious than the one I'd heard before.

The turntable was back. He'd just made it appear out of nothingness. The bulb in the ceiling had been switched off. The only remaining light in the basement came from the little fire he'd built. And there was no ash, no debris. The twigs blazed brightly, but did not disintegrate. Being around

Willets was like being in those dreams I'd mentioned. Cause and effect did not work the same.

The doctor and his bed were just pale shapes in the flickering dimness. But he looked up startledly as I came rattling down the stairs. Smaller outlines were still moving all around him. Tiny eyes were fixed on him. His bright red pupils winked like distant beacons in the gloom.

"You again?"

He sounded bemused. Maybe he'd been focused inwardly, and had not noticed I was coming back. But then he pointed at the record player.

"Cannonball Adderley," he told me, sounding rather pleased with himself. "'Alabama Concerto,' in four movements."

He made the discs pop into being, just like the plinth, just like the books. But I wasn't here for any music lesson, this time.

I just marched across to where he was seated. Reached down. Grabbed the collar of his jacket, and then hauled him to his feet.

He let out a strangled, angry yelp.

"*Man?* What do you think you're *doing*?"

Taking a real risk, and didn't I just know it. Cass would have had kittens, if she'd seen me treating him this way. Most people in town would. You didn't *behave* this way when dealing with a powerful adept. Alarm them or make them angry, and there was no telling how they might respond in the heat of the moment. And that was just the more respectable ones, who didn't have the history that Willets did.

I'd been one of the cops who'd had to clean up after the incident at the Iron Bridge. I tried not to think about it as I hung onto his struggling form. Those charred young bodies—no, I just put all of that out of my mind, and propelled him toward the metal staircase.

"You can't *treat* me like this!" he howled, the Emperor of Ice Cream being physically dragged off his throne. "Where on earth do you think you're taking me?"

I could tell that, just like Raine, he'd developed a fear of stepping outside.

"Back into the real world," I replied.

"Real . . . ?" He made a spluttering noise. *"Why?"*

"There's a war going on. And you've been conscripted."

And he finally got it. Dug his heels in, skidding to a halt.

"I've already *told* you!" He gawped stubbornly around at me. "I can't possibly beat that creature!"

He'd told me several times, in fact. But I wasn't ready to accept it.

"Didn't you hear?" I asked him. "It's not the winning that counts, it's the taking part."

I gave his scrawny neck a jerk, and we were heading for the stairs again.

I've already mentioned that he could have done all sorts of awful things to me. He certainly kept threatening them as we continued heading up.

"I'll turn you to a toadstool!"

His feet tried to scrabble backward on the risers, making a loud clanging noise.

"I'll . . . transmogrify you to a pile of dust!"

Which he could have managed easily. But I had my own opinion, when it came to Lehman Willets.

He still thought about those kids who had died every single day—I had no doubt of that. I would have been the same, if I were him. And there are vast forces at work in this town, almost all the time. But guilt can be the strongest of them. Can outweigh them all. He kept on squirming, issuing new threats. But my bet was, he didn't have the resolve left to back them up with action.

So, seeing that he wasn't going to frighten me, he tried to reason with me instead. And more fool him.

"There's absolutely *nothing* I can do!"

"No," I told him. "There's one thing. You can at least give it your best shot."

"And what'll *that* achieve?"

"More than sitting on your backside ever did."

"Really? Oh, *great*! Homespun philosophy!" He sounded like he wanted to spit. "I *knew* I should've never come to a dumb provincial town like this!"

If he'd stayed in Boston, then it might have been for the best, all things considered. But we needed him right now.

We finally reached the top. I turned him around to face me. He was glaring, breathing heavily, his features set like anthracite. I got out the two items that I'd fetched from my car.

There was a floppy denim hat—I used to wear it fishing on the Adderneck. It went over his gray head, the pressure of it making him shrink down surprisedly.

"What? What's that?"

"A fashion statement."

And the shades covered up his eyes, so that the glowing pupils were no longer visible. That was a mild relief.

I didn't even know how long it had been since he had last gone out into the daylight. Even a person as powerful as Willets needs protection sometimes. And these two simple objects were his.

He seemed to get what I had in mind, the plans I had for him. The look on his face became even more alarmed. He pawed at the dark glasses. And then, failing to dislodge them, tried to head back down the stairs again.

I stretched out and refastened my grip around his collar, then yanked the door open. A shaft of sunlight flooded over us. That made him stop struggling and hunker down. But I just pushed him out into the open.

When the bright daylight hit him, he cringed under the impact of it, his hands trying to shield him and his features creasing up more than they usually did. Was he in actual pain? I didn't want to hurt him, and I felt a solid twinge of guilt myself. But things had got too serious for personal considerations. Too many people had already suffered, and much worse than this. And I wasn't about to give up at this stage. So I kept propelling him along the crumbled sidewalk.

"Have you no decency, Devries?" He was stooped over

like a man twice his age, his hands still trying to keep the sunlight off his face. "For pity's sake, stop this!"

"I'll stop when we're done."

"You s.o.b.! I'll make you pay for this. Why, I'll create a werewolf and I'll set him on your hide!"

"Loaded my gun with silver bullets, just this morning," I informed him.

He pulled and twisted in my grasp. And his language became a good deal worse than a college professor's ought to be. But I got him into the passenger seat of my Caddy all the same, slamming the door shut behind him. He stared around the interior like he'd forgotten what an automobile was.

My own attention had gone elsewhere. The jackdaw that had first been there had company by now. The branches of the tree that it was sitting in were full of crows, magpies, and ravens, all of them gazing in the same direction. Ours. And I thought I could make out, below them, the shape of a weasel of some kind. The kind of power the doctor had attracted a good deal of notice.

It was pretty weird, feeling their inquiring gazes on me. I got in the other side.

"Put your seat belt on," I said.

He was all hunched up into a ball, the light still obviously causing him discomfort. But it wasn't that he couldn't move. He just didn't want to.

"Okay then. Your funeral."

I started the engine and swung us around.

"Where are we going?" he asked me, his voice all muffled up.

"To see the wizard."

Then his head came up a little. "Huh?"

"Someone just as powerful as you," I told him.

At which, his face rose fully into view, the expression on it filled with icy shock. He peered at me through his dark lenses. Out here in the light, I could see the faint carmine specks behind them.

"Who? What good'll that do? You're insane!" he hissed.

"Oh? I thought that was your bag."

"You're ridiculous! A consummate fool!"

Well, a poet called Carl Sandburg once wrote, "to never see a fool you lock yourself in your room and smash the looking-glass."

Which sounded about right. But it was far too late for that.

CHAPTER 33

When he saw where we were pulling up, he got so agitated I became concerned he might forget himself, and do something unpleasant to me.

"No . . . oh no! You're kidding, surely?"

He crammed himself back in his seat, and waved his bony hands. But I wasn't going to let this drop, so I steeled myself. If it happened, there was nothing I could really do about it.

"There is no way," he wailed at me, "that I am going in that place! There is no *way* I'm meeting with that nut-job! You can forget it, Devries! It simply isn't going to happen!"

I went around to his side and bundled him out. And then half dragged and half propelled him. This was getting to be a habit. As I yanked him past the gates, however, he finally seemed to lose it.

There was a crackling sound. And a stream of flaring light came rushing out from the center of his forehead, shooting upward. The top of one of the spindly, leafless trees caught fire. A few large dark birds flapped away alarmedly, and something heavy went stampeding through the undergrowth.

I watched, genuinely shocked, as the fire began spreading to the lower branches. That could have been me, goddamn it.

But I kept hold of him all the same. It was less of a problem this time, since he had gone slack in my grasp. I could tell that he was mortified as well. He hadn't meant to do that.

So I let go of the tension that had spread out through my body. And my tone, when I spoke to him again, was harsh.

"Is that nice? You're a guest here. Put that out."

He obediently raised his fingers, twitched them, and the fire completely vanished. But a few cinders were hissing down, there was a plume of smoke. This hadn't been like the flames in his basement. They'd been far more real.

"I'm sorry, Devries," he muttered, apparently disgusted with himself.

From this point, then, I was satisfied that I'd have no more trouble from him. He seemed rather lost and saddened. He had even managed to singe the brim of his hat.

Slowly, and still reluctantly on his part, we negotiated all the roots and saplings on the driveway till Raine Manor came in sight.

It looked rather different in the day. More solid, yes, and more distinct. But not completely either of those qualities. The mist around it was all gone. It seemed it only came during the hours of darkness. But the place as a whole still had an eerie, faded look that wouldn't go away entirely. Stare at it for long enough, and it might start crumbling away before your eyes.

The *W* on the high spire was casting a long shadow. The windows still gave onto pure blackness, despite the fact the sun was glinting on them. It just didn't seem to be allowed inside. And the gargoyles I'd seen moving on the roof were fast asleep along the gutters by this hour. Not one of them stirred.

A wind chime finally rattled, making me jump. Principally, because there was no wind at all this time.

"You can still forget it," Willets was informing me by this juncture. "I'm not going to fight you, but I'm not cooperating either."

Once I'd made my mind up about something, I wouldn't

take no for an answer. Didn't he even understand that? I dragged him up onto the porch. The front door was shut. And when I tried to turn the handle, it wouldn't budge an inch.

I thumped at the wood with the edge of my fist and yelled out, "Woody, let us in!"

He had to know that we were out here. And I doubted he was all that pleased about it. He had probably guessed what I had planned for him. And the thought of actually getting involved? There was nothing quite like a stiff dose of practicality to send our Woods into a sulk.

I yelled out, "You can't hide in there forever!"

Which was another questionable statement, and got no response at all. I thought about trying to ram my way in, but the woodwork looked too stout for that.

"You see?" Willets was saying. "We're wasting our time."

I told him to be quiet. Except I didn't exactly use those words.

Then I backed us both off half a dozen paces. Took the gun out of my pocket, and fired a round at the big brass lock.

It did nothing but make a hole. But it had the desired effect.

There was a clack. And then the door swung open half a dozen inches. In the pitch darkness beyond it, Hampton's broad, flat face appeared. He wasn't in full uniform. He had his livery pants on, but the shirt and jacket were gone, and he was in his undervest. I'd apparently interrupted him in the middle of grabbing a snack—there was a large blob of mayo sliding down his chin.

Those peculiar eyes of his narrowed at the sight of us, and a crease appeared in his wide brow.

"Mr. Devries? What do you think you're playing at?" he piped out. "Do you realize this door is made of the very finest Massachusetts oak?"

Unimpressed, I marched toward him, Willets still in tow. Hampton only saw his mistake too late. He hadn't even put the chain on. And when he tried to close the door again, I was there already, slamming it aside, then barging straight past his enormous bulk.

He started to protest, but I continued down the hallway, yelling, "Woody, show yourself!"

Willets's footsteps clattered and scrabbled on the wooden floor. He seemed to have gotten a second wind, and was trying to escape from me more determinedly than ever. But in physical terms, he's not all that strong, so I just hung on tightly. There was candlelight showing from the ballroom, once again. So that was where I went.

It was no different to the last time I had been in here. Woody obviously liked things just the way they were, all dismal and spooky—it probably suited his usual frame of mind. Dim, ephemeral shapes surrounded us, the portraits, and high chandeliers. It always felt, when I came here, like I'd fallen into someone else's semi-waking fantasy.

At the center of the room were several flames, a candelabra rather than a single light. The glow they cast combined, however, didn't even reach the walls.

We stepped into the thin pool of illumination. Willets had given up trying to protest and looked around nervously, his features rather awed.

"He's not here," he protested. His voice had taken on a noticeably tremulous edge. "He's probably just gibbering around in the attic, playing with his own feces or something."

"That's disgusting," came a voice that I already knew, although it was a touch sharper this time, a little more cut-glass to the tones.

We both spun around, but could see nothing.

"Is *that* what you think of me?" it went on. "Do you honestly believe that I could be so . . . ?"

Then it paused. A sigh rang out.

"Words fail me."

There was a humming sound above us, like some kind of massive hornet had appeared out of thin air. So he was obviously unhappy. And that's something about Woody that I haven't yet explained.

He never could get it into his head that certain people didn't like him. He always thought of himself as some kind of beloved leader, some revered benefactor. Mr. Popularity, with yellow eyes. And finding out that wasn't the case . . . it made him sad, or made him angry. It invariably threw him into a foul mood.

Except I very badly needed him on board. I wasn't even sure we could get anywhere very far, without his personal involvement. Damn Willets and his big mouth. I struggled to think how to retrieve the situation.

"It was just a turn of phrase, a joke," I called out.

He had so little understanding of the way that normal life worked that he might just buy it. I could only hope.

"Really?"

He sounded faintly intrigued. So I'd been right about that.

"A joke between friends," I told him, pressing the point home. "What's the world come to, if friends can't josh each other?"

"But we're not actually—"

"Comrades, then. Brothers in arms, united in a noble cause."

He'd go for that, surely, being painted as the good guy? I felt slightly dirty by this stage. I would have said almost anything to get him on our side, and knew it.

"Number twos, though, sport? The very thought is so unsavory."

"Bar-room humor," I explained, working hard to sound convincing. "Just a bunch of buddies, all potty-mouthed and yakking it up."

The only response I got was silence. So perhaps he didn't understand.

"It's a male-bonding thing," I tried. "Boys will be boys, you know."

"Oh!"

Which was followed by another pause. And then, "Yes, I see. I suppose they might."

Those golden, slitted cat eyes of his opened in the darkness. I heard Willets let out a stifled murmur.

The humming above us stopped. So Woody had apparently cheered up. I took a deep breath. For all his dottiness and eccentricity, he could be dangerous when roused.

Raine took a step in our direction. It sounded like he was barefooted this time.

"Ha, yes! Very convivial. What fun we shall have." He stared at me. "But I'm not sure I actually approve of your behavior, sport. Coming here completely uninvited? Shooting at my door? You are in my employ after all, and I believe I'm entitled to expect better of you."

Then he looked across at Willets.

"The good doctor, I presume. Pleased to make your acquaintance at long last. It so happens that we share a passion. I have a particular taste for the musicality of that great tunesmith Benny Goodman."

He made a few quick noises that were supposed to be a clarinet. Willets turned away, muttering some kind of anatomical suggestion underneath his breath. But I grabbed him by the collar again. Turned him around and then gave him another shake, reminding him to behave himself.

He got the message. Nodded politely. Even tried to force a smile.

"That's . . . well, that's good to hear."

He was still wearing his floppy hat and shades, and looked faintly ridiculous among all this dimmed-out grandeur. But when it comes to adepts, as I'd found out long ago, you never read them simply by appearances.

Raine turned his attention back to me.

"So—why have you disturbed me in this fashion, sport?"

"You must know what's going on?"

"Of course. But I thought we had a deal. You sort out this unpleasantness, and I reward you handsomely. It all seemed very simple at the time, as I recall."

"No, not good enough. I need your help."

His eyes narrowed even further. And a luster that was half puzzled and half amused crept into them.

"Mine, old chum? I don't get what you're driving at."

There was a hard set to my body. I'm not sure he even noticed that. But it was time to bring the Master of the Manor down to earth with a pretty hefty bump.

"You already know what we're up against," I told him flatly. "You must see that nothing I can do alone will stop it. But look where I am? Standing in the same room with the two strongest adepts in this town. And if we worked together, as a team . . . ?"

There was the faintest glint of comprehension from him, realism starting to bite home. But that didn't even start to mean he liked it.

"But I *hired* you! You're supposed to—"

"And that's what I'm doing," I broke across him. "My job, the best way I know how."

"Blast!"

He seemed lost for words for a short while after that. But then, in the soft glow of the candlelight, I caught a faint glimpse of a smile. It was perfectly neat and even this time. Except that, when I had last met him, his teeth had been slightly jagged. It was always this way with him, like watching a movie that kept altering the details of its plot.

All I ever felt like I was dealing with, around any of these guys, was an utter lack of definable substance. I was conversing with shadows. I was negotiating with creatures who dwelt far beyond the borders of the everyday, mundane. And if I kept on doing this, I wondered, would I eventually travel to that place myself, without so much as a ticket back?

"Can I take it, then," Raine asked, "that you're appealing to my better nature?"

I nodded. If it made him any happier, putting it that way, okay.

He blinked slowly. "Very well. What do you want from me?"

"Get both your heads together for a start," I told him. "Pool your knowledge. Try and find some way to at least slow Saruak down."

Willets's mouth popped open again. But I still had him by the collar, and he seemed to change his mind.

"More importantly, figure out some way to convince Levin and the others that they need to cancel the ceremony."

Woody seemed to lose the plot for a moment. He's remarkably good at doing that.

"But I love that ceremony. It's always such tremendous fun."

"Not this year, Woods. *Think* about it."

Which he did.

"Ah! You might have a point."

An air of frantic busyness seemed to overtake him as soon as he'd conceded that. Once he'd made up his mind about something, he usually threw himself into it with a passion. So he turned smartly around and took a few paces toward the furthest corner of the room, making a soft padding sound. Then he stopped and raised one arm, the palm held open wide. Something against the wall over there suddenly lifted itself into the dim, flickering air—it was massive and rectangular—and started to float toward the man.

"We'll need magic stuff. I've got plenty of that, most of it inherited." And he let out a small laugh. "In fact, I've got so much that I could actually go into the magic-stuff business. Wouldn't that be grand?"

The object was a chest, I could see, and was glinting faintly. It was hard to tell in this poor light, but it looked like mahogany inlaid with brass. It settled down in front of him—there was not the tiniest sound. The lid swung open without anybody touching it. Our host bent over and started rummaging through its contents.

Willets rolled his eyes, although he'd learned his lesson and didn't attempt anything more than that. His expression, a resigned one, hung there in the dimness. He had taken off his shades, and his red pupils glowed. He stared around at me like some despondent bloodhound.

"This might take a while," he pointed out.

"Which we don't have."

"There's no need to exaggerate. We've still got a whole day."

And there were times, I already understood, when good, effective magic?—it could simply not be rushed.

A cough from the doorway captured my attention. Hampton had appeared there, in full uniform, and was clutching another candle in a white porcelain holder. He stared at me as though he'd only just noticed I was there.

"Sir, if you would follow me?"

I hadn't planned on going anywhere, and told him that.

"It would perhaps be more appropriate if you allowed the gentlemen some time on their own. Some privacy, yes?"

In other words, it might be best if I went elsewhere while there was sorcery afoot.

"Might be the wisest course of action, Devries," Willets grumbled in my ear. "Once that we get going, well then, sparks might start to fly. Literally."

Which was the first positive thing I'd heard him say so far. People are just full of surprises, aren't they?

I stopped at the doorway and looked back at them. They were both leaning over the chest, mere shadows in the dimness, and were picking objects out of it, inspecting them, then casting them aside.

Two mighty magicians. One a sad, aimless recluse, his head all full of mad, chaotic music. And the other a Jesus wannabe, with barely the thinnest of grasps on the regular world at all.

Our whole survival might depend on them, within the next few hours.

And so, heaven help us all.

CHAPTER 34

Hampton led me through the wide, echoing passageways, our candle-broken shadows flickering around us. He was taking us on a convoluted route, but there seemed no escaping that. There were dozens of corridors, all tortuous. The enormous house seemed to get even darker, the further in we went, as though each step we took was sinking us deeper into a perpetual night. There were still shapes around us, but you couldn't even make out what they were.

We kept on passing light switches, however, polished brass ones. So, getting tired of this, I reached out and flicked at one. But nothing happened.

"Master Raine doesn't approve of electricity," the chauffeur informed me. "It makes him nervous."

He continued leading me inward, turning yet another corner.

"How do you even stand this?" I asked.

"When I'm off duty, I get out into the daylight, as much as I'm able."

Which explained the tan.

I thought about all those windows I'd seen on the outside of the mansion.

"Doesn't *any* light get in here?"

"If it manages, then I'm not sure where, or how. It certainly doesn't announce itself."

And then, as if by way of explanation, "Master Raine does all of his best thinking in the dark."

Which sounded pretty much like Woody. All theater and pose, and no real common sense.

We finally reached another doorway that we stopped in front of.

"The games room," the man announced.

He walked in and stooped down, applying the candle to a larger wick. Smoky amber light came spilling out, widening as the flame grew. There was a clattering as he replaced the glass. This was another oil lamp, like in DuMarr's office. It sometimes felt like we were living in the eighteenth century.

The glow it cast threw the room into dusky relief. Another crystal chandelier was tethered below the ornate ceiling, all the facets winking with the deep yellow light. Sporting scenes had been painted up there, from more elegant but rather crueler days. Aristocratic types in red coats hunted foxes, and there was a stag at bay. Hares were being coursed, and badgers baited. They used to call that stuff fun, which shows how definitions change.

Somebody was setting a falcon on some smaller birds.

Another thing struck me as odd. Everything around me, so far as I could make out, was spotlessly clean. The woodwork had a luster to it, and the fittings all gleamed. Woody's state of mind spoke of neglectfulness and disarray. I had imagined thick cobwebs and mildew. But it looked like this part of his home was all scrubbed up and neatly ordered, like the pantry of some spinster who took Bible class.

If the same was true throughout the mansion, then I doubted Hampton here was capable of doing this much work. Maybe brooms appeared on sticks, at regular occasions. And danced around the place to the strains of "The Sorcerer's Apprentice." Knowing Woody, it was not beyond the bounds of possibility.

Over in the corner, a huge red-and-green chessboard had been set up on a low desk—never quite my game. The larger pieces, carved from ivory, were around a foot tall. And I decided to avoid them as much as I could. Because the eyes of the facing row all seemed to follow me a little as I stepped into the room. Maybe that was only my imagination. But I wasn't taking any chances, not in this particular house.

Dominating the center was a full-sized billiards table. The baize on it was a deep navy blue. And all the balls were black. Terrific.

But there was a deep, comfortable-looking armchair, swathed in dark red damask, to the left of it, which Hampton led me to. The coffee table by its side had a heavy crystal ashtray on it, several coasters.

"I'll be back presently," he told me, once I'd settled down.

As soon as he was gone, I got busy. I already understood, perfectly well, that Raine didn't like the new technology. But he was fully occupied, and I supposed he wouldn't notice. So I pulled my cell phone out, and then rang Cass.

Her voice was slightly distant. "I thought you'd forgotten about me."

"No chance. Just been rather occupied. You?"

"I'm in *Easy Rider*'s sequel, *Tedious Rider*. Nothing's doing here. How are things going at your end?"

"I'm not sure you want to know."

I could imagine her pulling her mouth out of shape at the far end of the line.

"You be careful around those nuts," she admonished me. "I wouldn't trust either of them with a burnt-out matchstick."

"Yeah, I know the feeling."

Which was all that I could think to say.

"Want me to keep going?" Cassie asked.

She sounded genuinely fed up.

"That has to be your decision. But if there's really nothing happening, then maybe you should just go home."

Her voice became noticeably duller when I said that.

"That seems pretty pointless too," she answered. "I'll stay on it for a little while longer."

She was like most people who spend too long on the street,

in other words. She was there, mostly, because there was nowhere else she had to go.

Hampton came back in as I was pocketing the phone again.
He caught a glimpse of it, and looked uncomfortable. But that
went away, almost immediately, and he decided not to comment. In fact, the man seemed almost pleased with me. I was
doing stuff connected with the real business of the Landing,
things that had a genuine purpose. This was possibly the first
time in years that he'd been involved in anything useful.

He was carrying a large white china plate with an equally
large sandwich on it, and a tall and foaming glass. I looked
at them warily.

"My own speciality snack," he informed me, in those
piping tones of his. "Spanish-style serrano ham, romaine
lettuce hearts, and organic Honeycup mustard on lightly
toasted white bread. Do you know how hard it is to get ingredients like those round here?"

When he saw how cautious I still was, he made a reassuring clucking with his tongue.

"No need to worry, sir. I prepared this myself, and I do *all*
the grocery shopping. No magic involved." He took a quick
glance around, and then confided to me, "I like to make sure
that Master Raine at least eats well."

He set the glass down delicately on the little table.

"Ginger beer," he added. "I thought you'd want to keep
your head as clear as possible."

It was probably best if someone did. He handed me the
plate, and then went away again, did not return.

After the briefest sniff at it, I wolfed it down. It tasted absolutely fine. I drained half of the ginger beer, then fumbled
in my pocket and took out a cigarette.

And remembered what Cassie had said this morning.
About the way I'd somehow changed.

I could feel the muscles in my forearm tensing slightly.
And my hand stopped, halfway to my mouth. I peered at the
smoke, turning it over in my fingers. And then slid it back
into its pack again.

Which left me with not very much to do. I was just waiting for the others. How to pass the time?

The adrenaline that had been driving me, ever since Saruak had come into my home, had gone away completely. Lead seemed to be flowing through my veins. The dimness of the room was seeping through me. I leant back. My heart's beat sounded like the thudding of some distant ocean. How long was I going to have to sit here?

Any rest that I got seemed to be on chairs or couches, these days. I was starting to forget what it felt like being in a bed. But what the hell. I couldn't remain on the move forever.

I let my eyes slip closed. Then remembered where I was, and sat up sharply.

There was still no one here. And nothing—except for the chessboard, perhaps—to worry about. None of the pieces seemed to be watching me anymore. They were staring fixedly ahead.

I couldn't hear a sound, from the surrounding mansion. How could any place be so quiet? But I slid back again, a little more relaxed, and grayness filled my mind.

Except . . . there was a tiny point of light within it.

Colored light.

Electric blue.

That first time she had contacted me, back at St. Cleary's, it had only been the briefest of connections, a taut nudge at my consciousness, albeit one that had pushed me in the right direction, helping me save Cassie's hide.

This time, it was entirely different. A larger intrusion by far. She took form in my mind, and grew, till I could see her clearly. Her eyes were closed as usual. And she was rotating, which she nearly always seemed to do. I could have almost been standing in her room and looking at her. What was happening?

The electric blue glow that she cast off seemed to wash right through me. And her energy made my fine hairs prickle. I couldn't tell if this was a dream or something else entirely.

"Mr. Ross?"

I stared at her.

"Is that really you?"

"What do you mean?" she asked bemusedly, her high voice rather tight.

She always looked a touch annoyed when I managed to confuse her.

"You've never . . . come to me like this before."

Her smooth brow puckered.

"I took what you said to heart."

"Said?"

"What you thought, at least. What you've been thinking all this while. I've become," and she smiled, rather proud of herself, "more actively involved. A concerned citizen, doing what I can to help."

I shifted in my chair, not sure if that sounded like a good idea. But she was apparently trying her best. I felt it wise not to offend her.

"That's . . . that's good of you," I said.

And then I paused, thinking it over.

"What exactly are you doing?"

"Looking for the person Dr. Willets talked about. The Changer of Worlds. But I haven't found anyone like that yet."

It was something that was puzzling me as well. I directed my attention to the matter.

"Does it have to be a person?"

"How so?"

"It might be a thing?"

"No, I don't think so, Mr. Ross. To change a world, you have to want to. There has to be an active will, or what would be the purpose?"

I could see her point. And was impressed by how perceptive she was, for one who looked so very young.

"Maybe such a person wouldn't even know they had the power in them."

Which made her nod vigorously.

"Maybe."

"Or perhaps we just don't *have* a Changer. That sounds like a pretty massive thing. And—for all its strangeness—this is not a big or an important town."

Her face went noticeably sad, the way it might do if you told her that her birthday party had been canceled.

"Yes, that's possible as well. But I'll keep on trying. You're right about that, Mr. Ross. All we can ever do is try."

"Willets doesn't seem to agree. He reckons we're already beat."

"That's never true."

"So there's no Fate, no *kismet*?"

She studied that idea curiously.

"Maybe. Or perhaps there's only what we make."

But then, the speed of her rotations slowed. That only happens when there's something really bothering her. Her expression became very grave. As serious, in fact, as I had ever seen it.

"There is time, though. Nothing we can do can alter that."

Sure. And any way you looked at it, it was a commodity that we were always running out of.

"Faster than you think, Mr. Ross," she told me.

Once again, she'd listened to my thoughts. I'd got used to her doing that, so it did not surprise me. But what she'd said puzzled me. She sometimes speaks in partial riddles, and it's hard to know what she is driving at.

"Faster?" I asked. "How so?"

"If you want to know how powerful Saruak really is, then watch the moon tonight."

And, of all the references she'd made so far, this had to be the most obscure. I didn't have the first notion what she might be talking about.

"The . . . ? What am I supposed to see?"

"His impatience. And the scale of his ability. I'm sorry to tell you this. But if you're wise, you'll watch the moon."

Then she faded, and was gone out of my thoughts. And darkness filled my head again.

CHAPTER 35

It was getting fairly close to evening. The shadows were all stretching. And the sky was gently draining of its color, like blue ink fading in a massive tank.

Cass Mallory had headed west, an hour back, and begun patrolling Marshall Drive. She was heading slowly down the main street, her Harley making blatting noises underneath her as though it were a live animal, annoyed at being held back. She stopped at a corner, resting her boot on the curb.

Bethany Street lay up ahead of her. Cass felt her skin tingle, at the mere idea of going there. Stared in its direction for a moment, and then opted to turn down Gaines instead. She felt her shoulders relax and her breathing lighten, as she moved further away.

It was still there clearly in her memory, that first night she and Ross had found the Little Girl. And . . . bursting into that blue-lit room, gawking at that small, pale figure, just rotating in midair? She'd almost screamed. She'd thought that she was looking at her eldest daughter, Angel, but with fairer hair. A phantom in her shape, perhaps.

Cass had never gone back since. Had resolved not to, and was privately appalled that Ross still did. How on earth could you trust something that looked like a child, but probably wasn't?

Shaking her head briskly, now, she tried to put it right out of her mind.

She didn't believe she'd ever been down this particular street. It was much like all the others in this well-heeled neighborhood. Spacious, leafy, and with sprawling green front yards. Prosperous-looking without being overblown or ostentatious. The trees lining its verges had been neatly pollarded. Ivy clambered up most of the walls.

Out front of one house, there were nesting boxes and a fancy bird table with a thatched roof, a speckled starling perched on it. Down the side of another was a little sailboat on a trailer. It got used at Crealley Street Park, doubtless, or on the river, although the latter didn't really take you anywhere. Cass regarded it with just a touch of sadness. She had never even been on a boat.

Right deep down, she'd always hankered after living in a place like this.

The kids, she thought, would have simply loved it. Proper grass to play on, instead of the dirt out back of the diner. Banisters to slide on, trees to climb in, and a great big room for each of them.

They could have even bought a dog. Oh, wouldn't Cleveland have just loved that? Kevin had always wanted one, and a big one at that, a German shepherd or even a Great Dane. But "we can't have some huge slobbering mutt running around the diner," she had told him.

God, how she regretted that. If she ever got any of them back from wherever they'd gone—she often thought—then she would go down to the pound and get a *dozen* dogs, the biggest, sloppiest ones she could find.

A slight dampness was forming in the corners of her eyes, but Cassie just cruised on, ignoring it. If she spent her whole life dwelling on her past regrets, allowing them to overwhelm her every time they surfaced . . . then she'd never get anything done. And she'd structured her existence, since her family had disappeared, around doing things. Dealing with the problems that arose like mushrooms in this place, perhaps to distract her from her single biggest one.

There'd been an earlier period in her life when she had been like this.

After her parents had died, she had been completely alone. She hadn't got on well with her half sister, Pam, at that stage. There had been few other relatives. There was her folks' house, which was paid for, and a small sum of insurance money. So she'd had somewhere to live, something to eat, at least. But at seventeen, that isn't enough. You need stability, to make up for the inner turmoil. She had none. And so she'd wound up mostly on the streets.

O'Connell was the one that largely bothered her. Because every time she went down there at night, she would invariably run into some drunken older guy who wanted to do stuff with her. Try and touch her mostly. But her dad, as well as firearms, had taught her the basics of judo. So she didn't have all that much trouble fending them off. She carried a knife with her most days anyway. The incidents disturbed her, all the same.

But one bar in particular kept on drawing her attention.

It was simply called The Hole. There was just a red-lit doorway, and a long flight of stairs leading to a basement. She had never been inside. But she had noticed, several times, the small squadron of motorcycles parked outside it beyond ten o'clock. And she had always been attracted to those kinds of machines.

She'd finally steeled herself one evening, and gone down there. She was already tall, and looked older than she was, so it was no real problem.

Grunge music—Nirvana's "Aneurysm"—was playing from a tape deck. And it was so dark she could barely make out where she had wound up exactly. But there were people down there, seven of them, grouped around the bar. And all her age. They had stiffened when she'd walked toward them. But then one of them, a handsome-seeming young man with a close-cropped beard, had grinned at her.

"Who're you, sweetcheeks?" he asked her, in a lazy, throaty drawl.

She had already figured out the best way to approach these people was to be completely straight with them. "I'm Cassie."

He nodded politely.

"Rooster. You look like you're missing something."

"Maybe."

"Can you ride a bike?"

"I'd like to learn."

"Okay, then. I'll teach you." He patted the empty stool next to him. "In the meantime, you can ride on mine."

That seemed a whole lifetime ago. She had changed so much, since then. It wasn't that she'd become more respectable. It was simply that she had more respectable ambitions these days, as she'd recently been proving to herself. Kids changed you that way.

God, it was so quiet around here. That struck at her forcibly, the further she progressed. The whole town, in fact, had seemed at low ebb all day since that ruckus in the square. She'd seen no one run, or shout, create any kind of fuss or upset, all this afternoon. And it wasn't that the people of Raine's Landing usually swung from the nearest lamppost. But they'd seemed unnaturally placid for a good few hours.

Folks had largely finished work by this hour and come home. Lights were appearing in most of the windows surrounding her. She could see potted ferns on the sills, and china figurines. Through one pane, she could make out the portrait of a lady who was finely dressed, looked very cool and dignified.

Most of the driveways that she passed had cars parked on them. Their owners had disappeared indoors. And that had been the last she'd seen of them. No one reappeared to mow the lawn, water the roses. And there were no kids outdoors playing on the sidewalk, riding skateboards, pedaling their bikes.

On a summer's evening like this? She supposed that people were just really scared, after everything that had occurred the past couple of days. But the town seemed more than simply hushed around her. It appeared half dead.

How accurate was that? Cassie wondered. Could the place that she'd grown up in be nearing its End of Days?

The intersection with Beaumont came up, and she paused at it again. Another, vaguer, memory came drifting back into her thoughts. Had she dreamt it? Or had Ross hovered for a while over her bed, last night?

The idea made her throat go stiff. She wasn't quite certain how she felt about something like that. They were firm friends, and almost seemed to think along the same lines sometimes. He was the one person she trusted before anyone else, in fact. And she respected his quiet courage and his keen brain. But beyond that?

All she felt was a strange blankness when she tried to work it out. She'd chosen the wrong men so often—almost infallibly, she was forced to admit. When it came to that part of life, was she even capable of separating good ideas from bad ones?

One of her palms dropped from the handlebars. She looked up, and then stared around.

It was almost grating at her, by this juncture. *All* of the streets. So *very* quiet.

There was no sound in the slightest from the neat houses in her field of view, despite the fact that some windows were open. Not a television. Not a radio. No one was visible. There was not even any barking.

She was nearly at the point where it was starting to alarm her, when she finally heard a voice. Except . . . it seemed to be inside her own head. And she sat up very straight.

"Nothing for you here, Cassandra. Best if you go home."

And, yes. That did seem like a good idea. Cassie's frame relaxed.

Then, she turned her Harley back the other way, and finally gave vent to the throttle.

The roar of its twin-cam engine still hung on the air for a few seconds, after she was gone.

CHAPTER 36

In another hour, the light was beginning to fail properly.

Samuel Howard Aldous Levin—Judge Levin to almost all the town—didn't even switch on his desk lamp. He was seated in his study, which was underneath the gables of his home on Billings Avenue, just off Plymouth Drive. Going to the window, you could see the Vernon residence from here. Except he didn't go there now. He was almost motionless in the gathering twilight.

His hands were clasped around his chin again. His tired eyes gazed into thin space.

My God, he was exhausted. Hadn't slept a wink last night. And as for today? He kept going over the battle with that Saruak character in his mind. He had never come across anything that equaled the experience, the shock of it. Heaven's sake, he had torn at the creature with enormous claws. Felt them rend flesh and part sinew. And the fellow had shrieked with pain, hadn't he?

But then, this new intruder had stood up and laughed about it, like no harm in the slightest had been done. Had the screams merely been a sham? Or was the creature like the surface of a pond? You could disturb it, part its outer skin. But then it simply closed over and calmed down again, like nothing at all had happened.

He had never been made to feel so utterly ineffective. It was far from the most comfortable sensation, wholly alien to him. His family had enjoyed great power in Raine's Landing for so many generations. And, outcast stock though they once had been, they had worked very hard at fitting in, making themselves acceptable.

He let his gaze drift about slightly. Just look at this study, for a case in point.

It was as archetypically New English in its character as any room could be. The furniture was American Classic, as was the china in the tall armoires. A collection of scrimshaw sat behind the leaded panes of glass as well. There were engravings of old-time whalers fastened to the walls, little rowboats after mighty beasts that could smash them with a brief flick of their tails.

There was even a stuffed moose head up above the door, its glass eyes shining down at him. And he didn't even hunt.

He was a gentleman of Massachusetts, then, his ancestors, those tinkers with their strange accents and foreign customs, long ago forgotten. He knew the law from back to front. Had studied the Constitution avidly, and grown to revere it. If anything kept this benighted town sane, it was people like himself—Levin was quite sure of that. It was his *raison d'être*, his whole justification.

Which made what had happened today all the more alarming. It wasn't just a darkness that had seeped into the Landing. It was insanity too, the breakdown of everything rational. And that was a quality more usually confined to the enormous manor further up the road.

He remembered Saruak, sitting in that tree beyond the border, dangling his legs and mocking, chortling. Exactly like some spiteful child, delighted at the mayhem it had caused. You couldn't even reason with a mind like that.

But combined with such enormous power? It was the most dangerous thing he could imagine.

Levin breathed out hard, trying to stop thinking about it for a little while, and totally failing.

The boys—he had two teenaged sons—were very quiet tonight. He couldn't hear a sound from the rooms below him. His wife, he knew, was helping Fran, their cook, prepare this evening's supper. And maybe a good meal would help. But he doubted it. He felt as if his insides had been hauled across some jagged rocks. And his limbs were aching. He was so horribly weary.

Although he couldn't fall asleep, or even doze. Didn't feel like he would ever get to rest his mind again—at least, until this was resolved one way or the other. What to do about it? Saruak was beyond his reach.

At his window, the last chink of daylight glimmered, and then disappeared. A charcoal grayness closed across it. The shadows in the study swelled, completely filling it. Levin didn't even move, just sat there listening to the dull sound of his own exhausted thoughts.

A sudden movement, in the corner of his eye, brought his narrow head swinging around. Had he imagined it? There was no doorway there.

But a figure had just entered the room.

It was tall. He couldn't quite make out its shape, beyond the fact it seemed to have a hat on. Gaspar, maybe? His old friend sometimes dropped in this way, unannounced.

The figure moved forward, and its left eye glinted.

Levin sat bolt upright in his chair.

And then, an icy whisper pushed out from between his lips.

"You!"

By the time that Saruak emerged from the front door, his dog at heel, night had closed its grip completely over Sycamore Hill. Crickets chirped on the summer breeze. Stars had begun to sparkle, and the moon was rising.

He peered up at it, a satisfied smile on his withered face. He had plenty more visits to make tonight. Lots more work to do. But what point was there, if you couldn't stop a moment, savor it all?

He could feel the power coursing through his body, growing stronger as each hour passed. The whole of Raine's

Landing was obsessed with him. The entire *town*, from the oldest to the youngest. Little kids were asking questions that their parents found uncomfortable to answer. Full-grown men were jumping at the sight of their own shadows. And in the older people's homes, the talk was muted when there was any at all, there was a grim air of finality.

Soon, this whole place would be his. But he felt impatience prick at him. Because soon was not really enough.

The moon was full, and rising like some dented silver buoy on a black tide. Its pale glow made his left eye gleam more brightly. He stared at it for another while, then stretched his hands toward its bulk.

He began to turn them in broad circles, clockwise. Sparks leapt from his fingers, crackling through the air. They lit up his face, making it shine. It was almost like he was trying to turn an enormous wheel, one that was invisible.

He threw his body into it, so that his whole frame shook and bucked. The motion grew faster. The atmosphere around him flickered with a bright electric charge. The wind hissed around him, curving past his narrow ribs. His ragged coat lifted, and the brim of his hat flapped.

He stopped abruptly, grinning again, pleased with himself. Because of what?

The sparks all died away. The gusts slowed down.

But next moment, a sound drifted toward him from the direction of Union Square. It was the clock on the Town Hall, ringing the hour. Nine. Although when he had started his hands moving, it had only been eight forty-five.

Saruak looked back at the moon, the way that it was traveling by now, and laughed again. Then he bent down and scratched his bulldog behind one distended ear.

"You see, Dralleg?" he murmured. "What they say is true. Time really does fly when you're having fun."

CHAPTER 37

Something was prodding, pretty hard, at my left shoulder. I dreamt for a moment that it was the Dralleg, jabbing at me with its claws. And, in my dream, lashed out at it.

"Ow! Mr. Devries?"

My eyes came partly open, and the dim lighting of the games room seeped back into my consciousness. Then I focused on the large expanse of midnight blue material— Hampton's uniform—in front of me. His dual-tone eyes were watering when he hunkered down and peered into my face.

"Are you okay, sir?"

He was asking the wrong person.

"Did I hurt you?"

"No."

You couldn't help but rather like a man who told white lies like that. He had a faint mark down one side of his cheek.

Then I looked at my watch, and saw that it was nighttime. There was no other way to tell, in a place like this. I sat upright sharply. How could I have slept so long, with all this going on?

Except I hadn't just been sleeping. There'd been my self-appointed new associate, namely the Little Girl.

Hampton gazed at me like he was wondering what I was thinking about. Then he told me, "Master Raine and the doctor request your presence, sir."

So they had finally come up with something. Or at least I hoped so.

The man had another candle, and he led me back along the blackened, echoing corridors. I thought I could make out a few of the shapes better this time. Wasn't that the Raine coat of arms, a unicorn dueling with a satyr?

A few more candles were shining in the ballroom, when I got there. It was slightly better lit. Hampton paused. I stepped inside.

My gaze fell on Willets immediately. You could see how bloodless his face had become. His eyes looked hollow, there was perspiration on his lip. Whatever else the doctor might be, he was still—deep down—an intelligent, perceptive man. And several hours spent in Raine's company had apparently taken their toll.

He looked quickly around at me, and seemed to deflate a little, like he'd been holding himself very stiffly for a good while now. When you considered all the tangents that his host's mind kept on going off at, I could understand that.

Of Raine himself there was no sign at all, but I was sure that he was still around.

"You kids been having fun?" I asked.

Willets only scowled at me. But a pair of golden eyes came open, just behind his shoulder.

"Oh, tremendous fun, old chum. I really wish I'd got to know the doctor sooner."

Willets pulled the same kind of face as a little boy who had been forced to swallow medicine. I stepped in closer.

"What've you come up with?"

"In the matter of defeating Saruak," Willets told me dryly, "nothing whatsoever, I'm afraid. It's not just physically that we can't reach him. Not even our magic spells extend beyond the borders of this town."

But that didn't apply to him entirely. He hadn't been born here, and was not bound by the curse. So he could walk out any time he liked.

I pointed that out to him. But all he did was stare at me as though I were insane.

"You're proposing I take on a fully fledged Destroyer single-handed?" His hot red gaze filled with displeasure. "Did nothing that I said this morning have the slightest impact?"

"We think," Woody added quickly, trying for once to be diplomatic, "that he might have popped back into town a few times in the last couple of hours."

Popped back . . . what in blazes?

"He was too fast for us, unfortunately," Raine continued.

And he nearly looked apologetic, which was difficult for somebody with such a high opinion of himself.

"He always seemed to choose a moment when our focus was elsewhere. Crafty bugger, I have to say."

They could have confronted him, and had failed to, in other words. The idea of it nagged at me. But I already knew how slippery Saruak could be. I couldn't claim to have made any better headway with him. And both these guys were trying their level best. There was no point taking my frustration out on them.

"So, any idea what he was up to?" I inquired calmly.

That might be a help, at least.

I couldn't even see Raine's shoulders in the dimness. But his head tilted a little when he shrugged them.

"I'm afraid not."

I turned my attention back to Willets. He looked equally at a loss.

"How about tomorrow's ceremony?"

His bitter expression transformed almost—not quite—to a smile.

"Now," he breathed. "That's a different story."

"You wanted proof?" he went on, once he had my full attention. "Well, there's an expression that you probably don't even know. 'I'm from Missouri—show me.'"

I did know it, in fact. But this seemed to be important, so I just let him continue on.

"The best way to prove anything, in other words, is to simply demonstrate it."

Okay, I'd got that.

Then Raine held something up into the guttering candle-light. They were like a pair of performers, it struck me, treating me to some kind of rehearsed show. Whatever he was holding caught the tiny flames, and threw their glow back a dozen times more fiercely. And they were not yellow anymore, but pure white light, broken to a thousand fragments. I was dazzled by it at first, and I glanced away.

But when I managed to look back, I could see it was a large, transparently white jewel, the size of an egg, a symmetrical oblong in shape, intricately cut. A golden chain dangled from one end of it. It was some kind of big pendant, nothing like the one at home.

"It's Greek," Raine informed me. "One of the many artifacts my forebears acquired before they sailed for the New World. It's called the Eye of Hermaneus."

And what did it do? I stared at Willets again.

"The wearer of it," he told me, "can prophesy the future. Which is obviously of little use, since Levin and the others wouldn't take our word for that. So we tinkered with the thing a bit, and managed to adapt its function."

Raine let go of the jewel. It did not fall. It simply lifted higher in the air, till it was drifting above our heads. Its facets seemed to chew the light up and then spit it out. Both of the magicians took a couple of steps back. I followed suit.

"What did they used to call this when I was at school?" Willets pondered. "Ah, yes. Show and Tell."

They spread their arms, and whispered a few words in time with each other, so softly I could barely make them out. But I could hear they were not English, mostly sibilants and lengthened vowels. Like the sounds a gathering storm would make, if it ever came alive and spoke.

The jewel seemed to draw even more light into its depths, but was not letting go of it anymore. We were standing in absolute darkness. The brightness churned at its core, massively compressed, like it was being distilled somehow.

And then it was released, in a wide, shimmering cone that stretched down to the parquet floor.

Within it, a picture coalesced. It was fully colored, fully detailed, but cut hugely down to scale.

I recognized the scene immediately. This, again, was Union Square.

But not as I had ever seen the place. The sun was high in the sky; this was supposed to be tomorrow. It was hours before the ceremony. But the place was already full to bursting. Why was everyone there so early?

They had crammed into the doorways of every last surrounding building, mine included. They were sitting on the roofs of the few cars that were still parked there. There were even people standing on the plinth of Theodore Raine's statue and clinging to his great bronze bulk. I thought there was some kind of bylaw against that.

More of them were trying to get in. The streets that opened out onto the square were uniformly choked. The banners flapped above them in what seemed a very agitated manner. And the few small clouds were drifting overhead rather too quickly. I stared across at the adepts.

"It seems to be," the doctor explained, "a sped-up version of events. We've no real idea why that is."

Raine looked slightly embarrassed at that, but even he could see this was no time for wounded pride.

When I looked back at the pyramid of light, the little yellow sun was moving westward like a bird.

Was there no sound to this? Or was the crowd—a truly massive one—just absolutely silent? They were motionless, all standing very calmly. There wasn't even anyone on stage yet. It struck me as pretty damned bizarre. What had made them gather so far in advance?

I could see a few blue uniforms at the edges of the vast throng. There was no telling if Saul Hobart was present. As for myself, and Cassie . . . ?

I felt rather glad I couldn't make out either of us. That would have been just too weird. I relaxed, and simply watched the scene unfold.

The sun drifted toward the far horizon. Then, as it began to drop, two things happened.

Mayor Aldernay emerged from the Town Hall, flanked by his assistant and his deputies. They went briskly down the steps and up onto the stage.

Then, swift shadows moved across the heavens, all of them coming from the same direction. Gaspar Vernon sprung into being beside the mayor. Then Levin, both of the McGinley sisters, and a smiling, nodding Kurt van Friesling.

A few lesser adepts appeared too. I thought I recognized Cobb Walters from his waistcoat and bow tie. And was that Martha Howard-Brett, the Hill's most elegant beauty?

A huge ripple went through the crowd, and some people applauded, although it turned out that there really *was* no sound. The adepts took it as their due. Vernon and Judge Levin nodded mildly. Kurt and the McGinleys waved. Chairs had been set up for each of them, but none of them sat down.

Aldernay took center stage behind a microphone, produced a sheaf of papers and—so far as I could make out— launched into a speech.

"Fortunately, this is sped up too," Raine murmured.

The sun was halfway down by the time that he had finished, and had turned a harsh crimson. Shadows sprawled across the crowd. Thousands of eyes glinted—hopeful, pleading—in the dimness.

Gaspar Vernon raised his arms. And, on that signal, hundreds of torches were lifted among the throng. Smaller flames were applied to them, and they began to blaze.

I began to see what they were doing. Hadn't there been torches used when Regan Farrow had been burned alive?

Most of the faces looked ghostly in the firelight, like they were already standing in Death's door. And there were other points of brightness appearing in the crowd. Glitters, twinklings, of precious metal and of crystal.

Most people had brought their own magic along, their favorite amulets and charms. The entire, combined potential of the town was there, in other words, all concentrated in one place and focused on one goal.

The sun had almost gone. Up on stage, the adepts formed a semicircle and joined hands.

Then, in the sky above them? There had only been a few small clouds until this point. But a massive one began to form, completely out of nowhere, like a spreading, jet black inkblot on the darkened firmament.

Lightning started to dance within it.

Back behind the adepts, Aldernay pointed at it, his feet almost stamping with excitement.

"You see?" I imagined he was calling out. He gestured at the townsfolk. "It's working! I always *knew* it would!"

The vapor churned, densening even further.

The last ray of sunlight winked away, at the world's edge. But no stars came out.

In the depths of the cloud, Saruak's face appeared, the same way Gaspar Vernon's had done, but far more massive. It was leering down, its eyes ablaze. Another stir ran through the people below, but not of anticipation this time. Mouths came open, and I could almost hear the screams.

His hat was gone, as was his beard. His hair was tied back in a ponytail. His eyes were a bright, sickly green, and the points of his long, sharp teeth glinted when he smiled.

It was a delighted one. He had the town's complete attention, right up close. Which was what he'd wanted all along.

There was a mass of writhing tentacles beneath him. Scaled ones, like I'd seen when he'd revealed himself to me that first time. One of them lashed down and ripped a banner away. Another knocked Mayor Aldernay off his feet and halfway across the stage.

Nobody else was moving yet. The crowd simply couldn't— they were far too tightly packed. And the adepts were just staring up, bewildered and seemingly helpless.

But then fire began to rain down from the blackened sky. And there was pandemonium, after that.

I felt glad that there was no sound, because it would have been plain awful to listen to. The people up on the stage got off quite lightly, since they had a clear run at the Town Hall steps.

But the people below them were a different story. There was a terrified stampede in a bare few seconds. People were pushing in every direction, trying desperately to get out. Small children were being lifted overhead. The weak were already falling.

The whole square began to shake, caught up in the grip of some tremendous earthquake. Splits appeared along the flagstones. Then a chasm, about a yard wide, opened up. That only made the chaos worse. Sections of the crowd were falling into it.

They were too small to make out their faces, but some of them had to be people that I knew. I had to look away a moment.

Willets and Raine muttered a few more words. The glow within the white jewel faded. And the scene, thankfully, went away.

Sweat was running down my face. My mind was still trying to take in what it had seen—a large part of it didn't even want to.

Finally, I peered at my companions. Even Woodard Raine looked grave.

"You have to show this to Levin," I told them.

It was the judge who'd asked for proof this morning, after all. What more did he need? And I trusted him a lot more than the rest of them. Watching this, he'd call the ceremony off, whatever the opposition. He'd demand it.

The jewel on its gold chain was still floating in midair. Willets stepped forward and snatched it down, a determined gleam in his red-flecked eyes.

"I'll do it right away," he offered. "He's at home in his study, and alone."

He dissolved into a murky shadow, vanishing completely.

Which left me alone with Woody in the dancing candle-light. A sad, wistful expression spread across his features, and his golden eyes took on a hint of dampness.

"I wish . . ." he whispered, almost to himself, "I could do more."

I gazed at him. And I had never seen him look quite so ill at ease.

"I wish . . . I could have gone with the doctor, at the very least. It seems ridiculous really, when I think about it. All this power at my fingertips, and I'm afraid to . . . to even . . ."

And then his voice trailed away.

That whole ghastly spectacle—he'd had to watch it twice, I knew—had obviously shaken him. And perhaps even worked something loose inside that crazy head of his. Self-knowledge? Was that possible?

His eyes slipped shut. You could only see a vague shape where he stood. It shuddered, going through some kind of powerful inner torment.

I felt almost sorry for him. But then, I'd be feeling sorry for all of us, if things unfolded in the way I'd seen. Our best hope was the judge, by this hour.

Lehman Willets reappeared.

And announced, "Something's wrong!"

His face was like a detailed map of a place called Dismay.

"I—he—the judge was sitting at his desk, just as I thought. I appeared right in front of him. He didn't even seem to notice me, Devries. He stared right through me. And when I spoke to him, it was like he couldn't hear."

My head reeled slightly as I tried to take that in.

"Was one of his pupils larger than the other?"

Willets's head shook briskly.

In which case, it was really Levin. But his mind had been invaded, just the same way Cassie's had.

"Try the rest," I told the doctor. "Vernon, the McGinleys, anyone who can get this stopped. He can't have gotten to them all."

But could he? There appeared to be nothing stopping him. Willets nodded all the same.

"And you?" he asked me. "How about you?"

"I'm going to visit the judge myself, and try to snap him out of it."

I'd already managed it with Cass, although I wasn't planning to use the same tactics.

But Saruak was holding all of the trump cards. And there had to be something I could do to win a few of the good ones back.

CHAPTER 38

It wasn't too far from here to the Levin residence. But I was in a hurry, so I drove, my route taking me down avenues so lush with greenery they almost resembled public parks.

It was very quiet up here. But then, it usually was. There were no stores, no malls, no movie houses. Plain nowhere for anyone to go. What was it about the rich, I wondered, that made them want to live in neighborhoods defined by their properties and little else?

I drove on through a spidery maze of silver light and shadow. Then remembered what the Little Girl had told me earlier. And so I started glancing upward at the moon. It was sailing high above the gathered branches. And there was nothing wrong with it at all, that I could see. What had she been trying to warn me of?

I came to a hairpin bend, on a lofty ridge in the hill's side. And slowed down a little, gazing at the town beneath me. There was nothing moving on its straight, broad boulevards. No headlamps showed at all. There was no sign of a light in any yard, despite the fact the weather was still warm. Far fewer lights in general, in fact.

No activity up here was one thing. But down among the ordinary people? It might just be that everyone was anxious and afraid. I got a gut feeling, though, that there was something else involved.

That instinct grew worse when I drew up outside Levin's home.

There was no security around it, never had been. No bars or hedgerows or high fences. I suppose he—and his forefathers—had always made a logical assumption. That if anyone was crazy enough to come after them, with all the power that they had, then a few bricks or pieces of iron were not going to stop them.

And besides, it would have looked all wrong. The judge's was the most beautiful wood-built house in the entire town, all eaves and gables and scalloping and flower baskets. The conical turret in the roof even had a weather vane perched on it, an iron cockerel.

A dim light was showing, underneath the tiles up there. And I already knew that it was coming from the study. I'd been up there a few times in my old job, fetching warrants late at night.

No one answered when I yanked on the bellpull. Which was curious, since other lights were on downstairs. I could see them through the leaded windows, despite the fact that the drapes were closed. He had a family and servants, and they couldn't all be out. So why did nobody respond?

I finally got out my pocketknife—feeling a little uneasy doing it—and applied it to the latch. It clicked open after a few seconds. And then I put the blade away, and pulled out my gun instead. The judge would have a blue fit if he saw me waving it around his premises. But I could now feel something like a twitching in my bones. Something wasn't right. And so, there was nothing else that I could think to do.

The murmur of a TV set came to me, as I stepped into the hallway. It wasn't at all loud. They'd still have been able to hear the bell. So why had no one even noticed me?

There were large prints, sketches of the Civil War, on the walls all around me. This town had missed out on that completely. A framed copy of the Declaration of Independence sat behind a pane of glass. And several gleaming flintlock muskets were suspended from brass hooks.

A grandfather clock, more than a century old, clucked to itself over in the far, dim corner.

All of the lampshades here were opalescent, and the lighting very mild, subdued. I edged through the soft mist of it toward the doorway of the living room.

Fleur Levin and her two sons—Thad and Darius, both nearly grown-up—were sprawled across the couch and the matching high-backed chairs, gazing frozenly at the TV screen. Their attention was fixed on . . .

Nothing much at all, in point of fact. A program about home improvements, which I didn't suppose they really needed to watch. It was being broadcast from a small apartment in the Boston area somewhere, hardly the kind of place they might be interested in. All the same, they were staring at it like shopwindow dummies.

I stepped fully into view. But they didn't even seem to take in the fact I was there. Not even when I called to them.

It brought back very unpleasant memories. This was far too much like going into the house next-door to mine, and finding Mrs. McGaffrey, silent, in her chair. Almost exactly the same, in fact. Only the jabber of the show's presenters made it any different.

I could feel my palm becoming slightly damp against the grip of my revolver. And a bug seemed to be crawling down my neck again. Should I try to rouse them, bring them back to life? But that was not what I had come here for.

Quietly, I headed up, then went along the corridor. There were more prints of battles, redcoats against blues this time. The thick, patterned carpet made my footfalls almost silent. The door to Levin's room was closed.

I rapped at it briefly with my knuckles.

"Judge?"

No answer. So I tried again.

"It's Ross Devries."

I went in. Only one small light was on, casting a pool of canary yellow around him. Judge Levin was seated behind a magnificent four-panel cherrywood desk. Its fittings had an almost unreal luster. The lamp sitting on it was a black one, apothecary-style, with a big round shade.

The top was dark green leather—golden scrolling around its edges—the color of which precisely matched the swivel chair that he was seated on. The man was in his rolled-up shirtsleeves—pinstripes, blue on white—his jacket flung behind him and his cufflinks to one side. He was in the act of lighting a long, thick cigar. Smoke swirled around the lamp bulb. His huge diary, also leather-bound, was opened up in front of him. The date of the page that he was looking at was Friday. Tomorrow. Just a few hours away.

Practically today, I told myself.

He didn't look up at me. And maybe he was simply lost in thought. I'd known him get that way before, so I stepped in a little closer.

He *still* didn't notice, despite the fact that I was standing right in front of him. He shifted the cigar to the grasp of his left fingers, then picked up an ornate fountain pen, and began scribbling quickly.

I peered upside-down at the words that he was writing.

They were all the same word, repeated in a constant row in that perfect, copperplate script of his.

Reunion.

I felt a chill run through me.

"Judge?" I tried.

His head remained down and he kept on at it.

"Judge Levin? Can you even hear me?"

I put my gun away. There was no need for it. But . . . what had Saruak done to him?

His hand paused. And his gaze came slightly up. It avoided me completely, going over to the darkened window of the room instead.

"It must all go perfectly," he murmured.

That was not for my benefit. He'd taken on a musing look, and he was talking to himself.

"Not a hitch," he whispered. "Not the slightest small mistake. It's vital, if we are to leave this place."

I'd had enough. If—as with Cassie—physical force was the only way, then that was what I'd have to resort to. I wasn't going to hit the man exactly. But I marched around his desk.

Reached for his starched white collar. I could at least try to shake some sense back into him.

My fingertips passed straight through the linen, without feeling anything there at all.

My shadow was sloping across him, and he didn't even notice that. His gaze remained on the windowpane.

"It must go like clockwork. Must." He sighed. "It is our only hope."

If he seemed completely calm, I felt anything but. My fingers twitched involuntarily, as they withdrew. They felt as if I'd plunged them into an ice bucket. What had just gone on?

Very carefully, I reached out again. Then tried to settle my grip on Levin's narrow shoulder.

It passed straight into his body, although I could still see it. My hand and the corner of his shoulder looked superimposed, two images drawn on glass and laid across each other. And I could still feel nothing there. No resistance in the slightest, not even the faintest pressure. Was Levin really here at all?

The cigar continued smoldering in his left hand. I reached across and dabbed at it. And I could smell the smoke. It was real enough.

So was the pen, when I brushed my fingertips across that. Perfectly solid, cool enamel. Judge Levin seemed oblivious to everything I did. But if he was an illusion, then I couldn't see how he could hold real objects. It just wasn't possible. So I tried to touch the man again.

I passed my palm across his gaze first. His eyes didn't waver, holding on the window. I seemed totally invisible to him.

Then, cautiously, I set my fingers against the side of his face.

Or tried to. Like before, they went right through.

His attention dropped back to the diary. And he started writing something else. It wasn't just a single word, repeated, this time. It was a message that was being spelled out. And not his words either, at a guess.

Having a problem, Mr. Devries? it asked.

I looked around quickly, but there was no sign of the Manitou.

Levin's hand continued moving.

Maybe the people in this town have stopped believing in you. They believe in me, though . . . utterly.

Which told me all I really needed to know. Levin was still with me. But was totally in Saruak's grasp.

And there seemed to be no way that I could wrest him out of it again.

CHAPTER 39

Outside . . . another minute, and I couldn't wait to get outside. We might have had our disagreements in the past, but I couldn't bear to see the judge like this. A massively smart man, of shrewd and independent thought, rendered to a puppet and an implement.

A substantial man in every way, made wholly insubstantial.

I stumbled out onto the porch. My head hurt from the pressure in my temples. And I reached for the cigarette pack in my pocket, but didn't complete the motion.

The fragrance of night-blooming honeysuckle, from the trellises on the facade, swept over me, but only made things worse. The cloying sweetness filled my head and made me want to vomit. I stepped down onto the clippered front lawn, trying to escape the smell, and pressed my eyelids shut.

Was *I* the one who was losing it? Or worse, was I already lost, drifting on a sea of passing time, with a sharp reef—my final moments—looming up ahead of me?

Then I took in something else. I didn't like magic, no. But—whatever problems this town had faced in its checkered past—it had always relied, and been able to fall back upon, the powers of its adepts.

Without them, what was there left? Me? Just one man with a gun?

I suddenly felt terribly alone, even more than I had during the past couple of years. This was a different thing, like being completely severed from the life that I had known. There was a horrible inertia to it, like I'd dropped abruptly from the edge of a great cliff.

A sudden gust of wind made my head lift and my eyes come back open. And I looked at the night sky once more. There was another thin dusting of cloud up there. Some of the stars were obscured. But I could see the moon clearly enough. And I kept on going over what the Little Girl had said to me.

I squinted puzzledly. There seemed nothing odd or different about it. Just the same old moon that had shone down on the Landing since I'd been a kid, as familiar as one of my own hands.

And then I saw what the problem was.

My God, was the motion of the clouds deceiving me?

I watched closer, and became convinced that that was not the case. And why hadn't I noticed this before? I'd been in my car, that was why. I too had been traveling at speed. And because of that, I hadn't seen . . .

The moon was drifting through the blackened heavens like some great spherical zeppelin. You couldn't call it hurtling exactly, but I could now see that it was moving far too quickly. Completing its celestial arc at much too fast a rate.

As I watched, it reached its zenith, and then started coming down the other side.

My heart thudding, I looked at my wristwatch. The second hand was turning twice as quickly as it ought to. And the minute hand was following along like some dog on a tight leash.

I had believed—until this moment—that we had almost a day left before the ceremony. That we still had time to come up with something, even though I wasn't quite sure what.

It seemed that Saruak wasn't even going to allow us that.

He had already taken over nearly the whole town. And by this stage in the proceedings, even time itself was bending to his will.

I watched the big mottled disk slipping down toward the far horizon. And could almost hear the spirit's laughter, ringing through my head again.

Willets had returned to the Manor, when I got back there. He had noticed what was going on as well. And the realization had thrown him into a blue funk.

He was pacing the ballroom furiously, his hands knotting and unknotting and his head tucked down. And he kept on mumbling to himself. I'd not seen him this agitated in a while.

Was it possible that he was awed as well, or even humbled? What Saruak had just achieved—not even the doctor could pull something like that off.

"The same happened at every house I went to," he told me. The red of his pupils glinted.

"Vernon, van Friesling. Hell, the sisters. Tried to touch them, just like you did. Tried to use some of my own powers on them—it didn't work. I even visited old Lucas Tollburn. He was fast asleep, and there was nothing I could do to wake him up."

For his own part, Woody had become extremely quiet and still again. His eyes remained open, shining in the dark. His gaze seemed to be very tightly focused, as though he were concentrating, hard, on something just in front of him. But there was nothing there at all, at least, that I could see.

I started to become alarmed. Could Saruak have gotten to him as well. But no. He blinked, next second. He had simply been musing.

"I wonder," he murmured. "Is it they who have become like ghosts, impossible to touch? Or is it us?"

So far as I could figure out, it didn't really matter either way. But he'd just put his finger on something, hadn't he?

"Why *not* us?" I pointed out. "How come everyone in town, even the strongest, is under his power in some way, and the three of us are still operating freely?"

Or maybe we were just kidding ourselves. It might only be an illusion that we were. But I explained to them my gut feeling, about the general quietness that had gripped the Landing.

Willets nodded. "Yes, I sensed that too."

I took out my cell phone. As I had expected, Raine inclined his head toward it and then looked unhappy.

"Sorry, but I've got to do this."

And he nodded.

"Perfectly all right, under the circumstances."

Even he could see how serious this was. He still squinted uncomfortably as I punched the speed-dial button. And he murmured something about thumbs. By the pricking of them, perhaps?

Cassie answered on the second ring, which seemed to indicate she was still *compos mentis*.

"You okay?" I asked.

"Fine, unless there's anything that I don't know about."

"Where are you?"

"At home."

Her voice sounded as lively as it usually did, no hint of torpor in it. So whatever had overcome the rest of the Landing wasn't affecting her either.

"Anything much happening down there?"

"Down . . . where are *you*?"

I told her, and she made her usual grumbling noise.

"It's quieter than a funeral home on Christmas Day," she told me. "I keep hoping that's a good thing."

Which was setting too much store by hope. I brought her up to speed with what was going on, warned her to be on her guard, then dialed another number.

Saul was at the station house, and in his office. He too picked up on the second ring.

"Hobart," he announced.

Just saying his name, he sounded anxious. Glad, perhaps, of something new to occupy his mind.

"What's up?" I asked him.

"Ross? Where did you get to?"

"I've been busy. Magic stuff. And you?"

"Precisely the opposite. There's nothing going on—except the clocks are moving faster."

"Yes, I know. How are your guys?"

"Meaning what exactly?" he asked.

His tone was wary straightaway. The safety of his people was always one of his top priorities.

"Do they seem . . . well, normal?"

"They're in limbo. Simultaneously tense and bored as hell, if that's what you're referring to. Otherwise, they're perfectly okay."

He paused.

"You know what this feels like to me? The proverbial calm before the storm. And I left my umbrella at home this morning."

Yeah, I knew the feeling.

Once I'd rung off, Willets put his two cents in.

"I think I know what's happening. And it's all down to our visitor's psychology. His frame of mind."

Okay, Sigmund Freud, I thought. *Let's hear it.*

He peered hard at me, unamused.

"What use is a victory, without anyone to watch it happen? What use a triumph without someone else experiencing defeat? The way this Saruak's mind works . . . he's a gloater, yes?"

I nodded. I'd had plenty of that from him.

"So this is his way of saying, 'You are the most important here. You are the controlling forces, the authorities, the powers-that-be. And still, you cannot stop me.'"

He had left us twisting in the wind, in other words. Incapable of doing anything but watching.

"For heaven's sake," Raine muttered. "This is ludicrous. There must be something . . . ?"

But if there was, I couldn't think of it. And neither, by their expressions, could the others. Willets just looked blank. Raine had an expression on his face like he was astonished something of this nature could descend on him at all.

All three of us were lost for words. The candles in the ballroom kept on flickering. But there was no other movement.

CHAPTER 40

It was, quite literally, the shortest night of my whole life. Although in a lot of ways, the longest one as well. I got no sleep at all. How could I possibly? I spent most of my time out on the mansion's sprawling porch.

The moon had disappeared completely. It had sunk so rapidly from view, it might have been trying to run away from this town and its troubles. But most of the clouds had gone as well. The sky was clear and filled with stars. And they were moving too. Not so quickly, but they wheeled against the heavens in a graceful and ethereal ballet. Billions of years old, they were, and I felt very insignificant beneath them. Just a minuscule, dim spark. And one that might, before much longer, be snuffed out completely.

Every so often, I would go back in and check up on the adepts. They had given up on magic spells. After all, look how far that had gotten us. And were doing what the Little Girl had already begun—searching for some other power, unknown, that might help us in these final hours.

It was like they were asleep, but standing up. Raine in particular looked odd that way. Their brightly pigmented eyes were closed. Their hands were spread out to the sides, and their heads leant slightly backward.

If they'd found anything, it wasn't apparent, since their faces were still barren of expression.

How rapidly was time progressing? The hands of my watch were still turning at the same accelerated rate. But as to exactly *how* fast? I had nothing to measure it against, since every timepiece—Hampton's watch, a clock out in the hallway—had all sped up in the same way.

I wandered back outside, looked eastward.

The blackness of the sky had phased to an increasingly pale charcoal, steely-edged along its base. And I had seen those hues a thousand times before. The gradual approach of dawn. The nearness of the sun out on the distant, low horizon.

But I had never till this morning seen it all happen so fast.

The silver spread, then turned to a pale lemon shade. That deepened as I watched.

A ray of golden light sprang up. And then . . .

It had always been a joyous thing, watching that intensely bright disc start to reappear. But this time, as its top edge came boiling up, I felt my insides clench.

Long shadows were cast at first, so that the ground was dark even in newborn daylight. But the sun came rushing up behind them like a juggernaut. A thousand windows shone with its brightness. Color flooded out across the landscape. There was a load of green down there, a lot of brown and red roofs, and the big lake glinted blue.

The town remained as motionless as it had been all night. No kids on bikes appeared, delivering newspapers. Nobody emerged to walk their dog. The little oblong dots of cars sat unused on their driveways.

But then, finally, I spotted someone who'd come walking out. He or she—it was impossible to tell from this far away—moved along the front of a short row of houses, over by Crealley Street Park. Paused for a few seconds on the sidewalk, and then started heading for Union Square.

Others were joining in, before much longer. All over the town, people were emerging and then heading in the same direction. They seemed to move mechanically. It was almost like watching ants at work. The bottom edge of the sun had cleared the horizon, and I looked back at my watch.

Seven o'clock already, dammit. Were the hands moving even faster, or was that just my frame of mind, lending them some extra impetus?

The first person I'd seen emerge had almost reached the square. Entered it a minute later, going around the barriers that had been set up, walking at an even speed, moving toward the stage. The figure came gently to a halt, in front of it. Then settled down, and moved no more.

I went back inside and managed to rouse Willets.

"Can you see what's happening?"

"Yes, I can! Just leave me be!"

He couldn't affect it in any way. That was what was making him so angry. All that he was capable of was trying to find someone else who could.

About a dozen tiny dots were clustered on the flagstones, when I went outside again. And here was another unpleasant surprise. A bus was rolling up from the far suburbs, trundling to a halt on the corner near the public records office. It seemed to be full. All the passengers started disembarking.

There was nothing I could do about it either, I kept on telling myself.

Hell, there was *definitely* nothing I could do from up here. All this going on, and I was just sitting around?

I headed for my car.

I was forced to slow down when I reached the streets leading directly into the square. They were absolutely *full* of people, all walking at the same even pace, and gazing in the same direction. Flowing like a river around the lampposts and mailboxes. Going past the stores and eateries as though they were not even there. And not all of them, by any means, were sticking to the sidewalks.

Apart from the fact that this was starting to look like a jaywalkers' convention, there was nothing odd I could see about any of them, in spite of their behavior. They had, apparently, got up and washed and shaved, or combed their hair. Got neatly dressed. Then simply come down here, like they had some kind of appointment. Not a single one of them looked troubled. Not a single one of them, I noticed too, was making any sound.

More were arriving all the time. Another bus went trundling by. I wound my window down and gazed at the faces behind me, dozens of them. They didn't look transfixed in any blank-faced kind of way. Rather, like Judge Levin, they seemed thoughtful. Placid and even slightly expectant. Like—it struck me—they were hoping for good things to emerge from this particular day.

A community of passive wishful thinkers, then. That was what these people had become. And there were finally so many of them, I was forced to abandon my car, get out and walk myself.

I finally reached Union Square. The barriers had all been pushed aside. And I could feel my eyes widen as I stared around.

It had only taken me a matter of minutes to get down here. But in that time, hundreds more had arrived. They had all sat down on the hard, smooth flagstones. Their eyes were raised, as one, toward the empty, waiting stage.

There were townsfolk of all ages and professions. Workmen in jeans and overalls. Guys in smart gray suits. High school kids in T-shirts. And the women were got up in everything from sweats to floral dresses.

I recognized our postman, some of the people who worked at Jacklin's Family Restaurant, a couple of regulars from the diner I frequented. And there were Joe Norton and Jack Stroud.

The square, despite their numbers, was not anywhere near filled up as yet. As I said, it's a pretty large one. But newcomers were flooding in the entire time. They were arriving from all of the surrounding avenues, and pouring in a steady stream across the bridges on the Adderneck.

There were whole families, I could see. Little kids being led by the hand or carried. And *they* were completely silent too, which was the eeriest thing of all.

I caught sight of Saul Hobart with a couple of his men, over by my office building's doorway, so I made my way across to him. He was slack-jawed, and his pupils glittered with astonishment.

"What the hell are they doing?" he asked. "The ceremony's not till eight."

Which was not so far away as it had once been, and he fully understood that.

"They're being controlled by Saruak," I told him. "The whole town is, even most of the high adepts."

He cursed quietly. He had obviously been afraid that was the case.

"There's something else you have to do. Once the ceremony starts, there's going to be a big stampede."

You'd have thought I'd just grown an extra head. "There's what?"

"Everybody's going to try and leave here, all at once. Not without good reason. And these"—I gestured—"are just the start of it. There's going to be thousands more, the entire square filled to bursting."

He gave me a look that asked, *How do you know any of this?* Which hardly mattered, right now. If we got out of this in one piece, I would explain it to him then.

"Listen, you've got to get the streets around here all cleared out, and I mean completely. Every obstruction. Every parked car. The mailboxes, if you can. Anything that people can be crushed against. It's vital, Saul."

His gaze flickered again. He'd already told me from whom he didn't take instructions. But I kept on remembering, vividly, that final scene the white jewel had revealed, and I wasn't in any mood to argue.

"Hundreds will be trampled otherwise. For God's sake, would I steer you wrong about something like this? Can you afford to take that risk?"

It must have been my tone of voice. His expression got all furrowed up. He stared across the growing crowd perplexedly.

And then he said, "I'll get right on it."

His head ducked, and he began consulting on his phone.

A familiar deep growling brought my head around. Cassie

had arrived, and was picking her way through the clumps of people on her Harley, taking care to steer wide of the littler kids. Her expression was the same as Saul's had been. She seemed to half believe she was hallucinating all of this.

"What *is* this?" she called out as she reached me.

I quickly outlined what was going on.

"And your highfalutin friends up on the Hill can't do anything about it?"

I described everything that I'd been doing since we'd last met up. When I told her about Levin and the rest, she whistled. Saruak had finally impressed her, I could see.

"I *knew* those nuts would be no use," she came back at me, loudly. "And what the *hell's* a Changer of Worlds, when it's at home?"

Apparently, it wasn't. I was pretty sure, by this stage, we had no such being in our town. In which case, the others were going down a route that was entirely pointless.

Cassie chewed the whole thing over, and seemed to come up with something. Like I've said, she can be pretty shrewd.

"The bum who made my kids . . . you know. He certainly changed *my* world. Have you thought of that?"

I hadn't, until now. Perhaps I'd shied away from the idea. But she was right, so I gave it some consideration.

The guy who she was talking about? She'd only ever mentioned his name once, and it had been when she'd been pretty drunk. Tom Larson. I'd known the man. I had arrested him for burglary one time. And he had *definitely* turned her world upside-down, the same way Jason Goad had done to mine.

But my mind rebelled against the whole idea. It *couldn't* be either of them. Apart from any other matter, they had both completely disappeared, in the self-same moment that our families had.

Something, though, was murmuring, deep in the background of my thoughts. Something . . .

No. I wasn't sure. I couldn't put my finger on it yet.

We both gazed out across the square. The sun had climbed

above the Town Hall roof. The flags there cast gently drifting shadows, just the same way that the banners were doing with the crowd. There were a few white clouds up in the sky beyond them, just as I had seen back at the Manor. A lazy breeze was towing them along.

About a hundred more people had arrived and sat down, by the time that I looked back.

They didn't move at all. If they were even blinking, it was hard to tell. Their gazes all shone dully in the sunlight. Did they know that we were there at all?

I wondered what was going through their minds. Perhaps they could hear Saruak's voice, telling them that everything would be just fine. The ceremony would work. They'd be out of Raine's Landing by late evening.

They remained completely motionless, and looked comfortable enough, in spite of the hard stone that they were sitting on. For all the world like they were waiting for a concert to begin.

But there would only be one instrument, I knew. The Final Trump.

"Maybe I could scare them up a little, fire some shots into the air?" Cass suggested.

But that didn't sound like too much of a good idea. I was trying to think of a better one, when a harsh bark of a laugh rang out.

I recognized it straightaway, and swiveled around in its direction.

Saruak was marching toward me from beneath the shadows of the stage. How long had he been there, skulking in his leery way? Or had he just arrived? Once again, there was no way to tell.

The tattered hems of his coat flapped. There were threads hanging from its edge that almost reached the ground. His boots looked grimier than before, from his trip to the great outdoors. His hat still covered half his face in obfuscating shade.

The Dralleg was shambling along at his heels, hunched over and snuffling. Its claws were out. I felt a sharp pang of unease, watching it move through all these helpless, placid folks. It could easily repeat what it had done on that bus yesterday, re-creating all that mayhem twenty-fold or more.

But it seemed to just ignore the humans. Its green eyes were duller in the sunlight, and the thing looked rather witless, with no real intelligence of its own. Its gaze was fixed on its master's back, and it stuck closely to him, the same way that it had done in its bulldog form.

"You're like a fly, a bluebottle, all buzzing and pesky, Mr. Devries!" Saruak shouted. "You just keep showing up in the same annoying manner!"

He seemed to think about that, and then grinned unpleasantly, displaying the off-white spikes of his teeth.

"I've put up with it long enough. I think the time has come to finally swat you."

CHAPTER 41

His voice was as coarse and dry as ever, ringing with contempt and spite. And he didn't sound even remotely like he was kidding this time. I remembered just how powerful he'd already become, and felt my body draw away from him.

Which was more than you could say for Cass. She had already stepped over to her bike. She snatched her carbine up. And, between one heartbeat and the next, was aiming it.

I lunged across and caught hold of her elbow.

"Cassie, no!"

She looked around at me, slightly annoyed at first.

"With all these people around? Jesus!"

Her expression told me that she saw my point. Her eyes narrowed frustratedly. But she started moving back with me, as quickly as we could, to the edges of the crowd.

Out of the corner of my eye, I saw Hobart and his men start to come to life as well, moving toward us. I just held a palm out flat, signaling to them to remain where they were. And, thank God, they took the hint, although Saul did it pretty grudgingly.

"Trying to *run*?" Saruak called to me.

His dusty boots thumped on the flagstones. He seemed heavier than he had been. And it wasn't just a matter of him putting on physical weight.

"You forget, Mr. Devries. There is nowhere *to* run, thanks to this fascinating curse of yours. You're like a goldfish in a bowl, and you can only go in circles."

He leaned his head a little to one side.

"Think of me as a big cat, about to dip its claws in."

He was mixing his metaphors slightly, but no matter. I had got used to these snarling, mocking diatribes of his. And paid what he was saying very little real attention. What I *was* noticing, as he advanced, what struck at me most forcibly . . .

Was the effect that he was having on the crowd around him. All these waiting townsfolk.

Nothing had seemed to impinge on their attention, so far. Nothing we had done had made them look around, or even stir. They'd simply sat there, peering up at the empty stage, their faces pensive and their eyes like tarnished glass.

But right now?

It wasn't that they looked directly at him. Their expressions stayed impassive, and their eyes remained locked on the stage. But their faces . . . they turned slightly in his direction as he passed. Mouths hardened a little. Thoughtful creases appeared in otherwise placid brows. As though they had just heard a sound, a voice, much too far away to understand what it was saying.

They were noticing him, in other words, but not on any fully conscious level. They were like somnambulists. And he was a figment in the dreamworld they had entered.

The Dralleg was another matter. People didn't shift their heads toward the thing at all. No gazes went in its direction, despite its enormous bulk. It might as well have been invisible, stalking along behind its master, dragging its heavy limbs.

But the sun was halfway up to its peak. The creature cast an elongated shadow. And as that darkness swept across the crowd, their features became stony. Their shoulders hunched, a little like its. Their gazes became vaguely anxious. And a few small children stood up and looked almost on the verge of crying, except that not a whimper could be heard.

I recalled what the Little Girl had said. "An expanding

and engulfing nightmare." That was how she'd described the spirit as his powers grew. And his monster was a part of that, the venom in the scorpion's tail.

The Manitou voiced the threat. And his creature provided most of the muscle with which to back it up. They'd been a team so far, I could see, each depending on the other.

I knew that my hopes of doing Saruak any genuine harm were limited. He had already grown stronger than I could have imagined, just a couple of days back. But me and Cassie had already hurt the Dralleg several times. And I knew we could repeat the trick. So I began to consider the possibility of taking the damned thing down for good. Between us, I was certain we could manage it.

That would put its master's nose badly out of joint, at least. And I'd pay good money to see that happen.

We were still backing away through all the seated, hunkered figures. We had almost reached the outer edge. Were not having to step so carefully, and were beginning to speed up.

Townsfolk were still coming in and drifting blankly past us, sure. But a few more seconds, and we'd be pretty much out in the open. We'd have a chance of fighting back without too many civilians getting caught up in the crossfire.

Cassie realized the same thing. I saw her knuckles stiffen on the dark grips of her carbine.

We fell into step together, taking the final paces back in almost perfect unison.

But where to make our stand?

"Sidewalk," I muttered. "Up behind us."

And she nodded briskly, getting what I meant.

"Now!"

The word was still dropping from my lips, when I just turned around and sprinted. Cassie did the same. From behind us came another bark of laughter. Saruak thought that we were trying to get away from him. I just ignored him, kept on going, slipping around a few more inward-coming folks.

My shoes and Cassie's black boots hit the curb at the exact same time. We both wheeled around again, took one more backward step.

And then, mainly because we had no other place to go, we drew ourselves up and stood our ground.

Saruak, as he had done from the start, looked cruelly amused by our antics. He kept pushing on toward us at the same unbroken rate. The smirk across his lower face was like a big, loosely healed scar.

There had to be *some* way he could be thrown off balance, at the very least.

"Stand or run, Mr. Devries," he was snarling. "Make your mind up, one way or the other. I'm easy because, either way, it'll make no difference in the least."

Way off behind him, I could see, Saul had drawn his weapon and was squinting down the muzzle of it. Both his men had followed suit. They hadn't done anything apart from that, were just holding themselves at the ready, waiting to see if their help was going to be needed.

Not a single other person was looking in our direction. There was more than half the town here, and there might as well have only been the seven of us.

My attention returned to the Manitou. He drew up to within two yards of me, and finally stopped. The Dralleg stayed behind him, the same way it had the last time. It was like a wide, distorted shadow of the man himself. I could hear it growling faintly underneath its breath. But it made no attempt to get at us.

I supposed that it would do whatever its master wanted. Would attack us in an instant, if he told it to. So, whatever Saruak had planned for us this time, maybe he was planning to do it himself.

That big left pupil of his glinted at me, once again. Half in shadow as they were, those narrow, bearded features of his looked like two sections of different faces, one light and one dark. It served to remind me he was not a man at all. In which case, why'd his body aged? I had not thought of that before.

His nostrils flared. His lips skinned back a little from his sharply pointed teeth. His pale eyes studied me curiously, drinking in the sight of me all over again. You'd think that he'd never even seen me before. What *was* it about me that fascinated him?

His left hand started coming up, the long fingernails curling. But then he seemed to think better of it, let his whole arm swing back down. There were liver spots on the back of the palm, I noticed. Just how long had he been in human form?

His stare intensified a little. It was almost as if he was searching for something in *my* eyes, on my own face.

I seemed to . . . what was it exactly? Seemed to puzzle him. I kept on thinking of the way that he'd come after me. Concentrating on me. Probing at me, when there were far more significant individuals in town.

He was somehow being drawn to me, again and again, like I posed some kind of riddle he could not completely solve. Why *was* that? I was just a simple man, with no mystique, no magic. Was it the sheer lack of that which kept him coming back to me?

But I couldn't see what sense that made.

His gaze hardened next moment. It grew flinty, rather bored. If I was a puzzle to him, then he seemed to give up on it.

"How many people would just stand here, nose to nose with me?" he hissed. "Foolishly courageous to the last, Mr. Devries."

"If you say so."

"Oh, I do, I do!"

His pallid irises flicked slightly to the side.

"You know, I think that when I've killed you, I will keep this nasty little girl you drag around behind you for my own amusement. Nice long legs, I see."

He was about to add something more, when a triple-thud broke across him. Three tightly grouped holes, smoldering a little at their edges, had appeared in the front of his coat, pretty much where his heart ought to be.

I looked around. Cass had dropped her carbine to her hip, and let off a burst at point-blank range. It was probably the remark about her legs that had pissed her off. She has no sense of humor about things like that.

The slugs should have lifted Saruak up off his feet. But the Manitou didn't even rock. Didn't even wince, in fact. The holes in the fabric were the only damage he'd sustained.

His lean face snapped toward her. Even Cassie froze beneath his gaze. The muzzle of her carbine was still smoking. It was the only movement that I was aware of. Everything seemed frozen in place.

"Very spiteful!" he complained.

The muscles in her arms went tense. Her dark eyes didn't waver, boring into his.

"Look what you've done to my coat!"

When he saw she wasn't going to reply, he returned his baleful gaze to me.

"You've done better than you ought so far, with this one by your side," he told me.

And what was he going to do with her?

"Let's see how you manage without dear Cassandra."

Without even thinking about it, I started pushing forward. If I could only get close enough to take a decent swipe at him. I'd fight him to the death before I let him hurt her.

Saruak extended his right palm. I staggered to a halt. Both of my legs had turned rigid at the knees. And I could not go forward any more, however hard I tried to. It was like being trapped in an invisible cage.

He raised his left arm toward Cass. And, at first, the hand was balled into a fist, all bony knuckles and thick veins. It didn't stay like that for very long. He extended a grimy index finger.

Raised it.

Cassie let out a frightened yelp as she followed the motion, lifting off the ground.

In an instant, she was at head height, as if she'd been suspended there by strings. Her boots were kicking, a couple of feet in front of my face. She was wriggling wildly, like a small fish, hooked.

She tried to bring her carbine back to bear, but lost her grip. It came whirling down, clattering on the sidewalk.

Saul and his people started edging in our direction again, but I waved them off a second time. Although I still couldn't go any further forward, however desperately I tried. I could only stare helplessly at Cassie, shocked by the horrified expression on her face.

"Let her *go*! It's *me* you're after!"

"Altruistic to the last." He grinned.

Cass drifted a little closer to me. I tried to stretch out, grab hold of her ankle. But the fingers of his right hand twitched. And suddenly, my arms were pinned down by my sides, I couldn't even lift them.

When she saw I couldn't help her, her whole manner changed. Fright gave way to renewed hate. She drifted slightly to the right, till she was staring down at the guy's battered hat. She spat down at it defiantly, then let out a stream of language that she'd definitely not learned at any Sunday school.

Saruak peered up at her, mimicking shock, although his eyes were laughing.

"Such a lack of manners. Such a load of hatred too. But you're mistaken, dear Cassandra. Try to see things from my point of view."

He abruptly made a sweeping motion with his arm, a high arc through the clear, bright air. And—she was howling again, and I couldn't blame her—Cassie's body followed it. She went sailing off into the heavens, all her long limbs flailing. Ice replaced the blood in my whole body. I was certain he was going to let her fall.

But that didn't turn out to be what he had planned for her. He was simply showing off his powers again. Cass went hurtling right over the square, the podium, the flapping banners.

She wound up on the high, gray-green roof of the Town Hall, where he'd been yesterday morning.

So he hadn't killed her. Maybe he was serious about keeping her when I was gone.

I could hear the rattle as her boots hit slate. She only paused a short while, crouching, getting back her breath. It was hard for her to take in what had happened. Then she straightened, and began casting around for the best way down from there.

She was probably safe for the time being at least. I felt the pressure in my chest relax a little. Off to the side of the square, Saul was pointing, shouting orders to his men. They holstered their weapons, then ran across to help her, sprinting up the Town Hall steps.

They disappeared inside. So I looked back at our visitor, our grim tormentor.

But his back was turned to me. Perhaps, for the moment, he'd forgotten all about me. He was gazing at the high roof, watching Cassie move across it. And the spectacle seemed to fill him with malicious glee. His shoulders were quivering with silent laughter. Damn him. I had never hated anyone more.

I noticed that my arms had started moving slightly once again. And when I pushed hard, I found that I'd regained the ability to move forward. I *had* just dropped beneath his radar, hadn't I? I seemed to have slipped from his attention temporarily.

Perhaps I ought to draw my own gun, press it to his skull. And keep on firing till it was empty. I doubted it would do any more good than Cassie had. But maybe I ought to try.

Then I remembered something else.

I still had a pocketknife on me, the one I'd used to break into the judge's home. Would I do any better with that, if I took him by surprise?

The Dralleg was peering in the same direction he was. It was like the thing responded to, obeyed, his every thought.

As gently as I could, I pulled the knife out and unfolded it. And then, I stepped forward. And plunged the metal into Saruak's neck, driving it right in through the spine.

There was no blood. And there was no response at all, except the mildest shudder.

Saruak's gaze was toxic as he took in what I'd done, and swiveled around.

CHAPTER 42

He reached swiftly around and yanked the blade out—it was still completely clean. Then tossed it to one side with a dismissive flick of his wrist. It had been a useless gesture, but I still felt glad I'd done it.

"I'm disappointed in you, Mr. Devries," his voice rang out. "You pretend to be some kind of paragon, an upholder of order. And then—hypocrite that you are—you try a stupid trick like that, just like some common thug."

He began taking a step toward me, then seemed to think better of it. What was holding him back?

I forgot about him for a moment, glancing up over his head. Cassie was still trying to find her way down from the roof. There had to be one, or else how did the flags get raised and lowered? But it was probably a concealed hatch, she hadn't come across it yet.

As I watched, she went up to the guttering, which had never looked that steady. Then slipped her lower body out into the void, making desperate kicking motions, trying to grab a drainpipe with her legs.

My teeth ground. *For God's sake!* She was so anxious to get back down here it was making her even more reckless than usual.

I wanted to help her. But Saruak and his creature stood

between us. I had to get around them first. It wasn't exactly going to be an easy job. I fixed him with what I hoped was a discriminating eye.

"Seriously, why not come and get me?"

He drew himself up rather proudly, pulling both his shoulders back and puffing out his chest.

"I, who have lived so long and caused so much destruction? Should I even dirty my hands, dealing with a pest like you? I think not. This is one job that I'm going to delegate."

I took a step back, not liking the sound of that at all. The Dralleg had turned to me as well. It seemed more alert than it had been before. A rumbling was coming from its throat, and its luminous eyes were pinned on me intently.

Saruak's gaze shone brightly, and the skin around his cheeks had taken on a little extra color. Oh, he was enjoying this.

"How do you plan to win this time," he asked, "without your little friend around?"

The humor left the features, and he bared his teeth again. His arms spread a few inches from his sides.

I glanced briefly back up at the Town Hall roof. Cass was trying to do something pretty stupid with the ropes around the flagpoles. But one of the cop's heads had now appeared, thank God.

Saul Hobart had moved halfway toward us by this time, his legs apart, his gun still out in front of him. I tried to signal to him with my eyes. *Don't interfere. Stay back.*

"You end here, Mr. Devries!" Saruak was saying, yanking my attention back. "Well, any last words?"

I pulled a face. "What difference does it make?"

"You're quite right. No difference at all."

All his cool triumphalism vanished like a morning mist. He seemed to breathe outrage and petulance.

I was already moving away from him. There was a lightness to my step there had not been before. A lithe springiness, my heels barely touching the ground. The fingers of both my hands were all curled up and twitching.

Saruak swung around and faced the Dralleg. And then pointed in my direction, siccing the thing on me.

And I started to run.

I'd never gone so fast in my life, as though a storm were after me. The Adderneck bobbed up ahead. As did the Iron Bridge, still full of approaching people.

But here's the odd thing. When it had first appeared today, shambling along behind its master, only the Dralleg's shadow had caused people to react.

Now that it was active, moving at full speed, a sudden shock went through the citizens around us. Again, it wasn't that they looked at it directly. But it was almost like they sensed the creature. Were aware of it as a strong vibration. Felt the violence of its motion, like a rumble of thunder out of nowhere. And it affected how they were behaving.

Those who were about to mount the bridge paused, looking uncertain what to do. Those at the end stepped quickly off. The others, spaced along the middle, all shrank back to allow us through.

And once again, thank God for that. The thought of the creature getting in among those spellbound people—I'd do anything to avoid that.

The Dralleg was right up behind me. I could hear its pounding tread, and almost feel its breath hissing across my neck. There was suddenly a high-pitched singing noise back there, the air being parted. I lurched forward hard, almost stumbling over. Something brushed against my collar, but did not connect. Had the thing just swiped at me? I didn't doubt it.

Didn't dare pause either. But I pulled out my gun and tucked it under my left arm, firing backward blindly.

The thing let out a wail. And I think it staggered briefly to a halt. Then, it kept on coming.

My foot clanked down on metal. I was in among the girders now. The Iron Bridge was far more stoutly constructed than it genuinely needed to be, a symbol of the new industrial age in which it had been built. A plaque on it read

"1899." And it wasn't really iron at all, despite the name. It was made of two matching webs of steel, the crossway clamped in between them, riveted along its entire length and painted glossy black.

The crowd still on it had abandoned the right-hand side. So I went in that direction, clambering up and swinging myself across the framework. And, clinging to the outside of a girder, finally turned around.

The bridge had emptied out almost completely, I was pleased to see. No one else had stepped onto it, and the last few shapes were now retreating. Another bare handful of seconds, and we were alone above the river.

The creature had stopped too, looking puzzled. It hadn't been expecting this. Perhaps it thought I'd just keep running until it caught up with me. If it was an extension of its master's consciousness, it was a pretty stupid one. Maybe this was the animal aspect of him, the brainless, primal beast.

It stared at me with those faintly glowing, pale green eyes. Its brow was furrowed once again. Its mouth was slightly open, so that I could see the rows of fangs. The whole of its body, from waist to neck, was hunched completely over.

But I already knew what it could do. I smiled bitterly at it, more like a grimace really. And then fired two shots directly at the center of its face.

It went flailing back a yard or so, pawing at its ugly features, howling.

But then the Dralleg just recovered, and it flung itself at me.

I barely got out of the way in time. Sparks flew from the girders as its long claws struck them, scraping along. One set whistled above my head. I started to edge away still further. Maybe this wasn't such a good idea, but it had been the only one available. I couldn't move and aim my gun at the same time. It was either one or the other.

So I stopped and fired again. I managed to hurt it, sure. But much less badly than the last time. Or perhaps the creature had grown more determined. Moisture blew out of its nostrils. Then it lunged toward me very quickly. One of its arms came snaking out through a gap in the ironwork, the claws almost catching me across the middle.

I had to hang right out over the water to avoid the blow, in point of fact. Which meant using both my hands again. And then I went scuttling sideways, toward the far bank of the river.

We could keep this up, backward and forward, all day, I supposed. Or at least till one of us got too exhausted to continue. And it didn't take a genius to figure out who that would be.

But Saruak had moved up to the bank by this time. He was watching us very closely. His sangfroid of before had returned. All of the rage had left his features. His expression was a calculating one.

"Dralleg?" I heard him murmur.

And the creature stopped and peered around at him. I could only wait and see what they were going to do.

A few more words dropped from the spirit's lips, in that curious language that I'd heard him use before. I had no idea what they meant. But the monster seemed to understand. It craned its neck toward him for a second, then looked back at me.

And in the next moment, it was climbing out itself, vaulting across the girders and then scuttling in my direction.

There was nowhere else left to go.

So I pocketed the gun, and then gave in to gravity, letting myself drop.

CHAPTER 43

Despite the fact that it is not a particularly significant river, the currents of the Adderneck run strong. It is much deeper down the middle than it looks, a good couple of fathoms. And its waters are cold, whatever the season.

The shock of it hit me as I went plunging in, but it wasn't an unpleasant sensation. More like a purging, a release.

Bubbles swarmed around me, clinging to me like a shoal of fish. They tried to push their way up through my nostrils, and they crackled in my ears. My eyes came open. I could see the dark outline of the bridge above me. Beyond that, the sun looked slightly shapeless, rather weak.

It seemed so far away, a wavering smudge of brightness. Maybe, if I stayed down here, then all this awfulness would pass on by me. But my lungs weren't buying into that.

I broke back through the surface. Gasped. It sounded like old timbers, creaking. Wavelets were splashing up around me. Dampness spilled across my face. The world went blurry for a few seconds.

But when it cleared, and took on proper shape?

I had already been towed about twenty feet or so from the bridge. Saruak was still there on the river's bank, and following me along. There was a jauntiness to his tread, and he seemed cheerful. So perhaps I had only postponed the inevitable.

He drew level with me, and pointed at my bobbing head. I only had a split instant to wonder why.

There was a sudden, large dark movement in the corner of my eye. And then, a massive churning, an enormous splash that sent far bigger waves rushing out.

Only one thing could have done that. The Dralleg had plunged in after me.

My first instinct was to swim away from it. And first instincts are usually good, so I went with it. I must have taken twenty strokes before I slid to an uncomfortable halt. Then, treading water, I turned back around.

I had expected it to come after me. But the beast was nowhere to be seen. I scanned around quickly. There was nothing. No pale gray head moving in my direction. And no further commotion of any kind. Had the river simply swallowed it? Where had the monster gone?

The coldness of the water had seeped right into my skin. But that wasn't bothering me. Not knowing what was happening did, not even being able to see. What was going on? Something, I was sure of that.

I tried to circle around and take another glance at Saruak.

Something tugged, very briefly, at the left hem of my waterlogged pants, drawing my attention down. Maybe it had been a clump of weed or a piece of sunken debris.

But the sensation was replaced by a searing pain next moment. I struggled upward wildly, dragging myself free of it. My body cleared the surface halfway to my waist. Then I flopped back down and floundered.

My ankle was killing me. It smarted like darning needles had been driven right through it. I knew what had caused it immediately. Something had just cut me, badly. And it didn't take me very long to figure out precisely what.

I wasn't swimming anymore, but the current was still dragging me along. I raised my lower body as much as I was able, keeping it horizontal in the drift, putting as much distance as possible between my legs and the bottom. And then, I gazed downward.

A vague shape was on the move, in the depths below me. It was sunk too far to make out any proper details. Just a vague silhouette, that was all. But there were two luminous glimmers down there, keeping the same distance from each other. Two inhuman, glowing eyes.

I saw what the truth of the matter was. The Dralleg, apparently, couldn't swim, or even float. But it had walked along the riverbed, and caught up with me that way.

There were two thin streams of bubbles coming from its nostrils. They were bursting just in front of me. I wondered if it even needed oxygen, a thing like that. Or was it simply holding its breath?

The creature lashed at me again. But it couldn't seem to reach me this time. I paddled away from it, kicking gently with my unharmed leg and staying belly-down, trying to ignore the pain now spreading through the other one. I wasn't sure how badly I was bleeding. But in waters as cold as this, it wasn't going to be long before my body temperature began to drop.

The current was still bearing me along, and tugging at me even harder. We were entering the fastest stretch. The monster kept on after me. But, satisfied it couldn't hurt me for a while, I took a few more seconds to absorb my surroundings.

Union Square was fading off into the distance. The Town Hall had dwindled, the crowd in front of it lost from view. Ordinary houses were beginning to appear around me—the suburbs of East Crealley and Pilgrim's Plot on either side— although I could tell that most of them were empty. There was no help coming from that direction, then.

Saruak was still following me, pacing down the river's footpath like a bloodhound on a scent. He reached a little rowboat tethered to a pole. And looked like he was considering using it, coming after me that way.

All he did, in the end, was stop where he was and shove his hands into his pockets. His gaze on me was very taut. He was silent, but his whole mood seemed expectant. Why?

All I needed to do, I thought, was strike out for the far side of the river. Except my head seemed to have become rather light. My gaze lost a little of its focus. The pain in my leg . . . ?

Had gone away almost completely. It was not that it had gotten any better. No, the limb was growing increasingly hard to feel. I started shivering gently.

How deeply had those claws cut? And, if the wound was as bad as I suspected, how much had I already bled out? It was impossible to tell while I was in the water. But I felt my insides lurch.

Memories came rushing back at me. I'd used to fish this stretch of river with my father, when I'd been a kid. Night crawlers and lures, we'd used. He'd had this thing about "fly-fishing snobbery." And . . .

Didn't it get much shallower, around these parts? The best area, as I recalled, for catching trout?

I turned over in the current awkwardly, wondering where the Dralleg was by this time. It had disappeared from view again, despite the fact that I could make out the bottom clearly.

I could see some large rocks in the filtered sunlight. I could make out clumps of flowing weed. There had to be eight feet of water underneath me at the very most. Which made me a far easier target. But I could see no hulking shape at all. No pale green gaze mirrored my own. Where in blazes had the creature gone?

When my head came back up, I'd been turned around once more and was facing the Iron Bridge, a jet black cobweb in the distance. Some instinct made me look the other way.

And I remembered it all clearly. My father and I, out for an evening's fishing? We had waded in the margins, on this section of the river. The central channel, which I was still in, had to be only some five or six feet deep.

Twenty yards downriver from me, a huge, pale head was emerging. Unable to reach me from the depths, the Dralleg had made its way up there to cut me off. Its enormous shoulders burst free of the surface, water spilling off them. Then its powerful forearms came out, the claws catching the light and shining.

But there was something else I could see. As it emerged, the creature blew a huge plume of vapor from its muzzle. And its mouth was hanging open wide. Its ribs were heaving.

It had stayed down there a good long while, I figured out. But it still had to breathe eventually. And maybe I could use that. How?

The current became faster still. I was being swept toward the thing.

Again, I tried to swim away. Except the only thing that really swam was my own head. My insides seemed to turn to Jell-O. I thought I'd be sick. The numbness from my left leg had spread out into my whole lower body. When I tried to kick, it was like trying to pull my limbs through mud, not water.

How close was I to passing out? I worked my good leg hard, and some sensation returned.

The flow dragged at me insistently. But I had little strength to fight it. Cassie was going to have to finish this all by herself. I knew that she could, didn't I?

The Dralleg's shape—which kept on blurring—was getting closer every time I blinked. In a few more moments, I'd be cut to shreds.

But there was still some feeling in my arms. And dammit, I wasn't going out this way. I took a long breath, and then began hauling breaststroke. At first, nothing seemed to happen. Then I broke free of the pressure on me, and began to make some progress to the side.

The Dralleg let out an enraged wail and came after me, flailing wildly. But we'd entered deeper water, before too much longer. I was letting it carry me downstream again.

I didn't dare go near the bank anymore, that much was obvious. I doubted I'd even be able to stand up if I reached it. The beast would catch up with me easily, and that would be the end of that. So I kept on paddling uncomfortably till I'd completely passed the shallows, and then headed back for the central drift.

I took another glance across my shoulder, just in time to watch the Dralleg suck in another lungful of air.

And then its head went back under.

CHAPTER 44

My head was becoming light again. I shook it, struggling to hold myself together. I was barely paddling at all, just letting the flow carry me. And it was doing that quickly enough.

But when I swung around a little and looked back, a trail of bubbles was still following me. It seemed to be catching up.

We were going around a shallow bend. And, once I'd passed it, a strange shape loomed in front of me, breaking up the water and distorting its reflection. I remembered something else.

I was now looking at what I'd always thought of, in capital letters, as the Fallen Oak. I'd lost more hooks near it than in the rest of the river combined. Around forty feet tall, and wide enough around its trunk to take in a couple of automobiles, the massive tree had crashed into the river back when I'd been nine. A colossal storm had torn it from its roots.

It lay halfway across the Adderneck, at a slight angle. I could still recall how the authorities had tried to pull it out. They'd used tractors, bulldozers, any vehicle that could push or tow. And barely managed to budge it an inch. Its branches had lodged into the bed—it wasn't going anywhere. And as for moving it by magic? It was just a tree, for heaven's sake. Nobody had even had the nerve to ask the adepts.

The amazing thing was, after all these years, the thing

was still alive. It was half buried in water, wasn't it? There was a scattering of green leaves on the branches that were not submerged. New shoots pushed out all the time. I'd even seen squirrels and raccoons climbing along it. The tree had made itself a part of the Adderneck, the same way it had once been part of the dry land.

When I looked back, the bubbles were getting closer. Saruak was nowhere to be seen. He'd perhaps assumed that I was finished, and returned his attention to more important matters. I stared at the oak again.

I could haul myself up onto it. But I didn't see what good that would do. The Dralleg would follow me, and it would all be over, just the same way as if I tried to climb the bank.

I'd been close to fainting not so long ago. But now, I felt slightly revitalized. A second wind? But no. It seemed to be far more than that. More sensation flowed back into my limbs, and it felt like an extra surge of energy had rushed into my body. But I couldn't tell from where.

And this wasn't the moment to start worrying about it. Another notion came to me.

I swam in toward the side a few yards. Then I halted just short of the protruding branches, treading water, waiting for the bubbles to approach.

And when they were close enough, I went under myself.

Another swarm of bubbles frothed around me. I added to them this time, breathing out very gently. If you keep your lungs moving, you can stay under for longer. I had learned that long ago.

The water was slightly murky here, with a faint brown tinge. Up ahead of me, I could make out the submerged branches. Unlike the ones in the air, they were completely leafless. Weeds and mold had gathered on them. I could make out silver minnows flitting around.

When I turned back the other way, there were twin green glimmers closing in on me. And at first, they looked a good distance away. But then, a shape resolved itself. The Dralleg had to be a few yards from me at the very most.

I immediately shot up to the surface, and took in more air. And then I flipped my one good leg above me, and was heading down toward the bottom.

I could still see the beast, and it was getting closer all the time. It almost looked at home, down here. Its body was a dim gray shape. Its gaze seemed more iridescent than ever. Its mouth was shut, only the tips of its fangs in view. But its claws were still extended, its arms scything back and forth as it progressed. It was bouncing along with a weightless, easy tread.

I returned my attention to the sunken half of the great oak. Everywhere I looked, there was a canopy of narrow twigs. No way to get past the thing without clambering out.

Then a section of the main trunk came in view. It was completely buried in silt. I cursed inwardly, and just kept pushing myself along. It might be pointless, but this was my only hope.

I could almost *feel* the Dralleg moving in on me. Its great bulk changed the currents slightly. I thought that something snatched at my right foot, though it did not take hold. That just made me swim harder.

I was running out of air by now. My ribs were beginning to ache. If I didn't find what I was looking for, and soon . . .

Something grabbed at my foot again. The sole split, and my shoe fell away.

And then I saw what I was after. A shallow gap, between the tree trunk and the bottom. And it was gravel down there, not silt.

It didn't look quite wide enough to let me through. And that had not been the idea. But the creature was still coming up behind me, literally on my heels. And so there was no other direction to take.

My strength seemed to be failing again. I gathered up the last of it, then drove myself, as fast as I could, toward the opening, my good leg kicking furiously.

Went underneath. I stuck for a moment. Chunks of bark had snagged my clothing. There were dozens of twigs grasping at my face.

I just grabbed hold of the trunk with both my hands, and hauled. Everything was very tight and painful for a second.

And then, I was bobbing up the other side, water sluicing down across me. I was gasping frantically for breath, but still alive.

I wiped my eyes clear, stared at the emerging branches.

They all shivered, and then lurched.

I knew why. The Dralleg had tried to follow me.

I made it back to shallower water, closer to the bank. Till finally, I could prop myself up on one foot, staying upright by moving my arms. I was shivering hard, my teeth chattering. But I kept on watching what was happening now.

The great tree trunk continued to bump up and down. The branches that still had leaves on quivered, rustled. It seemed to go on for an endless while. The creature was trapped beneath them. The gap had barely been wide enough to allow me through. And for a monster of that size?

But it kept on trying. At one point, the entire trunk lifted practically a foot out of the current. But its weight was too imposing. The great boughs all dropped back again.

It was still for a while after that, and I became afraid the Dralleg had either got through or had managed to back out. I started hunting for my gun, but I seemed to have lost it.

The branches started shivering again, more feebly on this occasion. It had to be five minutes, in total, before the movement stopped completely. In that time, a freezing chill took over my whole body. I could feel neither of my legs anymore. And my arms and fingertips all ached like crazy.

I stared at the motionless branches. Surely the thing was dead? But I had to be certain.

So I balled up what little strength I had left. And then went under for a final look.

CHAPTER 45

It was completely still. There was not the slightest twitch left in its body, I could see. It had only gotten halfway through, and then become wedged solidly. Its great arms were stretched out in front of it. Without any doubt, it had been scrabbling to escape until the end. And its claws were still in view, but they were rendered harmless now.

A few large bubbles escaped from its open jaws. I remembered the way the thing had hissed and roared. Down here, there was no sound except the flowing of the Adderneck. The creature had finally been plunged into silence.

Its eyes were still glowing very faintly. And I wondered, would that ever stop?

A crawfish scuttled over its left shoulder, and then vanished with a flick of its broad tail.

I swam in a little closer. It looked almost pathetic, trapped this way. But considering the suffering it had caused, there was nothing in me that felt any pity for it.

I must have drifted closer in without even noticing it, an eddy towing me along.

Its right hand suddenly lashed up at me, the claws gashing my forearm. I propelled myself away, with shock. When I looked back, the light had gone completely from its eyes. A few silver bubbles were still clinging to its nostrils, that was all.

But the water around me was becoming stained with red. I was losing even more blood, and I'd already lost enough.

The current snatched at me again. I let myself drift back up to the surface. But then I recognized the truth. All of the additional strength I'd felt was gone, used up completely. I barely had enough energy left even to tread water any longer. I just wasn't going to make it back to dry land. It all ended here.

The sky looked very blue, with puffs of white. The coolness of the river seemed to calm me. My head felt extremely light, almost like I was dozing with my eyes wide open. A broader eddy had carried me over toward the other bank. And I was lying on my back in it, just gazing upward.

I drew another breath, just in time. The water closed back over my face.

I tried to drag myself up through the surface, using just my arms. I was scarcely able to move them at all, and only half succeeded. The top of my face broke through. I managed to snatch a scrap of air. And then I was sinking again, the water pushing into my skull. My legs were like dead weights towing me down. The surface of the river looked like a receding mirror.

It felt like I'd been anchored to a truck. However hard I tried, I couldn't seem to make my body rise.

But it wasn't that. I was just making extremely slow progress.

Finally, I felt the crown of my head come out again. I tipped right back and tried to breathe in through my nose. The river hauled me under, for perhaps the final time.

Fear spread through me. I was staring upward desperately, trying to will myself back up.

When I felt a hand close around my collar, then start pulling me toward the shore.

I thought I recognized the voice. But I was coughing so furiously that I could barely make it out.

"Are you all right, sir?"

I choked and spluttered for another while, then gave up on that in favor of a heavy wheezing sound.

"Sir?"

It was Hampton. I managed to get my head around, and squinted up the bank. The Silver Shadow was parked higher along it. Then I looked directly up.

A pair of eyes, one green, one yellow, stared down at me worriedly from a tanned, round face. The question that he'd asked me was still burning in them.

How to answer? It didn't matter. I had lost far too much blood, and was in the grip of hypothermia. If nothing happened soon, then I was pretty well done for.

I was half in and half out of the river, lying in its margins like a piece of driftwood. Crouched above me, Hampton was stripped right down to his underwear and socks. He had forgotten to remove his chauffeur's cap, which struck me as faintly ludicrous. I glanced past his shoulder at the sun, which was on its way to the west horizon. It looked to be somewhere around four or five o'clock.

Hampton didn't seem to understand exactly what was going on. He's a chauffeur, not a doctor, so you couldn't blame him.

"Master Raine saw what was happening, and sent me down to help," he was explaining. "And it's just as well, I have to say. You look in an awful state."

I felt my eyes start to roll back. And then I noticed that the back door of the Rolls was open. That made me cling on to consciousness a little harder. I could make out a lined, gray face, framed by a familiar hat and big dark glasses.

Hampton glanced in that direction.

"Dr. Willets asked to come as well."

Which was a partial revelation. So he wasn't as remote from all this as he usually tried to pretend.

Hampton was inspecting my damaged arm, and looking very puzzled.

"It's not even bleeding any more. Should it be this color?"

He gave it a gentle twitch.

"Can you get up, sir?"

I didn't think so.

"You're so cold. Good Lord, you're freezing!"

And then his attention went to my lower body. He rolled up the pants leg as far as he could, then jerked his fingers back.

"Good *Heavens!*"

But I wasn't even looking at him anymore. Barely clinging on I might be, but I was staring evenly at Willets. He saw most things, I already knew. And he had to understand the condition I was in.

I didn't even voice the question. Didn't have the energy. I just kept peering at him, waiting for him to respond. He'd gotten people out of wheelchairs in the old days, hadn't he? Pulled out tumors? Saved lives?

The doctor got out of the car in an ungainly fashion, trying to evade my gaze at first. He looked up at the sky, then down. He'd taken off the hat, was fiddling with it, running its soft brim through his fingertips.

Finally, he looked across, then took a step toward me. There was something like anger—but not quite that—on his features.

"For God's sake, Devries?" he shouted. "Do you know what you're asking of me?"

I continued watching him, even though he was fading to a silhouette before my very eyes. That wasn't any magic on his part, I knew. I was finally passing out.

"This was how it started for me last time. All the madness. All the . . . dying."

I fought to hang on. Pushed open my eyelids, which were starting to slide shut. *So you're going to walk away now?* my gaze asked.

By this time, Hampton was glowering at him too.

"Sir?" his voice piped up. "Sir, you *are* a doctor."

Not that kind, I knew. But his reproachful tone seemed to do the trick.

Willets's face was sweating. He wiped it with his palm. He was remembering stuff, I understood that. The faces of those youngsters. And the screams. This had to be a torment for him, yes. But there were larger issues at stake, and he had to acknowledge that too.

He drew himself up straight at last, his face hardening with determination.

"Okay, then. Can you hold yourself extremely still, Devries?"

I didn't imagine that would be too difficult. The doctor began walking toward me, his shoes scuffing through the grass.

"It's not simply a matter of closing up the wounds."

His voice had gone very deep and serious. It had been a while since he had sounded quite as solemn as this.

"I'm going to have to raise your body temperature. And conjure blood into your veins as well, several pints of it. You have to be told, I've never done the latter."

But I felt sure he could.

"I swear," I could hear him muttering under his breath, just before he bent over me. "I'm putting a padlock on my door in the future, and keeping it that way."

Then he took the dark glasses off.

The bright red of his pupils had spilled out, and filled up both his eyes from lid to lid.

CHAPTER 46

Half an hour later—we had all piled back into the Rolls by then—I was still aching like all hell, my wounded arm and leg especially. It felt like it would never stop, a constant, subcutaneous throbbing like I had been worked at with a tenderizer by some culinary-minded giant.

But I was back on my feet and moving around. And the good doctor had even made the scars fade away. That was the upside. On the down, I had never felt such a nauseated sense of panic as when he'd directed his powers into my veins, refilling them. I'd felt them stretch and move, as if there were insects shuffling around my body's secret passageways.

I forced myself to just forget it. *Worry about the future*, I told myself. But that wasn't particularly comfortable either.

The sun was still descending like a faded yellow volleyball.

In the back of the Silver Shadow—they'd popped into existence as we'd climbed into it—were a change of clothes for me, and a big pile of towels, courtesy of Woodard Raine, without a doubt. So at least he'd not lost interest in us yet. His focus seemed to be in the right place, for once.

I was drying myself down, then struggling into them. And I had to admit that the new shirt and pants fit perfectly, the shoes were pretty good ones.

I checked through my other clothes, the soaked ones, retrieving useful things like sets of keys. But my gun was definitely not there.

Up front in the driver's seat, Hampton had been provided for as well. He was wearing a thick, voluminous bathrobe over his dripping underclothes, the same color as his uniform. And a pair of dark blue flip-flops that he seemed a little puzzled by. The Rolls was moving rather jerkily. He was finding it difficult to work the pedals.

As for Willets, the doctor gazed at me suspiciously while I did up my cuffs. I slipped my brand-new jacket on, then did something I almost never do. I tried out a gentle smile on him, of gratitude.

Willets just frowned back. His sour, despondent mood had returned, crinkling his features.

"So, one small victory, and a tenuous one at that. Do you really still believe you have a chance?"

I looked at him without replying. Was he still trying to talk me out of this?

"You've bested his creature, true enough," he granted me.

But he looked unimpressed.

"Stopping the one who created it in the first place will be infinitely harder."

"Yes, I know that," I replied.

But he had hit the nail directly on the head. Time was slipping away far too quickly, faster than was natural. And I still didn't have even a basic plan for dealing with Saruak.

We were humming through the inner suburbs. Hampton's footwork on the pedals seemed to have got more assured. And—once more—there was not a sign of life. Some of the house's doors were hanging vacantly ajar. The yards in front of them were all abandoned. There was no one on the sidewalks, and no other traffic on the streets. Which made our progress easier, at least.

What Cassie had said came back to me. A load more people tinkered with magic than you might expect. Most of them had to do it secretly. And were they *all* at Union Square? Hampton had to know more about it than I did, so I leant across and asked him.

"Pretty much the whole town's there, sir," he informed me. "I could see it from up on the Hill. The square is full beyond capacity. Those who can't get into it have clogged up the surrounding streets."

Exactly as the jewel had shown me. The look in his eyes, reflected in the rearview mirror said it all. They had taken on a sharp, tight gleam of apprehension.

"So many of them?" I asked. "They all . . . ?"

"Yes. Of course."

I suppose that, if you're just an ordinary person and you live here in the Landing, the temptation becomes too great after a while. Which had left almost everybody vulnerable. I looked back at Willets, with a question in my own gaze. He just pulled another tired face at me, knowing what I wanted of him.

"I've done all that I possibly can, Devries."

I ought to have got angry with him. But he had just saved my life, so I held off a little.

"Really? You're quite sure of that?"

"I'm certain, believe me. From here on in, you're on your own."

Then he put back on the dark glasses I'd given him, and turned his face away from me, refusing to look back.

We went across another intersection. The taller buildings of the town center were drawing into view. And still, there was nobody around. Shop doorways hung open—nothing moved beyond them. A few lights ought to have been coming on in the rooms above, but the windows remained darkened to the last.

That added to the sense of deepening gloom. It looked to me as though the entire place was trying to fade from view, in spite of the fact it was still day.

We turned another corner. There was just a block to go. But then Hampton stamped hard on the brake. The Rolls skidded to a halt.

I righted myself and peered ahead of us, at a dense wall running across the entire street. Except that it wasn't made of bricks and mortar. It was people, jammed shoulder-to-shoulder, back-to-belly, as far as my eyes could go.

When I'd last been here, the townsfolk had been sitting down. But there was no room for that anymore. It looked to me like they were all trying to press a little further forward, something drawing them in that direction. And, despite the fact that they were making no sound, there was a tense air to them.

Something was coming, and they seemed to feel it in their bones.

Hampton slumped back in his seat.

"Good Lord!" he said again.

I took another glance at my watch. Six o'clock. Two hours to go. Except the hands were moving even quicker. In real terms, how much time was left?

Saul Hobart—I could see, staring around—had been as good as his word. There were no obstructions remaining on this street, not so much as a skateboard. I wondered how much would that help when the terror really started kicking in.

I was still trying to think what to do next, when there was an abrupt, sharp clank, just above my head. An object rattled to the pavement.

Something had just struck the roof. A stone or suchlike. Thrown deliberately?

Hampton's reaction was immediate and fierce. He seemed to forget all about the crowds in front of us, the situation we were in. He snorted angrily, then got out, the entire car lurching.

His only concern was for the Rolls's paintwork. I just wound a window down and stuck my head out, trying to find out what was happening now.

There was a whistle from above. I tipped my face in that direction. Four stories up, a narrow head was poking out across the edge of the nearest building's roof.

It was Cassie.

CHAPTER 47

Going up the fire escape, stretching out my aching muscles all over again, wasn't exactly pleasant. But it turned out to be worth the effort.

By the look on Cassie's face, once I'd got up there, I wasn't the only one who felt deeply relieved. Her face had gone paler than ever, the cheekbones stark as marble, but her eyes glittered. She looked like she was going to let out a whoop any second.

You'd have thought that she was sick of rooftops, after her recent experience with them. But she'd obviously come up here to keep an eye on things. It was far too crowded for that, down below us.

"You thought I was *dead*?" I asked her, as I stepped onto the wide expanse of tar paper. "Have you no faith in me at all?"

Her head did something in between a shake and nod. She released a breath and put a hand across her chest.

"Stop that! I . . . I wasn't sure."

I hadn't been either, for a while there. So I could see her point of view.

"I watched you jump into the river. And the Dralleg go in too. Once I'd got back down, I headed after you. But there was no sign of you, or anyone else. I just assumed . . ."

But that didn't sound exactly right. I recalled the way that Saruak had stalked me down the towpath. Even though he hadn't followed me the entire way, where'd he been while she was doing that?

"He seems to have disappeared again," Cass told me.

The rise and fall of her chest was starting to slow down, at last. I was glad that she was so pleased. But, my thoughts revolving around our visitor again, I became increasingly uncomfortable. He was preparing himself for his finale, doubtless.

"How about the Dralleg?" Cassie asked.

"A goner," I told her. "But it wasn't easy. That damned thing was hard to kill."

She nodded with approval, but that didn't lighten my mood at all. I knew what an enormous gap there was between "hard" and "impossible." And Saruak still answered to the latter, any way I looked at it.

I gazed over the roof's lip at the street I'd just climbed up from. There seemed no point in hiding. There were hundreds of people there. The light was weakening slightly. All their clustered faces were like pools of growing shade. The silence was enduring and profound. They still looked like they were moving very gently, trying to push a little further forward. That was all.

You could hear the swishing noise the breeze made as it sifted through the rooftops. You could hear the flapping of a nearby bird. There were little kids down there, and even babies. They were not letting out so much as a murmur or a cough.

Then, the thrumming of a motor brought my head around. The Rolls was performing a three-point turn, then heading off through the barren streets, carrying Willets with it.

"Second time in that thing," Cass remarked, glancing at me sideways. "Getting used to luxury in your old age?"

She'd no idea what had been going on. Not the whole story. So I just let the jibe slide by me.

My gaze wandered to the people jam-packed further up

the street. The scene that had been revealed to me came back, in all its shrieking awfulness.

But it hadn't been enacted here. I wanted to see what was happening down on Union Square itself.

Every eye down there was still fixed on the platform. We studied it all from the roof's front edge.

Hot droplets of sweat formed on my lip. Once more, the scene was precisely as the white jewel had predicted it. The banners flapped. Every spare inch of space was filled, right down to the last small alcove. There were cops stringing nervously along the edges of the crowd—I recognized Jenny Pearce's white-blond hair. But what they could do seemed pretty limited, to put it mildly. There were so many people pressed up around them, even moving anywhere was difficult. And most of them had given up trying.

One thing was different. I took that in almost right away. In the scene the jewel had shown me, there were civilians standing on the statue's plinth, clinging to our founder's big bronze hems, God bless him. That part of the prophecy hadn't been correct. Just one person occupied that spot.

It was Saul Hobart. He had cleared the others off, made some room up there that he could work with. I thought I could make out a walkie-talkie clipped onto his belt. And he had a riot gun propped up in front of him against the statue. What good he thought that might do, I had no real idea.

He kept glancing between the stage in front of him, and then the sky above. Ready for whatever happened. And the man had to have some notion of just how bad, how devastating, that was going to be. I'd already warned him about the stampede. But . . . run away? He'd rather die first.

I stood as tall as I was able, and tried to see what else was new. There was nothing. Events were traveling along the same dark route I'd watched before.

Off to the far side, the sun had almost reached the top of the wide gray buildings. Shadows were stretching everywhere. They swept over the clustered people. Countless eyes glittered dully from them.

"Jesus," Cassie murmured, her tone breathless. "Look at all the little kids down there."

There were toddlers, borne up on shoulders. Older children, trying to stand as tall as their dads, their moms. But what could we do about it? My heart became so heavy that it felt like it was going to stop.

My gaze went back to the lieutenant, and I turned that over once again. It was just a small detail, but he had managed to make a difference. The Eye of Hermaneus had not shown me that. And the question came immediately. If that could be altered, what else?

How, though? *How?*

The bottom edge of the sun was touching the rooftop opposite me. And a rattling sound, then urgent movement, brought me jerking around to the north.

Mayor Aldernay, a small stout shape flanked by his assistant and his deputies, had just emerged from the Town Hall. As I watched, they all came briskly down the steps and then went up onto the stage, the mayor taking his place behind a microphone.

He cleared his throat. The sound rang out loudly through the speaker system.

Oh my God, it was beginning.

CHAPTER 48

The sky was turning red again, the color spilling out across it and then thickening, getting darker. And the crowd started to come properly alive. It had been half asleep all day. Now some of them were blinking curiously at the mayor. Others were looking upward and around, wondering how they had even got there.

They all seemed to accept their circumstances in the end. And they stayed put.

My gaze darted across to the huge, dimming bulk of Sycamore Hill. And sure enough, the adepts were on their way. They were coming, in the form of swiftly moving black smudges against the darkening firmament. They seemed to swell as they approached. Swept above us in formation. Then, passing over the Town Hall's roof, they turned and plummeted toward the stage.

Gaspar Vernon and Judge Levin both appeared there. Followed quickly by the McGinley sisters, Kurt van Friesling, Cobb Walters, and Martha Howard-Brett.

A huge ripple swept through the crowd. But this was a completely different experience to seeing it relayed by the white jewel. For starters, there was sound this time. Some people applauded. A few children shouted out, either happy or astonished. But the generalized murmur that swept across the square was far louder than that. A solid thrum of conversation rose toward us, as the townsfolk wondered, speculated, hoped.

It wasn't just what reached my eardrums, though. It was what touched my nerves and heart. Minutes ago, all these people had been silent, passive. But between one moment and the next?

You could feel the excitement from up here, and it was growing all the while. The townsfolk felt certain something was going to be achieved. And they seemed to be convinced that it was something good.

If only they could understand the truth. Could see what I had witnessed.

Mayor Aldernay had already launched into his speech. The loudspeakers were blaring with it, overloading slightly. He was standing too close to the microphone. I racked my brains again.

A Changer of Worlds might be our only answer. But *what* Changer of Worlds?

Cassie had said something, hadn't she, back when we had talked about this? She'd pointed something out. Her world had been changed completely by the guy who'd robbed her of her family. The same was true of my life. But that *couldn't* be the answer. She'd been talking about our personal histories, not the entire town's.

I gazed down, feeling increasingly helpless and baffled.

The sun, half sunk away, had taken on a harsh carmine glow that made you squint. There was now more shade than light in front of the stage. The smaller children had already become so lost in the dimness you could barely see them. And the adults all around them looked only semi-real. You could pick out heads, and make out individual features. But the rest was just a formless mass, the gathering night trying to absorb it all.

They had fallen silent as the mayor continued talking. But they looked on edge, expecting marvelous things to happen once the sun was gone.

The best magic always did happen in the dark. The adepts spent most of their life in it, after all.

Their mood hadn't infected Saul Hobart, I could see. He was expecting something too, but not as optimistically as them. As I watched, he crouched a little further down, and spoke to his own people on his walkie-talkie.

I looked back at the general crowd. And . . . what might change *their* world? I was still trying to think of something. What might alter it completely? My mind hunted for an answer.

What had changed our whole town in the past? The coming to Raine's Landing of the Salem witches? Certainly that was true, but I couldn't see how that was any use.

Aldernay had finally stopped. Most of the audience clapped—this has always been a polite community. But the sense of impatience grew stronger. They wanted to get on with it. Proceed. Cast the strongest spells they'd ever managed in their entire lives, and free this place from . . .

Was *that* it?

I remembered more of what the jewel had shown. And I already knew what was going to become apparent next. The mayor would take a pace back. Gaspar Vernon would step forward. He would raise his arms.

And on that signal, hundreds of torches would be lifted from the throng. Flames would be applied to them, in memory of . . .

Yes, I *had* it.

So I reached across, grabbing Cassie by her wrist. She winced at me surprisedly, her mouth agape.

"Where's your bike?" I shouted.

"Parked out back," she answered. "Why?"

"I have to get back to Raine Manor, Cass. I have to get back *now*."

CHAPTER 49

We crested the Hill with the Harley's needle teetering around one-fifty. I kept thinking, Saul would have a fit if he saw this. Raine Manor was looming up ahead of us. You could see its peculiar spire beyond the tangled mass of trees.

Cass finally slowed down, then skidded to a halt beside the open gates. The driveway ahead was so overgrown, even she would have real trouble negotiating it at any serious speed. But that wasn't why she'd stopped. Whatever might be happening now, she didn't want to go any further. Dealing with the likes of Woody was my territory, not hers.

I looked back. I had a perfect view of the center of the town from here. Torches, hundreds of the things, were blazing in Union Square. They gave the place an almost medieval look, as if the bad old days had just come back. I could not make out the townspeople any longer. They were lost among the fire and darkness. The ceremony was well under way.

So I slid off the pillion.

"Wait here," I told her.

"Suits me!" I heard her shout, as I began to run.

The house grew larger in front of me. The front door swung open as I reached the porch, Hampton standing just behind it, and back in his full uniform. So it seemed that Raine had known that I was coming.

I went past the chauffeur, skidding to another halt. Once more, there was faint candlelight coming from the ballroom. There were plenty of other rooms in this place. Did he spend his entire life in there?

I got a fresh surprise when I reentered, because Woody's narrow shape was not the only one that I could see. Willets was still there as well, a surly outline in the shadows. He'd come back, in spite of all his earlier protests. His red-flecked gaze returned mine challengingly.

"I just thought that there was no sense going home, with all this happening," he said.

And let's face it, a little while longer and we might not have any homes left to go back to.

"I decided to wait it out, in case . . ."

He faltered, seemingly embarrassed. I finished the sentence for him soundlessly inside my head. *In case he was needed again.* He *did* want to get involved after all. He just found it difficult to rationalize that, or explain it.

Woody, naturally, had no such trouble, since normal concepts like that didn't even come into the equation.

"Nice of you to drop in again. But what do you want now, old chum?"

His solemn manner of before had vanished. His tone was breezy, like we were all at a picnic. What was taking place seemed rather lost on him. And I would have got annoyed with him again, but this wasn't the moment for it.

"The Eye of Whosis. You made it look into the future, sure. But can it look into the past?"

His features went completely unreadable. He'd obviously never even thought of that. And then, he began pacing gently around, turning the concept over.

"That's an interesting question. Gosh, I wonder if that's possible?"

He and Willets exchanged glances.

"Um . . . I suppose we could take a stab at it."

He lifted his right arm, and the jewel came floating to his grasp. Woody balanced it delicately in his open palm, as though it were a living thing, a butterfly. And it behaved like that, next instant, rising up again into the air between them.

He and Willets spread their arms, the same way that they'd done before. Its facets all started to wink, sucking in the candlelight and increasing its glow.

But they didn't seem sure what they were supposed to do after that. This was a brand-new feat of magic I was asking for. They tried out a few different incantations, which had no effect at all. I just ground my palms together, wondering what was happening back in the square. How far had the ceremony gone? It was entirely possible that, whatever they managed, it was going to be too late.

But then, I heard the adepts go back to the first spell that they'd tried. They simply said it backward.

"Got it!" announced Woodard Raine.

I looked around at what they'd done.

The pyramid of light had reappeared beneath the stone. And, within it, the events of the past few days were being replayed, in reverse. There were me and Hobart, speeding to St. Cleary's to do battle with the Dralleg. There I was, being chauffeured up here the first time around.

Raine beamed at me delightedly, looking atrociously pleased with himself. I just ignored that, nodding.

"That's impressive."

"Isn't it just? So, sport, how far back exactly do you want to look?"

And when I told him, even his big golden eyes became a whole lot larger.

It was night, pitch-dark above. The mob was beating at her door. The women in it—and there were plenty of those—wore shawls and white bonnets tightly fitted. And the men had on those high, wide-brimmed felt hats that I thought were called sugarloafs, in spite of the fact that they were uniformly black.

It was nearly the close of the sixteen hundreds. And practically the end of a certain woman's life. Probably the most famous event in all the Landing's history. Certainly the most familiar name.

Some of the crowd were carrying blazing torches, just like the folks down in Union Square. And a few of them had pitchforks too, as my grandfather had supposed. Their faces were lumpen and their eyes dull in the amber glow, their expressions savage and twisted. It was frightening to see how hatred became magnified as soon as it was shared.

There was no sound, just like earlier. But these ancestors from our past had to be baying like a pack of hounds. I stepped around the pyramid of light anxiously, watching the dying moments of the person who had genuinely changed this town, for centuries to come.

It was a cabin that the crowd was pressed around, out on the edge of what had merely been a good-sized village. It had stout log walls, but only a thatched roof. The door was obviously barred from the inside. The mob kept pounding at it furiously.

I became uncomfortably aware of Willets's gaze on me, and glanced across at him a moment. What exactly was I looking for? We were *both* wondering that. I'd only know it when it came in view.

So I returned my attention to the scene.

The cabin door crashed inward the next second. And the outraged mob went spilling through.

They emerged, a short while later, dragging someone with them. A woman, in her early thirties by the look of her. I hadn't understood, until now, just how beautiful Regan Farrow had been. She was absolutely striking, in spite of the way her face was twisted up with fear. She was very tall and slender. She had tousled auburn hair that ran halfway down her back. Her eyes were olive green, and had a brilliant sparkle to them. Her complexion was extremely pale.

There was a long gray cloak on over her day clothes, like she'd been planning on going somewhere. The hood was thrown back. And, as she was dragged clear of her front door, she began to scream.

The crowd had her by the wrists and shoulders, and were towing her remorselessly along. Some of the fury had gone from their expressions. It had turned to something even worse, a sadistic amusement. I could see a few of them were even laughing.

One of them lobbed his torch onto the cabin's roof. The flames took hold, crackling fiercely.

The rest of the mob paid it no attention whatsoever, hauling Regan off toward the common. Where the stake was waiting, and the piles of kindling. And a priest was standing there.

I remembered what I had been told, all those years ago. It was the site of Union Square these days.

I felt pretty uncomfortable, watching the scene unfold. And it wasn't just the horror of it. What if I was wrong about this? If it was *merely* Regan Farrow who had been the Changer of our World, then there was nowhere left to take this thing.

Or . . . could there have been something else involved, not merely her? All I could do was keep on watching, almost shaking by this stage.

Regan had stopped screaming and—just like in the legend—she was pleading with the crowd instead. I couldn't hear the words that she was speaking, but remembered what they were.

"I'll go away, and never come back. You'll never hear of me again."

The mob's answer was more laughter and jeers.

She began struggling furiously, but there were far too many of them. They just hoisted her up against the stake, and tied her there with lengths of thick rope, wrapping it tightly around her upper arms and body. They had left her forearms free, I saw.

"They did that," Willets explained, stepping quietly up beside me, "so that, in her final moments, the witch could put her hands together and pray for forgiveness. Ugly, ain't it?"

Yes, it was. I set my teeth.

Woody had stepped in closer too, his face illuminated by the cone of light. And even he looked strangely moved. Did he identify with her, I wondered, one sorcerer to another?

Regan Farrow was still begging with her captors as they piled the kindling around her. But it did no good at all. They were not listening. They were moving practically like automatons, absolutely certain that what they were doing was just and proper. It struck me what an awful thing belief like that had been.

As they started to apply the flames, she went stiff and stopped begging. Regan seemed to understand that there was no talking her way out of this. I could see it by the coldness that swept over her fine features and her olive gaze. She realized that she was done for.

Her expression filled with anger and defiance. And she stared around at her tormentors, showing them they'd not get the better of her. She'd not spend her final moments sobbing like a child.

The flames were climbing up around her. They were scorching the hems of her cloak. The heat had to be washing over her, because her features creased with pain. Then she pushed her head forward, and her whole face caught the light and seemed to shine.

I watched, aghast, as she began to mouth the words that had cast this town into its solitary abyss. I'd never thought I'd get to see this.

"If I cannot leave, then none of you ever shall. And you shall dwell alone here."

It was so much a part of our heritage. Those words?—they had made Raine's Landing what it was today. I felt light-headed, watching her actually speak them.

But what was *that*? My gaze jerked, and I tried to understand what I was looking at.

The witch was clutching at something just below her throat with her right hand. I couldn't make out what it was. The cloak was hiding it. And something had happened to her features. They seemed blurrier than they'd been before. Was that the fire? Or perhaps the spell was going wrong somehow?

Next instant, the flames spread up her cloak. She howled, and her grip let go.

"Poor girl," I heard Woody sigh.

But I had caught sight of the briefest glitter, just above her breastbone.

An instant later, Regan Farrow's entire body was engulfed in flame.

It was sickening to watch. But I was not here simply to be horrified. I had to find out what she'd had her palm pressed to.

"Can you run it back?" I asked, in an urgent tone.

When Woodard Raine stared up at me, I could see that there was dampness in the corners of his eyes, glistening like liquid gold. A line of it ran down one cheek. His face was oddly rigid, except his lips were trembling slightly.

So he did have a human side. His voice was very hushed when he replied.

"This isn't a VCR, old chum."

But then he looked across at Willets.

"We can start the scene again, though, I suppose."

"We can take it from the point where they begin to burn her," Willets added, nodding quickly.

There was a curious look on his own face. So he had probably spotted something too.

They both raised their hands, and shouted a few words. The scene disappeared. I began to pace, massively frustrated, while they prepared themselves again.

Then Raine whispered, "Ready."

They resumed their backward chanting. And I stopped dead still. We were back to the point where they'd applied the flames.

I knew what the problem was. Why I'd missed the things I had been looking for. I'd been so fascinated, watching Regan mouth her curse, I hadn't taken too much notice of the other things that were going on.

But I knew exactly where to look on this occasion. I went around a little to the side, anticipating it. The pictures in front of me were not flat, like a movie screen. They were three-dimensional. And I needed to see under her cloak a little better.

Just before she spoke those words, something happened that amazed me. I'd noticed her face becoming less distinct before. But now I could see that it wasn't only that. It didn't simply blur.

I squinted. Willets did as well.

Then I drew in a sharp breath. It had happened in an instant, but . . . there seemed to be another face, superimposed over hers. Who was that?

It was smaller and far narrower, and looked very old. Creases covered it, and there was gray hair hanging down from its scalp, the same dry texture as straw. A woman's face, though, definitely that. But my guess was, not European. This looked native. The cheekbones were flatter, the temples more prominent, and the nose was hooked. The eyes were almost black, and they looked very sad and wise.

There was a double scar below her left ear too, which looked as if it had been carved into the flesh deliberately. And she wore large earrings. They seemed to be made of bone.

All of her features were faintly realized. Just a phantom image, superimposed over the more solid one. But the lips appeared to be mumbling gently, in perfect time with Regan Farrow's.

And, as soon as the curse was out, the older face disappeared. I had not been expecting anything like that. A profound sense of shock rushed through me.

Regan's hand was still inside her cloak. I stepped a little further around, the doctor following me.

He let out a puzzled sound. But I just bent in, and stared harder.

She was wearing a gemstone pendant in there, on a narrow silver chain.

The same pendant that Jason Goad had been wearing, on the day my family had disappeared.

The same one that had stayed behind, when they were gone.

And was now sitting in the living room of my own house.

CHAPTER 50

I pounded back along the driveway. Cassie came in sight. She wasn't looking in my direction, in spite of the fact that she had to be able to hear me coming. No, she had her back to me instead. She was facing out across the town. A quick glance beyond her told me why.

The daylight was almost completely gone, only a few faint glimmers of it remaining. And, directly over Union Square, a huge cloud had begun to form.

First, it just drew in the smaller clouds around it, merging them into a greater whole. But then it started taking on a life of its own, churning and expanding.

The darkness below it grew even thicker. The torches seemed to shine even more brightly in it. How much longer until Saruak snuffed them out?

Cass swung around sharply as I made the last few yards. "What now?"

"My place!" I yelled at her.

She peered at me cockeyed. But we both got on the bike.

Normally, we would have headed through the middle of the Landing, but that was impossible. We peeled back down the hill, the tall hedgerows and high walls melting to blurs around us. And then, hitting Sandhurst Avenue, we started heading north.

The shrieking of the engine was a sharp physical presence around me. The air battered at my face so hard that I could barely breathe. I tucked my head down and hung on to Cassie's waist. And tried desperately to figure all this out.

A gemstone. A material object. Could it be the Changer we'd been looking for? But I'd been told that couldn't happen. How about the woman that I'd seen?

There was a blue glow deep inside my head. And the Little Girl reappeared there, a floating, childlike image.

She was not rotating anymore. And it was hard to tell with her eyes closed, but she seemed to be just as surprised as I was.

"Is the pendant it?" I asked her breathlessly. "The Changer of Worlds that Willets talked about?"

She seemed to be concentrating intently, as though she were trying to study something very far away. Then her mouth dropped open a little, and her tiny white teeth gleamed.

"I think it might be, Mr. Ross."

"But you told me it cannot *be* an object. That it has to *want* to change things. Has to have a will, you said."

There was so much noise around us, Cassie didn't even notice that I was talking to anyone. She was peering straight ahead, concentrating on covering the distances as rapidly as she could. The Little Girl had my complete attention, and was pondering the matter, her whole face slightly twisted.

Then, her narrow eyebrows lifted. And amazement spread across her features. What exactly was she seeing, the closer she looked?

"It seems . . . the crystal is aware. It has a consciousness."

And then she almost drew back in the air.

And cried out, "Oh, Mr. Ross!"

"Yes?"

"There's the soul of a *lady* in it! She is trapped in there, I think!"

I tried to get my mind around that.

"Regan Farrow?"

"No."

Her tiny head shook. She looked pretty breathless now.

"It's someone from an earlier time, a good deal further back. She is sorry for what happened to your family. And, ever since they disappeared . . ."

Even she seemed to be having trouble taking all this in.

"I think she's been watching over you, Mr. Ross! I think she's been trying to protect you! You must fetch her now!"

"I'm doing that!"

"She will try and help you," the Girl told me. "I am sure of that. And I wish you the best of luck."

And with those words, her image vanished. My surroundings came flooding back.

Trapped in her room as she seemed to be, the Little Girl could only point me in the right direction. Although I felt very grateful that she had.

We were turning onto Colver Street, and heading east.

Below us, to our right, the cloud was spreading even wider. It was black as tar, an amorphous hole cut in reality. And as I watched, a few thin strands of lightning began flashing deep within it. So the Manitou's endgame was well under way, just as the jewel had predicted.

When this had been shown to me before, it had been all sped up. So I had no idea what the genuine timeframe might be. How long was it before Saruak appeared?—before Union Square began to shake and fall apart, taking a load of people with it?

Cassie didn't need any encouraging. She already had the throttle to its limit, gunning the Harley forward as hard as she could. Its engine let out a bone-vibrating shudder. The houses going by us seemed to merge into each other, like they had been drawn in wet paint and it had started raining.

My head was still tucked down. And I was still thinking about everything the Little Girl had said.

Someone in the crystal, trying to protect me. Why?

Cass's words came back to me, after the fight at her place. How she believed that I had changed, post Goad. The ways that I seemed different to the person I had been.

And then there was the way that Saruak had kept returning to me. Peering at me curiously, almost every time. I'd been wondering why he did that, ever since I'd met him.

Had he sensed something about me, from the very start? Had he seen that I was different to most humans he encountered?

All of it seemed to fit. But another question raised its ugly head. *Why me?*

I could only hope there'd be the chance to answer that one later.

Cassie slowed again, the needle dropping to seventy. We both leaned over to the side as she went around another corner. And then we were heading up my own street. I remembered—it felt like a lifetime ago—standing out here, talking idly with one of my neighbors. Only a few days back. Ancient history, by this stage of the game.

This district was just as deserted as the rest of town. A curious bleakness overcame me as I peered along it. Could it ever be put back the way it had been once?

But then we were screeching up outside my house. And, leaving Cassie behind, I was off the pillion and running again.

CHAPTER 51

It was dark inside. All the drapes were still pulled shut, the way I'd left them. But I didn't waste time switching on the lights. I simply went into my living room, and flung open the cabinet.

The gemstone sparkled gently when I stared at it, as though it could create illumination all by itself. For the first time since I'd brought it here, I put my fingers to the chain and picked it up.

Something like a freezing blast of air went through me. *Maybe I'm just imagining this*, I told myself.

The pendant swung in front of me, the clear, bright facets of the jewel glistening. I could see the small black flaw inside, and the tiny markings around the setting. There were plenty of magical devices more impressive to the eye than this—I'd had some of them shown to me the past couple of days. But sometimes it was the simplest-looking ones that were really the strongest.

Regan Farrow had worn the thing, and so had Jason Goad. And look what they had done. I peered at it a moment longer and then, steeling myself, grasped it in my palm.

"No!"

The voice came out of nowhere, hissing through my skull.

But it wasn't the Little Girl this time. I looked around, and could see no one.

"You must not do that!" it told me, sounding extremely insistent.

It was old and husky, with the strangest accent to it. Very flat, for all its urgency. It echoed in my head. It had to belong to the woman I'd seen, I had no doubt of that. But there were more questions than answers here.

Despite the fact that it was what I'd come here for, it still alarmed me badly. And my first reaction was an instinctive one, devoid of any common sense. I shook my head fiercely, like I was trying to rid myself of it or weaken it a little. But it turned out to be no use. It would not quiet down or go away.

"You must not use magic. You are the Defender. It is prophesied."

I forced myself to calm down. It had to be coming from inside the pendant, that much I was certain of. But it was using words that had no meaning in the slightest to me. Defender? And a prophecy? What in Christ's name was this about?

I opened my hand again, and peered at the jewel uncertainly.

Without any warning, changes started to come over me. My temples began pounding badly. Pressure was building behind them. And the details of the room around me became vague, then actually began to fade away.

I thought I could smell a wood fire somewhere, and hear a distant murmuring on the air. Almost as if there were others watching us from somewhere that I could not even see.

My whole body appeared to sway. It was a struggle just to keep my footing. Or was I imagining that too?

"Who are you?" I managed to ask.

"I am Amashta," it replied.

Which didn't even help a little bit. I couldn't seem to get a grasp on anything that was happening.

I kept on trying, though.

"What are you?"

"A leader, in my day."

And when had that been?

"I've had this pendant two years! Why am I only hearing you now?"

"It is time."

More riddles. I felt so dizzy I could barely think.

"What does that mean?"

"It is time for action. The world has turned sufficiently. The Final Hour is drawing near."

What was she referring to? The threat imposed by Saruak? My skull began to ache severely, and I clutched my free hand to it. God, it felt like someone had gone at it with a power drill. I couldn't make out my surroundings at all anymore. A blurry haze had filled my vision.

Then it cleared a little. But the room was completely gone.

A shudder ran down my spine. I seemed to be out in the open air, and on a plain of some kind. I thought that I could make out the outline of vast rocks, off in the distance. Where exactly had I traveled to?

The scene remained there a short while. Then the details of the room came back. It tried to let go of the pendant, but couldn't seem to manage it. It seemed to be clinging to my hand, even when my fingers let it go. The chain swung below it, quivering, letting out a tiny rattling noise. The tiny jewel glowed brighter still.

There was a rumble from the distance, off in the direction of the square. I hoped that it was only thunder. All those people, still in danger. That consumed my thoughts now, driving out all the bewilderment.

I managed to get my head straight finally. I was trying to save this town, and all the people in it. Anything else was a distraction. And I wasn't about to be told what I could and couldn't do, not even by this strange being.

"If I can't use magic, where the hell am I supposed to take this?"

"Release me," she replied.

"What?"

"Release me, while we still have time."

But could I even trust her, if I went that route? Look what she'd brought down on us so far.

Except . . . it isn't any worse than what the Manitou is bringing, I now told myself.

I wasn't even sure that I could do what she was asking. Surely such a thing had to involve some kind of spell?

"How do I do that?" I asked.

But the voice did not come back to me. There was only silence in my head, backed up by a faint rushing sound, like something had been in there. The pain had stopped, which I supposed I was grateful for.

This woman, this Amashta, had told me what she wanted. But apparently, it was up to me to figure out the rest for myself. And where was the sense in that? I got the feeling, all over again, that I was being played with.

There was nothing else that I could think of, though. So I lifted the gemstone closer to my face. It looked as solid as a diamond. Would it even break, if I smashed it against something? But that seemed a rather crude approach. I held it between my forefinger and thumb, and turned it over.

And it started to become a little clearer in my frantic thoughts. Trapped, the Little Girl had said. And, surely, trapped by sorcery. The setting was oversized, and it *did* look like a grasping claw. I'd noticed that several times already. And all those crude little markings around it . . . might they form some kind of spell that was holding the woman prisoner in there?

I didn't even have my pocketknife left. The only tools remaining were my own bare hands. So I started pushing at the silver with my thumbnail, trying to work the gemstone loose.

It should have been easy for a man of my strength, but it proved to be anything but. At first, it wouldn't budge the tiniest fraction. All I got for my efforts was a drop of blood, springing up under my nail.

Something happened that was so bizarre I almost dropped the pendant. The bead of red touched the gemstone's setting. And was absorbed by it, soaking in and vanishing.

I halted nervously for a long moment. What the blazes was going on now? Then I got to work again.

There was the faintest crunching sound, and I pushed even harder. It felt like I was trying to drive the jewel in through the surface of my skin.

The gemstone shifted, glinting wildly, And then dropped into my palm.

Next moment, there was a white flash so intense it seared right through my eyelids, even when I closed them. And, accompanying it, a massive cracking sound. Something warm spilled out across my palm like water. But when I looked down, there was nothing there at all.

The jewel had split in two halves, right across the flaw I'd seen.

Despite the fact I was indoors, the newspapers on the couch started to rustle, moving gently, and the corners of my drapes began to flap. It was no longer dark in here. A yellow glow was spreading out directly above my head. It seemed to have sparks of other colors in it, like some unworldly kaleidoscope.

Amashta's voice filled up my head once more.

"I must use you now, Defender."

At which I stumbled back, afraid I really had been tricked. But her voice was reassuring.

"There must be a physical presence to do what I must, and I have none anymore. You may not cast spells yourself, but you can be my conduit."

I took that in as quickly as I could. And acknowledged that I'd come this far unharmed. More thunder was erupting from the center of town. So I was simply going to have to trust her, I could see.

I stood straight, ready for whatever happened next. When the glow started to descend toward me, I kept myself completely still, not even flinching.

I felt the light pour into me. And there was warmth accompanying it again, filling up my whole body and making it seem to expand. All my tiredness dropped away, and all my doubt at the same time. Don't ask me how, but I now *knew* she wasn't going to harm me. I flexed my fingers, raised my arms.

There was brand-new strength in them, just like in the river, but more powerful.

"Are you ready?" the voice asked.

As ready as I'd ever be.

The room began to whirl around me, growing dark again.

Then becoming almost black.

Then it was gone.

CHAPTER 52

The darkness lifted. There had been only the vaguest sense of motion, like the world had tilted very slightly underneath my feet. But when my surroundings came back, I really was outdoors this time, on another rooftop on the west side of the square. I almost lost my balance but I held myself together, then gazed down at Union Square.

There was something else the Eye of Hermaneus hadn't shown me. In the scene I'd watched, the banners had been flapping agitatedly for sure. There had obviously been a heavy wind.

But up here, closer to the spreading cloud, the air was moving with the violence of a hurricane. It howled and tore at me, ripping at my hair and clothes, dragging across my cheeks. I pushed against it, managing to remain upright.

The ceremony was in full flow. Aldernay had taken a backseat. And the major adepts had stepped forward, forming a broad semicircle, stretching out their arms and joining hands. Each one had a microphone in front of them, and they were leading a slow, sonorous chant that was being repeated by the crowd. It seemed that everybody knew the words. Perhaps that was a touch of magic too. They rang across the broad square like the chiming of a bell.

Half the sorcerers, the judge included, were crying out in

English. But Gaspar Vernon was using Ancient Greek, his great voice booming. I'd heard him cast spells in it before. The McGinley sisters were speaking in some kind of Celtic tongue. And Kurt van Friesling? Dutch or Flemish, something along those lines.

And I supposed the different languages gave an added dimension to the witchcraft. But it sounded like Babel below me.

There was not the slightest hesitancy that I could make out. Not the tiniest awareness that they might be headed in the wrong direction. I had almost got to Levin before, making him reconsider. But all of that had been swept away. The adepts looked totally engrossed, the same way that the ordinary folks were, wrapped up in the solemnity and power of the moment. Their voices reverberated from the speaker system, certain and unstoppable.

I swung my attention to the crowd. Saul Hobart was still there, high up on the statue's plinth. He had his riot gun in both hands and was, unlike everyone around him, staring directly upward. He'd figured which direction the trouble, when it arrived, was going to come from. And I wasn't sure what he hoped to achieve. But it didn't even occur to the man to back off.

Among all those townsfolk, I had never seen the big lieutenant look so very tiny. And had never seen him stand so very tall.

Some things are revealed in desperate circumstances. Like the true nature of someone that you only *thought* you knew.

In the torchlight, I could see the way the other faces had become. They were still happy, but looked less dreamy than before, and more intent. All this chanting was their ticket out of this place, yes, their passage to a safer life. They seemed quite convinced of that.

There was so much glittering down there. The bright winking of metal, and the languid flash of crystal. Almost every person had brought something magical along. Pendants and amulets, talismans, fetishes, and charms. Some of them must have been bought only a few days ago. Others had, doubtless, been in people's families for generations. Individually, they counted for nothing all that much. But all massed in one place?

It was—they didn't even know it—a part of the engine that was driving them toward their own destruction.

I inclined my head back, staring at the cloud above.

It seemed to be no more than a dozen yards above me. Either it had simply thickened, or the thing had actually dropped lower in the sky. Its black vapors rolled and swirled, but its darkness was not absolute. Dazzling bolts of lightning were passing through it the entire time, and more thunderclaps rang out.

It could only be moments until Saruak's face appeared. And what was supposed to happen? How was I supposed to stop it.

The voice of Amashta drifted through my head again.

"I cannot fully destroy your enemies, Defender. That is your task. I can help you, but I cannot save you."

In which case, I wondered why she'd even bothered bringing me here. And all that talk about me being her conduit?

"It is a matter of free will. In time, you will come to understand. But you must make the choices and decisions. What would you do now?"

And that was all the explanation that she gave me. Did she expect me just to have faith in her?

A dozen thoughts all tumbled through my brain at once. I'd like Saruak gone. I'd like everything put back the way it had been. But how much of that was possible?

I kept staring at the crowd. And began to see what the right answer was.

"You've held yourself aloof and distant for so very long a time, Defender," the strange voice went on. *"You have made a shell of your own anguish, curling up inside it. You must let go, if you want to save these people. Think about them all as though they were your own."*

I felt my eyes widen as I gazed at them. Families, the same as mine, all squeezed together tightly by the pressure of the throng. And if anything bad happened to one of them, they'd hurt no less than I . . .

Than I . . . ?

"What do you genuinely want to happen?"

And I knew what the first task was, the most important one.

"Get all of these people out of here."

"Agreed."

A strange emptiness overcame me, for a moment. Then the warmth I'd felt was surging through my arms again. I started to understand it. She wanted to use me as a lightning rod. And so I lifted them toward the mass of people, tipping back my palms the way I had seen Kurt van Friesling do.

Thousands of glittering points of brightness—little golden sparks—came flowing from them the next instant. It wasn't me making this happen, whatever it might look like from below.

They were no larger than motes of dust, but the wind that was still buffeting at me had no effect on them whatever. They moved in a perfectly straight line at first, pouring evenly outward. Then, when they were over the crowd, they began to spread. Until the whole of Union Square was covered with a gossamer-thin brilliance, a shining golden veil.

I was almost breathless as I watched what happened next. The sparks began descending, breaking off into groups of two as they did so.

Each pair found the eyes of a congregant. Stopped there, winking for a moment in that person's gaze. Then vanished, as though drawn inside. It wasn't just selected people. It was happening throughout the crowd. Only the adepts were untouched.

The chanting subsided, then drifted to a total halt. The townspeople's content expressions were all gone in the next instant. Most of them looked startled. All of them were peering around. The kids were beginning to get frightened. There were wails, and then a loud, scared murmuring started up.

On the stage, the adepts kept on calling out for a few more seconds. Then they took in the fact that nobody was listening to them anymore. And they too faltered and stopped. They seemed to come around all by themselves.

Urgency swept over me. These people had been freed, for sure. But they were still packed in like cattle. If a panic did start up?

It would be the same result as I'd seen at the manor, except that I'd be partially responsible.

I struggled to think what to do about it, then snatched out my cell phone. And, my fingers shaking, dialed Saul Hobart's number.

He looked astonished anyone was calling him right now, but he fished into his pocket all the same.

"Saul!"

I watched him hunker over slightly.

"Ross? Where are you?"

"You and your men have to clear the square! As quickly as you can, but without any melodrama! Can you manage that?"

He was staring around, and I could see how worried he'd become. It finally occurred to him to look up, and he saw me.

"Hell, we've never dealt with anything on this scale, Ross. But we can try."

Then he forgot all about me, and got on his walkie-talkie. Blue uniforms began pushing their way among the stunned, unhappy people, whispering instructions, picking infants up. Presumably, the cops on the surrounding streets were doing the same thing, because the pressure on the mob decreased a little as the folks along the edges started filtering away.

There were so *many* of them. If this was going to work, then it was going take a while. At least not many people were turning their attention upward, where the black cloud was still rumbling.

I craned around at the figures on the platform.

If the common folks had seemed bewildered, then the adepts all looked thunderstruck. They were wandering gently about on the stage, their expressions disbelieving.

Gaspar Vernon and Martha Howard-Brett stepped forward unsteadily, wanting to do something, although they didn't seem sure what. But Judge Levin, who was standing tautly, spotted me immediately. He seemed to figure out, extremely quickly, what was going on. He grabbed the others by their elbows, drawing them both back.

Whispers passed between the little group. And then the whole bunch of them began retreating toward the Town Hall, Aldernay leading the way.

A gap appeared at the center of the throng, as the crowd grew thinner. The flagstones around the statue had almost completely emptied out. Saul had stepped down, and was ushering folks in the direction of the bridges, which were already filled to capacity, a mass of people pouring off the other end.

I tipped my own head back again. The cloud was still pitch-dark, still filled with lightning. But it had shrunk to about a tenth the size that it had been before.

People were not thinking about him anymore. He no longer held their attention in the way he'd done. And his power had already been drained a good deal, I could see.

But not all the way, by any means.

Saruak's face appeared up there.

CHAPTER 53

He was exactly how the white jewel had depicted him. His gaze was no longer pallid, but a sickly, venomous green. It immediately fastened on me. Which was fine, I thought. Just so long as his attention was diverted from the people down below. More of them were managing to get away as the crowd thinned, the whole square clearing out. The streets beyond it were full of motion, I could see. All of it heading away from here. So my focus went back to him.

"You!" he howled.

His voice was as loud as the screeching wind around me. Almost a part of it, the way it shrieked. His disembodied features drew up nearer to me, the cloud becoming even smaller.

Any pretence at humanity was gone. His teeth looked more like the sharpened fangs his monster had displayed. They jutted across his upper lip, the same way that the Dralleg's had. His left pupil was about four times the size of his right one by now. Fumes seemed to be rising from him, mingling with the cloud. And a great mass of scaled tentacles writhed where his body ought to be.

But I'd seen all of this before, and I was not so badly shocked as I had been the first time.

One thing struck me oddly. In this form, he had no wrinkles. His beard was gone. And his face was completely smooth, with not the tiniest line or crease. It almost looked like plastic, it was so unnatural. There was not a sign of aging.

And his hair, tied back into a ponytail, was dark and lustrous, not gray. That made sense. Why on earth would a tree spirit grow old the same way humans did?

But the way he usually appeared? I had even noticed liver spots. So it began occurring to me . . . was it possible that he'd been living in a human's body all this time? Was that how he'd managed to leave New England in the first place?

A couple of his tentacles came burrowing toward me like enormous snakes. But they stopped short, waving in the air at me.

"What have you done with my Dralleg?" he yelled.

He'd drawn to within about twenty feet of the rooftop. And the cloud around him was still diminishing. *Which didn't mean,* I told myself, *I ought to underestimate him any time soon.* He'd already had some degree of power when he'd first shown up in the Landing. Even in this weakened state, he was still pretty dangerous.

Proof of that came in the very next instant. Saruak seemed to understand that, if I was still standing here, then his creature wasn't alive any longer. He let out a disgusted moan. One of his tentacles stopped shifting, and then pointed in my general direction. But it didn't try to grab me. It just lifted in the air instead.

Just like Cassie, gravity abandoned me. I was yanked off my feet like an invisible hand had caught hold of me. Everything inside me seemed to lurch.

A second later, I was sailing out across the rooftop's edge. The sidewalk, four stories down, pitched giddily below me. It was no mere show of petulance this time. Saruak was furious, and he was going to let me fall.

The heat came surging back into my left arm. And, an instinct taking hold of me, I pointed it where I'd been standing.

And I heard Amashta's voice again.

"You must hold fast."

Another shower of sparks flew out, bright platinum ones this time. They did not spread out the way the gold ones had. They stretched between my arm and the roof like some kind of shining rope. And they had pretty much the same effect.

I felt my momentum change. Instead of falling, I just swung around in a wide arc. My feet hit the tar paper a mere couple of yards from where they'd first been.

My heart was pumping, fierce and hard. What had just happened had shaken me badly. But there were other concerns than my own safety, and I forced myself to concentrate on that. My attention went toward the ground again.

A kind of herd mentality had taken over. Most of the people fleeing from the square were going south, or east across the river. Very few had headed past the platform and the Town Hall. And I wanted to keep Saruak away from them for as long as was humanly possible. So I turned in that direction and began to run.

A thick, protruding metal pipe—part of a flue or something like that—groaned and broke off, at a muttered word from his lips. It came hurtling toward my face. I simply ducked it.

But when a couple of loose bricks off a cornice did the same, I could see the same evasion wasn't going to work a second time. I was caught between them. I felt the energy pulse and raised my hands. There was a flash between my palms. The chunks of brick were deflected in midair, crashing harmlessly to either side of me.

Saruak was rushing up behind me, I could see when I glanced back. More of his tentacles were reaching for me. The edge of the roof was coming up. It was only about four feet to the next one, so I didn't hesitate. I jumped.

This one was aged, all of brittle slates, its incline heavily tilted. Which meant I landed on it at an awkward angle. I skidded and wobbled for a moment, then righted myself. Several tiles broke free and clattered away.

His shape was almost over me, so I continued running.

Saruak let out an enraged bellow that made the whole roof shake.

Suddenly, all the tiles I'd passed across were springing up behind me. Being lifted into the air simply by the violence of his yell. I heard the massive clashing noise as they broke free, and chanced another swift glance back.

It was like they'd all been turned to playing cards, and some great arm was sweeping them along. A wave of jagged, broken slate was surging up at me. And I could feel the ones underneath my feet starting to tear free—they seemed to squirm as though they'd come alive. I stumbled, my footing becoming unsteady.

The next roof was a good eight feet away, and had a high cornice into the bargain. But this one was coming further apart with every passing second. How much longer before the whole thing collapsed? There was no staying here. I flung myself across the gap.

There was a dizzy moment of inertia. My arms were stretched as far as they would go, my hands grasping desperately for something—anything—to hold on to. Then they found the ledge, and curled across it. The rest of my body slammed into the brickwork. A harsh jolt of agony went through my knees and ribs.

I put that behind me quickly, scrabbling and hauling myself up.

Union Square tipped like a seesaw, below me. And it was almost empty now. I couldn't even see Saul Hobart.

I swung my legs across the side. My feet came down on weathered gravel, and I realized where I'd wound up. This was the roof of my own office building, practically where this whole thing had started. We had come face-to-face out front of here.

Which seemed fitting. But could I do any better this time? Could I actually stop him, finish him?

I spun around, then backed off a little, satisfied the crowd was safe. Saruak's huge features were still advancing on me.

He stopped, about ten feet above me. One of the largest of his tentacles lashed out and caught me solidly across my jaw.

The blow sent me flying. I came crashing down, and rolled a couple of times. White light filled my head, but not the magic sort.

I just took hold of my jaw carefully, making sure it wasn't broken. Then I got to my feet and steadied myself. And simply faced him down.

The warm energy had come back. It had started rising through my entire body, not simply my arms. And so, as I had done before, I thrust out my palms at him.

That strangely accented old voice went through my head again. Although, this time around, the words seemed to be directed at the Manitou, not me.

"A spirit you are, but not merely that. Show me the other things that you are made of, Saruak."

Again, I felt hollow momentarily. My body didn't even seem to belong to me when that happened.

The sparks that flew, on this occasion, were far larger. And translucent, almost colorless. They moved in a different way to the others.

They circled him, then wrapped themselves around him like a shifting ball of gel, smothering his features. Then they tightened, pressing down.

His tentacles tried to shove them away, but he couldn't seem to get free of them. They kept spinning away and then returning. His expression became distinctly alarmed, and the fire died out in his bilious green eyes.

And then, the remnants of the cloud around him all began to funnel downward, drawing him along with them. The night sky reappeared, above. The vapor hit the rooftop, billowing and evaporating a few yards ahead of me.

And when the last of it cleared, he was standing there. No fangs anymore. No long appendages. His human body had returned, and he was still wearing that ragged coat, although the hat was gone. The gray hair and beard were back, and all those wrinkles I'd become familiar with. Which made me remember what I had figured out before.

This was no disguise at all. It really was the way he looked most of the time.

But there was something else as well, the spell had done to him. Something that I genuinely hadn't been expecting.

It was hard to tell straightaway, in the dark. But some of his wrinkles weren't that any longer. Some of his skin, patches of it on his face and hands, had been replaced with what appeared to be bark.

Yes, it was exactly that. His fingers looked more spindly than ever, and a dull brown color. The long nails had disappeared.

They were twisted. They looked more like twigs than digits. Which was when I finally understood what Amashta had done.

Saruak was mostly spirit. But was partly man as well, and partly tree. And she'd reduced him to those elements, the human who he had possessed, and the oak that had birthed him.

He was looking down astonishedly at himself, bewildered by the changes to his body. He hardly seemed to be aware that I was there at all. All the rage had left him, and been replaced by stunned horror.

"I have done what I can, Defender," the voice told me. *"It is up to you now."*

It paused for a second.

Then it added, *"Now it genuinely begins."*

It faded to utter silence, and I knew that it was gone.

I gazed at Saruak coolly for the first time since I had arrived here. In either form, tree or human, he could now be harmed, couldn't he?

So I decided to test that theory out, and started to move in on him.

CHAPTER 54

He finally noticed me again, as I stepped in closer to him. And began screeching at me furiously, quivering with rage. His shape might have become largely human, but his anger was far more extreme than that. He was so apoplectic, howling like an animal that had gone totally insane.

Some of his hair had come loose, and it swirled around him in the wind. His shoulders were hunched up, the way the Dralleg's had once been. His hands were raised in front of him, the weird-looking fingers bunched like hooks. Spittle was appearing in damp flecks across his beard.

Nothing that he shouted was in English. He had dropped back into that same language I'd heard him use earlier.

I just closed the distance and my fist went back.

I was about to take a swing at him, when he threw himself at me. He was slightly taller and, despite the fact he'd been diminished, proved to be extremely strong. Maybe that was the tree part of him.

One arm wrapped itself around my shoulders. Then the free hand clawed across my face, the fingers rigid and scratchy, trying to push their way into my eyes. They felt like wood.

I shifted my head, preventing him from doing that. But I could feel the skin around my temples being scored. I paid no notice to that either. Pushed at the arm gripping me, trying to loosen it and get some room to maneuver. Then I lunged up with my knee, slamming it into his hip. But it probably hurt me just as much as him. It was like banging up against a post.

His grip loosened a touch further, and I made a stab at shoving him away. He wouldn't budge, though, and was all over me again in the next moment, trying to actually bite. His pointed teeth snapped inches from my cheek, his hot, sour breath wheezing up against me.

I just wasn't going to let him do that. So I hit him with my knee again, twice more, on the exact same spot. It wasn't any more pleasant than the first time. He let out a stifled yell, however. His gaze blurred with pain. Then it cleared again, turning bright with malice.

"You can't stop me like this!" he shrieked. "Are you so ignorant?"

A hand grasped me underneath my chin, and he started squeezing. He wasn't just trying to choke me. He was trying to crush my windpipe.

One of my arms got clear at last. I drove my fist into the crook of his elbow, making his arm buckle. Then I slammed my forearm, hard, into his throat.

His eyes widened. He finally went staggering backward, making heavy, ratcheting, gasping sounds. But I wasn't going to let him get out of my reach. There was no way that was going to happen.

I grabbed hold of his collar. Swung my right arm back again. When I punched him squarely in the middle of the face, I felt the vibration of it right up to my shoulder, and my knuckles felt like they'd been skinned.

It was still the most satisfying thing I'd done in days, so I kept on repeating it.

The second time, I felt his nose break with a snap like a dry branch.

On the fourth blow, he went lurching out of my grasp, staggering across the gravel roof in the direction of the square. He collapsed just before he reached the cornice, and lay there, barely moving.

My fist was throbbing, blood oozing up into the wounds, but I barely registered that. I just stared down at the Manitou.

He was sprawled out on his belly, twitching. God, he looked a total wreck. Frayed, torn clothing. Limbs as spindly as poles. As I watched, he tried to raise his head, and only partially succeeded.

His own blood spattered down onto the rooftop from his nostrils. And he'd never bled before, not even when I'd stuck a blade into him. So his powers really *were* at a low ebb.

"See. You've a human side after all," I murmured.

But the liquid was viscous, and looked a strange color, a peculiar mix of red and green.

I stepped forward again, reaching out, already knowing what my next move was. I was going to pick him up and hurl him off this roof.

His peculiar, misshapen hands pressed down. He raised his upper body, and then lifted his face toward mine. But it wasn't that which made me halt. It was a sudden additional motion.

There was a bulge now, in the skin of his throat. It was moving up toward his mouth, not downward. He appeared to be disgorging something.

His lips shifted, something foreign pushing them apart.

I recalled the arrowhead he'd swallowed that first day we'd met. The sharp tip glinted dully as it slid out into view.

His right hand darted to it, turning it over and gripping it around the base. The fingers became narrower and less normal-looking than ever. Shorter too. They shrank around the bottom of the arrowhead, and then fused together.

His sleeve had fallen back, revealing most of his forearm. It was covered entirely with dense bark, not a scrap of skin visible any longer.

All of his pathos of before had disappeared, like the illusion it had always been. His nose was off at a curious angle, blood still running down his lip. But his eyes were burning again.

He hissed, inspected the sharp spear that his right arm had become, then grinned. It looked especially feral with the blood oozing between his teeth.

He started getting to his feet.

"You've put up a good fight, Devries, but a pointless one. I am forever. There will always be another road, another town, and more humans to play with. Once I've finished with these, of course."

His head went from side to side.

"And that will take a while."

Then he came at me, the flint spike pointed at my chest. It was all that I could manage to deflect it. I couldn't stop the power of his charge, and I went backward, crashing down onto the roof with Saruak on top of me.

I heard a rip, and felt more pain. The arrowhead had gone through a sleeve and gouged the side of my arm.

Still kneeling on my chest, with one hand around my throat again, he drew the weapon back.

"Give my regards to all those others I've sent to the after-life!"

I got both hands where his wrist ought to be, and tried to force his arm back. But it wasn't like trying to move flesh and bone at all. There was an unyielding stiffness.

The tip began edging down again, in the direction of my face. I couldn't seem to stop it, much less push it to one side. My arms were shuddering, with precisely no result.

I tried to use my knees, like last time. But he had got wise to that. He'd positioned himself so that I could not lift them. My legs jerked ineffectually.

"Helpless at last? How excellent. It does my old heart good."

Mine was beating like a drum. The arrowhead was growing larger in my sight. I tried my best to angle it away from me, but it was like trying to push a branch. It went a little way, then just bounced back. Nothing I could do made any difference.

Before much longer, it was just a few inches away. I could see Saruak's grin behind it. His features were glowing with delight.

Why'd Amashta brought me so far, only to abandon me? I couldn't understand it.

I let go of his arm with one hand, and tried to grab at his face. But he simply moved it away. My palm quivered inches short of him.

"Barely worth the effort, Devries. Where is your protector now?"

He leaned in, bringing all his weight to bear. And, even though I grabbed it with both hands again, he pushed his arm down smoothly, till it was hovering just above my eyes.

"First the anticipation," he was saying. "Then the pain. Then nothingness. And won't that be nice?"

His body lifted over me. He was readying himself for one final push. And I wasn't going to be able to stop him. I knew that, but I still hung on.

"Not said your prayers?" he yelled. "Too late!"

A sudden shot rang out.

It came from our left, the next rooftop along. And was the loud boom of a shotgun, not a pistol.

The impact sent Saruak lurching off me. He staggered away several paces, although he remained on his feet. A wide, tattered hole had appeared in one side of his coat, that strangely hued blood leaking through it from his ribs. And had splinters been scattered across the rooftop? It looked like it. They were soaked in the gore too.

His hand went to the wound. His face screwed up with anguish, and his eyes squeezed shut a moment. His legs started to buckle. I began getting up myself.

But he wasn't finished yet. He righted himself when he saw what I was doing, and his gaze returned to me.

He lifted his right arm. Pointed the tip at me again.

And, with a ferocious bellow, hurled his entire bulk in my direction.

I wasn't even fully up. I raised a hand, trying to fend him off.

The next shot came from behind me. An even louder roar, which split the evening air apart.

There was no messing this time. No mere peppering of buckshot. The slug—a BRI saboted one—lifted Saruak off his feet so hard he almost left his boots behind.

As I watched, his body spun around in the air. And then came down with a wet slap on the cornice.

It was just a narrow concrete one. He hung there for an instant, then went sliding off, dropping the entire four stories to the ground below, leaving a wide, mud-colored smear behind.

I let out the breath that I'd been holding. Got the rest of the way up. And then, rather shakily, made my way forward and peered over the ledge.

There were no illusions left at all. He might have still been powerful a few moments ago. But no man can survive that, even if he's partly tree.

Saruak lay motionless, quite tiny from this distance. A rumpled figure surrounded with blood, his limbs flung out at impossible angles. I watched him for what seemed like an age. Long enough to satisfy myself entirely.

He didn't move a muscle. He was gone.

My limbs were trembling again, my chest still heaving.

Footsteps started coming up behind me. There was no need to look around to know to whom they belonged.

My gaze went to the sky instead. The wind had died down. It was completely back to normal. There were more clouds than there'd been earlier on. But in between their bulk, the evening stars shone down.

I looked across at the dark silhouette of Saul Hobart on the adjacent rooftop, still holding his riot gun. Raised a hand to acknowledge him. He simply nodded back.

And then a palm descended gently on my shoulder.

"Thanks, Cassie," I think I muttered.

I could feel it when she shrugged.

"It's what I do," she said. "I watch your back."

CHAPTER 55

On the way back down the fire escape, the air got a little cooler around us. And then, gently at first, it began to rain. It had dampened everything by the time we reached the ground, the whole of Union Square glistening in the dark.

All the flagstones shone. And the bright globes on the streetlamps seemed to melt a little, their shapes going slightly blurry. Moisture was dripping off the statue in the middle, and the stone lions by the Town Hall steps seemed to shift gently beneath its flow. A gutter was overflowing too; there was a little stream of droplets pattering down.

My clothes were getting damp too, but I didn't care about that. I was simply relieved it was all over. Most parts of my body hurt like hell.

So I just gazed around me and watched nature washing our surroundings clean.

"How did you know I'd come here?" I asked Cass.

I had left her behind, after all, when I had vanished from the house.

"A voice in my head told me," she said, very matter-of-factly.

She'd been gazing at me oddly for a good while, by this time.

"An old woman's voice?"

Her eyebrows lifted. "Yeah. In case you hadn't noticed, stuff like that happens around here all the time." She pulled at her lip. "Who was she?"

"I'm not really sure."

Which was the truth, and she seemed to accept it for now.

The wind had done one final piece of damage. One of the banners over Union Square had fallen halfway down. It read, "285TH REUNI."

"Roll on the two hundred eighty-sixth." I walked along the sidewalk, limping gently toward Saruak's corpse. "This one didn't exactly go as planned."

"What does round here?" Saul Hobart asked, coming toward us from the other side.

I didn't answer him, though. As I got closer, I began to notice something odd. It was difficult to tell in the dim ochre light, the wetness, but . . .

The cadaver was no longer its usual colors. Even the blood splashed around it had gone duller. When I'd peered down from the rooftop, everything had looked the way it ought. Not anymore.

I came to a halt. Even his texture had changed. And everything—his skin, his clothes—had turned to a uniformly dismal color, mostly grayish brown, with just a hint of green.

The rain was leaving pit marks all over him. I prodded at him gently with a toe. A piece dropped abruptly off, and crumbled into fine particles, which the drizzle sluiced away.

I remembered that leaf mold in the churches. Every final ounce of him had turned to that.

When I gave him a second prod, his body fell apart completely. And the water took it in a thin gray wash across the paving stones. It began running off into a gently gurgling storm drain.

Cassie let out a derisive snort.

"Ashes to ashes," Saul remarked.

"Dust to dust," I finished for him.

He looked at my injuries, then went away for about a minute. He came back with a first aid kit, from his own car presumably. Moved me into the shelter of a doorway, and started dabbing disinfectant on my wounds, then binding up my arm and damaged fist.

All the while he did that, they were both peering at me with the same stupidly inquiring expression on their faces.

"Well?" the lieutenant asked.

"Well what?"

My head was hurting worse than any other part of me, and it wasn't the fight that had caused that. I was thinking about everything that had happened to me, and trying to understand it. And it wasn't in the least bit easy. There weren't many points where my mind could get a grip. So what kind of answer did they want from me?

"What the hell was that about? And you, of all people. Magic, man?"

I jutted out my lower lip. "It wasn't me."

He looked unconvinced, seeming to believe that I was trying to duck the issue.

"It sure looked like you."

"Appearances can be deceptive. You must have learnt that by now?"

His eyes went narrow. So I sighed and looked away from him.

"There's plenty of time for this later, Saul. To tell you the truth, I've a lot of figuring out to do."

Then something else occurred to me. All the while I'd been Amashta's lightning rod, I'd felt disconnected, torn apart from who I really was. And that hadn't left me at all comfortable or happy. It was like something had been robbed from me, rather than added. I felt pretty sure I didn't ever want to repeat that.

"If it's any consolation," I told them both, "I *still* don't like magic. It . . ."

I fumbled for the correct words.

"It just didn't feel right."

And then I quickly changed the subject.

"Is everyone okay?" I asked. "The townspeople, I mean."

The big lieutenant just smiled quietly.

"One teenager fainted on the Iron Bridge. Her boyfriend's probably still performing mouth-to-mouth resuscitation on her as we speak. That apart?"

He gave the laziest shrug I'd ever seen, his shoulders rising like a pair of hills.

"Everyone's just fine."

"What are you going to do now?" Cass asked me, obviously concerned about the state that I was in.

The edges of the world were getting faded by this juncture, sheer exhaustion closing in around me.

"Go home," I murmured. "Sleep for a week."

But then the cell phone started ringing in my pocket. And so someone, obviously, had other plans.

"Hand them over, Devries."

Wasn't this just typical?

A few hours ago, almost all the major adepts of Sycamore Hill had been very firmly under Saruak's power. Not too far back, as I recalled, they had actually run away from him. And now here we were again, in Gaspar Vernon's study. And, stern and patrician to the last, they were acting like nothing had happened.

The status quo had been restored, and that was what genuinely mattered to them.

As it had been last time, only one small lamp was on. The room was half shrouded in blackness. Behind the desk sat Levin, Kurt van Friesling, and Cynthia McGinley. Her sister Dido, Cobb Walters, and Martha Howard-Brett were standing in the deep shadows behind them, barely visible at all.

Vernon himself was on his feet in front of me, chewing at the fringe of his moustache, a hand the size of a dinner plate extended toward me.

"The gemstone, and its setting. Give them up."

How they'd learnt of their existence, I wasn't quite sure. Divined it, maybe. I'd detoured home and collected the pieces off my living room floor, understanding that they wanted to examine them. But there was such a thing as asking nicely.

"A slightly less aggressive tone might be appropriate," Judge Levin intervened, with a faint, thoughtful smile.

So at least I had one of the great and good on my side.

"In the first place, we owe Mr. Devries and his friends an awful lot. In the second . . ."

And he eyed me mildly through his rimless spectacles.

"I believe that he has other concerns, regarding the object in question."

"Like what?" Vernon asked. "Good God, this stuff? It could be the key to lifting Regan's Curse. We're the real magicians here. He has no right to hang on—"

"They might also be the key," I pointed out, breaking across him, "to getting my family back. And if I'm going to leave them in your care, I'll need your word on that."

"You have *my* word," the judge told me firmly. "On my life, on the lives of my sons, and on every principle that I hold dear."

His gaze held mine like a vise.

"Is that good enough for you?"

I supposed it had to be. And so I got the pieces of broken jewel and silver out, and then surrendered them.

The halves of gemstone flashed in the weak light as Vernon turned them over. Then he peered warily at the marks engraved into the setting.

"I've never seen anything like these," he grumbled. Even his voice was subdued. "How on earth did Jason Goad get hold of something like this?"

"Did he find it here, do you suppose?" Cynthia McGinley wondered. "Or in Vegas?"

"If the latter, then it poses an even bigger question," Levin said. "This thing, as I understand it, was with Regan Farrow when she put her curse on us. It must have lain there with her ashes. Which meant that nobody in town could leave from that point on. So who carried it out of here?"

The metal caught the glow of the lamp, and seemed to change the quality of it a little.

Did they even know about the woman's voice, Amashta? Apparently not. They hadn't mentioned it. It hadn't come to me again, not since the rooftop. But I didn't want them studying me as well, so I decided to just hold my tongue about that whole business. Or at least till it was more appropriate.

For now, let them stay convinced it was the pendant that had aided me, the same way their talismans and crystals did.

"All such questions will be answered," Vernon barked out confidently. "We'll get to the bottom of this, you mark my word."

It was Kurt van Friesling's turn to address me.

"I must say, I'm surprised by the course you took this evening, Devries. Not like you at all."

"When needs must," I told him.

"Well, exactly. How pragmatic. We're prepared to reward you for your services," he said. "And Cassandra Mallory as well, of course."

My mouth came open. But he held a palm up, stopping me.

"No objections, please. You have to keep body and soul together. After all, there might be more you can do for us in the future."

I didn't doubt there would be. And the prospect of that made me even tireder than I already was. The whole room seemed to drift a little.

"Is that it?" I asked.

Gaspar Vernon's moustache bristled like I'd just offended him. But then, he simply nodded

"For now," he growled at me quietly. "For now."

I was still turning it over during the drive home, the windscreen wipers marking time. All those strange things Amashta had told me. The way she had described it seemed bizarre. It was as though she were alluding to some kind of plan that I was part of. Some grand scheme, beyond my understanding as yet.

Did destiny have a role for me? In which case, it was one I'd prefer to turn down. All I'd ever been, or wanted to be, was an ordinary man.

But perhaps I wasn't going to be allowed that luxury.

The house was still dark when I finally got back. I clicked on the hallway light. And immediately, the quietness of the place began to seep, all over again, through my skin and into my body. This had once been such a noisy place. So full of life and love.

I leant against the doorframe wearily. And then turned it all over for a last few seconds.

Defender? What did *that* even mean?

Now it genuinely begins? But I thought that we'd come to the end. Could it be possible I was wrong about that?

I was far too tired to think about it anymore, and so I went into the kitchen. I switched the light on there, and I noticed something on the table.

It was a massive wicker hamper, piled to overflowing with a variety of foodstuffs. There were cans of clam chowder and lobster bisque. Pots of caviar. Brown packages filled with truffles. Baguettes, cheeses, and even a bottle of champagne.

"Food on your table for a year," Woodard Raine had said.

He had even stuck a handwritten note in the top of it.

A deal's a deal, sport.

It was signed with a simple *W*.

I picked up a muffin curiously and bit into it. Then I went across to the sink and spat it out. The same thing happened when I tried a bunch of fat red grapes.

It wasn't that they tasted bad. It was just that he'd forgotten to give them any flavor whatsoever.

Which, again, was pretty typical. The hell with magic. It was too confusing, too capricious. I preferred a simpler life.

I went across to the fridge and got a bottle of beer out. Took a pull at it, but then I stopped.

I couldn't drink right now, because I needed to use my car again. I'd realized I had one more place left to visit.

CHAPTER 56

The steady electric blue glow washed over me again as I stepped into the upstairs nursery at 51 Bethany. The rain was tapping on her window from behind the drapes. And the Little Girl was still rotating in midair, as she had done since I'd first found her, concepts like sleep or play completely alien to her, which continued to make me think she wasn't a real child at all.

Her slightly echoey, distant voice was high-pitched, just the way an infant's should be. But it sounded worried.

"You ought to be resting, Mr. Ross. You're tired, and you have bruises, cuts, on you."

"All true. But I had to come and thank you."

She looked surprised. Which was odd since . . . couldn't she read my mind? Not all of it, apparently.

"Why?"

I smiled at her. "You got genuinely involved, this time. You really helped."

"I only . . ."

"Couldn't have done it without you, kid. You led me in the right direction."

She gave that some more thought. And then her lashes, which were still closed, quivered very delicately.

"Then I'm pleased. All those other children? All their

mothers and their fathers? I am glad that I could do something to protect them."

She sounded genuine enough. But she still appeared to be troubled, even at this late hour. As I said at the start of all this, it's hard to read a person properly when you can't see their eyes. But I'd known the Little Girl for long enough to sense when she was not at ease.

"What's up?" I asked.

"I'm up. In the air," she said.

She got like this sometimes, answering questions far too literally. Or perhaps she was just trying to avoid the question. I was too exhausted for such games. I leant against the wall and sighed.

"Seeing as you're being so perceptive, can you tell me what's really been going on? Who was that?"

"The lady? She is Amashta."

"I know that. *What* is she?"

"She is mysterious, even to me. I did not know that she was there before. And now that I do, I cannot see inside her."

"Did you hear the things she said to me?"

"No, Mr. Ross. Only your replies. Her words were meant for your ears alone."

So I told her everything that had passed between us, even that remark about a Final Hour. Had the woman been talking about tonight, or was there something else?

The Little Girl turned slowly in thin air, taking it all in. She considered what I'd said, then pulled a face that was indecipherable.

"I don't understand what any of these things mean. But I suppose we will find out."

Which was philosophical, surely, but one hell of a frustrating answer, any way you looked at it.

Her pale expression was still grave. What was wrong with her? I couldn't remember the last time I had seen her looking so unhappy.

"Really, what's the problem?" I asked. "Hey, we won, didn't we?"

She finally decided to come out with it.

"You've beaten Saruak, yes. But . . ."

Her lips tightened. And then she forced the words out.

"I can feel it pushing forward through the darkness of the night now. I can feel it pressing up against the high walls of our world. I hate to be the one to tell you this, Mr. Ross, but . . . something else, something new, is coming toward Raine's Landing."

She stopped rotating, facing me. And her voice, by this time, had become reduced to an anxious, hissing whisper.

"Something even worse."